In the Passion of the Night

She awoke to the feel of him. The light that still burned and the suddenness of awakening put panic in her eyes; they opened to find his face hovering above hers, his eyes topaz chips that smoldered with dark destructive passions. Her gaze fled. The panic caused her to struggle briefly, and he jerked both her hands above her head, pinning them together beneath one bandaged palm. He used his freed hand to bracket her jaw, dragging her eye back to him.

"Don't fight me," he said thickly. "For the love of heaven, don't fight me now. Don't make me stop."

She moaned. "I won't fight you. I'll let you, Daniel, but—"

He freed her wrists and sank his white-swathed fingers into her hair. "Then kiss me," he commanded.

Other Avon Books by
Araby Scott

WILD SWEET WITCH

HEART OF THE FLAME
ARABY SCOTT

#0006374

HEART OF THE FLAME is an original publication of Avon
Books. This work has never before appeared in book form.

AVON BOOKS
A division of
The Hearst Corporation
959 Eighth Avenue
New York, New York 10019

First Avon Printing, May, 1982

AVON TRADEMARK REG. U. S. PAT. OFF. AND IN
OTHER COUNTRIES, MARCA RESGISTRADA, HECHO EN
U. S. A.

Printed in the U. S. A.

WFH 10 9 8 7 6 5 4 3 2 1

BOOK I

The Weapon

PROLOGUE

In the year 1858, ten years before he acquired his first railroad, and more than a quarter of a century before he became known as the Man in the Iron Fist, Julian Gow had his first manifestation of the recurring vision that was to haunt him until his death.

It happened in New York, in the shank of a warm April night. He had had visions before, visions of power; and because these visions gave him pleasure, and because they always came at this hour, he had always welcomed the fact that he needed so little sleep.

On that particular night in 1858, being then in his twenty-seventh year, he lay in bed, staring unblinkingly at the blankness of his ceiling, and waiting for a vision. It came.

He was in a boardroom, at the head of a table. On the table and stretching its full length lay a great double-edged sword, silvery and shining, its hilt toward his hand. The chairs along the sides of the table were empty. At the far end of the table a shadowy figure stood. The figure was clad in shapeless black, the face was hidden in the shadow of a hood.

"Who are you?" he asked.

"I am Revenge," came the whispered answer, and he knew it was a woman. A cold chill touched Julian Gow, like a presage of his own doom.

"I am Revenge," repeated that faint inexorable voice.

He felt chilled to the bone. Sweat broke out on his brow and ran sideways in rivulets, darkening his ashen hair. He began to blink rapidly, willing the vision to vanish, but he could not wrest his eyes away. The vision was more real than reality.

"I am Revenge," she said for the third time.

"You are only a woman." He trembled. "You cannot destroy me."

"I have the weapon," she whispered. "I have the will. I have the way."

And he saw that the woman bore a seed in her belly, and

3

that she was great with child. And he knew that the seed was of his own sowing.

He reached for the sword without taking his eyes from the ceiling. He screamed. He looked down at his fingers, and saw blood. With a horror too great for words, he realized that the hilt was no longer at his hand, but at hers.

When the vision vanished, the blood remained. Julian Gow had bitten through his own hand, nearly to the bone.

In the morning, for he was a rich man even then, he hired a team of Italian artisans to paint scenes on his bedroom ceiling, scenes that would remind him what a woman was for.

1

The man in the lower berth stirred, pleasurably. The fluted wail of the steam whistle, the rocking of this dark enclosed world he inhabited, the rhythmic clack-clack-clack of great metal wheels on steel—they were all pleasant adjuncts to the dream he had been having. And so was the feel of someone's silken hair cradled against his shoulder, and someone's velvety flesh pressing down upon his arm.

Whose flesh? He came wide awake at once, but without alarm. Memories of last night seeped back. The parlor car. The dim, intimate lighting: In this year of 1875, gas light had not yet come to the railway coaches. The glow of Cordovan leather and the gleam of inlaid Honduran mahogany. The bottle of brandy. The woman.

Without disturbing her, he shifted slightly so his free arm could adjust the wooden slats of the venetian blind to admit slivers of light. It was morning—not long past dawn, he guessed—and the sun rose early in June. Because of the tilt of slats he could see nothing outside the window. Where would they be now? Two or three hours from Saratoga Springs?

His head turned again, and his tawny eyes connected with a woman's long auburn hair in early-morning disarray. Sophie. Very pretty. He did not remember her last name. He had met her some years before, when she had been mistress to a friend of his; the chance encounter on the train last night had finally led to the intimacies she had tried to encourage during the earlier acquaintance.

A quick glance at his pocket watch, hanging by its fob on a hook near his head, told him it was before six o'clock. With a smile that transformed the deep clefts of his cheeks from cynical to sensuous, he bent his head into the woman's throat.

"What time is it?" murmured Sophie, waking with a thrill at the sense of returning danger.

"Early. Not yet six. Still two hours to Saratoga Springs," the man reassured her quietly, coming up on one elbow. His was a body that might have spelled danger to any woman. His shoulders were broad, his legs long, his stomach flat and athletic. Sun had streaked his hair to a dark bronze, turning it shades paler than the crisp dusting elsewhere on his well-sinewed frame. But the eyes, those reckless gold-flecked eyes—that was where the real danger signals gleamed.

"Good." Sophie smiled in a lazy, leisurely way, and laced long fingernails into his hair. "There's time, Daniel."

The man's eyes smoldered as they swept the curves he had possessed last night. A hand well-versed in ways to arouse a woman drifted down to find a silken hip. His head was still bent to her breast when a rustling noise redirected his attention. Without lifting his mouth, he raised his eyes and saw a stirring at the heavy wine curtains that enclosed Sophie's berth. With no more warning, a hand came through the opening and connected with Sophie's hip. Long bony fingers, attached to a somber black sleeve, missed Daniel's tanned hand by inches.

"Wake up," came a muffled voice from the aisle.

"I'm awake," called Sophie without missing a beat. "I'm just about to get dressed."

"Who was that?" Daniel whispered as soon as the hand had been withdrawn.

"My husband," came a low throaty whisper.

"Your husband," Daniel groaned briefly. "Christ. Why didn't you tell me you were married? And that your husband was on the train?"

"I thought you might turn me down." Sophie smiled a slow feline smile. Certainly it had been dangerous, but then, she had always known this lean, bronzed, good-looking face spelled danger, one way or another. "You used to turn me down, and I wasn't even married then. Would you have come to my berth if you'd known my husband was sleeping just across the aisle?"

Without answering, Daniel levered his long lean body across hers, no mean feat in the cramped space, and glimpsed through a careful quarter-inch opening in the curtains. The berth across the aisle had already been made up. Seated in the chair was a sallow sanctimonious man with a prominent Adam's apple, already clad for the day in somber black frock coat and stiff starched collar. He looked every inch a man of the cloth.

"What will your husband do if he finds me in your berth?"

whispered Daniel, sinking back into the small dim space he shared with Sophie.

"He'll kill both of us," she returned without a flicker of hesitation. "Ezra is a very jealous man."

"And how did you expect me to get out of your berth unseen?" asked Daniel in a dry whisper. "Jump out the window?"

"Of course," she murmured languidly, moistening her upper lip with the tip of her tongue. "It can't be any more dangerous than what you do for a living."

"Like hell," came the sardonic reply.

Sophie pulled his hand to her mouth and bit the heel of the thumb softly. "With luck the train will stop somewhere soon. But don't get dressed yet, I have something in mind. . . ."

Thus it was that some twenty minutes later, at an hour when most passengers were still sleeping an untroubled sleep, a pair of long athletic legs, now clad in tweed, emerged from the window of a sleeping car in northern New York State. Moments before, the hiss of air brakes had been heard; now the train was losing its forward impetus. Through the raised window a second ribbon of rail came into view. A station? No, decided Daniel; there were no signs of a settlement. No doubt they had pulled onto a siding to allow some other train to pass; most of the line was single track. Luck was with him after all. It should be easy enough to get back on the train, moments from now, by more conventional methods.

"Good-bye," he whispered to Sophie. His strong mouth curved into a conspiratorial smile. "And thanks . . . for everything."

Seconds later Daniel dropped onto the dry packed earth between the rusty rail of the siding and the smoother rail of the main line where another train would soon pass by. He straightened and strolled at once to the end of the train, where a brakeman was throwing the switch that had guided them onto the siding.

"Where did you come from?" the brakeman asked, narrowing his eyes.

"Just off the train for a morning stroll."

"Didn't see you come off," said the brakeman suspiciously.

"Check with the sleeping car porter if you wish," said Daniel blandly. "Or with my partner who's still aboard, Mr. Yancy Brody. My name's Savage, Daniel Savage."

"I've met Mr. Brody." The brakeman relaxed a little; this

must be a railwayman, too. "Can't be too careful with Mr. Gow's train about to go by. Got a lot of enemies, Mr. Gow has. A mighty lot of enemies."

"Why is Gow passing us? I thought he was headed for Saratoga Springs, same as we are."

"He is." The brakeman tilted his cap back. "Saratoga's first stop on his special trip, an' he don't want to be late. Telegraphed ahead to clear the tracks. Railway president kin do a thing like that."

Daniel had read newspaper accounts of this proposed special trip, a three-week tour planned ostensibly for the patriotic reason of commemorating five years of coast-to-coast rail travel in the United States. Actually, six years had passed since the linking of track between east and west had taken place at Promontory, Utah; but the first single coast-to-coast train had not made the journey until the following year, 1870. That event had been greeted with much waving of flags and setting off of fireworks. Julian Gow, the railway president referred to, now promised to re-create that trip—Boston to San Francisco—with minor alterations in route and timetable to accommodate various pleasure stops and watering holes, such as Saratoga Springs.

However, Daniel suspected that Gow's trip had very little to do with nostalgia, and a very great deal to do with publicity. Julian Gow's railway—the New York and Chicago Trunk, or The Trunk, as it was unaffectionately known—had at last lived up to its name, by greedily swallowing yet another competitor. Now, The Trunk's Chicago to New York run, which would be encompassed in the return trip, could be accomplished entirely on The Trunk's own tracks.

That fact, along with The Trunk's numerous other acquisitions westward as far as Omaha, had made Julian Gow's railroad empire a powerful rival to other eastern lines. Even that old fox Cornelius Vanderbilt had not been able to stop the rapid growth of The Trunk, but then, Vanderbilt was near eighty now, and Gow was in his prime. The Trunk was the newest giant among giants, and Julian Gow one of that new breed of men Daniel did not like: the railroad baron.

There was a reason for Daniel's scorn. To his way of thinking, The Trunk had been constructed out of mergers and shady stock maneuvers in the gleaming boardrooms of Wall Street. Gow was not a railwayman but a financier, and a questionable one at that. Most of his fortune had been built by supplying faulty armaments to both sides during the Civil War, and for that, too, Daniel had reason to dislike Gow.

Explosives and tunneling were Daniel's specialties, and his interest lay in building railways, not buying them. His hard-earned expertise had led to many footloose and hazardous years, including some time spent in the service of the Union Pacific during the race to meet the Central Pacific, and join the continent by rail. After tunneling in the Wasatch Range of Utah and down the descent of the Weber River canyon to Ogden, through territory where the snow could cover the telegraph wires, Daniel had been present at the golden spike ceremonies at Promontory, six years before.

There he had by chance met a seasoned railroad man by the name of Yancy Brody, who had earned something of a reputation during the construction of the rival Central Pacific. A maverick, Yancy had for years been outspoken in his disagreement with his bosses over the lack of consideration for Chinese life; countless hordes of imported coolies had been sacrificed in the fight to claw through the Sierras.

"Figger the Central Pacific could use a feeder line or two, back in California," Yancy had drawled on that fateful day. "Sure hate to see Crocker an' Huntington an' all take over the whole dang state. Got me a backer or two, an' a helluva track gang lookin' fer work. Could use an explosives man."

"A partner?"

"You got money?"

"Some," said Daniel guardedly. Because of the special expertise he had brought back to America after a year of working in Sweden, in an explosives factory near Stockholm, the Union Pacific had agreed to pay Daniel off in land grants. It happened that one of them had become the site for the briefly booming town of Cheyenne, where $250 lots had zoomed to $2,500 in five days when the railroad crew had wintered there.

Yancy had looked at him suspiciously for a full sixty seconds. "Yer too young, an' I don't know a dang thing about you, an' I ain't seen the color o' yer cash," he said at last. "But I seen you waggin' chins today with one o' my yeller boys. Figger we'll talk turkey."

Soon thereafter the matter had been settled on a hand-shake, and the following year they had agreed on a route for a feeder line through the rugged Sierra Nevada range.

But railroads cost money, more money than Daniel's and

Yancy's pooled resources had produced. He and Yancy had come east to seek financing for their partly built and still inoperative line. But these were difficult times: carpetbaggers and scalawags bleeding the South; scandals in the White House; and now the whole country in the grip of a severe depression. That the depression had been triggered by the failure of the Northern Pacific Railway and its Wall Street backers made railroad financing a very difficult thing to find. The fruitless search had taken Daniel and Yancy from New York to the financial houses of Boston; now they were on their way to Chicago to try again.

"Up bright and early this morning, ain't you?" came a voice from the observation platform at the rear of the train, and Daniel turned to find the pouched poached-egg eyes and doleful visage of Yancy Brody himself. Yancy was a long string bean of a man, cautious and competent, and nearly a dozen years older than Daniel, although with his prematurely grizzled head he looked even older. He swung down off the ornate rear platform, and ambled toward Daniel and the brakeman, who had now visibly relaxed.

"Hello, Sam," Yancy said to the brakeman. "What the hell's goin' on here, anyways?"

Sam delivered the explanation, to Yancy's deep disapproval.

"Already late on the run," he grumbled. "Special train be danged. Gow should be tendin' to his reg'lar runs."

"Ah well, he's not a real railwayman like you," said Daniel dryly. "Thank God, it doesn't matter to us if we're late into Saratoga Springs. We're not making connections until tomorrow."

"Ain't no way to run a railroad," snorted Yancy. "An' if you think it is, then I'm hitched to the wrong locomotive. Might as well team up with Julian Gow hisself. An' I hear he's more'n half tetched in the head. Here comes the sonuvabitch now," said Yancy, as their attention was distracted by the tremble of track and the building of sound in the distance. A plume of smoke crested over the wooded hills, and moments later a crack train streamed proudly into view around a bend. It accelerated as it came into the straight stretch. Like an impetuous metal monster it flung itself at the track, the red protruding teeth of its cowcatcher devouring the twin streaks of steel. Its great steam whistle flooded the morning with imperative sound: two longs, a short, another long—rising, mounting, martial. The engine's gaudy gilding glinted in the sun and the very earth quaked underfoot as the train screamed past in a blur of spokes and a pounding of rods—a deafening thunder of sound.

But in the instant before the locomotive burst past, it was the gleaming mahogany cab that riveted Daniel's attention. The cab, and the person in it—one hand on the throttle, one on the whistle cord—glimpsed briefly but clearly imprinted on his mind.

"By crikey, now I know Gow's outta his senses," muttered Yancy disgustedly.

"You may be right," agreed Daniel, but the appreciative gleam in his eye did not exactly match the sentiment.

Yancy rolled his pouched eyes heavenward. "What's the railroad business comin' to now? A girl!"

And what a girl, thought Daniel. That unfettered black hair, streaming free in the wind; the young golden sheen of her skin and the joyous bloom of excitement; the glowing eyes—silvery gray, he was sure; the face . . . Good Lord, the girl was already a knockout. A little on the slender side, to be sure, but then she couldn't be more than sixteen or so. Give her a few more years, and . . . but what the *hell* was she doing driving Gow's special train?

It was a question that Julian Gow himself might have asked.

"Och now, Miss Cat, look at ye! Soot on your dress and grime on your face. Why, ye might have come from a coal bin!"

The young woman who spoke was in her late twenties; her Scottish ancestry was written into every homely feature and every flaming hair of her head. She was plain faced, plain shaped, plain spoken, and plainly dressed. At the moment she stood with arms akimbo, legs belligerently braced against the motion of the train, in a small, exquisitely appointed compartment—the bedroom of the person to whom she spoke. Clearly, she was a servant, but she addressed her charge with the manner of a mother whose patience has been strained too far.

"Where *have* ye been?" she demanded.

"Sight-seeing," said the girl, who had just entered the compartment with an ingenuous widening of lashes that did wonderful things for the silvery eyes Daniel Savage had sighted not fifteen minutes before. The girl was considerably dirtier now than she had been then, but even the smudges of coal dust could not conceal skin like golden syrup and finely winged brows; and the hair, though badly tangled by wind, was a glorious dark cloud framing a face no man would soon forget. It was a face in which no detail was perfect according to the fashions of the day. The mouth was a trifle too wide, the chin a trifle too stubborn, the eyes a trifle too bold, but there was something in the overall effect that transcended passing modes. She was, without question and despite the fact that she was easily two inches taller than the fashion, an extraordinarily striking girl. And she had the bones that promised the best of her beauty was yet to be.

"Sight-seeing! Whisht! Do na' be skirting the truth, Miss Cat. If I had na' come to your room to lay out clothes, ye'd have changed and washed and tucked that dress to the bottom of your trunk for the next three weeks, with none the wiser. And out and about without your proper underpinnings, too! Ye've been up to no guid, Miss Cathryn Kinross, so do na' pretend innocence with me. Well, out with it!"

The girl called Cathryn sighed and spread her dirtied hands in a mock-helpless gesture. "You've caught me red-handed, Hannah. Yes, it's true. I've been at it again."

Hannah drew her plain mouth into a long-suffering line. "Ye're too old to be a tomboy now," she said tartly. "Och! If your grandfather knew, he'd curse the day he ever lifted ye into an engine cab, when ye were no more than knee-high to a grasshopper. It was an ill day he allowed ye to come along on Mr. Gow's trip! Who's the engineer *this* time?"

"Uncle Ernie," said Cathryn. The engineer was not her real uncle, but she had known him—and many other engineers who had once worked for her grandfather—for too many years to use the formal manner of address usually accorded to that much respected profession. "But don't blame him . . . I tricked him into it."

"He's na' the one I blame," snorted Hannah. "And how did ye get that muck all over ye?"

"I climbed over the tender on the way back," admitted Cathryn, "to avoid a brakeman I didn't know." She took a belatedly repentant look at the black coal smudges on her dress; they would cause Hannah some hard minutes at the washboard.

Hannah glared. "Have ye learned nothing at that fine

12

finishing school ye've been at? Why, it's made no more dint in your tomfool ways than the years I raised ye myself!"

Nine years before, when Cathryn Kinross's parents had died during the first of the recurrent cholera epidemics that struck New York after the Civil War, Cathryn, then eight, had gone to live with her grandfather in his country home some miles north of the city. Hannah McBride's father worked at this home; and Hannah—then at the marriageable age of eighteen, but without a suitor—had taken over the task of raising Jared Kinross's high-spirited granddaughter.

For the past few years, Hannah's supervision had been replaced by that of a very proper young ladies' boarding school not far from Boston. Cathryn had finished her last term only days before, defying all dire predictions that her irrepressible spirits would cause expulsion long before graduation. It was for this unexpected success, as much as anything, that her grandfather had indulged her by bringing her along on this trip.

"Well, Hannah, I don't want to wait all day for my punishment." Cathryn blinked, innocently, and cocked her head to one side in a waiting attitude. "Go and tell grandpapa right now. Let's get it over with!"

Hannah rewarded her with a sour old-fashioned look, and went to the door. "Strip your clothes off," she sniffed, without answering the challenge directly. "I've already put out some clean things and drawn a bath, for I knew full well where ye'd be. And this time, when we get back home, ye'll wash the dress yourself!"

And at last, with Hannah gone, Cathryn—Cat to her friends—did a little dance step to give vent to her delight. An impish grin spread over her begrimed features as she flung off her clothes. Hannah would not tell; and even the prospect of an hour spent at the hated tasks of washing and ironing could not blunt Cat's pleasure; that was too far in the future to worry about!

Cat Kinross had been teethed on trains. Her father had been a railway man, and her grandfather was a railway man. The small line Jared Kinross had built some forty years before—the Peekskill and Tarrytown—now existed only on paper; it had been leased to The Trunk two years ago, at the start of the depression, when Jared Kinross and many other railroad owners had fallen on hard times. The Trunk had taken over the Peekskill and Tarrytown's tracks and rolling

13

stock, and its employees, too—that was something about which Cathryn's grandfather had been adamant. Julian Gow had not liked the terms of the lease, which included keeping Jared Kinross on his board of directors. But with Gow still in the process of building his railway empire, the small local railroad had provided some vital rights-of-way east of the Hudson River, in territory otherwise preempted by Cornelius Vanderbilt's lines. Linked with Gow's other lines by a railroad bridge some fifty miles north of New York, the Peekskill and Tarrytown provided The Trunk with access to Manhattan.

A deal had been struck, but allowing little girls to drive trains was not part of it. For the past two years, Cat had had to indulge her passion on the sly. Last night, when she had seen that the engineer on Julian Gow's special train was an old and trusted friend, the opportunity had been too tempting to resist. This morning she had risen before dawn; and now, even Hannah's displeasure could not dim Cat's delight in the escapade that had just taken place.

Hannah's grumblings had not come to an end. They started again a short time later, in the tiny bathroom that served this part of the train. The bathroom was far more luxurious and well fitted than those that had served the travelers on the historic transcontinental trip of five years ago. It even enjoyed that luxury seldom seen on trains a century later—a tub.

"Satan's doings," Hannah said with a shake of her fiery head. Despite her passion for cleanliness, she did not entirely approve of the bathroom: It was not spartan enough for her tastes. "Marble bathtubs! Brass pumps! *Hot water!* Who ever heard of such things on trains? The devil's own luxuries they are!"

"Heavenly," sighed Cat, and sank a little farther into the foam, an action which deranged the pinnings of her hair, and drenched the little dark tendrils clinging to her neck. The hair had already been washed at the sink, and thoroughly toweled, an occasion which had allowed Hannah to vent some of her spleen, at the expense of Cathryn's scalp. "Now pump some more hot water in, will you, Hannah? We're traveling smoothly enough."

"'Tis a train of iniquity, mark my words," said Hannah direly, although she obliged the request and punctuated her warnings with several fierce thrusts at the pump handle. "And bound straight for hell at sixty miles an hour."

14

"I think it could do seventy on a long straight stretch," Cat corrected, with a dreaming look in her eye. "And it's the finest one I've ever driven."

"Och! I'm na' talking about that lump of iron in front. I'm talking about the *train*. Two pipe organs! Sofas and chairs soft as sin, and gilt and mirrors and fancy inlays on the wood! A dining car fit for a . . . a bawdy house! Bedrooms na' much better! A flatcar just for Mr. Gow's fine carriage, and a horsecar for his team! Barbershops and smokers for the men! Ladies' maids for the fancy women! Aye, I've marked, if ye have na' done so, Miss Cat, that half the fine women aboard this train wear rings as big as roses, but nary a one for the finger an honest woman thinks about. Your grandfather was na' thinking straight when he allowed ye along on this trip. It's a sight too much fine living for an impressionable bairn like yourself, Miss Cat, and I've said the same words to your grandfather, straight to his face."

"I'm not a *bairn* anymore, Hannah, or hadn't you noticed?" With wicked intent, Cat slid herself up to a sitting position in the tub, bringing the upper half of her body out of the bubbles. Water streamed over breasts that were youthfully firm, but with the ripeness of newly found womanhood. "I'm quite full grown, thank you."

Hannah averted her eyes with a pained expression. "Have ye no modesty? Seventeen years of age, but ye're na' full grown in the head. Looking at ye is no pleasure!"

"Some of the men on this train don't seem to agree with you," Cat said with a fine nonchalance, sliding back under a veil of bubbles that sloshed gently with the train's motion. "Didn't you notice the outrageous way they were flirting with me last night, after we boarded?"

"What I remarked," said Hannah with asperity, "was the outrageous way ye were flirting with *them*. Lord alone knows how ye'll act when your tomboy days are done! From hellion to hoyden with nary a moment's peace between, I'll wager."

"Oh, Hannah," protested Cat, "I was not flirting. I wouldn't know how. All I did was smile."

"Humph," returned Hannah disbelievingly. "Ye've a bad failing, Miss Cat, and that's vanity, and why the Lord gave a weak-spined thing like yourself the wherewithal to catch a man's eye, I'll never know." There was no jealousy in Hannah's tone; she had long since accepted the fact that nature, with its unequal hand, had bestowed on Cathryn all

15

the gifts it had withheld from her. But her scrawny spinster's breast still ached, at times, for home and husband and children of her own, and it was the knowledge that she would never have them that put some ferocity in the scrubbing-brush she now applied to Cathryn Kinross's shapely spine.

"Ouch," howled Cat.

"The things ye let them say to addle your wits, and ye lap it up like a kitten with a saucer o' cream. Eyes like a morning mist indeed!"

"Hannah, you were listening!" The gray morning mist eyes stared indignantly at the homely red-haired woman. It had never occurred to Cat that Hannah might be anything but content with her role in life. Hannah was more mother than servant, and one did not think of a mother in terms of having longings and frustrations. Just as the thought of jealousy had never occurred to Hannah, so had it never occurred to Cat. But she knew Hannah was punishing her for something. "I suppose you saw that young man try to kiss me, too!"

"Aye, that I did, for if ye choose the observation platform for flirtations, then ye're bound to be observed."

"Well, then!" returned Cat airily, laving the bubbles over her breasts and indulging in a little of the vanity of which she was, indeed, guilty. "You must have noticed I didn't let him do it."

"When ye let a man get that close, Miss Cat, sooner or later he'll succeed." Hannah's voice warned gloom and doom. "That's why I say Mr. Jared was na' thinking of his own granddaughter's guid when he brought ye along."

"Perhaps grandpapa knows there'll never be a chance like this again. Why, half of America would die to be on this train," said Cat with an exaggeration that reminded one just how young she really was. "Flags waving! Speeches when we left Boston! Photographers with big black cameras! One of them took my picture."

"If ten of them took your picture," sniffed Hannah, who knew that was closer to the truth, "ye won't be making the history books. It's na' sae notable as the first coast-to-coast trip."

"*I* won't make the history books," agreed Cat, "but maybe hot water on trains will. Can you please pump some more in, Hannah?"

"No, for it's time ye were out of the tub," replied Hannah, seizing the dry towel that had been set out in readiness.

16

"And Mr. Gow certainly won't be forgotten in years to come," mused Cat. She wriggled a now-spotless toe above the surface of the water, as if to inspect it. "I wonder if I'll ever meet him? So far, he hasn't set foot off his private car at the end of the train."

"And now ye know why they say the devil takes the hindmost. Come on, Miss Lazybones, out with ye, or ye'll miss breakfast."

"Not yet," said Cat, and with her foot she gave a final thrust to the hot water pump, causing a sudden gush of water. But at that moment the train lurched, and so did Hannah; and the water that had been intended for the tub ended up on the towel in Hannah's hands.

"Now look what ye've done!" glared Hannah, holding up the dripping towel in disgust. And to the tune of Cat's apology, which sounded too unrepentant for Hannah's liking, she busied herself for a few moments searching through the small rosewood-paneled cupboard built in beside the sink. "Och, those maids! Fresh flannels from thin air every time ye wash a little finger, but na' an extra towel on the shelves! I'll be fetching ye one, Miss Cat, though ye deserve to dry yourself on a handkerchief. It'll take me but a twinkling of an eye. Do na' be adding more hot water now, for it's a sin to waste!"

Cat made a face. "Go away with you, Hannah," she said, and then called as Hannah's spare frame bustled out the door: "*Two* towels, Hannah! I feel like sinning!"

At Cat's sunny laugh, the door which had just been shut was immediately thrust open. Cat sat bolt upright to defend herself, for she knew there was sure to be another well-deserved reprimand.

"I didn't mean it, Ha—" But the words died in her throat, and the smile on her face.

In the narrow corridor of the train, Hannah stood shock-eyed, pressed against the far window; a man of enormous bulk prevented her return. But for the moment Cat was far too paralyzed to see that.

Her attention was riveted by the other man—the fortyish one who stood in the doorway of the bathroom. He was a pale, strongly built, well-preserved man. Power had corrupted the mouth and turned the eyes cruel, but he was handsome in a ruthless way. His gaze slid downward and found her bare breasts; lust licked out and touched her like a

17

living thing. A frozen moment passed before Cat found the presence of mind to cover herself, and sink into the water.

"Mr. Gow," she whispered.

Without taking his pale ice-blue eyes off Cathryn, Julian Gow raised one gloved hand in the gesture of a man accustomed to total and instant obedience. "Towels for the young lady," he commanded, evidently to some lackey standing out of sight along the corridor. "See to it that she does not lack again, for anything. Fire the maid who services the linens in this part of the train. Which of my directors has been assigned to these quarters?"

"Mr. Jared Kinross, Mr. Gow," came an immediate and obsequious answer, in a voice Cat recognized as the functionary in charge of arrangements for the trip.

Now Julian Gow took a backward step, and his eyes at last left Cat. Another man's hand came in from limbo to close the door. "And his traveling companion is . . . ?"

But the answer was lost in the click of the closing door, leaving Cat with a heart that hammered as loudly as the pounding of great metal wheels on steel.

2

"Yer outta yer ever-lovin' senses," said Yancy, staring at Daniel as if he did not believe his eyes or his ears. "I think you *like* living dangerously. An' what with his missus cosyin' up like you was a hot blanket on a cole night—"

"Now *there*," said Daniel Savage emphatically, easing his arms into a dove-gray frock coat, "is a lady who likes to live on the edge."

He turned to the cheval glass in his hotel room, and spent some moments adjusting his frock coat to smoothness. The clothes he wore tonight, more formal than those he had worn on the train that morning, did not transform him to a city man. If anything, they emphasized the depth of his tan, the breadth of his chest, and the length of his muscular legs.

"Christ. You sure can pick em," Yancy said disgustedly.

"Do I detect a hint of envy . . . or is it disapproval? Ah, Yancy, just because you're a good family man yourself. But don't worry, Sophie won't be there tonight."

"It ain't her I'm fidgety about," said Yancy. "It's *him*."

After leaving the train this morning, Yancy and Daniel had checked into separate but adjoining rooms in the huge new United States Hotel, pride of Saratoga Springs. In the morning each man had gone his separate way, but they had spent the afternoon together at the racetrack, and it was there that they had connected again with Sophie and her husband, and been introduced properly.

"Ezra Lowe," Yancy gloomed. "High Stakes Lowe. Hear tell he carries a little pepperpot up his sleeve, an' he put a load o' lead into one feller back in Baton Rouge, jest fer hintin' he ran a crooked game. An' then in Dodge, he . . . Fer Chrissakes, Dan'l, if you knew who he was, why'd you let yerself be sucked into a card game with *him*?"

Daniel tucked a small object into the watch pocket of his waistcoat. "Simmer down, Yancy," he said easily. "If I lose,

19

well, hell, it's only what I won at the racetrack this afternoon. And maybe I can parlay it into enough to cover a payroll or two."

Yancy watched as Daniel strode to the door. "An' you ain't even got a good black suit to be laid out in," he said lugubriously, then called after his departing friend: "Second thoughts, mebbe a big black hankychiff will do."

Ten minutes later, Daniel and several other men were in the small private dining room that had been booked by Ezra Lowe, having followed the instructions given to them earlier this afternoon.

"Well, gentlemen, do we all understand the rules? I believe you all checked your money at the hotel desk—"

"Guns, too," said one of the men at the round leather-topped table.

"Good, good," said Ezra Lowe, rubbing his hands. "We want no trouble in this game."

In this room with its red-flocked walls and single brass gas light chandelier, Lowe appeared even more jaundiced and more pious than he had this morning. But if High Stakes Lowe had the mien of a missionary, he also had the aim of a rattlesnake. Now, with soulful expression and fingers steepled as if in prayer, he regarded the participants in tonight's poker game with satisfaction. Although nothing in his manner had betrayed it, his attention during these past few minutes had been directed to only two of the men at the table; the other two, despite their honest faces and open manners, were his own shills. They would both appear to lose tonight. But the other two . . .

The tall man. Sophie's choice. Mouth hard, face cynical. Name of Daniel Savage. Sophie had a good eye for unscrupulous men, and although Ezra Lowe had not quite liked the way she looked at this one, he knew Savage would serve his purpose, especially as his name was known in railway circles. Savage would be allowed to win—not a huge amount, but enough.

And the other one. An older man, mid-sixties. He had been pulled in through an acquaintance in Julian Gow's retinue. That was really why Ezra Lowe was in Saratoga Springs: because the special train, with its burden of rich and super-rich, would be standing on a siding overnight. There were good pickings on The Trunk's board of directors, and this man looked like a suitable choice. An honest, proud, honorable face, the sort of man who could be counted on to pay his gambling debts. Tonight's victim.

"Cigar, Mr. Kinross?" offered one of the shills, pushing a box forward, and leaving it on the table, while Lowe looked on disapprovingly. "Help yourselves, gentlemen," said the shill.

"No, thank you," said Jared Kinross. He enjoyed a cigar, but they had been forbidden by his doctor. Now, he smoked only under extreme stress.

Jared Kinross had a strong face, craggy-boned but too tired. Battles not lost but never won had left their mark in the seams of his forehead and the snow of his hair. Life had held too many bitter disappointments for him: the death of his wife in childbirth; the death of his only son from cholera; the financial troubles that had plagued him for a quarter of a century; and finally the loss of his life's work to Gow, two years ago.

He had known his small railway was an anachronism for many years before he had agreed to lease it. In the East at least, the days of the small railway had passed. Starting back in mid-century, most little local lines had gradually ceased to exist as they became unprofitable. There had been offers to buy over the years—the rights-of-way were valuable, especially as they gave access to New York—but Jared Kinross had long refused to sell, preferring to see his handiwork fall into total bankruptcy than to have it swallowed by a huge, impersonal octopus of a company. But there were employees to think about, too, and so Kinross had finally submitted to the compromise of a lease arrangement with The Trunk. The arrangement was not overly rewarding financially. In the hammering out of the terms of the lease, Kinross had devoted most of his attention to clauses about the disposition of the line he loved, and the job security of valued employees in these depression years.

But if Kinross had not grown rich in his financial dealings with Gow, neither had he suffered unduly. The lease produced a sizable and steady income that might have, in time, paid off the crushing burden of debt that had been accumulating over so many years—except for one thing. Jared Kinross had a heart condition, and for the past few years he had known his time was running out. He was in a hurry: He wanted to die leaving no debts for his granddaughter to pay off.

"Poker isn't my usual form of poison." He smiled now at the other men gathered around the table. Wall Street was where Jared Kinross did most of his gambling, but tonight he felt lucky, and he knew in his bones he could double the windfall coup he had made at the racetrack this afternoon.

"Then we'll keep the stakes low," said Ezra unctuously, indicating the chips. "Red is one, blue is two, white is five. You may each sign notes, gentlemen, for whatever number you wish; we'll settle at the end of the evening. Perhaps Mr. . . . ah . . ."

"Fallon," said one of Ezra's own shills.

"Perhaps you would be kind enough to count the chips and accept everyone's notes. Shall we cut for deal, gentlemen?"

Jared Kinross extracted a card from the fresh deck that had just been fanned out, and smiled to see that he had won the deal. A good omen.

And for the first hour, as the smoke in the room thickened and drifted up to meet the flame of the chandelier, it seemed to Kinross that his bones had told no lies. Yes, by God, a lucky day.

Perhaps if he had known about his granddaughter's escapades of this morning, he would not have been so confident. But neither Hannah nor Cat had revealed to him any part of what had taken place; and, as yet, Jared Kinross had no reason to know that the missive he had been carrying in his pocket since shortly after breakfast—an invitation to dine with Julian Gow tomorrow night, in his private railway car—meant that this was not a lucky day at all.

Ezra Lowe fixed tonight's victim with a sad and ministerial eye. "A debt is a debt, Mr. Kinross. Strange that none of the others misunderstood me. Mr. Fallon and Mr. . . . er . . . Snow have already settled their losses. Do you refuse to settle yours? Your note states it quite clearly. Forty chips each color. A total of thirty-two thousand dollars, all told."

"Three hundred and twenty," said Kinross whitely, looking to Daniel Savage for confirmation. He had heard of Savage before, and although he had come to the inescapable conclusion that the other three were in a conspiracy to cheat, he hoped this man might support him. But all he saw were enigmatic dark gold eyes and a large stack of chips.

"Three hundred and twenty," Kinross repeated desperately. "Surely Mr. Savage can testify to that."

"Mr. Savage has done very well for himself tonight." Ezra Lowe turned his eyes to the pile of chips in front of Daniel Savage with some well-concealed chagrin. Savage had done far too well for Ezra's liking. The man's bidding had been reckless early in the game, and Ezra had allowed him to win heavily, certain that he could recoup most of the chips as the game progressed. But it had not worked that way. Savage had changed tactics midstream, playing close to the vest and bidding little. Now, he sat watchful and relaxed, saying nothing, a small smile playing over his lips.

"Mr. Savage has won close to thirteen thousand dollars. Surely, Kinross, you don't expect him to settle for a hundred and thirty? I stated it quite clearly: red one hundred, blue two hundred, white five hundred. Your hearing must be at fault. You heard me, didn't you, Mr. Savage?"

"I certainly did," said Savage coolly.

Kinross glared at Daniel with hatred in his heart, then turned back to Lowe. "Even if I wanted to pay I couldn't. Three hundred and twenty is all I have." He placed the bankroll, recently retrieved from the hotel desk, on the table.

"Then I'll take your note," said Ezra coldly, reaching for the bills. "And also the three hundred and twenty, as interest. I expect payment within the month. A gambling debt is a debt of honor, Mr. Kinross. I'm sure Mr. Savage will support me if the matter should come to court."

"I'll sign no note!" declared Kinross hotly.

"You won't leave this room until you do."

"I'll do no such . . ." But Jared Kinross's voice trailed off as he found himself looking into the business end of a small but lethal pepperpot pistol.

"Better sign the note, Kinross," said Daniel Savage, stretching lazily. Casually, he extracted a cigar from the box on the table, without lighting it. He watched Kinross, noting the tightening of knuckles, the sway of the body, the thin white line around that proud old mouth. "Sign it and get out of the room," he suggested.

"I won't," said Kinross fiercely. "I won't knuckle under to this kind of thing. I'd rather be shot than cheated!"

"In that case I can't guarantee your safety." Daniel Savage sighed heavily, and touched a match to his cigar. He inhaled deeply, conscious that several pairs of eyes had turned in his direction. He found one pair—Ezra's—and smiled. "One dollar, two dollars, five dollars. I heard you perfectly clearly, Lowe."

"You just cost yourself a lot of money, Savage," Lowe replied in a threatening voice, and the pepperpot pistol turned in a new direction, just as Daniel's fingers emerged from his watch pocket with the small object he had placed there earlier this evening.

"If I were you, Lowe," said Daniel coolly, coming to his feet, "I'd put that toy away. Here, catch."

Instinctively, Ezra Lowe and others pulled back in their chairs as Daniel tossed the small object toward the poker table, aiming for none of the men. It exploded on contact, scattering poker chips and leaving a black, smoking scar on the table surface.

"A detonator cap," Savage said calmly. "They've been known to blow a man's hand off . . . even kill him, if they're close enough to his vitals. Very lethal little things, and easy to set off. I have them concealed all over my clothing."

Lowe recovered quickly. "How unfortunate for you," he sneered, leveling the pepperpot once again.

"All attached to dynamite," added Daniel.

"I don't believe you."

"Shoot if you want, Lowe, but remember that little pepperpot of yours sprays shot all over the place. You won't hit me without setting off the dynamite."

"I still don't believe you!" Lowe's finger tightened on the trigger.

"Don't you?" Daniel flashed open one lapel of his frock coat, displaying very visible evidence. From the end of one stick jammed into an inner pocket, he pulled out something that resembled a cord. "Now I suggest you let Mr. Kinross leave the room," he directed conversationally.

Lowe's eyes narrowed, and his gun turned back to Kinross. "He stays. There are two other witnesses to say he owes me money. You wouldn't light that thing."

"Oh, no?" The end of Daniel's cigar connected with the cord, which started to sizzle at once, slowly. "Let him go . . . but first, give him back the three hundred and twenty dollars. You were cheating, Lowe."

Ezra Lowe turned lemon yellow; his Adam's apple worked. "You wouldn't blow yourself up just to—"

"Not only me, Lowe," corrected Savage. His eyes glinted

24

dangerously. "You, me, your two accomplices here . . . Kinross, too, seeing as he didn't have sense to leave. Now give him his money. And hurry; this is a very short fuse."

"You wouldn't—"

"Wouldn't I?" Daniel leaned closer to Ezra Lowe, and grinned, although his eyes remained hard. *"Now,"* he ordered, "or say a last prayer . . . a quick one."

A few minutes later Jared Kinross and Daniel Savage were standing in the sumptuous hotel lobby. Outside, the doorman was hailing a hansom cab to take Kinross back to Julian Gow's special train.

"Here's my card," Kinross said, his war horse expression replaced by one of genuine friendship. "About that railway you're building . . . perhaps I can help in some way. You must look me up next time you're around New York way."

"I'll do that," promised Daniel.

"Why did you go to all that trouble," Kinross asked, "if you didn't plan to take your winnings?"

"Ah, but I did plan to take them . . . if you had left the room. I'd have collected my winnings, and then your note."

"You could have taken your winnings anyway," Kinross pointed out. "All that money Lowe collected from his accomplices . . . he had it in his pockets."

"If I'd waited to collect," Daniel said coolly, "we'd have all collected a quick trip to hell. We had about one second left."

"Then you weren't bluffing."

"No."

Kinross's eyes traveled warily to the dove-gray frock coat. "Do you always travel around like a walking arsenal?"

The facial grooves deepened into a somewhat cynical smile. "No, I borrowed these small surprises this morning, from a friend in Saratoga Springs. I was expecting trouble tonight."

The older man's white and bushy brows lifted in some surprise. "But you told me you didn't meet Lowe until late this afternoon."

"Ah, but I knew I would meet him, and I knew he'd include me in the game. I also knew I'd win. Someone told me about his modus operandi."

Again, Kinross looked puzzled.

"Inside information," Savage explained, just as the doorman indicated that a hansom cab had been found. He steered Jared Kinross toward the exit. "It seems," he smiled, "that someone wanted me to win. Will you forgive me for not accompanying you to the train? She's up in my room now, waiting for me."

3

From under a veil of lashes, Cat watched Julian Gow's right hand with the same kind of fascination she might have accorded to a snake. How odd that he should wear a glove on one hand only! How odd that he should not remove it, even for the meal! At the moment his naked left hand rested on his lap, and his kid-encased right hand fingered the stem of his crystal wine goblet in an oddly cruel gesture, as if he stroked it only in preparation for snapping it.

"A cigar, Mr. Kinross?" offered Gow, lifting a finger to one of the several hulking bodyguards who had hovered nearby throughout the meal.

"Thank you, no," said Jared Kinross, although he eyed them longingly. Tonight, he was disturbed about this dinner in a way he-had not been yesterday. His fears had started upon arrival in Julian Gow's private car, when he had realized that none of the other directors on the train had been invited to share this intimate meal.

Gow did not take his meals in the luxuriously appointed dining car that had been provided for his guests, and which was doubtless even now—with the train once more thundering toward Chicago—crowded with the fashionably clad occupants of the train. Instead he ate here, in the resplendent private car that had been designed and built especially for him at the astounding cost of a hundred thousand dollars, four times the amount most men earned in a lifetime. Where the rest of the train was darkly paneled, with much use of marquetry, Gow's car was different—pale classical frescoes, and a lavish use of ormulu, marble, and mirrors.

Surrounded by such splendors, Julian Gow looked much like a latter-day Roman emperor, as in a way he was. He had been called a handsome man, but his looks were not to Cat's taste. His eyes were too cold and colorless and his mouth too ruthless, and the whitish blond hair clinging to his temples contributed to an overall effect that she found chilling. And the worst thing was he seldom blinked.

Despite all this, the terrible apprehensions of yesterday had been somewhat allayed. For the past two hours, through an elaborate meal of many courses, Mr. Gow had shown no particular interest in her. In fact, he had spoken to her no more than he had spoken to the meek and startlingly beautiful girl who had completed the foursome at the table, and who, Cat had decided at once, must be Julian Gow's mistress. Deirdre, a raven-haired beauty with eyes like emeralds, was no older than Cat herself. She wore a velvet-trimmed white tarlatan gown cut so low that Cat felt embarrassed for her, partly because she received the distinct impression that Deirdre felt humbled by her décolletage—and that Julian Gow enjoyed that humiliation. All the same, with a lovely young thing like Deirdre what interest could Julian Gow possibly have in *her?*

"Take Miss Kinross to your bedroom, Deirdre," Gow ordered curtly, his tone that of a man addressing the lowliest of subordinates. The gloved hand waved a peremptory command. "Stay out of my sight until further notice. Mr. Kinross and I have things to discuss."

In the seventeen years since the first manifestation of his vision, Julian Gow had developed a number of idiosyncracies, and the glove was only one of these. Many of his fetishes revolved around the care and cleanliness of his person. His kid glove was changed several times a day, whenever he washed his hands. He had also become obsessed with virginity, as evidence of cleanliness in a woman. Pregnant females were not allowed within his sight, and he took care, through various means, that he himself should father no child. He would have preferred to dispense with women altogether, but his powerful and well-preserved body was racked to an unusual degree with needs he could not control. He found maturity in a woman distasteful; untried girls were more submissive to his demands. And so, because his jaded tastes required frequent change, there was always a young companion like Deirdre in his life.

"As you wish, Julian," said Deirdre in the meekest of voices, and stood up to go.

"Ask one of the guards to open the safe so that you may show Miss Kinross the Bombay emerald. It's an amusing bauble."

At this last directive, Jared Kinross stirred uncomfortably in his chair. "You mustn't give my granddaughter notions,

28

Mr. Gow. Famous emeralds are not within the reach of every man."

"I'm aware of that." Julian Gow turned his pale unblinking gaze toward Jared Kinross. Those who had seen him in process of acquiring new railroads might have recognized the cold-eyed appraisal as dangerous, and Jared Kinross did.

"Perhaps I'll have that cigar after all," he said with a frown.

Gow stirred a lifted finger, and a man leapt to do his bidding. "I have them made for me in Cuba," he noted in a remote tone, but Cat heard no more, for already Deirdre had started to lead her along the length of the car.

"Well, that's a relief," Deirdre sighed as she entered the bedroom. Cat stared in surprise; Deirdre's whole demeanor had changed in a single eyeblink. Now the green eyes danced with merriment and mischief, and Deirdre seemed gaily at ease in her low-cut gown. "I didn't think I could bear another word of that boring railway talk!" she lilted.

The bedroom was grand beyond all belief, considering the space limitations on any train. At least fifteen feet of the car's seventy-foot length had been assigned to this one compartment. Cat's first impression was white and light, gilt and silk, satin and softness and space—and the bed. It was the largest bed she had ever seen on a train. There was something subtly chilling about the room despite the cloying warmth that emanated from a pot-bellied stove, well-stoked although on this warm June night it should not have been necessary.

"What do you think of my little love nest?"

Monstrous . . . the word popped unbidden to Cat's mind. "Very nice," she said out loud.

"Then I guess you haven't noticed my ceiling," Deirdre said with feigned innocence.

Cat's eyes traveled upward and immediately skittered back to safety. Her heart pounded and her palms grew damp.

"You're blushing!" Mischievous laughter bubbled into Deirdre's pretty throat. "I'll admit I wanted to shock you. The ceiling affected me that way, too, at first. Now it only makes me laugh. Would you believe I was an innocent when I first came here? Wide-eyed Deirdre O'Brien, a poor little orphan right off the boat from Ireland!"

"An orphan?" Cat fastened on the thought—something, anything, to keep her mind from dwelling on that one glimpse of the ceiling. "I'm sorry. Did your parents die recently?"

"Last year. There was a famine . . . oh, not a total crop

29

failure, but it was bad in our county. My parents were evicted from their farm. My father starved to death and my mother died of fever, from eating rotten potatoes."

Cat's throat contracted. "How terrible that must have been," she whispered, thinking of her own sheltered upbringing.

Deirdre brightened almost immediately. "It's all in the past now, so you don't need to feel sorry for me. I came over in January, and I'm doing very well for myself now."

"You don't have much accent for someone who's been here such a short time."

"Oh, I was born in the States. My parents came over during the *big* famine, twenty-five years ago. They went back to County Donegal when I was fourteen, but I still have relatives in this country. An uncle, for one. That's why I came over. Uncle Ryan sent money to help my parents when he heard about the eviction, but it didn't arrive until it was too late . . . for them. But it wasn't too late for me!" Deirdre's very bright green eyes turned defiant. "The money paid my fare over here. I was on my way to throw myself on Uncle Ryan's mercy when Julian Gow caught sight of me, boarding an immigrant train for California."

"Your uncle lives in California?"

"Yes, in San Francisco. He owns a gaming house on the fringes of the Barbary Coast. The One-Eyed Irishman, it's called. Oh, it's quite decent really, compared to most of the places out there. Uncle Ryan is a gentleman at heart."

"Doesn't your uncle mind that you—" Cat bit back the words, realizing that her observation was less than tactful, but Deirdre seemed unoffended.

"He doesn't know where I am," Deirdre admitted cheerfully. "Julian won't let me write to him. Not that I'd want to, right now! Oh, someday I'll join Uncle Ryan, but not until Julian is through with me. Come along, I'll show you my gowns."

She led Cat through a door into another, smaller room. An apprehensive upward glance revealed, to Cat's relief, that here there was no fresco of contorted, naked bodies.

This compartment was all gilt and mirrors, and filled with racks of clothes. Evidently, it was a wardrobe and dressing room, and a very splendid one, although Deirdre pointed out at once that most of her gowns were kept on the next car forward.

"Nearly all my gowns are white . . . oyster, champagne, pearl, old ivory. Julian's favorite color is white. Silly, isn't it?" She lowered her voice conspiratorially. "Oh, he's a dreadful man to live with; he won't touch anything that isn't clean. And he won't let me go anywhere without a bodyguard watching my every move. As if I'd want to run away from this bed of roses!" The lilting voice returned to normal. "Julian buys me so many nice things. If you knew how I used to yearn for such things! For silks and satins and soft beds . . . Oh, you don't know what it's like, living in a scalpeen that's little more than a hole in the ground, sleeping on bracken, hunger gnawing at your belly and rain drizzling through the gaps in the furze roof, and . . . but that's all behind me now," she finished firmly. "Now look at this! It's a Worth gown, he's the very *best* you know, and those seed pearls are quite real. Isn't it divine?"

It was not impossible to understand why Deirdre had chosen to live this life. All the same, thought Cat, how could she stand it? The cloying wealth, the restrictions on liberty, the bedroom where Deirdre must undoubtedly be at her protector's beck and call, the *ceiling* . . . Cat's mind fled from that thought, and she turned her attention, determinedly, back to the gowns and jewels that Deirdre was showing off with such evident delight.

Cat's grandfather gave her no suggestion of what he and Mr. Gow had discussed over cigars. His only reference to the evening was a mild: "What did you think of Mr. Gow, Cat?"

"I didn't like him," she confided with a tiny shudder. They were back in their own compartments now, having been dismissed immediately after the inspection of the gowns. After the unpleasant formality of Julian Gow's quarters, the dark Honduran mahogany and ball-fringed portières of the Pullman Palace Car seemed warm and welcoming. "He makes me feel . . . crawly. Perhaps it's that glove. Does he wear it all the time?"

"Yes."

"How can you bear to be on his board of directors, grandpapa?"

"I'm a railway man, Cat." Did her grandfather look grayer and more tired this evening? Cat wondered with a lurch of concern. But he smiled as if nothing were amiss, and began to reminisce.

31

"I've been a railway man since the days when trains were no more than tea kettles on wheels! Ten, twelve miles an hour . . . why, a horse could go as fast. My first locomotive had a whiskey barrel for a water tank, and leather water pipes stitched up by a local shoemaker! We also made boiler tubing out of musket barrels in those days, and used the open carriages from horse-drawn streetcars for our passengers. The passengers carried umbrellas to protect them from flying cinders. Even so, sometimes their clothing caught on fire. Then we tried stagecoach bodies, but that was hardly better. Finally the cars became little clapboard cabins on wheels, boiling hot near the stove end, freezing everywhere else, in winter at least. The crews used to come in sheathed in ice. But there was no stopping the trains once people discovered they could cover in one day the distance that used to take them four or five."

Cat, seeing the faraway look in her grandfather's eye, did not interrupt. She had heard these reminiscences before, and others; and tales of the early days of railroading fascinated her.

"I doubt there was five hundred miles of track in the whole country back when I built my little line. Oh, the railroads then! The Camden and Amboy didn't have a single steam engine at first . . . they used horses to pull their train. And then, when they finished building their line between Philadelphia and New York, that little trip took six and a half hours. Longer in winter when the ferryboat wasn't running, for their passengers had to walk across the Delaware on the ice! So many of the old lines have gone now, Cat . . . the New York and Harlem, the Mohawk and Hudson, the Baltimore and Susquehanna, the South Carolina Canal and Rail Road Company. . . ."

"Oh, grandpapa, I think you miss those days."

"Parts of them, Cat, parts of them! But not everything. I don't miss the old dangers. That early track . . . no more than wood topped by an iron strap. The ends used to curl up . . . we called them 'snakeheads.' Sometimes those snakeheads would derail a whole train, or even worse, rip right up through the floor of the cars where the passengers sat. And we didn't have the telegraph then, and that caused crashes, bad head-on crashes if a train was even a few minutes late. . . ."

"But not on *your* line," Cat reminded him quickly.

"No, I was lucky." Kinross was silent for a moment, musing. "We didn't have headlights then, either. If we wanted to run at night, we had to push a flatcar ahead of the locomotive, with a fire of pine knots on it. And we only had bells, until my friend George Whistler built an engine with a whistle on it, back in '36. And would you believe it, Cat, George was Whistler's *father*. Yes, indeed, he was!"

Cat laughed delightedly, although she had heard the story a thousand times.

"When your father was a tad, I used to take him up into the cab of the locomotive, just as I used to do with you. Then I'd let him hold the throttle. Do you remember how you used to enjoy that? 'Someday,' I used to tell him, 'everyone will travel this way. Trains are going to build this country. And it's my railway, son, all mine . . . mine and yours.' It's still my railway, Cat, and someday it'll be *yours*."

Cat indulged her grandfather with a smile and an appropriate murmur, although she knew his words were just wishful thinking. The Trunk's lease was a long one—nine hundred and ninety-nine years.

"It's still mine, Cat." There was something grim in her grandfather's voice, as though he had sensed her thoughts. "I own the stock. Gow may control it, but he owns none of it. He wanted to buy me out, but I told him I'd rather go bankrupt and tear up the line. Nothing on earth would make me sell the Peekskill and Tarrytown!"

Cat angled a quick look at her grandfather, and wondered exactly what had happened tonight, while she and Deirdre had been looking at gowns. "Has Mr. Gow been making things difficult for you, grandpapa?"

Jared Kinross looked at her affectionately, and smiled. "No, Cat. He hasn't been making things difficult. I'm still my own man."

And that was all that had been said. Even Hannah had maintained a closed mouth on the subject of Mr. Julian Gow, and if she was alarmed about the scene in the bathtub, she chose not to comment on it.

Cathryn Kinross and her grandfather were not invited to dine with Julian Gow again during the weeks of travel that followed. Only one other thing happened during the trip that gave Cat a peculiar feeling, and that was the sudden evaporation of the persevering young admirers of the first evening.

"Och!" Hannah had said crossly when Cat remarked on

33

the phenomenon, "I told ye this trip would swell your head! What admirers? There's na' a man in his right mind would take a fancy to an addlepated tomboy such as ye. No doubt their eyes fell elsewhere . . . there's half a dozen prettier lasses aboard. Ye're not as irresistible as ye think, Miss Cathryn high-and-mighty Kinross!"

But Hannah had taken to sleeping in Cat's compartment, all the same; and Cat had not asked her why.

And had there been any more reason for alarm? Not really, Cat decided a little less than three weeks later. The transcontinental tour was over. The train had discharged them at a small country whistlestop not far from Croton-on-Hudson, north of New York City, and now she and her grandfather and Hannah were on the way home over the rutted back roads that led to their country home, Kirklands.

They had been met at the train by the young stablehand who was one of the three servants, other than Hannah and her father, who worked at the Kinross home. It was not an extravagant number of servants, even in these depression years, for a place the size of Kirklands. The household had once supported three times as many, and all were strictly necessary in an age when washday meant scrubboards and lye soap and elbow grease; when basement kitchens were the order of the day, and meals must be hauled upstairs on heavy trays; when raisins must be seeded and bread dough kneaded; when even simple tasks like dusting meant much lifting of antimacassars and doilies; when water must be pumped and fires stoked and grates cleaned; when the only real labor-saving device of the day was Mr. Singer's wonderful treadle sewing machine. No conveniences of gas light or plumbing reached this isolated country estate. Jared Kinross could ill afford the five servants on an income which must also stretch to meet the payment of his debts. Nor could he afford to do without them, short of selling the old homestead—an act as unthinkable, to a man of his particular ilk, as selling the little railway would have been. Somehow, he had always managed to make ends meet. And the stablehand did not cost so very much: a dollar a week and board.

"Could do with a new buggy," frowned Jared Kinross. The one-horse vehicle was too shabby to be fashionable, and too small to take luggage on the same trip. It was also uncomfortably sprung, and to his old bones the jolting ride seemed particularly insulting after the luxuries of Julian Gow's private train. Gow: The very thought of him was a maggot in the mind.

"Yes, isn't this awful?" agreed Cat cheerfully. But in truth, she hardly noticed the bumpy ride in the excitement of coming home. To Cat, every greening field and every wooded hill held the memories of childhood, and although it had been fun to play at being grown up for the past three weeks, there was still enough tomboy in her that she looked forward to the prospect of a summer spent, tangle-haired, in favorite haunts.

At last, the buggy rounded a dusty drive, and came to a jingling halt at the front door of a large, rambling frame residence. A man emerged, his red hair peppered with gray, and even a stranger might have guessed that this plain beaming face belonged to Hannah's father. From the back of the house, a dog barked joyfully.

Cat's spirits soared, and the last of her misgivings evaporated in the bright July air. Home! No matter that the aging colonial dowager of a house was badly in need of repair; no matter that there were no longer enough sheep to keep the grass closely shorn. It was home and it was wonderful to be here!

"Well, now, my little Cat, you look mighty happy to be back home," chuckled her grandfather, handing her down from the buggy. "Next time I'm offered a trip like that, I think I'll just leave you here."

"Don't you dare!" she called back at him as she flew up the front steps, skirts held high in a way that caused Hannah, still in the buggy, to cast her long-suffering eyes to heaven. "I loved every minute of it, especially San Francisco. I'd like to do it all over again!"

It was two months before she had reason to regret her words.

4

By September the trip was no more than a distant memory; Cat's mind was far too preoccupied with her own dreams and plans to give Julian Gow a single thought. She had hoped to attend one of the new colleges for women—Smith or Wellesley, both of which were opening just this year in Massachusetts. But her grandfather had vetoed all schemes—for financial reasons, he said.

"Then I'll take a job," Cat had suggested, "and earn my own way."

"I won't have a Kinross woman working!" her grandfather had bellowed.

"Well, then, I'll go to Normal College in New York City. That's for women only . . . and it's *free.*"

"I won't have it! You're only seventeen. Eighteen's time enough to leave home." Jared Kinross's beetle brows bristled with disapproval. "And if I'd brought you up properly, you'd be thinking about marriage, not college. Why, if you gave that nice young Anderson boy half an ounce of encouragement—"

"Stop trying to matchmake, grandpapa!" she had stormed time and again. "I intend to go to college and that's that!"

The argument had gone on all summer, and at last Cat had won a grudging agreement from her grandfather. The following year, once she had turned eighteen, she would be allowed to attend the free college in New York City that would someday be known as Hunter. It was arranged that at that time she would be given shelter in New York by her godfather who, like Jared Kinross, was a member of The Trunk's board of directors.

Despite this concession, the approach of autumn filled her with a deep restlessness; she longed to be off and doing. Thus it was that she daydreamed too long one fine September afternoon. It was already near dusk when she arrived at the back entrance to Kirklands, breathless and covered with burrs from her rambles through the woods, her face warm with exertion and with the ripe golden glow put the by summer's sun.

Hannah was waiting for her at the door, her plain honest face screwed with worry, aging her to something beyond her twenty-seven years. On Hannah's face, the sun had produced only freckles, large ones that ran together like brown rain puddles on her normally very white skin.

"I've been quite safe, Hannah," Cat protested to forestall the coming lecture, which was sure to be a stern one. "I lost track of the time. And as you see, I had Prince with me. Good dog! Go get your supper!" She rewarded the huge Great Dane with an affectionate tousle of his ears, and Prince trotted off obediently to find his meal.

Oddly, there was no lecture forthcoming. "Go and change, Miss Cat," Hannah said in a voice that was unusually dispirited for her. "There's company for dinner."

"Oh? I didn't see a carriage." But Cat was unsurprised. Company was a frequent occurrence at the Kinross home; there was always room for extra guests at the table. And no doubt the visitor's equipage was in the carriage house, which was a large one, legacy of palmier days. "Don't look so glum about it, Hannah!"

"Mr. Julian Gow is here," said Hannah without further preamble. "And ye're to put on a clean dress. I've laid out the brown calico."

"I have more suitable things than that," Cat said automatically, although alarm bells were jangling through her system, and she had gone a little pale under the sun-honeyed skin.

"Ye'll na' wear them tonight," Hannah dictated firmly, ushering Cat through the door and toward the back stairs. "The calico's a decent, sober dress, and nobody by the honest name of Kinross puts on airs for any soul alive. Would ye have Mr. Julian Gow looking at ye as if ye were that fancy lady o' his? Up the stairs ye get, and look sharp about it!"

Was it all in the imagination, Cat wondered—her imagination, and Hannah's? Throughout the dinner Mr. Gow, as remote and as overpowering as ever, hardly looked in Cat's direction. She earned no more attention than the ever-present bodyguards who remained stationed beyond his shoulder throughout the meal, or the two maids of the household, country girls both of them, whose flustered manner this evening betrayed their nervousness in the presence of one so important as Julian Gow.

37

Cat ate with eyes lowered toward her high neckline, with a demure silence that was not natural in one normally so ebullient. The conversation was carried entirely by the two men. After the meal Cat was dismissed with a few words, and Mr. Gow and her grandfather retired to the library, which opened off the front hall. One bodyguard entered the room a few paces behind his master; two more stationed themselves just outside the door, and watched Cat impassively as she started upstairs.

No, it was not imagination, Cat decided as she reached the upper landing. Julian Gow's visit had something to do with her, and she intended to find out what. With hardly a missed beat, she directed her footsteps toward the servants' stairs, and moments later she was slipping, undetected, through the back door, and into the night.

The library was a dingy room, darkly furnished with old-fashioned Georgian furniture that was far too simple for most men's tastes in this Victorian era. Julian Gow had refused the offer of a chair, a maneuver which forced the older man to remain standing, too; but Jared Kinross, for all that his elderly bones complained at the deliberate discourtesy, managed to stand erect. His white-crowned head was unbowed, his seamed face defiant at the frightening ultimatum which Julian Gow had just finished delivering.

"You've sold short many a time, Gow. It's no crime to sell stock shares you don't own! Why, you made a small fortune on doing just that during the Panic of '73. And with stock prices still tumbling every year, it seems—"

"Failing to deliver the shares *is* a crime," came Gow's foreboding answer.

"Great God, Gow. A thousand shares of a low-priced stock . . . that can't break me even if the price doubles. I'm not a rich man, but I have some assets. I'll deliver the stock . . . somehow."

"Will you? You sold short, Kinross, and I think by tomorrow you'll find there's not a share available on Wall Street. That little company now belongs to me . . . every share. I took a corner some weeks ago."

Kinross paled. "You've been up to Vanderbilt's tricks," he said whitely, referring to a famous page in the history of stock market manipulation. Back during the Civil War, a group of investors including Daniel Drew, then president of the Erie Railroad, had sold shares they did not own in the faltering New York and Hudson River Railroad, the shares to be delivered at a future date. Drew, a past master at the technique of "selling short," had believed the shares were due to tumble in price. However, Vanderbilt had, on the sly, acquired every single share available; and as Drew continued to sell non-existent shares, Vanderbilt continued to buy them. In the end, in order to deliver, Drew and his cohorts had had to pay nearly three hundred dollars a share to buy from Vanderbilt, only in order to deliver the very same shares—*to* Vanderbilt.

"Vanderbilt!" scoffed Julian Gow. "Don't compare me with that soft old fool. He should have ruined Drew completely, when he had the chance . . . just as I intend to ruin you."

Kinross swayed, visibly, and wondered briefly if Julian Gow had played a part in Drew's revenge on Vanderbilt, as was rumored on Wall Street. Shortly after Vanderbilt's coup, Drew and his equally unprincipled cohorts, James Fisk and Jay Gould, finding their rival in the market for Erie shares, had obliged by printing new share certificates as fast as Vanderbilt could buy them. Certainly, that unsavory episode in Wall Street history had marked Gow's entry into railroading, and it had also earned Cornelius Vanderbilt's famous growl: "Learned me it never pays to kick a skunk."

"If it's any consolation to you, Kinross, you're not the only man who will be ruined. By tomorrow a dozen others will be scrambling to buy shares at any price."

There was a painful pause, as the changing expressions on the older man's well-mapped face registered incredulity, then a sudden alarm. "Arbuckle gave me that market tip," Kinross groaned, naming his most trusted associate, a friend of many years. "You must have ruined him, too. Oh, God—"

"Only a fool trusts inside information," Gow answered disdainfully, "even when it comes from his best friend. Arbuckle did very well out of the transaction."

Kinross's face whitened as he considered the implications of that statement. Betrayed by his best friend—the man who had been godfather to his own son, and to Cathryn, too! Sold for Gow's silver! The blow was a severe one, and at last he gave in to the demands of age and shock, and sank into a solid-looking chair. He buried his head in his hands, and it was a few moments before he spoke. "What do you want from me?" he whispered at last.

"I believe you already know, but we'll leave that for the moment. For the shares . . . let me see. Three hundred thousand dollars might pay for the considerable effort I've gone to on your behalf."

"Three hundred dollars a share!" gasped Kinross. "They were selling for four or five dollars, a few days ago."

"When one has a monopoly," Gow retorted coldly, "one can charge what one likes. There are no other shares to be bought, only mine."

"Damn"

"It would take me at least a week to raise that much," came the muffled answer. Kinross was buying time; he knew he could not raise the money.

"Only a week, Kinross? I think you'll find your bank will be less than agreeable. In a week, or in a year." With no compassion, Gow savored the humbling of the hunched figure on the chair. "However, I'm willing to give you the benefit of an extension. Two weeks. Fortunate, is it not, that you sold the shares to *me?*"

"Good God, man." The aged head came up again, the look of a fighter once again restored in the pugnacious tilt of the jaw. "It's no better than legalized robbery."

"Do not refer to me as *man.*" Gow's voice was steely. "Nor as robber. I'm a businessman, Kinross. Three hundred thousand dollars, two weeks from now. Otherwise the matter will be up to the courts. Or would you prefer to pay tonight?"

"You know I can't, unless—" The pained voice made Kinross sound even older than his years. What his next offer cost him could only be guessed at. "The Peekskill and Tarrytown. You can have my railroad shares."

"Kinross, you're a fool! Those shares are worthless. Once I wanted to buy them, and you refused to sell. Now, there's no reason to buy. The Peekskill and Tarrytown gave up existence two years ago, when you leased it. Oh, perhaps in nine-hundred-odd years, when that curious lease comes due, the shares will have a value beyond that of framing, but frankly I have no interest in future generations. To control, Kinross, to *control* . . . that is what matters. I already control your ridiculous little line. The shares mean nothing to me."

Gow paused, and in the ensuing silence was a menace more

40

deadly than words. "You don't understand me too well, Kinross. Had you acquiesced when I broached the matter of Cathryn—"

"You can't have Cathryn," growled her grandfather. "I won't even put the matter to her. You're forty-four, Gow. She's seventeen. What kind of marriage would it be?"

"The offer was never marriage," Gow snapped. "You must have misunderstood me, Kinross. I intend to make her my mistress."

"Your mistress!" roared Jared Kinross. "Cat will never be your mistress! I won't allow it!" He came to his feet and lunged across the room. "Damn you, Gow . . . damn you, damn you, damn you . . ."

Kinross had forgotten the omnipresent shadow of a bodyguard that lurked just inside the door. Six foot two of brawn burst across the room, and a fist connected sickeningly with aging stomach tissue. Kinross gasped in pain.

Gow was breathing faster now, and his pale eyes flickered. His gloved hand brushed the spot where Kinross had connected. "How dare you touch me! For that foolish attempt, Kinross, you will also have to pay. Cathryn, in *one* week . . . or *four* hundred thousand dollars! I'll see you a ruined man, Kinross! Ruined!"

The only answer was a low moan, and retching sounds from the sunken figure on the floor.

"Leave him, Olin," Gow directed his bodyguard curtly. He strode to the door, and moments later stalked into the night, followed by the hulking shapes of his strongmen.

In the circular driveway of Kirklands, the carriage lamps of his waiting equipage gleamed on crested panels, on pale, pearl-gray liveries, on the sleek flanks of the four matched grays that were the envy and desperation of every admirer of horseflesh along Fifth Avenue. They, and the fine brougham, had been brought north from New York on Gow's private train.

Even before Gow's men had mounted into the carriage, a slender figure had detached itself from the shadows at the side of the house, and was racing for the back door. Once inside, Cat could hear sounds of consternation coming from the second floor. She took the ill-lighted back stairs two at a time, heart in her mouth lest she had been missed.

Hannah met her on the landing, and at once launched into

41

a tirade. "Where have ye been, Miss Cat? Have ye na' heard me calling? Och! Your grandfather in a state, sick to his stomach, he's that bad."

The household's two maids were also on the landing, and Cat brushed past them, hurrying toward her grandfather's room. The door stood open, and Cat went right in, followed by the energetic Scotswoman.

Jared Kinross, ashen-faced, sat on a chair by the window, with Angus McBride, Hannah's father, attending to him.

"Are you all right, grandpapa?"

"Yes," came the answer, with some effort.

"I'm sorry, I've been with Prince all this time," Cat lied. "He seemed restless, so I took him for a short romp. Then I heard Mr. Gow's carriage leave, and . . . Hannah said you were feeling ill. Has something happened to upset you?"

Hannah started to speak, but Jared Kinross stayed her with a raised hand. "Nothing, Cat. Nothing! A touch of dyspepsia. Angus is going to help me to bed now. I'll be fine by morning."

It was some time before the servants dispersed to their sleeping quarters in the rear of the house, and Cat found herself in her own bedroom, alone at last. Her nightgown had been donned, her hair brushed out for the night; the coal-oil lamps had been extinguished; Hannah had departed for her own room in the servants' quarters. Silently, Cat left her bed and went to the window. She pushed aside the curtains and gazed out.

So, she thought, her grandfather intended to tell her nothing of Julian Gow's threats and demands. With no tears, but with a very real fear touching her face, Cat gazed down on the east terrace below her bedroom window, from which she had heard every word of tonight's conversation. The light of the crescent moon silvering her eyes made them appear pale and oddly incandescent in contrast to the darkness of lashes and hair—almost like the eyes of the animal whose name she shared.

Fear. Was that what Julian Gow really wanted from her grandfather? From Deirdre? From herself? From everyone?

Fear . . .

5

The lone roan stallion that reined in at Kirklands five days later bore little resemblance to the mannerly animals that had been driven by Julian Gow's coachman. This creature reared and snorted, for he was skittish from languishing too long in the livery stables from which he had been hired not an hour before.

A strong bronzed hand gentled him back to docility, and a low voice spoke some deep soothing words. Daniel Savage was still dismounting when others appeared—the young lad who served as the household's stablehand, and, from the front door, a young girl who was older, but not by very much.

There was some distance between the hitching posts and the front door. In the September sunshine, Daniel watched the slender figure of the girl as she descended the broad front steps, dark green skirts a-swish. Now, why did she look so familiar? That beautiful coloring, those startling silver-gray eyes—by God, it was the girl he'd seen on Julian Gow's special train. The one who had been driving the engine. Well, it was not an astonishing coincidence, was it? Jared Kinross had been on that train, too. Could this be some relative of his?

"Are you Mr. Savage . . . Mr. Daniel Savage?" she asked, and when he acknowledged that he was, she managed a smile that seemed too strained. Daniel noted, too, that the beautiful eyes looked smudged, as though she had spent too much time partying of late. "I'm Cathryn Kinross. A few days ago my grandfather received your letter saying you might arrive, but he had urgent business in New York. I'm afraid he's been there most of the week."

Daniel frowned, considering that. A communication from Jared Kinross, written some time ago, had reminded him of his promise to pay a call. Daniel had decided to follow through. He had other business in the East; a group of New York investors had finally agreed to put up venture capital for the California railroad.

"It seems I've come at the wrong time," he muttered.

"Not really. Tomorrow's Saturday, and grandpapa should be returning by this evening, or at the latest, tomorrow morning. In any case, he'd expect you to stay overnight."

Cat knew, without being told, that her grandfather had gone to New York in a last-ditch attempt to raise money. He had not yet conceded defeat to Julian Gow; he was made of sterner stuff than that. The day after Gow's visit he had been back on his feet, ready to go out fighting. Cat did not know about Jared Kinross's heart condition, but his do-or-die determination had given her hope where once there had been none. All this week she had wondered if some miracle might make it unnecessary for her to go through with a course of action that filled her with a nameless dread.

"I have an idea grandpapa wants to speak to you," Cat said; and at last Daniel acquiesced. He turned to relinquish the bridle, and give instructions to the stablehand.

Cat watched him as he spoke, and hoped she had managed to conceal the bitter disappointment she had felt on first meeting him. The kindling of warmth in her grandfather's eyes, when he had received the message that this man would be arriving to visit, had led her to believe that there might be some hope of financial salvation from the mysterious Mr. Savage—a railroad builder from California, she had been told, and a man with a very cavalier disregard for danger.

But all her hopes had been dashed on first sight of the man himself. Although grandpapa had said this man played for high stakes, very evidently he was not enormously wealthy. True, his clothes were of good quality, and tailored to show his tall athletic build to advantage. The frock coat sat easily over muscular shoulders, and the waistcoat lay smoothly over a stomach that looked hard and flat, and his shirt was a good silky cotton. But a hired horse? Not even a hired carriage? No silk hat? Gentlemen of means always wore silk hats. And they did not have a tan like *that*, so deep that a sunburst of paler crinkles showed around the eyes. Nor did they have eyes like that—untamed eyes that had raked her, briefly, in a way she had already learned to recognize. Recklessness glinted in those eyes, and, seeing them, it was not so very hard to believe the story her grandfather had told her about this man.

Well, thought Cat despondently, as she led her disappointing guest toward the house, it seemed that destiny had no reprieves to offer. And in two days . . .

At the very thought of what would happen in two days, Cat's stomach tied itself into a gigantic knot. The worst part would be telling her grandfather of her intentions. There was always the possibility that he would try to prevent her from going in Julian Gow's carriage, but Cat did not think he would, once she had told him the lies she had decided upon.

But did it have to be all lies? As the thought occurred to her for the first time, Cat cast a speculative sideways glance at the tall bronzed stranger whose footsteps crunched beside hers on the driveway. *He* looked as if he would not have cruel hands. The fingers looked long, hard, and capable, but they had been gentle on the horse—she had seen that. And he was younger than Julian Gow, not yet thirty, she guessed. Twenty-eight, twenty-nine? Still too old, of course, but at least he was not forty-four! This man had a fit, well-knit body and a way of moving that was lithe and loose-limbed and very self-assured. Too self-assured? He looked as though he had few scruples. An adventurer, Cat guessed. The type of man who would make love to a woman one day and not remember her the next.

"Do you often drive trains?" he asked as they reached the house and started up the steps. Then, in answer to the puzzled look she darted at his face, he added: "I saw you from a siding, when you were driving Julian Gow's train."

"You must be mistaken," Cat said absently, and did not even bother to add an injunction for him to maintain secrecy. In the light of more recent happenings, the minor infractions of three months ago seemed unimportant.

The mouth—she looked at it again, surreptitiously. What would it be like to be kissed by that mouth? It looked cynical. Or was that just the effect of the deep clefts that ran down his cheeks, definite as scars, although they were not? The mouth frightened her, but in a way that was not entirely unpleasant. Would it feel softer than it looked? She could not quite imagine what it would be like to have those lips pressing on hers. But then, how *could* she imagine such a thing? She had never been kissed by a man.

No! she thought, backing away from the insanity of the idea that had presented itself, full-blown, to her mind. It was unthinkable, even if her grandfather did remain overnight in New York. How could she have contemplated such a thing? She had had no experience in seduction, and this man looked as if he had had all too much. She couldn't. She couldn't. She *couldn't!*

And yet, could she bear for Julian Gow to be the first?

The speculation came to a halt when Angus McBride appeared, and more practical matters had to be attended to. Daniel Savage was assigned the large guest room, which was next to Jared Kinross's quarters. Despite its size, it was an unimposing room, with warm wallpaper and friendly furniture.

"I could use a bath," Daniel informed Angus once Cat had departed. Now why, he thought to himself, had she suddenly gone so strange and tongue-tied? She had seemed quite self-possessed at first. Ah, well, young ladies were a class all to themselves; and with a little shake of his head as though to dismiss her from his thoughts, Daniel turned to the matter of washing away the dust of travel.

Dinner for Cat and her guest was served after dusk, in the dining room. In later years, Cat always remembered the dining room best for that one silent hour: candlelight flickering on dark oak, picking out the great gray cabbage roses of the wallpaper, casting changing shadows into the deep clefts of a man's face, and transforming lips that had looked hard by sunlight into a softer, more sensuous line. Did it matter that he was a stranger? No: Perhaps that was best. It could be done and it could be forgotten; she would likely never see him again. Alternately fascinated and repelled by the outrageousness of her thoughts, she hardly noted the awkward lulls in conversation that followed Daniel's attempts to set her at her ease.

And when the meal came to an end, she had just, for the thousandth time, decided she could not possibly be so bold.

"I think I heard the buggy drive in," she mumbled with a lack of composure undeserved by such a simple observation. Angus had gone to the whistle-stop to meet the last train from New York; by now Cat hoped against hope that her grandfather would be on it. His presence tonight would put all speculations into the realm of the impossible.

Clumsily, she pushed her chair back from the table, not waiting for her guest's help. By this time she was sure that if her flesh came into accidental contact with his, it would burn. She felt incapable of looking at him directly; she was afraid her eyes would betray the intimacy of the imaginings she had been entertaining throughout the meal.

Daniel Savage pushed his chair back, too. And because Cat could not meet his face, her gaze was directed lower. *Why* did she have to notice the fabric of his trousers, taut over powerfully muscled thighs, revealed by the casual lay of the jacket as he sat? He stood up—no, uncoiled, thought Cat—and the frock coat fell back in place, but not before she had glimpsed the smooth bulge of fabric in a place where proper young ladies were not supposed to cast their eyes.

She felt curiously breathless—flustered—embarrassed; and she was sure he had seen the direction of her stare.

"I'll wander out and see if your grandfather's arrived," Daniel suggested, by now frankly relieved at the prospect of getting away from this uncomfortable meal. Could this inarticulate creature with the evasive eyes really be the same girl who had been driving a hundred and twenty tons of locomotive with such joyous abandon?

"I'll come and see, too," said Cat awkwardly, with downcast eyes. "I hope he's here."

Jared Kinross had indeed arrived on the train, but his condition gave Cat no comfort. He came in leaning on Angus McBride's shoulder, his eyes glazed and his mumblings incoherent. It was obvious that he had been drinking, and heavily—an uncommon occurrence for him, and one that boded no good tidings. Now, concern for her grandfather overcame the temerity that had assailed Cat throughout the meal just past.

"Take him to bed at once, Angus," she instructed. She turned to Daniel, eyes grave and once more level. "Grandpapa won't be able to talk to you tonight. I won't apologize for his condition; he's had a difficult week. Your business will have to wait until tomorrow. Now, if you'll excuse me, Angus may need my help."

"That's a man's job," Daniel said; and together he and Angus spent some minutes settling Jared Kinross into bed, while Cat hovered in the hall.

"I think I'll retire, too," she said as soon as the two men emerged from her grandfather's room. She looked white-lipped now, Daniel noted, but composed. The flustered girl had vanished, but she had not been replaced by the joyous one, either. There was something new in her manner now—a decisiveness that had not been there before.

"Angus, would you please tell Hannah and the maids that I won't be down to help with the clearing up tonight?" Then

47

Cat turned to Daniel. "There's no need for you to go to bed until you wish, Mr. Savage. Angus will show you to the library."

"I think I'll go for a walk. I may be late . . . if it's no trouble."

"The front door is never locked. But we do bed down early here. Perhaps Angus can leave a light burning for you."

"Aye," agreed Angus, his brogue reminiscent of Hannah's, but thicker. "I'll leave a wee lantern by the front door, for ye'll na' see a thing with the lights oot."

"And before you go to bed, Angus," instructed Cat calmly, "set out a bottle of brandy for Mr. Savage. In his bedroom."

It was more than two hours later, and nearly midnight, when Daniel returned from his moonlight walk. Inside the sleeping house all was silence and darkness, except for a faint glow emanating from a window near the front door. The walk had been a brisk one, and it was a warm night; Daniel had removed his jacket, and it now hung over one shoulder, slung by a finger. He found himself looking forward to the moment when he could pull off his dusty boots and settle down for a last cheroot, and the brandy Angus had been instructed to leave in his bedroom.

"Damn," muttered Daniel on a sudden thought. Would smoking be allowed in this house? He could not remember seeing Jared Kinross with a cigar on that night in Saratoga Springs. It was a practice frowned upon by many in this Victorian era; although cuspidors were omnipresent, ashtrays were not. And he had forgotten to put the question to Angus or to Miss Kinross.

He withdrew his hand from the doorknob, and redirected his feet toward the terrace he had noted earlier, at the east side of the house. He needed no lantern, any more than he had needed one on the walk. Tonight a globe of a moon hung in the sky, bathing the hushed flagstone terrace, casting silver on stone and white on flowering sweet clematis. From the garden below the terrace, a potpourri of sleepy autumn scents spiced the warm night air. After extracting a cheroot from his cigar case, Daniel threw his jacket over a parapet; and soon a new aroma drifted through the night.

Moments later the jacket was joined by the waistcoat whose confines he no longer wanted. He thrust away thoughts of a thorny tunneling problem, too, that had occupied him during his walk. There was no use thinking more of what the

48

future might bring. At times, a man must live for the present. He leaned forward, propping his elbows on the parapet overlooking the garden, and abandoned himself to enjoyment of the moment.

The silent footsteps on flagstone took him by surprise; they were nearly upon him when the soft stirrings sifted through to his drifting consciousness. He did not whirl around, for in the moment he heard the sounds he knew they were made by a woman.

Cat saw the tensing of muscles beneath the soft fabric of his shirt, and knew he had heard her. Unable to find the words for what she wanted to say, she touched his shoulder—a feather-light touch, tentative and suggestive all at once.

It was strange how some people had an aura, thought Daniel. Although there had been other females in the house, and one of the serving maids in particular had been quite come-hither in her glances during dinner, he knew who this was as surely as if he had already turned. It wasn't a perfume—she wore none; he'd noted that earlier.

"Why are you still up?" he demanded quietly, turning at last. Moon-silvered eyes looked back up at him, devoid of shyness, but devoid of flirtatiousness, too. They were serious, and so was her face. He saw that she had changed out of the simple forest green gown that she had worn earlier.

"You shouldn't be out here dressed like that," he said more roughly, although he kept his voice low. Oh, God—was it the moonlight playing tricks, or was she moistening her lips as though she wanted to be kissed? At the moment she looked about sixteen. Why did she have to be so damn beautiful? Why did she have to be so damn *young?*

"You should be in bed," he said gruffly when she did not answer.

"I was in bed." Her voice, like his, was lowered, for although the servants' bedrooms were at the rear of the house with no windows giving on this terrace, sounds traveled in the night. "I couldn't sleep. I was beginning to think you were never coming in."

There was a long moment's silence, during which she fought the impulse to lower her lashes. But the primitive thing she saw in his eyes was what she wanted to see, wasn't it? Despite the night's warmth, little shivers traveled over her skin beneath the flimsy wrapper and nightgown she wore.

"I can't think why you should care," came the abrupt answer, as he turned away toward the parapet again.

"Please kiss me," Cat braved on. Her voice was soft as a whisper of silk this time; even to her own ears it might have been imagination. "You want to kiss me. I saw it in your face, a moment ago."

"Go away, Miss Kinross," he said in a tight voice. His anger was evident, even in the lowness of his tones. "I'm too old for kissing games."

"A kiss. Is that so much to ask?" Cat replied, more bravely this time, though her heart felt as if it would explode in her chest, and her palms had grown damp. "To a man your age, a kiss must be nothing."

"That's right, it's nothing. Young girls don't interest me, Miss Kinross. When I play, I play for larger game."

"Please." Her hand touched his shirt again. This time it lingered, finding the corded muscles of his shoulder, taut with suppressed violence. Why was he so angry? Cat wetted her lips again, trying to find the courage to issue an outright invitation for what she wanted, but the brazen words would not come out. But if he kissed her, everything else would follow naturally, wouldn't it? And so she repeated: "Please kiss me."

Daniel found himself sweating, and cursed the dull throbbing that had begun to take possession of his groin. "Christ," he muttered savagely, and moved further along the parapet, but she—and her hand—followed.

"It's not just an impulse," she said. "I wanted to kiss you earlier."

Her face was so close he could feel the warm breath of her on his spine. And those slender fingers exploring his arm—bold and hesitant all at once. He pushed them away, roughly.

"Go away, little girl," Daniel commanded, his voice deliberately rude. He cursed himself for removing his jacket earlier: The narrow cut of his trousers outlined all too clearly the telltale swelling that his body was beginning to produce in defiance of his mind's command. And so he kept his back turned to her, and hunched his shoulders testily when the smooth small hand once more slid tentatively up his spine.

"I'm not a little girl, Mr. Savage. I'm old enough to be kissed."

"You're a little girl to me." The rasp of his voice held a suppressed rage. "Good God, girl! I haven't stopped at *kissing* since about the time you toddled off to school in pinafores. So back off. Go to your bedroom and stop playing with fire!"

"I want to play with fire," Cat whispered, breathless with her own daring. She was so close now that she could feel the knocking of his heart through the musculature of his shoulders. Oh, why did he make this so difficult for her? Dredging up courage, she let her arms slide around his waist.

"Dammit, stop that," he grated. He sucked his breath through gritted teeth, and his knuckles tightened for an involuntary instant on the balustrade. When he moved it was already too late; her hands were molded over the cursed outlines he had hoped to conceal. And his hands, disobedient to his brain, covered her fingers, clasping her to him, adding impetus to the arousal he had been trying so desperately to fight.

Cat felt the sudden springing surge of his body, and her senses swam. She was not so naive that she did not know something of what happened to a man in moments of passion—but *that* much? For the first time she realized the full enormity of the path she had chosen for herself, and the realization unleashed a trembling weakness in her lower limbs.

Reflexively she started to snatch her hands away, and in the next moment found herself gathered, with a groan, into a pair of strong arms. Iron bands encircled her; she could not have obeyed the instinct to flee now, even if she had tried. His mouth crushed down recklessly over hers. So that was how a man's lips felt! But how could they be hard and soft at the same time—the press of them so warm, the texture of them so demanding?

Her mouth remained closed against his, not in resistance but in ignorance. Daniel lifted his head away a few inches, conscious of her lack of response. But she was not fighting him: Her eyes, widely opened and sheened by moonlight, told him that. And so, in defiance of everything he knew to be right, he lowered his mouth again, this time tantalizing the closed lips with his tongue. His hands moved on her spine, feeling the slide of silky cotton; and his fingers that had known too many women knew that the skin beneath the wrapper would be silken, too.

Slowly the man-taste of him seeped through her closed lips. She understood the traceries of his tongue, and responded to

51

the message. Her lips parted, and he probed. Gently at first he explored the inner edges of her lips, the smooth polish of her teeth; and then, the secrets that lay behind, like sweet surprises, as her tongue began to take instruction from his.

Sensations never felt before began to lick little fires along her veins. But then, suddenly, with one brutal and explosive deepening of the kiss, he pushed her away and swiveled on his heel.

"For God's sake and your own, get away from me," he ground out between his teeth.

Faced with his uncompromising spine and unsteadied by this sudden change in him, Cat felt near to tears of frustration and humiliation. To her, it seemed that what had been happening between them, during the kiss, was justification for her earlier brazenness. Instinctively, she sensed that the first time for a woman should be tender, ardent, radiant, right. She also knew, instinctively, that with the man to whom she intended to give herself, it would not be so. Moreover, it had been instinct that had driven her to Daniel Savage tonight. Instinct had told her he would be very practiced, and very good, at making love. Instinct had told her he would take her with gentleness and ardor and consideration; that he would give her all the soothing words, the gentling caresses, the helping through hurt that she wanted for the very first time, and that she knew she would not receive from Julian Gow.

And a few moments ago, she had thought her instinct justified, in the slow probing way he had taught her to kiss, leashing his passions and seeking her own response before demanding more.

"Was I doing something wrong?" she whispered.

"Yes, you bloody well were!" His low vehement words came out with the force of a contained explosion. "I'm not interested in beginners' kisses. Now get the hell to bed, or I'll give you the paddling your grandfather should have given you long ago . . . preferably the first day you got into long skirts."

And with an oath that Cat could not understand, he flung himself away from her and strode down into the lower garden. With a feeling of sick shame in the pit of her stomach, and eyes huge with humiliation, Cat turned and ran, on silent bare feet, into the house.

Daniel thrust his hands fiercely into his pockets, and

groaned. So she wanted to learn about kissing? To test her burgeoning little sexual allures on a real live male? Or did she want the whole, unalterable, irreversible loss of virginity? Well, lose it she might, and lose it she soon would, if tonight was any sampling. But she wasn't going to lose it to *him*.

And certainly not with her grandfather in the offing! A budding Sophie, that's what she was. And he had no bloody intention of being caught in a compromising situation with a girl hardly out of the cradle. And totally inexperienced, too, despite those audacious hands. Poison!

All the same, the memory of those fingers, half shy, half bold, and the way they had found their goal before the kiss, wreaked havoc with his groin for some minutes after Cat went in the house. And the taste of her, the sweet girlhood taste of her, still taunted his tongue and his lips. The taste, the texture—and the fragrance. Why had he thought she had no fragrance?

From the lower garden, his eye caught a shuttered second floor window that must be hers. A faint yellow glow outlined it for a time, and then the light was extinguished. A half hour passed, then another. And when he was sure it was safe to do so, Daniel made his silent way to the front door; retrieved the low-burning coal-oil lantern that had been left out by Angus; went upstairs; and entered the bedroom that had been assigned to him.

And there, sound asleep on his bed, lay the girl he had spent this past hour trying to avoid.

6

She lay with no cover but the loose wrapper and nightgown she had worn in the garden; the patchwork quilt and bed-linens had been carefully folded to the foot of the bed. With her hair fanned out on the pillow, and the dark droop of lashes on her cheeks, she looked incredibly young. Too young.

And while Daniel stood grim-faced in the doorway, debating his next course of action, she awoke.

She woke without panic, lashes feathering open to reveal those pale, polished moonstone eyes. Something that was not quite a smile lifted the edges of her lips.

"You took a long time," she murmured, just as though this whole encounter had been prearranged.

Daniel closed the door behind him with a soft decisive snap. "Now look, Miss Kinross," he said with strained patience, "you came to the garden for a kiss, and damn you, you got it. Enough is enough! I don't go in for seducing half-grown girls. Go back to your bedroom like the good little virgin you are, and tomorrow I won't tell a soul you've been here."

"You're not seducing me," she pointed out, sitting up in bed. Her face was serious, like a child's. "I'm seducing you."

"No, you're not," he informed her tightly. "And certainly not with your grandfather in the next room."

"*You* saw him. You know he won't wake up. And the servants won't hear a thing. Their rooms are too far from here."

Daniel glowered at her, his grooved cheeks drawn into lines of disapproval that were deepened by the upward shadows of the lantern he held in his hand. "You don't know enough about sex to seduce a fly," he said gruffly. "Hasn't anyone told you, Miss Kinross, that making advances is a man's prerogative?"

"Does it have to be?" she countered. Her hands laced themselves around her knees—almost as if to prevent the knees from knocking. "And please call me Cathryn, or Cat, if you prefer. Do you mind if I call you Daniel? If we're going to be making love—"

"We . . . are . . . not . . . going . . . to make love," he ground out, each word deliberate and emphatic. "I make love when *I* choose, and to whom *I* choose. I don't choose to make love to a quaking little virgin who doesn't even know enough to part her lips for a kiss!"

"I do now," she pointed out with an ingenuous smile. "I'm a quick learner."

"Out," he gritted, waving his lantern toward the door.

"No." She hunched her shoulders defiantly, until her chin almost touched her knees—the gesture of a creature burrowing in for the night. "I could scream, you realize, and rip my nightgown. *That* would bring everyone running, and grandpapa would be sure to hear about it tomorrow."

Daniel compressed his lips, and walked farther into the room. He set the lantern down with a precise deliberation, and poured himself a full tumbler of the brandy Angus had left. He swallowed it at a draught, banged down the glass noisily, and turned to glare at her with folded arms and stern face.

"Start screaming," he ordered grimly.

For a silent moment tawny eyes battled with gray, and hers fell first. "It was just a thought," she admitted. "I wouldn't do it." Her mouth quivered a little. Doubt? Disappointment?

"Then go to your room," he directed more kindly, but with a weary note to his voice. His fingers ran a ragged pattern through his hair. "It must be one o'clock in the morning, and I'm damn tired of this nonsense."

And so, Cat slid to the edge of the bed, defeated and dispirited and shamed, and, to tell the truth, a little confused, too. He *had* wanted her; she had realized that earlier, as soon as she had returned to the house. His deliberately cruel words on the terrace, telling her she did not know how to kiss, had been a form of self-defense: That had come clear once she thought it through. He had rejected her, she was sure, only because he was not prepared to stop at kissing. Well, *she* didn't intend to stop at kissing either, and surely her presence in his bed, clad only in nightgown and wrapper, would advertise that fact? She had not been able to bring herself to remove her gown, nor could she now, though she was sure a true seductress would have done so.

55

Mr. Daniel Savage simply did not want what she was offering, and that humiliating fact had to be faced. Slowly, with head hung low and cheeks flaming, she started to pad across the room, then stopped near the door.

"I owe you an apology," she said to her feet. On the worn Brussels carpet they looked very naked and defenseless. Oh, *why* had she ever let those foolish feet bring her in here?

"Ah, all is forgiven," Daniel replied, relief evident in the soft exhalation of his breath. At ease now, he strolled toward the door with intentions of opening it for her. "And soon forgotten, too. By the morning I won't remember a thing."

No, thought Cat, he won't. "But I will," she said with a curious catch to her voice. "I'm sorry I came to your room. I'm sorry I forced you to kiss me against your will. I'm sorry I didn't . . . please you."

Daniel chuckled, relaxed now that he thought she had conceded. His hand caught her chin, cupping it and forcing her face to turn upward toward his. Her eyes, evasive once more, remained hidden behind their curtain of lashes.

"Don't be so impatient to grow up, little one. And don't worry, you'll please some man . . . someday. In fact, I think you'll please him very much. But not unless you save something to give him! Your feelings are hurt now, but someday you'll thank me for leaving you intact, and *he* will too, whoever he may be. Goodnight, Miss Ki—"

He was off guard when her arms suddenly wrapped themselves around his waist, and her tip-tilted mouth darted upward. She had learned her lesson well: This time it was her lips, and her tongue, that were the aggressors.

In the first outraged instant Daniel clamped his mouth against her persistent, pointed, probing tongue. He unlaced her fingers from behind his spine, and captured her hands in his, thrusting them firmly backward toward her hips.

His mind rejected her—so how was it that, moments later, he was dragging the length of her against him? That his hands were clasping her buttocks to mold the slender, sweet, perfumed body against his springing manhood? How was it that his lips had opened, and the kiss had become *his* aggression—a deep, intrusive, punishing kiss? There was a madness in him now, anger as well as hunger. A need for conquest thundered through his veins and his loins; and everything—the perfumed night, the silence of the house, the

56

yielding silk of her skin—they all conspired to drive the danger signals from his head.

Somehow, before the kiss ended, he had swept her back to the bed, torn off her wrapper, and levered himself beside the slender frame that was now clad only in a thin cotton nightdress.

Cat came out of the kiss gasping for air, shocked by the rough way he had thrown her on the bed, alarmed to find herself shackled by a pair of hands that were not gentle at all, as she had imagined they would be. The change of role was too sudden. In an eyeblink she had become the hunted, not the huntress; he had become the predator, not the prey.

And the way he was unfastening her nightgown now, so impatiently, tearing at the ribbons, pushing the bodice aside to reveal her breast . . . Oh, God, was this the same man who had kissed her on the terrace? His smoldering eyes possessed the rose-tipped ivory curves as he slid down farther on her body. The tanned face, mahogany against the milkiness of her, did not hesitate to violate the breast no man had touched before. There was a savagery in the mouth that claimed her nipple—punishing it, perhaps, for tempting him. And, merciful heaven, what was he doing with his hand? It rioted over her curves, burning its way down to the no-man's-land of her thighs, pushing the fabric roughly to her waist. His fingers tangled hurtfully in hair, and an instinctive cry came to her lips.

"Be quiet," Daniel ordered grimly, freeing her breast and moving upward on her body until the alcohol-scented breath of him mingled with her own. His harsh heavy breathing was punctuated by the thud of his heart through the thin shirt he still wore; his fingers dug patterns into her shoulders. "This is what you wanted, isn't it? Dammit, don't change your mind! A maidenhead is not my idea of a great trophy, but you've driven me too far, and now I won't be stopped."

Even as he spoke, he worked at the fastenings of his trousers, without removing them. Cat's eyes feathered closed to shut out the angers and the passions that burned in those primitive eyes. Every nerve in her body screamed revolt. Was this the way it always happened between a man and a woman? This—assault? And yet she would not fight. Did it matter who took her? It was either this hot-blooded man whose capacity for cruelty she had so badly misjudged, or another, very soon—and one whose cruelties she was sure would be worse. She tensed every muscle to accept what must surely come soon. Her own actions had led to this, and she would not try to escape now.

"Please be kind," she whispered as his mouth descended again.

"Oh, God," he groaned, and pulled back just as his knee had been about to intrude itself between hers. He paused—forced himself, with every ounce of will in his body, to pause. The fierce clench of her fists, the rigidity of her legs, the trembling of her lashes, the paleness of her cheeks, the ticking of a pulse in her throat—gradually he became aware of them all. What was he doing; what the hell was he doing? This was little better than rape. No matter that she lay there unresisting, like a blood-sacrifice; no matter that she had goaded him to heights of anger as well as of passion. With a low curse he bent his head into the soft satin of her throat, until the fires that blazed within him were banked enough to allow him to speak.

The huskiness of his voice was muffled against her skin. "If you slide out carefully you can still leave. Don't move too fast. Or too damn slowly, either."

"I don't want to leave. Please make love to me."

"I'm not making love, dammit! I'm practically raping you. Can't you tell? I'm angry that you've trapped me into this. You're a virgin, and good God, I'm a guest in your grandfather's house, and . . . Oh, *hell*," he groaned as her lips nibbled experimentally at his ear, "where did you learn to do *that?*"

Daniel jerked his head upward and glared down at the solemn face below him. Her eyes were wide open now, watchful and a little distrustful, but in no way telling him to stop. And suddenly he knew he wanted to see a different expression there. With an effort, he rolled his long-limbed body away from hers and adjusted his clothing to conceal his swollen manhood. It was a few moments before he spoke.

"I'm going to teach you to make love, Miss Cathryn Kinross," he said in a rough-soft voice, "as you're so bound and determined to learn. I shouldn't do it and I wouldn't do it if I had any sense. Are you sure you know what you're letting yourself in for?"

"Yes."

"I'm going to regret this for a long time," Daniel prophesied, sweeping her with his eyes, but the huskiness that now vibrated through his voice did not sound like regret. The arms that reached for her were kinder now. They gathered her close and slid down her spine, gentling it, stroking the flesh through the thin nightgown she still wore. He did no more until the tense shuddering stopped, and the rigidity began to leave her limbs.

"Don't be frightened, child," he murmured into her hair. "I won't grow angry again. And I won't do anything until you're ready."

Now he eased her onto her spine and hovered above her, his hands cupping her head, thumbs soothing the earlobes while he rained little kisses over her temples, her cheeks, the hollows of her eyes. The exquisite slow shiverings that began to take possession of her uninitiated flesh were nothing like the shudderings of before. This time, when he slid down to her throat and to her breast, there was no ferocity in his mouth. His tongue teased the nipple lazily, with a deliberate delicacy that was a torture of a different kind, and when the rise turned taut beneath his moist and expert feathering, he caught it briefly with strong teeth that did not forget to be gentle.

Drowning in the sea of sensations he was so skillfully arousing, she hardly knew his hands had done a different task, until a little coolness of air told her the nightgown had somehow been removed. But when long strong fingers broached the forbidden triangle of her thighs, her legs scissored together involuntarily, a virginal reflex in expectation of pain, and one she could not control.

"Don't tense up," he murmured, his mouth still at her breast. "I'm not going to hurt you. I promise I won't do that without warning you. I'm going to do something else, something that won't hurt at all. Now just relax."

"What are you . . . ? Oh . . ."

It was hard to remember what she had wanted to know with his hand touching her as it was. He did not try to ease her legs apart as she had expected. Instead, his seeking, stroking fingers found a part of her, a part exposed despite the rigid clench of thighs, loitering over it in a way that should have been soothing, but was not.

"I can't relax when you do that," gasped Cat, for something inside herself was beginning to squirm, causing unfamiliar sensations to shiver through her nether regions. There was

59

a restlessness in her thighs; they had begun to writhe of their own accord, allowing the hand to intrude farther between her legs.

Daniel raised his head from her breast long enough to look at her with eyes darkened to deepest hue by the passions he had leashed so well. His low smoky laugh was a tribute to the sensuality he felt burgeoning in the young body that lay beneath his hands, but there was something of triumph in it, too—the male animal mastering his mate. "Just let your body behave as it wants to," he instructed huskily, and his mouth returned to its appointed task. His hand still tarried at her thighs. Now, when he nudged her legs apart to allow his fingers full freedom, she obeyed the command of his hand that had become the command of her own consuming need. He felt the moistness of her inner thighs and the trembling readiness of her; and so he began with slow sure strokes to give pleasure to the pulsing crest of her passion.

Cat was witless with wanting. Moaning, writhing, she laced her fingers into his hair and pulled his head fiercely closer to her breast. No matter now if it hurt. Her body demanded him, and it demanded him urgently. An unfamiliar white heat centered in her loins, searing, surging, blazing. . . . She gasped and groaned and sobbed and twisted, and then, when she could bear it no longer, she clasped her slender hand convulsively over the strong one that roamed between her legs. Her arching hips strained upward, upward, upward . . . until the white hot core of her exploded, fragmenting into a thousand thousand shards of color and light.

"That's it, love, let yourself go—"

He held her closely while she floated back to reality. And when she was quiescent once more, he pushed the damp tendrils of hair from her forehead, and showered little kisses on the moisture that had gathered on her brow. How fiercely he wanted her now! But the acute and terrible need for his own assuagement must be put aside a little longer. He had not always been so patient with a woman's needs. But then, he was used to a different type of woman: Virgins were not within his normal ken. And as she was a virgin—of that he now had proof—male pride demanded that he teach her well.

"That's how beautiful it can be, sweetheart. You've learned something about your body. Now I'm going to teach you something about mine."

Rolling to the edge of the bed, he stood up and divested

himself of his shirt and trousers. While his back was turned, Cat pulled a sheet over her nakedness—less for modesty than for the chilly little tremors that now seized the flesh no longer heated by passion. Eyes large, she watched Daniel, glad that his back was turned so that she could surrender to the fascination of seeing a man naked for the first time. The little fearfulness she felt was not unpleasant now. The ripple of muscles across broad shoulders, the little dark hairs that roughened his arms, the hard pale polish of his flanks—it seemed right and natural that he should be as naked as she.

But when he turned to face her, her eyes darted away to find safer sights.

"Another lesson," he said, as he adjusted the wick of the coal-oil lantern to brighten it, "you're going to learn to look at what you're making love to. You've walked into this with your eyes open, Miss Cathryn Kinross, and I intend you to keep them that way."

And then he came down on the bed beside her, and his hand on her jaw firmly redirected her head. As yet, he did not pull away the skimpy covering of the sheet she had pulled over herself.

"Turn this way, woman," he said in a thrillingly low voice. "And yes, you are a woman, or you will be very soon. Look at me."

Try as she might, Cat was unable to force her eyes to travel openly the full length of him. But she saw. Even with her gaze riveted to the matted darkness of his chest, she saw.

"A man's body is not so frightening once you're used to it. It's hard where yours is soft, exposed where yours is hidden, rough where yours is smooth. Touch if you want, where you want. Don't worry, I won't let myself be driven to a frenzy by anything you do."

After a moment he chuckled softly, and took possession of the hand that had been clutching a sheet to her breasts. He pulled it toward the tangle of his chest.

"That's what your fingers were wanting to do, isn't it? Do you like the way it feels?"

"Yes," said Cat breathlessly. The crisp darkness, prickling and vital, was sending shock waves through her fingertips. "And your chest feels nice . . . all sinewy and warm."

Then, after a few minutes in which her hand did nothing, Daniel said: "Do you want to explore some more?"

"No."

"Then it's time you learned to let me look at you." He propped himself up on one elbow. "Fold back the sheet, Cathryn . . . Cat. Slowly if you like. I'll tell you when I'm going to touch."

And after she had obeyed, he added in a curiously thickened voice: "You're very beautiful, d'you know that? Now be patient with me for a time, because what I'm going to do next may hurt."

Hurt? Not those exquisite sensations that started once more to thread their way through her limbs and her loins as he aroused her anew. With expert fingers and knowing mouth he prepared her, taking his time until the moist signals of her thighs told him she was ready for the mounting. Now at last his bronzed body covered hers, and he found himself where he wanted so urgently to be. He guided himself a short distance into the virgin flesh. The palm of one hand, smoothing her hip, steadied her to receive his sex.

"I can't prevent hurting you now," Daniel said thickly. "I'm going to kiss you, Cathryn, so you won't cry out."

"I won't cry ou—" she started to say, but his mouth clamped down over hers, and a battering ram drove into her core. Involuntarily she tried to shrink away, but there was nowhere to go with the heavy weight of him pinning her down, and the hard hands shackling her hips. At first the thrusts met with no success, and perhaps, had her mouth not been silenced by his, she would have given vent to the cries that strained upward to her throat. Thrust, thrust—and then, suddenly, the battering ram exploded through. Cat went rigid, every nerve screaming with the pain of an entry more difficult than most.

Now contained within her, Daniel willed himself to grow still once more, resting against her hips, waiting for the worst of her pain to recede. Perspiration bathed his brow with the terrible urgency of his own need. And at last, when the softening of her mouth told him she no longer wanted to scream, he could wait no longer. He began to move, slowly at first, then faster, driving deeply until all was forgotten but the mightiness of his desire, and the moist tightness of her. He had considered her pain, but he was too far gone now to consider her pleasure. And so, while Cat still struggled to accustom herself to the fullness and the hurt, he entered some other plane without her.

After, they lay without words, naked, a little apart, bathed in dim light, two strangers who had learned each other's flesh and very little else. Cat's eyes were bolder now; they traveled over the open secrets of his man's body, and wondered that it could change so, with the passing of passion. Could any man's body frighten her now?

At last she touched him tentatively. "Thank you," she said.

"For what?" Daniel replied, cynical now with the return of sanity. "For something I shouldn't have done?"

"For making it right for me," she replied quietly.

"Do you still hurt?"

"Not really."

"You'll have to do something about these sheets," frowned Daniel, thinking for the first time how easy it would be for this girl to trap him into marriage. Damn! Why had he allowed himself to be inveigled into this situation?

"I already thought of that." Cat gave a soft embarrassed laugh. "I brought a fresh one in, when I arrived. I'll look after it before I go."

"Which should be right now," Daniel muttered, but with the relief of knowing she intended no snares, he pulled her into the crook of his arm.

"Not yet. It can't be much more than two in the morning. Nobody in the house gets up before six-thirty."

"And exactly what time do you plan to go back to your own bed?" he asked dryly.

"Six o'clock," she declared, turning her face against the furred chest to hide a sudden empty hopelessness inside. Despair mingled with the warm gratitude she felt. Would any man ever take her with as much kindness again? She knew that the hurt had not been his fault, and that it would not recur another time. She knew he had taken the time to teach her, patiently, the possibilities of her own body. She had always wondered if she had a passionate nature, and now she was sure she did. Would another man have troubled to let her find that out?

Daniel pulled her young face upward to his, and tasted the new-wine taste of her, and wanted more. "Cathryn," he murmured. "Little cat. I think you already like making love. Do you want to do it again? I'm sure it could be arranged."

"Yes," she confessed, with a secret thrill.

"We'll start slowly," he told her. "Lie still for a short time." And for a time they did—touching but not talking, lovers with discoveries still to make, each aware of the other with every shiver of the skin, every leap of the pulses, every tingle of the senses. And gradually, the caresses began, in slow motion.

"Now take me in your hand," Daniel instructed her in a low vibrant voice.

Cat held her breath and dared to run her fingers over the flat iron hardness of his belly and into the tangle below, but she could not do as he asked until his hand came to instruct her. She touched, and felt the warmth—and then, with sudden wantonness, she clasped and moved surely and smoothly, instinct telling her what to do. He groaned briefly and closed his eyes; she felt him swell beneath her hand—and saw.

"If you do that so well," he said thickly, after a time, "I can hardly wait to teach you other things."

"What other things?" she whispered, heady with a sense of her own power. "Teach me now."

His hand made a fist in her hair and urged her head downward. At the same time he started to twist his own face toward her thighs. Then, perhaps seeing her puzzled expression:

"Ah, hell . . . not the first night." And he pulled her fiercely upward, and kissed her in an ungentle way, bruising her lips apart with a ferocity that left her faint, and wondering at the sudden vehemence of his passion. He entered her without ending the kiss, taking her this time with a direct roughness that was almost brutal. Yet she found her own responses rising to meet his, and this time, at the end, the little outcry that broke from her lips had nothing to do with pain.

After it was over they lay close and spent: he with his mouth buried in the disarray of her long hair, she with hers burrowed into the dark forest of his chest.

"Now are you glad I was persistent at first?" she murmured, replete, happy for the moment, and grown impudent as her confidence in her own powers blossomed.

"Very."

"But I suppose you still think I should have allowed you to make the advances."

"From now on," he muttered into her hair, "I intend to."

"And do you still think I don't do it right?"

"Do what right?"

"Kissing."

"You always did do it right, from the very first time. God help me, I was lying. And you knew it, didn't you?"

"Yes," she said, wrinkling her nose and rubbing it into his sandpaper chin for the sheer joy of the discoveries she had made tonight. But moments later, Daniel felt a little wetness on his jaw, and wondered if she had shed a silent tear for the innocence that would never be hers again.

7

Morning brought a sudden shower, settling the dust of rutted roads, and rinsing the air country clean. Cat stayed in bed, and pleaded a woman's complaints. She *did*, after all, have to explain the sheet, which remained marked despite her efforts with the ewer of cold water and the china basin that were kept on a butternut washstand in her room.

Hannah, fortunately, remained unsuspicious; but of the indulgence of staying in bed, she did not approve.

"Oh, aye, there are those who take to vapors and fainting fits and smelling salts, but ye've na' been one of them . . . until now! I've no patience with ye, Miss Cat. Softness, it is, to tarry abed for such a reason. And your grandfather home from New York, and sobered up this morning! *He's* up and about, and with Mr. Savage now, though he's still na' quite himself. Now no more greeting about! Ye went to bed early enough last night, leaving Mr. Savage to fend for himself."

"I'll get up later, Hannah." Cat muffled her face into her pillow. Mr. Savage again! Did Hannah have to keep mentioning him? What had seemed right by night seemed wanton by day, and her cheeks burned with memories of the abandoned way she had behaved in the small hours of the morning. She wished to change none of it; she knew that, given the same choices, she would make the same decisions all over again. But she did not want to see Daniel Savage again, or hear his name.

And at this very moment, Daniel Savage might have said the same of her. But he was not to have his wish. In the library where he was now conversing with Jared Kinross, a dull angry flush was darkening his face as he listened to the older man's words.

"Marry her," Jared Kinross repeated. His craggy head was bowed so that Daniel Savage could not see his expression. It was costing Kinross a good deal to swallow his pride like this, but Cat's safety was all-important to him. He wanted to put her out of Julian Gow's reach before it was too late, and after the recent treachery of his best friend, there were few he wished to approach. In New York his old associates had been less than friendly; some of them had actively avoided him, perhaps smelling the smell of defeat that touched those who were tainted by Julian Gow's displeasure. Kinross could no longer think of any man he trusted—except this man. And perhaps it was the hand of fate that had brought Daniel Savage to this house at this time.

"She'd make a fine wife for a railroad builder," Kinross went on, blindly. He sensed the cold silent anger of the other man, but he could not stop himself now. "And she'd be a good wife for frontier country. Cat may look soft, but underneath there's a toughness and a strength. She's got stamina, Savage, and you'll never be bored by her. And you can't deny she's a treat for the eyes. Oh, still too much of a rebel at times, but perhaps you can tame her where I haven't succeeded. A firm hand, that's what she needs! And I think you're the man to give it to her. I promise you won't regret the day."

"Like hell," growled Daniel Savage, but the words were said under his breath, and Jared Kinross did not hear.

"I don't know what type of woman you associate with in that rough country, but I can guess. I've heard about the Hell-on-Wheels towns. Surely having Cat for wife would offer advantages, even to a man of the world like you. You're the type who needs a woman regularly, Savage; I can tell that. Are you going to settle for camp followers all your life? Cheap saloon girls?"

"At least, with them, a man knows where he stands," snapped Daniel.

"Cat would have a dowry. It's not much, but—"

"I won't be bought either," came the angry reply. Daniel stood up ready to leave, rage in every taut muscle of his long body. So much for Cathryn Kinross! The very thought of her turned his mouth sour. "I'm sorry to disappoint you, Kinross, but I'm damned if I'll be trapped into marrying your grand-daughter, no matter what the circumstances. I prefer women with more maturity . . . more honesty. Even if you drag me to the altar with a team of horses you can't make me say the words!"

Jared Kinross raised his head and stared at his guest, puzzled at the suppressed fury that seemed out of all proportion to what he had suggested. Well, he thought tiredly, it had been a very sudden suggestion, and one that had only occurred to him on the spur of the moment.

He sighed heavily. "I can see I've offended you, Savage, and I apologize. I'm sorry I mentioned marriage. The thought only occurred to me a few minutes ago, and it's not what I really intended to ask you. No doubt Cat would have refused in any case. She has a lot of new-fangled notions about going to college or getting a job, and she can be very stubborn when she chooses."

Daniel's mouth snapped shut, and he stared in amazement. Was it possible he had been mistaken?

"But I do have a different proposal to put to you, Savage, and one that won't involve marriage. I approach you because at the moment, for reasons I can't go into, you're the only man I can trust."

"*Trust!* Good God," Daniel muttered, half aghast and half flooded with relief that there would be no nasty recriminations about last night with this proud old man whom he liked.

"Yes, trust. Frankly I've been worried about Cat . . . again for reasons I can't explain. I have to send her away from home for a time, and I have nowhere to send her where . . . where she would be safe." Jared Kinross bowed his head to hide a twist of sorrow. "I need someone to look after her for a time. Someone strong, someone who can be trusted. A man like you."

"Go on," said Daniel grimly, after a few silent moments. What freak of fate had led Jared Kinross to trust *him?* And with his granddaughter?

"I'm asking you to take her back to California with you. Frankly the idea first occurred to me when your letter arrived, saying you'd be here this week. For one reason or another, there's nowhere else I can send her."

"Now, look—"

"Wait, Mr. Savage, before you say no! I'm prepared to give you something in return for your trouble . . . some income. You've heard about the railroad I built myself," he plunged on with a worried frown, not liking the unreceptive expression that greeted him, "The Peekskill and Tarrytown. It's leased to The Trunk, but it still exists. In fact P and T trains still operate on part of the line: local trains, to serve the area just north of New York. It's one of the terms of the lease."

It was one of those terms that Julian Gow had not liked. But Jared Kinross had been adamant: He had not wanted to see the maroon and black cars of The Trunk taking over his line entirely. A settlement had been reached with some acrimony. One train out of ten using that particular stretch of track was to bear the coloration and insignia of the old Peekskill and Tarrytown. The little local runs made very little money, but they continued to operate.

"I've seen the cars," Daniel said dryly. "Powder blue and gold. Very handsome, but—"

"I'd make some arrangement to sign the income over to you, for as long as you have Cat in your care. It would more than pay for your trouble."

"I can't accept your money. And I can't look after your granddaughter. Good God, you must see why I have to refuse. A young girl, and a lone man with inclinations you've already guessed."

"Are you suggesting you *do* have some . . . personal interest, shall we say . . . in my granddaughter, after all?" asked Kinross, hopefully.

"No, I'm not saying that!" Daniel replied too forcefully. "She can't be more than sixteen—"

"Cat turned seventeen in April, and I'm only asking you to look after her temporarily." And if the worse came to worst, and Savage took advantage of his granddaughter? Kinross was not an unworldly man; he knew it was possible, probable even. If Savage would not give up his independence out of choice, perhaps he would do so out of honor. And he would make a hell of a husband for Cat.

"I can't think of a man I'd trust more than you. Well, Savage, what do you say?"

"No."

Jared Kinross sighed deeply, unwilling to acknowledge defeat. "Well, then, I'll ask you something simpler. A promise to step in and . . . look after Cat under one unlikely circumstance, the circumstance that I should die." His eyes grew evasive with the lie he had told. "For one reason or another I can't trust her godfather. He was to have been her guardian."

"I can't promise that. Good God, Kinross. That's the kind of responsibility I've always avoided like the plague."

"I'm not exactly asking you to be her guardian. For one thing, I don't want to put anything in writing . . . anything that could betray her whereabouts. Think carefully before you refuse, Savage. I'm a strong man and I'm only sixty-six. I don't plan to die. Your promise would mean a great deal to me. Set my mind at rest. And Cat needs no care; she's very independent. Is it so much to ask? Is there some reason you can't do a small favor for an old man?"

Every reason, thought Daniel, dragging his mind from visions of that soft compliant body he had deflowered last night. But how could he tell that to her grandfather? "I won't do it," he said.

"Please," Kinross begged in a choked voice, throwing all of his pride to the winds. "I'll even give you the railroad. It's yours if you'll take Cat with you today."

"The answer is still no," Daniel said unsmilingly, looking the older man directly in the eye. "You've picked the wrong man. I can't be trusted with your granddaughter."

"I understand your reservations. But, well . . . if anything happened I'm sure you'd do the right thing by her."

"No," came the flat reply, "I wouldn't. I'll never take a wife; explosives and wives don't mix. But I might take a woman . . . I *would* take a woman. You see, Kinross, I haven't got quite as many scruples as you seem to think."

Cathryn's grandfather opened his mouth to reaffirm his faith, and then felt a sudden chilling doubt. Was it possible he had been mistaken in his assessment of this man? Well, he thought tiredly, better Daniel Savage than Julian Gow.

"I still want you to take her. Take her and . . . and be kind to her."

"*No*, Kinross," Daniel said firmly, standing up to go. "Don't you understand about my profession? I want no one dependent on me. Now if you don't mind, I have a train to catch."

The sight of the old man's defeated figure caused a moment of wavering, but Daniel firmed his resolve and walked to the door. On the threshold he paused and looked back. "What were you going to do if I agreed to look after her in the event of your death? Kill yourself?"

"Yes," came the strangled answer.

There was a long compassionate silence.

"I'm sorry," Daniel said, and left.

Daniel Savage had long since put Kirklands behind him when the crested coach-and-four arrived, late the same afternoon. A second carriage, less elegant, followed close behind, and half a dozen men spilled out. Hannah answered the door, and then ran in a flurry of apron to see Jared Kinross, who was in the library.

"And a full day early!" she cried in anguish. "He'll see ye in his carriage, Mr. Jared . . . You, or Miss Cat. Och, Mr. Jared, what are we to do? He'll na' take no for an answer, and the house already surrounded by his men. And this time he's brought the law with him, bribed no doubt, for there's nary a law to give him right, that I can tell—"

Cat pushed through the library door from behind Hannah. Her face was white, and she was carrying a hatbox which she had packed hastily at first sight of the carriage. "There's no need for you to see Mr. Gow, grandpapa," she said at once. "I'm going with him."

Thunderstruck, Jared Kinross rose from his chair and shook his head as if he had not heard right. *"What?"*

"I'm going with Mr. Gow."

"Wait outside, Hannah!" roared Cat's grandfather. And when they were alone, he turned to her, the map of his face etched with disbelief and fury. "How did you know about this? And if you have some silly notion of giving yourself to save me—"

"To save you? I don't know what you're talking about," she lied. "I'm going because I want to. I couldn't help hearing you yell at Mr. Gow the other day, about not letting me be his mistress. I knew he'd come back for me, sooner or later."

"I won't have that man laying his corrupt hands on my granddaughter!" The words were an explosion of righteous rage. "You don't know what he's like, Cat. A depraved man like Gow—"

"I want to be his mistress," Cat said stubbornly, with a surface calm that belied the sinking sensations inside. "I want the things he can give me."

"His price is too steep to pay!"

"Not for me."

Jared Kinross stared at her as if he had never seen her before. "And how long do you think you'd last?" he said finally. "The man takes a new mistress every few months. Always young, always untouched, always—"

"Not always," Cat interrupted in a low voice. For a moment the words clogged in her throat; the truth was harder to tell than lies would have been. "I'm not a virgin, grandpapa."

He sat down, speechless, and his face, already gray, turned to the color of white ash.

"I've lain with a man more than once," she added, to give weight to her argument.

"When did this happen?" he said, in a ghost of a voice. "What man?"

"I didn't say it was *one* man," Cat replied, with her heart and her knees misbehaving.

"Good God." The white-crowned head sank, and a hand worried at the deeply creased brow. Then his face came up again, slowly, and it seemed his eyes had aged to that of a man in his eighties. "I don't think I know you, Cat. I don't think I know you at all."

His expression tore at her heart, and she knew she must leave now—now or never. "Mr. Gow is waiting, grandpapa. Please don't worry. I'll be happy with him. And when he finishes with me, why, I'll come back to you, if you'll have me."

Her grandfather groaned and buried his head in his hands. Cat left hurriedly without the embrace she wanted, for she knew she could not ask for it now.

Hannah was waiting in the hall, along with two of Gow's bodyguards, tall timbers of men with granite-hard mouths. Hannah's homely face was white beneath its blotches; she was still swaying with shock.

"The devil's taken ye, Miss Cat," she said. "Have ye no thought for your grandfather? Ye'll break his heart."

"He didn't stop me."

"Then ye've both gone daft!"

"Good-bye, Hannah," Cat said hurriedly, and for the first time tears threatened to spill. She hurried to the opened front door where the musclemen stood waiting, watching the scene with unaffected eyes.

"Wait, Miss Cat!" called Hannah, snatching at Cat's skirts. One of the guards intervened at once, thrusting Hannah roughly aside. "Do na' touch me, you nasty brute of a man!" And then, to Cathryn: "If ye're set on Satan's course, I'll come along. I can pack in but a minute. A shoulder to cry on is what ye'll need, once your senses unscramble."

"No, Hannah," said Cat, turning away to hide the tears that now stung her lashes. What that offer must have cost Hannah! Dear, loyal, fearless, straight-laced Hannah, her true beauties hidden beneath a sharp tongue and a plain face.

How she would miss Hannah. But Cat did not want a witness to her degradation.

"No, Hannah." Cat put on a brave face and turned back, control restored, to face the spare undaunted figure of the young woman who had been so like a mother. "I'll come back as often as I can," she promised lightly.

"From hell there's na' a path leads home." Tears coursed freely down Hannah's worried cheeks. "But even if it's hell ye're in, if ye send for me I'll come. I'm a-feared for ye, Miss Cat."

Cat's throat tightened again. "Take care of grandpapa, Hannah," she whispered, and hurried down the steps to the waiting carriage.

8

"New load o' mail," noted Yancy, squinting at a slight young man who was working his way down a long rope ladder into the mountain gorge where huge timbers were being felled and the first trestles erected for an enormous railway bridge.

"Well hallelujah happy day!" rejoiced a workman.

"Hey, Jake, got any newspapers there?" cried another.

Daniel Savage, who had been about to depart up a different rope ladder that led to the site of the blasting operations, halted and turned his footsteps back to that part of the gorge where bridge foundations were being built. Normally, the track gang, under Yancy's supervision, and the tunneling gang under Daniel's, would have been many miles farther apart. But in this April day of 1876, Daniel had been working on one single tunnel for more than half a year. It was a tough job in hard rock, and one that had occupied him ever since his trip to the East. Even the snow-bound winter of the Sierras had not halted the railroad work altogether. Under pressure to finish the line, which was now beginning the long slow descent into Nevada, Daniel had continued tunneling throughout the winter months, with a reduced crew. Even Yancy's construction gang, although unable to lay track, had managed to occupy a good part of the winter by shoring tunnels and building snowsheds to protect the line from drifts that could reach thirty feet or more. With the snowsheds, supplies had been no problem; to winter in the Sierras was not the hazardous thing it once had been.

Aided by a mild spring, Yancy's men had laid track to the edge of the gorge, less than four miles from where Daniel's men were camped. But now, the bridge would slow them for a time; it would be some months before the rails could move along.

"Git the one you bin lookin' fer?" asked Yancy, watching Daniel tear open an unimportant letter.

"I'm not expecting a damn thing," Daniel lied, in a way that invited no prying; and moments later he was up the rope ladder and working his way along the trails that led to the blasting site.

Damn! Why hadn't he heard anything from Jared Kinross, despite the three letters he had written, the first of them nearly six months ago? This past half year had brought too many pangs of conscience for his liking, and they had all started one star-swept night last October, shortly after he had returned from New York. He had been at the main camp that day, going over various matters with Yancy, as he did once in a while. By nightfall the business was finished, and they had relaxed around a campfire with Yancy's family. But in time, Laura Brody had taken the brood of small children back to the converted wooden-sided railway coach that served as a portable home, leaving the men alone.

On that night so long ago, Yancy had watched Daniel brooding at the campfire for some time before he spoke. "You ain't bin yerself since that last trip east," he said at length. "You ain't been over to the cathouse fer a month. That nice little gal Inge is eatin' her heart out, an' so are you."

"Mind your own bloody business."

"You need a woman," Yancy had said stubbornly.

And that was the nub of it. Yet why had the prospect of casual sex lost so much of its savor? And why did the face of Jared Kinross's granddaughter keep appearing in the campfire?

"Dammit, Yancy, I don't need a wife!" Daniel had angled a stick viciously at the vision in the campfire.

"Sore-headed bastard," Yancy had replied. *"Yer* the one who said wife. I didn't." And he had left to find his own woman, disgusted at his friend's ill humor. What had happened to the easygoing man that Daniel Savage had been? Sonuvabitch!

Conscience was what had happened to Daniel Savage. He could not forget Cathryn Kinross, and he could not forget her grandfather. Jared Kinross had been a desperate man—a proud man—prepared to throw his pride, his money, and even his life to the winds in order to protect his granddaughter from . . . *what? From what?*

Daniel wanted no woman in his life, at least not as a permanent fixture; but some persistent inner voice kept telling him he should have listened more closely to Jared Kinross. Damn! Had he become so gun-shy of personal commitments that he could no longer listen to a cry from the soul of a desperate man?

To protect her from what? The question kept turning and turning in Daniel's mind. Shortly after that night by the campfire, he had written to Jared Kinross and asked for more information. There had been no answer to his letter, nor to the two that followed it. By now, even allowing for the uncertainties of communication, Daniel was sure there was something grievously wrong at Kirklands. Was Kinross seriously ill? Was the girl in desperate straits of some kind?

But what was the point of speculating? He needed to go east in person. He didn't quite like to leave that new foreman in charge; there was something about the man. . . .

Perhaps, if Daniel had known that Cathryn Kinross was ensconced in the lap of luxury on Fifth Avenue, he would not have worried so.

Fifth Avenue: Now that was an address!

Fifth Avenue, with its Italianate brownstones and its marble façades and its ballrooms and its gold dinner services and its stables on back streets, and its plumbing *indoors* . . . Fifth Avenue, that was the place to live.

Oh, yes, there were other wonderful things in New York. Wall Street! Broadway, even with its traffic jams! An elevated railroad, and more coming soon! Huge towers already erected for a giant bridge over the East River, to Brooklyn! The brand-new Central Park! Parades of fine carriages and sleighs! Delmonico's! Young bloods racing horses up Manhattan's country lanes!

But to live on Fifth Avenue, where the rich were buying properties almost as far north as Central Park—ah, that was the thing. To the south lay the city, more than a million dense. To the east lay eyesores of railtracks and switching yards, where Park Avenue would someday rise. To the west lay scabby open fields and shantytowns; and to the north the garbage dumps and goats still held odiferous sway. But Fifth Avenue! Fifth Avenue had the fine perfume of wealth.

And it was here, in the most fashionable stretch of the most fashionable avenue of the wealthiest city of the continent, that Julian Gow had built a many-roomed marble mansion whose luxuries were legend even on this street of wealthy men. It had been built two years ago for a reputed three million dollars, a cost that staggered the imagination of the workingmen who built it, most of whom raised whole families on ten or twelve dollars a week—and considered themselves lucky to have a job, when millions were out of work. Even now, the mansion's elaborate crystal chandeliers and solid gold taps and three-story entrance hall often came up for discussion in humbler homes.

And if a certain ceiling had also staggered the workmen's imaginations—well, this was one idiosyncracy that few of them would describe to their wives. How could they tell such things to an inhibited Victorian partner, who permitted only the simplest of liberties? But it did give a man something to think about as he made love himself, in the dark and in the same old way, to a wife who had come to bed in several layers of clothing, none of them to be removed. Was it true that Julian Gow had a similar fresco in his private railway car, and another in his summer mansion at Newport? And what kind of woman would permit those things?

To Cat the ceiling had long since lost its shock value. She lay now, resting on her bed, while a maid fussed in the dressing room next door, preparing her clothes for the evening, and although her eyes were open she did not even see the fresco. The indignities of reality had replaced the subtle horrors of apprehension. She knew exactly what was demanded of her; what had been demanded of her ever since the nightmare of that first night in Julian Gow's private railway car.

The first night . . . Her mind retreated from the memory. She knew what must have happened because she knew what had happened since; there was some knowledge her mind could not escape. But most of that first night was a merciful blank. Except the beginning . . .

In the compartment that had once been Deirdre's, she had prepared for the night with the help of a maid. After bathing she found that her clothes had been removed, her nightgown, too, and the coverings from the bed. She was naked, and with nothing to cover her nakedness. At last she understood the reason for the stifling heat in the car. Sick with foreboding she lay down, deliberately avoiding the ceiling with her eyes. Long hours of apprehension followed. She had the distinct and frightening sensation that she was being watched. Fear: Was that what Julian wanted?

She decided at last he would not come that night. She had tried, then, to extinguish the lights, smoking oil lamps as all trains had at the time, only to discover that they were locked behind glass; that they could not be extinguished. Fear . . .

She had drifted into troubled sleep at last. And then, suddenly, he had been beside her, materializing out of nowhere, the light shivering down the satin lapels of his robe and on his pale pale hair and on that pitiless face and in those lustful eyes. With a jolt she realized that a partition had slid aside to join her compartment to his. *Fear.*

And then, the callous, clinical investigation of her lower half. The pale, polished naked hardness of the aroused man beside her. He did not remove his glove. It crawled over legs, over buttocks, over the little mound of flesh where another man's hands had seemed so warm. The rigidity of her limbs; the chilling sweat on her brow; the teeth digging silence into her lip until she tasted blood. Julian had not kissed her.

"Dry, very dry." The curdling excited sound had not been a laugh, and the ice floes that were Julian's eyes had begun to blink very rapidly. But suddenly he had withdrawn his hand and a blow of stunning force had cracked across her breasts.

"Whore! Strumpet! You've already been with a man!"

Cat had cried out, denying it, claiming that a youthful accident had been at fault. She knew Julian could prove nothing, and to admit to prior contact with a man might only bring worse retribution on her head.

"Liar! I share passage with no man! Who took your virginity?"

Cat's head had ricocheted from side to side with the stunning force of his blows. "No . . . no . . . there was no man. . . ."

"Whore! You dare to come to me unclean!"

And after that, blackness, a merciful blackness of the mind, penetrated only by the words:

"Whore! Filth! I take no man's leavings! *I'll teach you to cheat me—*"

Julian had not forgotten nor forgiven. In time she had learned to submit without complaint to the caresses she was forced to endure. At least, recently, the humiliations had become less frequent. There were nights, now, when Julian did not appear in her bedroom; and although she still slept restlessly, waiting for the apparition to appear, she was grateful for the increasing number of times she was allowed to lie alone.

Cat had learned, too, to wear the clothes with which she

was provided, and to wear them in public. She was aware that her décolletage caused ripples of reaction wherever she went. Too often, opera glasses were trained in her direction as she sat, head held high, in theater boxes or at opera performances in the Academy of Music, where Julian had obtained a box despite the strong opposition of society's Old Guard. She knew that the seemingly icy man who sat at her side, negligently fingering his program, enjoyed in some sick way the scandalized whispers; they fed his vanity and his need for power. Did he want her to feel shame? Did he want her to beg for less revealing garments? If so, she refused to satisfy him. She learned to ignore the stares and concentrate on the performances, and proudness of carriage became a point of honor.

But even those outings had become few and far between. Julian was becoming jaded with her; she knew that, and it gave her hope. Would she soon be allowed to return home? Or would her grandfather allow her to return? There had been no answer to her many letters; the only news of Jared Kinross came through Julian Gow. But then, she had long ago suspected that her communications would be censored once she took up residence in this hated marble mausoleum on Fifth Avenue.

Julian was tired of her, and still he would not let her go. Why? Why? It was as though he was waiting for something: some final surrender of self that she was unwilling or unable to give.

"Mr. Gow says that you are to be downstairs early tonight, mum," said the maid, entering the bedroom and indicating that it was time to dress.

"Is there company for dinner tonight, Brigid?"

"No, Miss Kinross. Mr. Gow left no instructions for your wardrobe." The maid's reserved manner masked some pity. Although she had served a number of Julian Gow's mistresses and was too well-paid to be anything but discreet, she was not a totally unfeeling soul. How this one had suffered! Cathryn Kinross's eyes were now deeply shadowed; the once-mobile mouth seldom smiled. Even the hair that had been unfettered was now swept into a modish chignon, and a fringe of fashionable curls clung to that sad and shapely forehead. "So I put out your favorite gown, Miss Kinross . . . the ice-blue silk with the higher neckline."

"Thank you, Brigid," Cat said automatically, but despite

the reprieve from low necklines Brigid's news gave her little comfort. Julian entertained several times a month: railroad barons whose interests did not rival his own too closely; oil millionaires and cattlemen whose lucrative contracts he wished to obtain; men of power from Europe and the Middle East with whom Julian still trafficked in the armaments that had once supplied luckless soldiers in the Civil War; politicians and Wall Street financiers whose glittering names were synonymous with the moneyed interests of this Gilded Age. They were a diverse crowd, the famous and the infamous and the influential, and what little enjoyment Cat found in life centered around those dinners. No matter that wives with names like Astor and Goelet and Belmont generally chose not to attend, lest their attendance seem to condone Julian Gow's open liaison with a mistress. No matter that those who did attend conveyed a mixture of reactions in their covert glances—curiosity and disdain and malice and sometimes, worst of all, pity. All these could be borne, for when there was company at Julian Gow's table, Cat managed to find some small escape from her own troubles. Conversation from the corridors of power was fascinating, and Julian Gow, for all his omnipotence, could not prevent her ears from listening.

Julian was waiting in his study, a formal room whose decor stemmed from his rageful reaction to various visions. He had become obsessed with swords, and with his own need to master them. On the silk-lined walls hung an extraordinary collection. All were represented here: the swords of Toledo and Seville, of Solingen and Passau and Ferrara; the rapier, the broadsword, the poignard, the épée; the Scotch Claymore and the Indonesian kris; the Roman gladius and the Venetian *schiavone*. Most extraordinary was a bejewelled model of King Arthur's Excalibur, a sword so heavy that few men could draw it from its stone bed. It was a sword no woman could ever have mastered.

"I'll speak to you in private, Cathryn," Gow said coldly, and with a gesture dismissed the ever-present guards. Their eyes flickered impersonally over Cathryn Kinross as they left the room. She pulled her skirts aside to let them pass.

"Seven months, Cathryn," Julian started when they were alone. "In seven months any woman becomes less than interesting. You are no exception."

Cat sat with hands folded in her lap, schooling her expression to conceal the flutter of hope. Julian had a way of building expectations only to dash them again.

"I've already chosen my next mistress; I found her in a convent school. Her parents are . . . amenable. Are you distressed, Cathryn, to think of another woman usurping your position?"

Cat's lips felt stiff with the effort of showing nothing. Could this really be happening—the moment she had awaited for so long? "As usual, Julian, I bow to your wishes."

"For months, Cathryn, your grandfather has been begging me to let you go. Ah, that a man like Jared Kinross should so lower his pride as to beg. Curious, is it not?"

"Yes," said Cat levelly. Julian had told her the very same things a thousand times; it was one of his subtler punishments.

"Then you should be grateful to know that your grandfather's misery is coming to an end. I have decided to let you go."

Cat lowered her head to hide the quick joy his words awakened. "When shall I leave?" she said at last, with an unconcealed tremor to her voice.

Julian Gow's laugh was like a body blow. "Never . . . until you admit you came to me unclean. Who was the man who took your virginity?"

Cat paled. "I can't give you the name of someone who didn't exist," she said with a plummeting heart.

"I confess you astonish me, Cathryn. I thought the opportunity to return to your grandfather would be enough to make you surrender . . . but I see it is not." Julian regarded her with a growing annoyance. But along with the annoyance came something else; and suddenly, the need to humiliate her stirred little excitements in his loins. "Perhaps I have been wrong to let you lie alone so many nights." He paused, significantly, until the veiled threat became clear.

Oh, God, thought Cat. How could she *not* tell—yet how could she tell? By now she had learned a very great deal about Julian Gow's vindictiveness toward enemies both real and imagined. He would never forgive, or forget, and the arm of his vengeance was long. What right had she to make Daniel Savage suffer for a seduction he had not wanted to commit?

"You can't want me in this house if you have a new mistress," she said, trying to keep the desperation from her voice.

81

"Mistress?" Again that chilling laugh. "If you refuse to tell me now, I may even dismiss my new mistress . . . and keep you." Julian regarded her with unblinking eyes, savoring the moment of unconcealed consternation. So she could show feelings after all!

"I expect I may even take a renewed interest in our little diversions. Tonight, after dinner, you will go to your room. . . ."

It was not until much later that night that Cat understood why Julian had chosen tonight of all nights to make his threats and promises. It was all over by then, and he stood at the foot of the bed, wearing the silken robe he always wore when he came to her room. A cruel half-smile touched his sensuous lips as he contemplated her spent and naked body.

"Who was the man who made you a whore, Cathryn? Who was the man who defiled your body?"

"There never was another man." Oh, God—would that there never had been. Had she really once lain with a man, and enjoyed it?

"You have been a good actress these past months, Cathryn, but tonight you confessed more than you knew. I saw your expression earlier. I had no idea you found your duties here so repugnant. I confess it renews my pleasure to know that there are feelings behind that mask you wear. *Who made you a whore?*"

Cat lay staring stonily at the ceiling, unwilling to give him the satisfaction of answering again.

"As stubborn as your grandfather! A proud creature, tamed in bed but not entirely broken in spirit . . . not yet. But I will break your spirit, just as I broke his in the end. Irrevocably!"

This time, the deep shock could not be hidden as Cat's eyes flew to Julian's ice-blue ones, seeking confirmation of what he had implied.

Again Julian gave his chilling excuse for a laugh. "Do you really think I would have considered giving you your freedom, if Jared Kinross were still alive? I swore long ago he'd die knowing his granddaughter was a whore! Yes, Cathryn. Your grandfather had a heart attack; the news arrived this morning. Jared Kinross is dead . . . and he died a broken man."

9

"In the midst of life we are in death."

Cathryn Kinross stood dry-eyed by her grandfather's grave and tasted the bitter dregs of defeat. She knew now it had been a mistake to offer herself to Julian Gow. Might her grandfather have died seven months ago, his brave heart giving out under Julian's stern measures? Perhaps. But, bankrupt or no, he would have died with pride, and she had robbed him of that. What had these past months gained him but grief?

Julian had allowed her to come home for the day of the funeral, accompanied by two of his trusted henchmen. They were burly men built like trees, and Cat knew only too well that their powers were more than adequate to enforce Julian's orders. She had been unable to tell Hannah anything of her way of life, or of her desire to escape. What opportunity had there been, with the guards listening, narrow-eyed, at every turn?

"Mister Jared has been at death's door for months, Miss Cat," Hannah had told her this morning, glaring at the guards who were midway through searching Cat's bedroom, as instructed by Julian, before allowing Cat the privacy to rest and freshen. "Did ye na' hear? Mr. Gow's been told often enough. Your grandfather begged that ye be allowed home, even for a day. He spoke of ye when he died, and asked that ye be told he was sorry he did na' say a proper good-bye. He loved ye more than his own soul, Miss Cat."

"Oh, Hannah—" But the guards would report everything to Julian, as they had been ordered to do. And what could she say to Hannah, when it was her grandfather who should have heard the apologies? After that, while the guards continued their search under Hannah's hostile eyes, they talked of more mundane things: Angus McBride's approaching marriage to a widow with several small children; the house he had bought with his savings; Hannah's intention of going to live with her father in his new home. Prince, too, would be given shelter there. Jared Kinross was not discussed again, nor were Cat's present circumstances.

"Earth to earth . . ."

Cat watched in silence as the handful of dust consigned her grandfather to realms where no vengeance could reach. A bitter wind whipped at the black shawls and mantles of the women, and men turned their dark coat collars against an April chill. Cat pulled the hood of her own dolman mantle, richly embroidered as were no others here, more closely around her veiled head.

"Ashes to ashes . . ."

The dry earth scattered in the wind, together with the skeletons of last year's leaves. Hannah, her face swathed in veils and her head bowed beneath the hood of a plain black cloak, was weeping quietly. Would there be no opportunity to speak to Hannah in private? Even while Cat rested before the funeral, the guards had remained stationed outside her door. And Julian expected her to return to New York before nightfall. The reading of the will was to take place at the house very soon; after that, Cat was to leave for the train.

"Dust to dust."

At last the mourners turned away and began to file quietly through the country graveyard. By the gates a line of carriages waited, some no more than country buckboards, others grand, like the black landau that had been hired at the local livery stables for Cat's own use.

Cat hung back, seemingly reluctant to leave the scene. Hannah remained at her side; the guards were several paces behind.

Crack!

The explosion shattered the funereal silence like the report of a gun. A hundred startled faces turned to the empty fields behind the graveyard, from whence the sound had come. *Crack!* It sounded again, and then again. Crack—crack—crack!

The mourners had turned. The guards had turned, instantly alert, their hands reaching for their weapons. Of all those present, only Hannah and Cathryn Kinross ignored the sounds.

"Then ye got my note, Miss Cat," whispered Hannah nervously, as the two women hastily changed cloaks. The rat-tat-tat from the adjoining field covered their words. "I thought ye might look in the very place where ye left a note se'en month since."

"I had to know if it was gone," Cat said simply, as she pulled Hannah's plain hood close about her veiled face. Months ago, knowing her betrayal of everything Jared Kinross believed in might hurt him more than anything, she had written a letter that begged his forgiveness and told the truth of her motives. The letter had been left in her own room under the carpet, where Hannah, good housekeeper that she was, would soon find it.

"Mr. Jared read it when ye'd been gone no more than a week. He took comfort from it, what comfort he could. Now go, Miss Cat . . . quickly!"

In the adjoining field a small rocket soared into the air and exploded, followed closely by another. And another. And another.

"Fireworks," muttered one of the guards to his companion, disgustedly. Some young prankster, no doubt. No sense of propriety, these modern youngsters! He shifted so he could better keep Cathryn Kinross within view, while watching the display of pyrotechnics that was now beginning in earnest. Impersonally, he noted that his charge had at last given in to grief, and was prostrated beside the grave, sobbing—perhaps stung into emotion by the inappropriate display. So the cold bitch had some feelings, after all!

He paid no more than cursory attention to the other figure clad in an old-fashioned black cloak of much plainer cloth, moving now out of his line of vision. It was only that carrot-topped Scotswoman. And son of a sow's belly! He was not paid to pay attention to a whey-faced thing like *her*.

With hood pulled close and without so much as a backward glance, Cat hurried toward a plain black victoria, first in the line of carriages. Hannah's note, brief and to the point, had directed her to this vehicle with no further explanation. Instructions, she had been told, would await her in the victoria. Its calash top was raised, ready to conceal the face of any occupant from curious eyes. With some corner of her mind Cat noted the pair of long legs that protruded into vision, but there was no time for speculation. Nimbly, and with no hesitation, she climbed in.

"So the lost lamb returns to the fold," said a dry voice.

Cat's eyes came up and froze to find deeply grooved cheeks and eyes of a very distinctive hue. "Daniel," she whispered.

"I see your memory can't be faulted," he remarked.

Cat tried to steady her thoughts. Daniel Savage! What was he doing in the East . . . ? What was he doing *here?* Why had Hannah's note not mentioned his name? Why, why, why . . . ? A thousand questions formed without finding voice.

A part of the explanation came from Daniel as the victoria started to move along the dusty road, unnoted by the cluster of open-mouthed mourners in the graveyard. "Sorry if I startled you. Hannah didn't want to mention my name in the note, in case Gow's men got hold of it. I thought you might guess when you heard that gunpowder go. Some small diversions . . . not too fitting for the occasion, but effective."

Still, Cat did not answer. Too many turbulent thoughts were swirling through her head, and she was glad of the heavy veil that concealed her face. But moments later Daniel reached over and removed the dark covering. "You don't need this for now," he said quietly, "not while the coach-man's back is turned. Keep your voice low, that's all. I don't want him to hear."

As the veil lifted, Cat's expression masked over, offering a different kind of protection. "I thought you were on the other side of the continent. You weren't at the funeral."

"It seemed best to remain out of sight. I'm sorry about your grandfather, Cathryn. I came to see him a few days ago. I could see he was dying, so I stayed."

"I don't understand."

"Your grandfather was very ill. Hannah says he's been at death's door for months, and that only one thing was keeping him alive: the need to see you free of Julian Gow. I made him a promise." A small frown dug furrows deeper into Daniel's cheeks. The promise had been made against his better judgment; it was hard to refuse a dying man. "I promised I'd get you away, somehow, even if I had to kidnap you. It seemed to set your grandfather's mind at rest."

"But why, how . . . ?"

"Ah, Cat, your grandfather seemed to put some trust in me . . . or perhaps I should say he put trust in no one else. Before he died he told me many things."

The swaying of Cat's body was not entirely due to the

86

clip-clop rhythm of the carriage. "Then you know I didn't choose that life," she said in a low voice.

"On the contrary, I heard you did," came the cynical reply. "Although your grandfather seemed to impute many noble motives. Was he right?"

Cat turned her face away, until her pale profile was nearly concealed in the dark hood of Hannah's cloak. Her voice was toneless. "I hated Julian Gow and I hated every minute of my life with him, and everything my grandfather told you was the truth. Even the night I went to you—" She closed her eyes, willing away the memory of her utter shamelessness on that particular night, a night she had spent these past months regretting. "That, even that, was because of Julian. I couldn't bear to go to him untouched, to let him be the first."

In the silence that followed, Daniel seemed to be considering her words, but when he spoke he made no comment on what she had said. "Will Gow set up much of a hue and cry when he finds you're gone?"

In Cat's mind, there was no doubt. Julian was a vengeful and unforgiving man; she realized now he had never intended to let her go. "Julian will look for me," she said levelly.

"Ah, well, in a few months he'll forget. And he won't find you where I'm taking you."

"Where *are* you taking me?"

"To catch a train to Chicago, but not a Trunk train, and not at the local staion. I rented this carriage some distance away, so it would be harder to trace. We'll cross the Hudson and work our way west; you'll be safer on the Erie. And from Chicago . . . on to California."

California. Cat had liked California, seen nearly a year ago on the fateful railway trip. San Francisco had been an exciting, colorful city—a modern city, with wonderful new cable cars and tall redwood houses and cobblestone streets and a huge new hotel that was said to rival the one in Saratoga Springs. And Deirdre would be in San Francisco: Surely, if anyone could understand about these past months, it would be Deirdre.

"Your grandfather thought you'd be safe in California." Daniel's eyes were watchful on her face, and on the proud line of her throat, sensed if not seen beneath the covering cloak. How beautiful she was. The molding of her bones had only fined with time, and even those deep shadows beneath her eyes seemed merely to accentuate the startling silver-gray. Perhaps his promise to Jared Kinross had not been so unwilling after all.

"I'd like to go to California," Cat said. "I have a friend in San Francisco, and I'm sure she'd help me until I get a job."

"I promised your grandfather I'd keep you with me, in the Sierra Nevada."

"With *you*—" Cat cast him a brief startled look, then turned her eyes back to the passing countryside. "Grandpapa would never have asked you for such a promise if he'd known about that night."

"Wouldn't he?" Daniel said in a soft voice, with meanings that went beyond the words. At the last, not wanting to deceive a dying man, he had told Jared Kinross the truth about his relationship with Cat. Oddly, Kinross had not been upset, perhaps because he considered his granddaughter's virtue to be so thoroughly compromised by then.

Cat's eyes dropped swiftly from his darkening, deepening gaze. "You must forget that night," she said fiercely. "It would never happen again. It was a mistake."

"A mistake—" Daniel repeated, with a brief frown. This was not quite the reaction he had expected; he would have to change tactics. Thoughtfully, he listened as Cat continued.

"I was . . . pretending that night. I've told you why. Later, I was sorry I had been so forward. Believe me, I was sorry." The gray eyes rose again, serious, the shadows dark as bruises. "I can't stay with you, Daniel. I don't intend to exchange one protector for another. I want to be free to live a life of my own choosing. And if grandpapa knew, he'd never—"

"Let me set your mind at rest," Daniel interrupted calmly. "I'll tell you about the rail-laying camp. It's two camps, really. The camp for the men that lay track . . . that's where *you'll* stay. It's a small portable town, a town that travels on wheels, although it's settled in one place for the time being, as there's a big bridge to be constructed. My partner Yancy Brody is in charge of operations at that camp. He's a rough diamond, plain but upright, a married man with four children. The track gang are a hard-drinking crew but they're good men, or at least most of 'em are. They won't bother you if I give the word. There's a small cabin you can use. It's mine, and it's been standing empty for some time."

Daniel's frame was totally relaxed, his voice matter-of-fact and his eyes trained casually on the back of the coachman's spine. His expression revealed no more than he wanted it to reveal. Cat listened in silence, judging.

"The other camp is the one I'm in charge of," he went on, coolly. "The advance camp. We live in tents, for we're always some distance ahead of the others. No portable buildings, for we've no tracks to move 'em on. Blasting, tunneling, preparing the road bed . . . With your background, you must know enough to realize that those things move well ahead of the track-laying. I have a tent at the forward camp. That's where I've been sleeping."

"I see," Cat said thoughtfully.

"D'you think your grandfather would have asked me to undertake your care without some discussions along these lines?"

"No, I suppose not." Of course, she thought to herself. Her grandfather had not been a fool; he would have extracted assurances of some kind. Daniel's next words confirmed it.

"I made promises to your grandfather." Their eyes connected again. The depths of his were at the moment so honest, so unevasive that Cat sensed he could only be telling the truth. He smiled disarmingly. "I didn't deceive him in any way, for I intend to keep all my promises, starting with taking you to the Sierra Nevada. Well? Will you come willingly, knowing these things?"

Cat managed a cautious answering smile, less wholehearted than his. "Yes. Yes, I'll come willingly."

"Good." Daniel's eyes dropped to the curve of her lips. His hand came up and Cat tensed at once, for she thought he intended to touch her. But his intention was simpler.

"Better put the veil back in place," he said pleasantly, lowering the dark barrier once again. Then he leaned back against the carriage seat, stretched his long limbs, crossed his feet, closed his eyes, and smiled.

"Perhaps you'd better keep wearing it," he added with evident satisfaction, "until California. Eight days, Cathryn. . . . It's not so long to wait."

10

"Wake up. Wake up."

A hurtful hand shook at her shoulder. The light shone through her closed eyelids, but that was not unusual: The light always shone through her closed eyelids. It was so terrible sleeping with the light always on. It was so terrible knowing that Julian watched her in the night. Why did he need so little sleep himself? Why did he always wait until she had drowsed— appearing at the foot of her bed, or sometimes just sitting in a chair, and watching while she woke? There was always that moment of uncontrollable panic that came with a sudden jarring awakening. Even with her eyes closed she could feel Julian watching, and she could see him in her mind's eye—that small lascivious smile toying around his lips, the cruel enjoyment in his eyes. But if she kept her eyes closed for an extra fraction of time she could don her armor of ice, she could hide the panic, and Julian would not know. . . .

"Wake up, Cathryn. This is the end of the line. On your feet!"

The rough impatient voice was not Julian's. She opened her sleep-dazed eyes to find tawny ones regarding her narrowly, their expression as watchful and ambiguous as it had been every day for these past eight.

"I know you didn't get much sleep, but dammit, nobody does on these day coaches. I've been trying to wake you for five minutes. Now come along! From here we walk."

"Walk?" Cat repeated, still disoriented and numb from the spine-jolting vigil of last night, and curiously light-headed, too.

"You're not on Fifth Avenue now," came the dry observation. "You're far into mountain country, ma'am, or as much of it as we've conquered on this line. Now up you get, for I'm not about to carry you."

Still groggy, Cat turned to the train window. Overnight the gentler lowlands had given way to a rugged vista, the snow-capped spines and spires of the Sierra Nevada. This last part of the journey, since leaving the Central Pacific tracks at Sacramento, had been accomplished on Daniel's own railroad. Its amenities consisted of the old second-class day coach whose wooden benches had so punished her spine last night; a number of flatcars and boxcars used to transport materials to the construction site; a venerable engine; and a helper engine that had joined the train as it started up the steeper gradients. Late last night, before they boarded, Daniel had taken her to inspect the locomotive, but Cat had done so only half-heartedly. Trains held painful memories for her now; the old joy was gone.

Daniel was already laden with luggage. Cat came to her feet, murmured an apology, and followed him down the aisle. Here there was no footstool, no porter to aid the descent. Daniel deposited the baggage, and then a pair of strong hands seized Cat by the waist and swung her bodily down onto rough rock that showed the signs of recent blasting. The moment of contact chilled her.

They were some distance below the snowline; mountains towered on all sides. It was a chilly May morning, the sun thin and crisp. A group of Chinese laborers continued assiduously at their work of loading supplies from the boxcars onto a tatterdemalion assemblage of pack mules and crude wagons, but several others, roughly clad men of a number of nationalities, stopped and gawked openly at Cat.

"Jake!" Daniel hailed one of them, a slight, intense young man with bright blond hair. The youth put down the heavy crate he had been hoisting onto a wagon, and came hurriedly to the call. "This is Miss Kinross, Jake. She'll be staying here for a time, in my charge."

Cat smiled in acknowledgment of the endearingly shy grin that spread over the lad's handsome face. Jake looked to be no more than eighteen, Cat's own age. He appeared to be too thin beneath his rough flannel shirt, but then, perhaps he suffered by comparison with the bulging biceps and burly shoulders of the other men standing nearby. Certainly, the heft of the crate he had been shouldering moments ago suggested that his youth and thinness might be deceptive; he was apparently capable of doing a man's work.

"Jake's Mister Fetchit around here," Daniel explained. "He goes into town every Tuesday, by train, and returns the following morning. Anything you need, you ask him."

"I do errands for everyone," Jake elaborated in a soft

drawl. "Picking up newspapers, shoelaces, that sort of thing. You name it, Miss Kinross, I'll get it."

"That's good to know," smiled Cat, thinking of the pitifully few things she had bought during the short stopover in Chicago: some plain petticoats and underthings; sensible shoes; three dresses more practical than the tight and citified black silk she had worn at the funeral and still wore beneath Hannah's cloak; a few minor essentials. Daniel had looked surprised when she had tried to hand back most of the money he had given her for shopping. "Keep it," he had said offhandedly, and refused to take it. And when she persisted, he had told her, finally, that the money was her own, provided by her grandfather for her keep.

"Jake, take the portmanteau for Miss Kinross, will you? Bring it along on your mule. No need to make a special trip. We'll go on to the cabin."

Daniel picked up his own luggage that included a number of cylindrical metal map cases and other paraphernalia he had bought in Chicago, and strode toward the front of the train, with no more than a backward glance to see if Cat was following. She hurried after him, surveying the surroundings as she went.

The tracks in the level unloading area incorporated no turning arrangement for the locomotive; there was insufficient space on the blasted-out shelf of rock. This would pose no problem, Cat knew, for a train. A locomotive worked as well in reverse as it did in forward motion; it would merely shunt backward down the track until it reached a Y or a turntable elsewhere on the line.

A hundred yards to the fore of where the locomotive had come to a halt, the track branched in two directions. Directly ahead, in the route the line would eventually follow, there was a deep mountain gorge that broke down into the treeline, and at its rim the track came to an abrupt halt. A bridge was under construction; Cat could see a score of men laboring to swing a huge sequoia log into place. Their shouts reverberated through the mountains.

"They climb down to work by rope ladder," Daniel told her, when she paused briefly to view the construction. "On the other side of the gorge there's another rope ladder, and a trail that leads to the blasting site, and the other camp. At the moment supplies are a problem. They have to be carried down into the gorge, and up the other side. Mules can't make it."

The other branch of the track followed a slight upward gradient, and vanished in a twin shining ribbon around the roadbed that had been blasted out of the side of the mountain. It had been laid, Daniel explained, only in order to reach a level grade suitable for a townsite. Despite the morning chill, Cat felt overheated and winded by the time she caught sight of their goal.

"Hell-on-Wheels," Daniel said easily, evidently untroubled by the thin mountain air. "That's what they used to call the construction town that followed the track, back when the Union Pacific were laying. This one doesn't have a name, but it's much the same kind of thing . . . smaller, of course. Quite a change from your last residence."

The portable town had mushroomed around the end of the laid track, on a broad rocky plateau ringed in by the granite ribs of the mountain. For the most part it was deserted at the moment; the workmen were occupied elsewhere. Shacks, cabins, tents, workshops, and privies clung to whatever precarious perches they could find, but the core of the settlement was a string of several dilapidated wooden-sided railway coaches, all of a type that had not been used since mid-century. Most had hammocks slung beneath them, and tents pitched on top. The sides of one coach had been decorated, by an artist of questionable merit, with pastoral scenes and half-clothed demimondaines; the aging and peeling of paint gave it a certain faded grandeur it had probably not had when the colors were brash and new. Smoke wisped upward from the thin stovepipe chimneys of this, and the other coaches.

"Bunkhouses for the track gang," Daniel enlightened her with a wave in the general direction of the coaches. "Or most of 'em are. One belongs to my partner, Yancy Brody. A portable home, you might say. Yancy has a wife and children. You'll meet Laura later. I'm afraid she's about the only female companion you'll find around here."

"Is that her?" Cat asked, as a shapely figure topped by a long drift of straw-colored hair emerged from the painted coach, still at some distance, and started to pin some intimate garments to a makeshift clothesline.

"No."

Cat angled a swift glance at him, amused by his uncommunicativeness. "What is that painted coach?" she asked with pretended naiveté, although she was sure she already knew.

"A bordello," Daniel said briefly, expressionlessly. "The men would decamp without. Several of the tents serve a similar purpose. Others are saloons."

"For a town with a shortage of female companionship," Cat remarked, now seeing several other women moving about the site, "it seems you provide quite a lot."

"Of sorts," Daniel agreed with a faint smile.

"Which is your cabin?"

"Over there." He indicated a small, neat frame structure set a little apart from the others, and leveled with piles of loose rock. "It's portable, too. Put it on a flatcar, it moves right along the route of construction. Not fancy, but damn practical, and a sight more comfortable than my tent up at the advance camp."

"How far is the advance camp?"

"Oh . . ." He paused. "It depends. Sometimes we're fifty miles ahead, or more. But the tunnel we're working on is a bitch of a job, and the track gang is catching up, although that bridge will slow them now. We can't afford a separate crew of bridge monkeys."

They had continued to walk as they talked, and now their progress along the ties of the railroad track brought them close to where the painted coach was parked.

"Daniel!" cried a glad voice, and the girl with the straw-colored hair hurried forward, her eyes kindling with a light that faded somewhat as she drew closer.

"Oh, Daniel, you were gone so long." The girl darted a swift and not entirely friendly look in Cat's direction. "You said you'd be back several days ago."

"Hello, Inge." Daniel came to a halt, and greeted the girl nonchalantly, with less fervor than she had shown. But his smile was friendly enough, and under its warmth Inge blossomed again, visibly. She had marvelous, high cheekbones and a fresh Nordic complexion—not at all Cat's preconceived notion of the hardened woman she might have expected in these rough surroundings.

"This is Miss Kinross, Inge."

Inge turned a grudging smile in Cat's direction. "New girl?" she asked with no particular show of interest. "A replacement, I suppose. So many of them don't last, but then, this is rough country. You don't look like the type."

"No, Miss Kinross is not a replacement." Daniel's eyes feathered into signs of amusement, although his mouth remained straight. "She's just staying in camp for a while. A guest, you might say. My guest."

Inge's smile slackened. "Oh," she said, inspecting Cat with more decided animosity.

"I don't expect I'll stay too long," Cat remarked.

Inge's eyes dropped to the expensive silk that peeped out from beneath the dark cloak. "No, I don't expect you will."

"Come along, Miss Kinross," Daniel said crisply, using the more formal term of address in Inge's presence. "I'll show you to your cabin. Take care, Inge." And he strode off quickly, as if impatient with the subtleties of this feminine exchange.

Cat murmured a hasty good-bye, and followed, conscious of hostile eyes upon her spine. Well—Inge would find out soon enough that her fears were unfounded!

Daniel reached the small sugarpine cabin several paces ahead of Cat. He opened the door and stood aside, waiting for her to enter. "I'll have to arrange for a lock on this door," he remarked as she stepped inside.

The cabin was, as Cat had guessed, one room, but more generous in size than she had imagined from outside. A crude deal table and five chairs stood squarely in the center; a pile of buffalo hides and a bearskin rug were the only coverings on the rough plank floor. In one corner there was a single cot that looked comfortable enough, and in another a Franklin stove that some kind soul had lit in anticipation of Daniel's arrival. The air in the cabin was warm.

"I'll take your cloak," Daniel said.

He hung it on one of several nails driven haphazardly into the walls. Suspended from other nails were two kerosene lamps and some clothes—a heavy flannel jacket; a flannel shirt and old buckskin trousers; a bearskin coat for colder weather. Daniel's other possessions, if he had other possessions at this cabin, must be in the large oaken desk and the one old chest of drawers that stood beside the bed. There was no provision for cooking, but there was a washstand with enameled basin and ewer. All in all it was a bachelor space, starkly masculine, tidy enough but lacking the welcoming touches a woman might add. Cat began a mental measurement of windows; a cheap fresh gingham would look better than the gunnysacking that hung there now.

"Never noticed before how dingy those curtains look." Daniel frowned. "Takes a woman to make me realize."

"Maybe that's because you generally sleep up at the other camp. I suppose that's where you keep most of your things."

"Keep some here, too," came the laconic answer.

Cat sighed. "Well, it's very good of you to clear out like this. Will you have room in your tent for everything?"

"Everything I need up there."

"One drawer will do me for the time being . . . and perhaps a few more nails on the wall. You can leave some things here, if you want."

"Thanks." His reply was dry, and his eyes mildly amused. "I intend to. No sense carting everything to the forward camp, especially the city clothes." He cast a brief downward glance at the tweed suit he had worn on the train, a casual cut but still out of place in this rugged environment. "You can clean out that chest of drawers before Jake arrives with your things. I'll give you something to put the contents in."

Daniel walked to the bed. Kneeling, he pulled a couple of wooden crates from beneath its edge. He shoved them in Cat's direction, but not before removing something she had never seen before, yet recognized all the same—perhaps because of the warning stenciled on the sides of the crates.

"Do you always sleep on top of dynamite?" she asked, eyes widening at the sticks in his hand.

He grinned easily, the white emphasizing the depth of his tan. "I'm not quite that cavalier. I brought these here one day when Yancy needed some extra blasting done, and stored 'em in this cabin because it wasn't occupied. It's a long time since I've slept in this bed. Don't worry, I'll take the stuff with me when I go up to the forward camp."

"Please do," Cat requested dryly, and turned to the task of emptying one of the drawers. Its contents were spare: some neatly folded shirts, a few handkerchiefs, a warm woollen scarf, some personal knickknacks. She could hear Daniel moving about in the background, and guessed from the sounds that he was depositing the dynamite on his desk, along with the metal map cases.

"What do you do about meals? I see you have no provision for cooking."

"I generally eat with the men, camp style." A chair scraped against the floor, advertising his whereabouts. "If you don't have a taste for beans and bacon and flapjacks, you can start doing your own cooking. Laura Brody does. It shouldn't be hard to rig up some arrangement, and snaffle some dishes from the camp cook. I'm sure he can spare a couple of plates, and a mug or two, until there's a chance to buy something better. Jake can pick up supplies in town, if you give him a list. He can make a special trip tomorrow, if you like."

"I wouldn't want to put him to any trouble."

"Ah, hell, it's no trouble. The train goes in every day. It arrives here at nine in the morning, leaves at eleven, comes back on the overnight run. Jake's glad of the opportunity to be on it. His father lives in the valley, and he's an invalid. Gives Jake a chance to look in, see how he's getting along. Well, what'll it be? Cook it yourself, or make do with the track gang's grub?"

"Well—" Cat hesitated, unable to come to any decisions at the moment. Her head was beginning to pound, perhaps with the lack of sleep. She pushed the hair away from her eyes. Stray ends from her chignon had escaped over her ears, and the fringe on her forehead, now uncurled, wisped below her brows. Unaccustomed to the thinness of the mountain air, she felt exhausted with the small amount of energy she had expended in emptying the drawer. "I'll make up my mind tomorrow, if that's all right. For today, I'll take whatever food is offered."

She straightened from her task, sitting on her haunches while she closed the now-emptied drawer. "There, that gives me lots of room." She came to her feet and turned as she spoke. "I won't need more than—"

The words froze in her throat, and every defense mechanism developed during these past months was on instant alert.

"What's the matter? Surely by now you must be used to the sight of a naked man." Daniel paused with one hand reaching for the buckskins on the wall, making no effort to cover himself. "No ulterior motives at the moment; I'm only getting into my working gear. I'd go into the other room to change, ma'am, but as you see"—he gestured mockingly—"there's no other room to go into."

Slowly she redirected her vision. Well-practiced habits of

pride kept her from turning her back altogether; she could still see him with the corners of vision. "I didn't mean to stare. It's just that you took me by surprise."

"And I thought nothing fazed you anymore." With a chuckle, Daniel returned the buckskin trousers to their hook, and deliberately walked into the line of Cat's vision. He stood facing her fully, arms folded, the tan of muscular forearms dark against the paler flesh of his hard flat stomach. Amused, he studied her expressionless face.

"Quite a change from the young lady with the adventuresome eyes. You didn't mind looking me over then—and very thoroughly, as I recall, once you got used to it. I remember it as a very erotic experience."

"I can't think why," Cat said coldly.

"I hope to God you haven't gone coy since then. I don't have much use for modesty in a woman."

"And I don't like immodesty in a man." She stared at him stonily, refusing to redirect her gaze. "I see no reason for you to flaunt your masculine equipment."

Daniel's face broke into a slow grin. "Around here you'd better get used to men without their . . . how do you phrase it on Fifth Avenue . . . without their nether integuments. Here in God's country we say trousers, and men shed 'em with no compunction for a lady's tender sensibilities. Bathtime is a very public affair."

"You've already made it clear that most of the ladies around here don't have tender sensibilities. And it's just as well, if the men all behave like animals."

"By God, you have changed." Daniel's face tightened back into its cynical grooves, and the narrowed eyes swept her with something very like scorn. Then, to Cat's relief, he turned away, his long lithe body moving with an unself-consciousness that was indeed feral in its grace. But the sight of a naked man no longer intrigued her, as once it had.

He walked to where the buckskins hung, retrieved them, and levered himself into one leg, then the other, evidently scorning the use of underwear. Decency at last restored, he reached for the flannel shirt, and soon it, too, was in place, covering the muscular shoulders she did not want to see. Barefoot, and with the buttons of the shirt still unfastened to reveal more of the hair-roughened chest than comfort allowed, he walked back to Cat again. Arms akimbo, he regarded her measuringly.

"It seems I'm going to have to teach you some things all over again," he said in the softest of voices.

Cat tilted her chin defiantly. "Exactly what is that supposed to mean?"

"Exactly what you think it means." Daniel assessed her reaction from under hooded lids. "Nobody stays around this camp without serving some purpose. I intend to make you my woman."

"Your *woman*," she repeated, feeling a sharp chill of shock.

"You heard me," he said equably, a lazy mockery tugging at the corners of his mouth. He scratched his chest indolently through the opening of the shirt, and then began to fasten the buttons. "A man in my profession needs a woman to remind himself he's still alive at the end of the day. I've decided you'll do."

"I'll *do!* I'll do nothing of the sort."

"Look, Cathryn, I didn't ask to be saddled with you, but as I am I intend to make the best of it." Daniel rubbed lean brown fingers against the nape of his neck, in a rueful gesture. "It's no more than you've already done for another man. Hell, you don't even have to cook for me, unless you want to. A little relaxation at the end of a hard day's work, that's all I ask."

"You're just trying to shock me again," she said, staring at him disbelievingly. "This cabin's too far away from your . . . hard day's work . . . to make the trip worthwhile."

"Is it?" His eyes crinkled, mocking her. "I didn't say that; you assumed it. We're tunneling only four miles from here right now. I can make the trip in less than an hour, rope ladders, rocky trails, and all. And with someone waiting in a nice warm bed, it sounds quite worthwhile to me."

"I won't be waiting!"

"You did once," he reminded her softly. "Why so outraged now? I think we can have a very nice arrangement."

"If you want an arrangement get someone else! Whoever you used to . . . to *use* before I arrived." Cat's breath felt constricted, and the sensation was not entirely due to the mountain air. "That pretty girl we saw just now, surely she's obliged you before!"

"That's none of your business," he stated with matter-of-fact coolness. "For all you know I've been leading a celibate life. It must be obvious to you that there's been no woman living in this cabin."

"But a great number living in the camp. Use one of them!"

Daniel sighed. "Ah, Cat. At times a man gets a yen for a woman of his own."

"If that's what you want take a wife!"

"Proposing?" he mocked.

"No!"

"Good, because I'd have to refuse. A wife is the last thing I need. But a woman . . . Ah, Cathryn, you'll get used to the idea."

She glared at him. "I will not!"

"No?" A slow, sensuous smile took possession of his mouth, and his eyes grew lazy, dusk-dark, possessive. "I'll give you till sundown to get used to it."

"By sundown I'll be somewhere else. I'm getting on that train when it leaves. You might have been honest about your plans a week ago, and saved me the trouble of coming here!" She started toward the door, intending to retrieve the cloak, but Daniel's arm shot out and a hard hand manacled her wrist, twisting it behind her back until she was trapped against the muscular length of him.

"Oh, no you don't," he said in an amused voice. "I wasn't dishonest a week ago; you just made assumptions. I told your grandfather exactly how I would . . . ah . . . care for you if I ever undertook your protection. Oddly enough, he agreed."

The ice-cold sensations that always accompanied any close contact shivered down Cat's spine. "I don't believe you," she said rigidly. "Now will you please let me go? You're hurting me."

His hand that was coiled around her wrist relaxed its grip only slightly; the heat and the height of his body still stifled her. "First let's come to some agreement," he suggested in a tone of exaggerated reasonableness. "I promised your grandfather I'd look after you . . . in my own way. And look after you I will. I'm damned if I'll let you get on that train."

Her eyes and her chin defied him. "I won't stay here to be raped by you," she stated fiercely.

"Raped?" A smoky laugh deepened the semi-sunbursts around his eyes. His gaze traveled to her mouth and lingered there, in an intimate appraisal that turned Cat's lips dry. "I've never had to resort to rape yet, and I don't think I'll have to with you . . . of all people. You'll be willing enough when the time comes. Willing and wanting . . . Oh, yes, I have an excellent memory about some things, Cathryn. A tigercat if there ever was one."

"Then you're an alleycat!" Her limbs were stiff with indignation. "The morals of a tom! If you want a woman get one at the bordello."

"I told you," he said agreeably, "I don't want any of the whores. I have this crazy notion that I want one woman for the next while . . . you."

And with no more warning than a gleam in his eye, his lips closed over hers, taking her mouth by storm. She did not try to fight him physically—that was one lesson these months had taught her well. She knew those arms that enclosed her were far too strong; her mind still held unwilling visions of sweat-sheened skin and the ripple of tendons beneath. But she fought him silently with a lack of response, stiffening beneath his embrace. For several stifling moments she permitted the warm and expert tongue to invade the soft inner recesses of her mouth; but when he lifted away for a moment, and then returned to tease the curves with his lips, asking for response, she denied him a second entrance. His hand molded her breast, feeling for the nipple and finding it through the silk, but the deliberate way he worked it between his thumb and forefinger only added to her cold dislike of what he was trying to do to her. She felt as she had felt so often, as though her body were encased in arctic wastes while her mind looked on from a detached distance, with an icy distaste that was made greater by the pressure of his manhood growing into life against her belly.

At length he pulled away and regarded her with some irritability. "Maybe this is going to be more difficult than I thought," he muttered.

"I told you I was pretending that night."

"Ah, hell." He let her go and put a few feet between them before turning to face her again. He made no effort to conceal the bulge that tightened the buckskin over his powerful thighs. He stood raking his hair, rampant and totally unashamed of his arousal, contemplating her as if in deep thought.

Suddenly, unexpectedly, he smiled. "I wonder if I should put my brand on you right now," he said, and despite the lightness of his tone, the words struck a chill into Cat's marrow. "No reason we can't put that bed to use in mid-morning. It's not as though you were a callow virgin. No doubt you'll see things differently from a horizontal position."

"To get me there you'll have to tie me down."

"You shouldn't dare me, sweetheart, that's a very tempting thought." His eyes mocked her; it was clear he was confident in his power to arouse her later. "But perhaps I'll have to put off the pleasure, after all. I do have a few things to attend to. But when sundown comes—"

"I'll say no."

"We'll see." He shrugged. "I can take no for an answer . . . for a day or two. And I'll even get Jake to buy a bolt for that door, next time he goes into town."

"How reassuring."

"Jake sleeps within hailing distance, too," Daniel went on as if he had not noted her sarcasm. "He's one of those who prefers privacy to the dormitory life. His tent's no more than thirty yards from here. I'll ask him to keep an eye on you. He'll come at a run if you call, and unlike some of the other men, he can be trusted not to make passes."

"Unlike you," she corrected him witheringly.

"Most of all unlike me," he agreed, smiling and flexing his spine lazily, in an unashamedly sensual way. His body had at last become quiescent, but the pantherish movement and the light in his eye reminded Cat he still had intentions of mastering her tonight. "Females aren't in Jake's line. Or so the story goes."

As understanding gradually dawned, Cat felt a flicker of irritation. Her instinctive reaction to Jake had been one of trust and liking, and Daniel's innuendo annoyed her. "How can you say that? Why, I thought he was very nice. And he's hardly more than a boy."

"I like Jake, too, and I wouldn't make that sort of comment to anyone else. I tell you only because I want you to know I'll be leaving you in safe hands should you . . . ah . . . turn me down tonight. I've no knowledge of Jake's sexual preferences, or even if he has any, for I'm damned if I'll listen to camp gossip on that score. But I do know that of all the track gang, he's the only one who can't function when he's alone with a woman."

"And how," she asked sharply, "can you know a thing like that?"

Daniel's only answer was silence.

102

"Never mind," Cat said after a moment. "You don't have to draw me a diagram. Inge, I suppose, or—"

The soft rap at the door brought the thought to a halt. With a grimace, Daniel strode across the room and opened the door to Jake.

"Sorry I took so long, boss." Jake darted an irresolute smile in Cat's direction as he handed Daniel the portmanteau. "Mr. Brody yelled for spikes, and I had to lower a keg into the gorge. Couldn't hold up the work."

"That's all right, Jake."

"Mr. Brody said to tell you he'll be up in a few minutes. He wants to talk to you, something about the tunneling."

"Trouble?"

"I don't think so. It's going along like a house on fire, more than six feet a day since Mr. Mosley took over."

Oddly, Daniel frowned as if he did not quite like that news. "No need for Yancy to make the climb," he said thoughtfully. "I'll go down. I think I should get to the forward camp at once. But first, Jake—" Despite the fact that his words were addressed elsewhere, his eyes found Cat and turned languid again. "As of today you have a new responsibility. Whenever that train's in camp, you're relieved of other duties, and you're to watch Miss Kinross like a hawk. Let her get away, today or any day, and you're fired!"

Cat glared daggers as Daniel picked up the dynamite and headed for the door. As he brushed past her, he leaned down and murmured softly, for her benefit alone: "Sole support of his invalid father, Cat. You wouldn't do a thing like that to a nice boy like Jake, would you?" And then, with one last wide and wicked grin, he banged out the door. His cheerful whistle vanishing into the distance seemed the very final affront.

It was a moment before Jake spoke. "Shall I show you around the camp, Miss Kinross? If you'd prefer I can leave you alone, and keep watch from outside. Sometimes a person wants to be alone."

"No, I—" Composing herself, Cat turned to face Jake, the slight flush high on her cheekbones the only remaining sign of the frustration that gnawed, like acid, at the pit of her stomach. "I'd rather have a look about the camp, as you've been good enough to offer. But first I should change into more practical clothes."

"I'll wait outside, then." Jake smiled again with his eyes, brown and long-lashed, reminding Cat that beneath the unassuming exterior he was an extraordinarily handsome lad. Briefly, Cat wondered if Daniel's supposition had been true. Well, what if it was? It was a relief to be in the company of someone who was not overpoweringly male.

She smiled back, lowering one single layer of the formidable defenses these past months had given her against men. "If we're to spend two hours together every day," she said impulsively, "let's start off on an equal footing. I call you Jake. Why don't you call me Cathryn? Or Cat, if you prefer. We may as well be friends."

"If you like." Diffidently, as if expecting her to retract the offer, Jake turned toward the door, and opened it.

"No, if *you* like," said Cat. "I mean it, really. I think I'm going to need a friend."

Jake hesitated before stepping outside, and the expression of shy gratitude on his face was reward enough for the spontaneous gesture Cat had made.

"I've never been friends with a woman," he said quietly, his eyes warm. "I think I'd like that . . . Cathryn."

11

"God dammit, Mosley, I don't care what you did on your last assignment!"

At Daniel's words, Lafer Mosley clenched and unclenched his white beefy knuckles, and a dull red flush climbed from the collar of his flannel shirt up the normally pallid skin of his thick neck, and into the heavy jaw, shadowed as always with a blueish stubble that even the closest shave never removed.

"No one talks to me like that," Mosley said in an ominous voice. Who did Savage think he was, to dress a man down for merely doing a job, and a helluva good job at that? In the month he'd been in charge during Daniel's absence, Lafer reckoned he'd blasted every tunneling record in the book, considering the hardness of the rock. Yet here was Savage, treating him as if he'd been common dirt, with Yancy Brody standing by for witness, and those damn pig-tailed Orientals squatting nearby on the rock. They pretended they weren't listening, but they were, curse their yellow bellies and their blank-eyed faces and their damned eternal cups of tea. And several others, too; real men, not Chinks, gawking about as if this were their day's entertainment.

"Six feet a day in hard rock like this?" growled Mosley. "You've never bested that. You were only doing five before I came."

"And at five feet a day, no one died." Daniel's jaw worked. "Good Christ, Mosley, I regret the day I brought you in as foreman on this job."

"I know my business," came the sullen answer.

"You may know explosives but you don't know men. You didn't even report the deaths to Yancy."

"Who counts Chinks? Never did on my last job." Mosley slanted a scornful glance at the silent cluster of laborers, with special attention to the man he had been about to send into the tunnel. "They're not really men. And, hell, only four of 'em dead in four weeks. The others got out. Christ, it's no worse than putting a little firecracker under their yellow arses. Keeps 'em on their toes."

"By God, Mosley, I have half a mind to send you in with a short fuse yourself," exploded Daniel, staring at the other man as if he had turned up a rock and found a particularly slimy slug.

"Saves time," muttered Mosley mulishly, still trying to save face because of the several Occidentals lounging around, grinning openly. "'Specially now that we're a long way in. Crew can be clearing out a ton of rock in the time it takes to stand around picking noses and waiting for a blast to go."

"I won't save time at the expense of safety. Now get in that tunnel and replace the fuse."

The blue-stubbled jaw jutted out even further. "So make me. I've done my job. That fuse looked plenty long to me, even for those chicken-livered Chinks."

Daniel controlled an impulse to flatten that pugnacious jaw. "You're fired, Mosley. Be on the next train."

"Fire me and it'll cost you. I've got a contract, remember. Three months' pay! And don't forget to include the bonus I get for being ahead of schedule."

Daniel's eyes narrowed. "Then you're not fired," he snapped. "But from now on you have a new responsibility. Once the charges are set you're to ignite every single fuse . . . you personally. Now get in there and do it! Surely you're not less of a man than a . . . chicken-livered Chinaman?"

The color drained from Mosley's cheeks, slackening the jaw and emphasizing its blueish cast. "You bleeding sod," he muttered.

"I wouldn't ask any man to do anything I wouldn't do myself," Daniel said, his eyes hard. "You light that fuse now, I'll do one half the length as soon as the next charges are laid. Well, Mosley? Do you have the guts?"

Sullen silence greeted the taunt, so Daniel added coldly: "You can always quit, Mosley. Your contract allows you to do that if you don't like the responsibilities you're assigned. Now get in and light that fuse . . . or go and pack your belongings."

With grim satisfaction, Daniel watched as a furious Mosley turned away, making the choice. He headed not toward the tunnel but toward the site where the tents were pitched.

"Sonuvabitch," muttered Yancy from behind Daniel's

shoulder. "So that's why he was gittin' on like wildfire. Shoulda figgered it was too good to be true. Sorry."

"Ah, hell, you've had other problems on your mind, and you couldn't know what this rock was like." Daniel rubbed the back of his neck ruefully. "Next payroll, Yancy, I want every Chinaman on my crew to get a bonus for danger pay. They've earned it after a month with Mosley. Not really men, he says! By God, with the railroads they've built, the Chinese and the Irish have damn near built this country!"

Some time later, when the next blast rumbled through the mountains, spewing black rubble from the mouth of the tunnel and expelling one man-sized boulder as if fired from a cannon, Lafer Mosley was watching from a safe distance, and still rankling from his public humiliation. His things were packed, his tent ready to dismantle. But the memory of the day lay in his gut like black powder attached to a slow-burning fuse.

"I'll show you who's a man," he muttered ferociously.

"You," whispered Cat, jerking to a sitting position and staring with evidence of real panic at the tall apparition that had appeared at her bedside so soon after she had fallen asleep.

"I told you I'd be back." Daniel walked across the room and put his lantern on the deal table, noting with mild amusement the way it, and the desk, and several chairs as well, had been pushed against the closed door of the cabin. Retrieving one of the chairs, he carried it to Cat's bedside, straddled it, and folded his arms along the back. He smiled at her reassuringly. His eyes took in the hair brushed out and lying like a midnight cloud around her shoulders; the night-dress of heavy white cotton; the quick come-and-go of her breath that lifted the fabric at her breasts. He had caught her with her defenses down, just as he had intended to do, leaving his arrival until long after dusk, and waiting outside until some time after the light in the cabin had been extinguished.

But he had not expected the surfeit of panic he saw in those startled silver eyes. "I won't hurt you," he reassured her quietly.

Cat recovered quickly, the mask of composure returning to still the quiver of her lips. "How did you get in? I thought I'd hear you."

"So I see," he said dryly. "I expected something like that, so I came in the window."

"Why did you come back? I told you no this morning."

"How could I know you wouldn't change your mind?"

"I didn't think you'd come. It's so dark . . . and after seeing that climb you have to make—"

"Ah, hell, it's nothing."

"I was dizzy just watching the men go down to work in daylight. Doesn't danger mean anything to you? You could have killed yourself."

"Do I detect an element of concern for my safety?" His eyes teased her. "I'm flattered. In that case, you won't want me to make the return trip until morning."

Cat stiffened. "But you'll have to, won't you? You gave me your word that you'd take no for an answer."

Perversely, now that the mask was back in place Daniel wanted to disrupt it again. "Maybe I was too hasty," he said, his voice mocking her lazily. "I'd forgotten how beautiful you look with your hair down. And that nightdress . . . it reminds me of the first night. Did *you* take no for an answer then? Perhaps I should pay you back in kind."

"Please go," she told him coldly.

"I remember saying the same thing to you, once upon a time." Daniel came to his feet and approached the bed, loosening the buttons of his shirt as he came. "And what did you do? You kissed me, and destroyed all my best resolutions. Perhaps I can do the same for you. I think the scenario goes something like this—"

He crushed down onto the narrow bed beside her, easing her back against the pillow and smoothing the hair away from her temples. Her expression suggested nothing but a cold antagonism, although she made no effort to push him away. His face hovered above hers, not closing the last inches between them, the gloom of the room carving changing valleys of his eyes. Gradually, his smile faded, to be replaced by a smoking sensuousness.

"Oh, God, Cathryn, if you knew how many times I've thought of doing this," he said huskily, "you wouldn't say no. That night . . . that's why I went east again, not to see your grandfather, to see you. I tried to forget you. But I used to see your face in the campfire, in the darkness of a tunnel, in the shadows on a mountainside. . . ."

"And in the face of every woman you took to bed, I

suppose." Cat's face mirrored her distaste. "Do you always court women with words of love? Perhaps men are more honest on Fifth Avenue after all."

He was silent for a little too long, struggling to contain a sudden surge of anger—with her, for her deliberately cutting words, and perhaps even more with himself, for admitting more than he had wanted to admit.

"Love is a word I don't use," he said at last, tersely. "Not to you, not to any woman. What I'm talking about is mating instinct. One night with you gave me a taste for more, that's all. In my occupation I don't allow myself the indulgence of emotional ties. Physical ones are all I can handle." Then, pride salvaged, he added in a softer voice, wooing her again: "I'm sorry, Cathryn. That's a hell of a thing to say to a woman you want with every muscle, every bone, every fiber of your being. I want you . . . God, how I want you—"

His fingers cupped her face, brown against the pale flesh. He stroked her eyelids closed with his thumbs, and his mouth began the descent.

"The answer is no, Daniel," she said in a succinct voice, turning her head away without struggle, for Daniel's touch was light.

"Let me undress you," he said huskily. "Let me touch you . . . let me make love to you."

"No," she said icily, brushing away the fingers that stroked her earlobes. She remained rigid beneath the impress of the long limbs flung over hers on the small bed. The sheets and blankets remained between them, but even through these mounded coverings and her nightdress, Cat could feel the heat of his body attempting to melt the ice of hers. As always, she had a sense of detachment, of watching herself from a distance. There was no panic now. To feel panic you first had to feel; and she felt nothing, nothing, nothing.

"What did Gow do to you, Cat?" Daniel asked quietly. "What did he do to turn you away from lovemaking?"

"I don't like it, that's all. I submitted then because I had to, but I don't have to submit to you."

"Surely no moral reservations now."

"I'm cold, Daniel," she told him in a toneless voice. "I have been for a long time."

"Just because you couldn't feel anything with Gow doesn't mean—"

"I don't want to feel anything, ever again," she inter-

109

rupted. "Now will you please leave? This bed is too small for two."

"What did he do to you, Cat?" Daniel came to a sitting position and seized her shoulders, drawing her unresisting form upward in the bed.

The answer to Daniel's question came not in words, but in the darkness that fleeted across her eyes, like the wing shadow of a giant evil bird on the surface of a frozen silver pond.

"What the hell did he do? Rape?"

Now, her cool eyes betrayed nothing. They neither denied, nor confirmed, his guess. "Please remove your hands," she said.

"Did he take you by force?"

"Force isn't necessary when someone doesn't fight, is it? You might remember that, Mr. Savage. I'm not fighting you, any more than I fought then. So please stop hurting me!"

"Oh, God," groaned Daniel, realizing now that his fingers had been bruising into the soft flesh of her upper arms. He freed her and stood up, turning away to hide the rage and pity and other emotions that stormed his brain, some of them caused by ugly memories out of his own past. Rape—it must have been, initially at least. She denied fighting Gow, and perhaps she had not, after a time.

"What else did he do?" Daniel asked thickly.

"I don't care to talk about it. Now will you please go? I had very little sleep last night."

He turned to face her again, eyes somber. "Tell me, Cat."

"Nothing happened."

"I don't believe that."

"What is it you want me to tell you? All right, I was raped . . . once. I really don't remember the experience, I've blotted most of it right out of my mind." Her voice was totally dispassionate, as if the occasion had had little meaning for her. "After that, force wasn't necessary. I submitted. It's not hard to submit when you feel nothing."

Daniel made a compassionate gesture. "Cathryn, I'm sorry—"

She reacted as if stung, with more emotion than she had shown since his unexpected arrival in the cabin. "If you really want to do me a favor take your pity and get out of my sight!"

"I'm sorry I startled you tonight: That's what I was going to say. Now I understand. And I think I understand other things: those dark circles under your eyes, for instance. You never sleep well, do you?"

"I certainly can't sleep when I'm not left alone," she said pointedly.

"And the way you turn rigid whenever you're touched," he said thoughtfully.

"I told you, I'm cold."

And there had been that panic in her eyes. It had been quickly shuttered but it had been there. There was more to Cat's problem than coldness. "You're afraid of being touched," Daniel said slowly.

"I'm not afraid. I just don't like it."

"Afraid of being made to feel."

"I feel something right now: *tired*. Will you please leave?"

"Cathryn, you don't have any reason to be afraid of me. I won't force myself on you. In fact, I won't touch you again without your permission."

"And you'll never have that. Now go. *Please*."

"I'll go." Reluctantly, Daniel retrieved his lantern and moved toward the window. "I'll leave your arrangement at the door for tonight. And I'll have Jake buy latches for the windows, too. Will that help you sleep more soundly?"

"It might."

He paused with the window open. The chilly night air of the mountain invaded the cabin, causing Cat to shiver involuntarily.

"Trust me, Cat," he said softly; and with an arrogance born of too much success with women, he believed it would be only a matter of days until she did.

"I'll try," she answered, without meaning it.

"I'll drop by tomorrow afternoon, if I'm able," Daniel told her, and vanished into the spangled night, closing the window firmly behind him.

It was dawn before Cat slept.

12

May melted into June; June into July; July into August. The uncertain summer of the high mountain meadows brought blue lupine and Indian paintbrush to vie with cow parsnip and the pale yellow of evening primrose, and in the high reaches avalanche lilies stretched their heads to find what warmth they could. No eternal snows were melted, but under the suns of summer the white receded up the mountainsides.

Daniel was courting Cat. He would not have called it that, and he would have snarled at any man who told him so, but it was courtship of a kind all the same. What had begun as a challenge to masculine pride had become something more—something he would not yet admit to himself. The excuses he found to visit the track gang's rattletrap town could hardly be accounted for in any other way, and as the bridge was not yet completed, the trek down into the gorge and up the rope ladder on the other side was still an hour's haul each way—a two-hour trip, all told, with few rewards for his efforts. But now, he made the trip by daylight, leaving the blasting operations in the hands of a responsible foreman who had been called in to replace Mosley.

And then, the days of August shortened, and Daniel knew the time would soon come when the distance between the two camps would be too great for casual visits. The tunnel, like the bridge, was nearing completion; soon, the railway would be moving on.

"Take over, will you, Williams? I'm off to the other camp this morning. I need a few errands done in town, and this is Jake's day to go. Anything you want?"

"Spool of thread," came the answer, not surprising in this rough near-womanless forward camp where men must mostly look after their own needs. Williams was a solid man with a nice-ugly face; Daniel had learned he could be trusted implicitly.

"What color thread?"

"White will do," said Williams.

"If I get back in time," Daniel told him, "I may go and scout that next tunneling job, see what problems we may encounter."

"Should be easy enough after this brute," remarked Williams, turning his eyes toward an odd-shaped mountain about two miles distant, but quite clearly visible from where they were standing. Like Yosemite's famed Half Dome elsewhere in the Sierra Nevada, the peak presented a vertical rock face which looked as if some massive glacier of a million years ago had sheared away a half a mountain. An imposing wall of granite, seamed only by occasional fissures, rose perpendicularly from a base of jagged rock. Inhospitable as it looked, it provided less challenge than the difficult tunnel that had occupied Daniel's attention for the better part of a year. Although there was other blasting to be done, this next short job was the last of the tunnels on the line. After that, the rails would lead out of the mountains in a series of loops and switchbacks for which much of the preliminary work had been done.

"Want me to come along?" asked Williams. "Or will you take one of the other men?"

"I shouldn't need anyone. I'll probably camp there, too, for a night. It doesn't look far from here, but getting there takes several hours. I'll have to go around the long way . . . follow the back trails up the mountain's other side."

"Then you'd better have company."

Daniel turned his gaze away from the lonely peak. "I'd rather go alone," he decided, fatefully.

It was eleven o'clock in the morning when Daniel arrived at the track gang's camp. An accident on the bridge had delayed him: One of the workmen had missed his step on a stringer, and spent half an hour dangling, screaming, five hundred feet above ground with a dislocated arm, a painful retribution for his one misstep. Daniel had watched from down in the gorge until rescuers on ropes reached the hapless man, and restored him to safety. Only then did he make his way to the rope ladder, and as he started up the side he heard the wail of the train whistle announcing an imminent departure. As he came over the crest, he saw the locomotive churn into a slow start. With no more than mild irritation, Daniel watched it gather speed as it snaked backward out of sight, leaving its white plume to disperse against a blue sky.

He turned his footsteps at once to the branch of track that

113

led to the makeshift townsite, and a few minutes later, after exchanging civilities with several passing souls, he arrived at the door of his cabin. He knocked briefly but did not wait for an answer; he knew by now that Cat always bolted the door when she needed privacy.

"Very pretty," he said as soon as he opened the door.

Cat was standing on a chair, at a window, arms raised above her head. She looked over her shoulder at Daniel, then lowered her arms and removed the half-dozen pins that had been clamped between her lips. For reasons she could not have given a name to, a faint trace of color rose to her cheeks.

"I'm glad you like them," she said. "Jake ordered the fabric for me months ago, but it only came in last week. I'm sorry you came now, when they're not finished. I wanted to surprise you."

Daniel chuckled. "I didn't mean the curtains, although they're very nice, too. In fact, a vast improvement. But I meant you."

The stain deepened slightly, and Cat turned her back to hide it. Why, now, did Daniel always give her this feeling of vulnerability, of being off balance? True to his word, he had made no real attempts at intimacy, always conceding to her evident dislike of physical contact. In nearly four months, he had not touched her at all. Even Jake touched her at times—often taking her elbow to help her over rough patches in the trails, sometimes linking arms when they went exploring in mountain meadows, once rubbing her ankle when she had sprained it slightly. But then, she and Jake had developed a warm and comfortable friendship in which physical intimacy played no part.

Jake touched her, but Daniel did not. And yet, as the weeks and the days and the hours ticked by, she had become increasingly conscious, whenever Daniel was around, of his physical presence, and in a way that she did not like. There was a male-animal aura about him, a vitality and virility as distinctive as musk. The lack of touching may have been a conscious effort to gain her trust, and it had had some of that effect; but it had also produced, perversely, an even deeper wariness within her.

Daniel was a threat, and Jake was not.

"Need help?" Daniel asked, moving slowly closer as if to swing her off the chair.

"No, thanks," Cat replied quickly, and scrambled down

before he could reach her side. She turned to face him, rewarding him with a guarded smile as she often did now, in payment for the overtures he never made. "Why have you come today?"

"To borrow a spool of thread," he said. "I didn't manage to catch Jake before he took off for town. White, if you have it."

"White it is." She produced a spool from the pocket of the sewing apron she wore, and dropped it several inches' distance into Daniel's outstretched hand. "Any other things you wanted Jake to get? Surely you didn't come on an hour's hike just to order a spool of thread."

"I did want a few things, but there's nothing that can't wait for a week or two," said Daniel offhandedly, and strolled over to that part of the cabin that had been reorganized to serve as a kitchen. The potbellied stove had been replaced with a proper wood-burning cookstove. On crude shelves that Daniel had installed in his spare time weeks before, a small pile of cheerful blue and white willow-pattern dishes shared space with canisters of supplies.

"Wouldn't mind staying for lunch, though," Daniel added, "if you can handle a guest."

"It's your house," she reminded him, her manner perceptibly cooler.

"For the time being, it's—" Daniel stopped himself, and started again. "You're quite right. Why should I have to invite myself when I'm in my own cabin? I'll stay."

"Don't you have to be back at work?" came the pointed reminder.

"There's nothing Williams can't handle," Daniel said, deciding then and there that his trip could wait until the following day.

"It's quite a time until lunch." Now the voice was decidedly cold.

"Well, then, we'll go for a walk," Daniel said crisply. "Soon it won't be warm enough to enjoy that kind of outing. There's a grand mountain meadow not fifteen minutes from here, and the trail's quite easy."

"No, thanks. I have to finish the curtains. And besides, I've already seen the meadow, several times."

"With Jake?"

Cat nodded. "With Jake," and bent her head to hide a moment's inexplicable confusion.

"I won't touch you, Cat," Daniel said in a low voice. "Not

115

without some encouragement. Surely you know that by now. I won't touch you until you signify that . . . Ah, *hell,*" he finished, as some small portion of his frustration vented itself, like steam escaping from pistons under too much pressure, "I know you always go walking in the morning. Why make an exception today? Is it because I'm not *Jake?* Surely I've given you no cause to be afraid of me. Have all my efforts been for nothing?"

Cat's eyes came up again slowly, their millpond surface restored. "Of course I'm not afraid of you," she said, hiding behind the mask of a smile she reserved for use on Daniel. "Since you put it that way, I suppose the curtains can wait."

"That's a girl." Daniel broke into a relieved grin that took years from his face. "D'you know, I think you'll have to show me the way. It's been that long since I've seen the meadow . . . six years at least, back when we were first scouting for a route. Shall we take a simple picnic? Cheese and bread would be fine, and mountain water will do."

And because there seemed no good reason to say no, Cat agreed to that, too. Daniel packed the food she provided into a small rucksack which he slung over his shoulder. She followed him as he took off in the direction of the trail with a self-assurance that told Cat his sense of direction could in no way be faulted. The trail was downhill and only wide enough for single file; Daniel went ahead.

In the meadow they came to rest on a cool green grassy slope, and talked for a time about news from the East. Although discretion still dictated that no letters be written, Daniel had arranged for a trusted friend to call on Hannah, who was now living with Angus McBride in his new home, and helping to care for his several new stepchildren. Kirklands remained empty; there was talk of selling it to settle the estate, which consisted mostly of debt.

"I wish I could go East and try to save it," sighed Cat.

"Surely it's safe to do that by now."

"No," and then again: "No." She shook her head, and the shadow of Julian ghosted through her eyes.

"The best way to deal with a man like Gow is to face up to him, Cathryn. What can he do to you now? You'll never shake fear by running away for the rest of your life. I'll go East with you. We'll—"

"I never want to face Julian again," she interrupted.

116

"You don't seem to have trouble dealing with the men in camp, and they're a rough lot. What can Gow possibly do to you now? I imagine he's forgotten you."

"Perhaps." Cat toyed with a blade of grass. "Please, I don't want to talk about Julian. Why don't we eat?"

They did. Afterward, Daniel lay sprawled on his back, hands laced behind his head, looking contentedly at cotton-ball clouds scudding by. Cat, not quite relaxed, sat with elbows resting on bent knees, feet tucked well under long skirts. Despite the near-frost of last night the air was warm today. The meadow was in a valley protected from the wind that so often moaned through the higher mountaintops. Nearby a little stream babbled over rock, and the scent of mint, crushed by their bodies, drifted in the air.

"How did you choose tunneling as an occupation?" Cat asked, after a time.

"Stumbled into it by way of dynamite," Daniel said lightly.

"And how did you stumble into dynamite?"

"Ah, it's a boring story and not the best for a sunny day. I'd rather talk about you."

"I refuse to talk about me, and we have to talk about something, don't we? Or else go home. We've already covered the weather, and railroads, and Jake, and who got drunk on Saturday night. Please tell me about you. I'd like to hear."

Daniel rolled half over, onto his side. He propped his head on one hand and gave Cat a long searching look she did not understand; it was the kind of look that had nothing to do with desire. "Do you really want to know about me?" he asked at last, seriously. "You know, I have this odd compulsion to tell you, and it's not a story I tell readily. Yancy knows parts of it, but I've never told a woman. I've never thought a woman would want to hear."

"I promise I won't be bored."

Daniel heaved a sigh, and rolled onto his back. One arm came up, and the back of his hand came to rest loosely over his eyes. "It's not boring, it's just ugly. Or parts of it are ugly . . . the early parts. It's not a story for someone who's lived a protected life. But then, you . . ." But he did not want to bring up her time with Gow again, so he started into his recital matter-of-factly, with no more waiting to find out if she really wanted to hear.

"I didn't plan to get into explosives; it just happened. If it hadn't been for the Civil War I'd probably be a trapper or a guide today."

Daniel had grown up in Nebraska, then a territory. His father, a trapper and trader of unknown parentage, had been brought up by a small Pawnee band; the name Savage had been given to him upon his return to civilization, as a young man.

"My mother was a Boston girl, good family, good education. Society folk. Her parents were aghast when she took up with my father. She ran away with him, settled into a rough sod homestead along the Platte valley. One daughter, three sons. I was the youngest. My mother baked bread with one hand and taught us all with the other . . . reading, writing, arithmetic; history and philosophy, too. It was a rough life for someone with a soft upbringing, but she never complained, although my father was often off on long trips. She died just before the start of the Civil War. She, and my only sister."

"What happened?" asked Cat quietly, after some silence.

"Indians. Sioux, maybe? There were other massacres about that time. My father was away, with my older brothers. I'd gone off hunting small game by myself, angry that I was too young to be allowed to go along with the men. My mother and sister stayed at home. And when I got back, they . . . There was blood all over. They had been been staked to the ground."

There was another silence, longer this time, and uninterrupted by Cat. The hand over Daniel's eyes concealed a part of his face, but his mouth was in view, and its very expressionlessness told her that he was reliving a part of the horror now.

In time he resumed the narrative. At the beginning of the Civil War, Daniel's two brothers, both some years older, had enlisted. Finally, at fifteen, Daniel had run away from a home that, because of his father's frequent long absences, no longer really existed. His goal was the special unit to which his oldest brother was attached—a raiding unit whose task was to disrupt communications behind Confederate lines. Their targets were trains and bridges and supply depots; their weapons fire and explosives.

"It was shortly after the Battle of Shiloh. I worked my way through the lines until I found my brother's unit. He was out on a raiding party at the time. They brought him in when I'd been there four or five hours. He was still alive, horribly alive. One hand had been blown off and his face was no more than a red pudding. And his gut . . . The Rebs had caught him. They had taken away most of his blasting powder . . . there was no dynamite in those days . . . and forced him to set off the rest at gunpoint, without a fuse. They left him for dead, laughing as they went. His partner had been concealed, watching. It was he that put a tourniquet on my brother's arm and dragged him back to camp. Oh, God, how I hated the Rebs at that moment! I bunked in with the unit, a useless fifteen-year-old kid, but they let me hang around while my brother died."

The other brother had been serving under Farragut; his name appeared in the casualty lists during the week it took for Daniel's oldest brother to die.

"Explosives again, I later learned. A faulty shell."

Daniel had hung around the battlefront near the special unit, scrounging what food he could, and offering a service that was not too politely refused. Raiding parties behind enemy lines were not for young boys. But he was given odd jobs of fetching and carrying, and when the unit moved on to new assignments, Daniel had tagged along, too, a kind of mascot by then. The following year, when he was sixteen, the chance he had been begging for came at last. A captain named Hewitt, whose partner had been wounded, took Daniel along on an assignment. Under cover of night they had sneaked through Confederate lines.

"We reached the rail tracks about four o'clock in the morning; Hewitt told me a supply train was coming through at six. He'd been back-packing a big metal can of some liquid . . . a potent acid, he told me. He handled that can as though it had been made of Venetian glass. I begged to be allowed to use it, and at last he agreed, gave me detailed instructions. He told me the acid would eat through the track, derail the train."

In the ensuing pause Cat noticed that the hand over Daniel's eyes had been balled into a fist.

"It was a scene out of hell. The train came through just at dawn, one of those dawns when the sky seems like pink fire, the world all silent and rosy except for the whistle in the distance, then the sound building as the train comes closer and closer. . . . And then suddenly it was black again, black billowing smoke and so much noise you couldn't hear the screams, at least not until later. Bits of bodies flying through the air. It wasn't a supply train, it was a troop train. Hundreds of men."

"You couldn't know," Cat said quietly.

"Well, it's just a matter of degree, isn't it? I knew men would die when I used that nitroglycerin."

"But you didn't know it was nitroglycerin."

"Yes, I did," he confessed. "I didn't have to be told. I wasn't that stupid; I'd been around explosives some at that point, and I'd heard of nitro though I'd never seen it before. I guessed as soon as I smelled the stuff. And I knew it didn't need a detonator; nitro explodes at the slightest jolt."

"All the same, you couldn't know so many would die."

"No. And that filled me with a terrible anger against the horrors of war. From then on, I couldn't hate, and I didn't want to kill."

"And you left the unit then?"

"No," he said in a level voice. "I stayed with them. That was just my initiation; they kept me on after that, in spite of my age. Even got me a uniform. But I confined my activities to less horrible things . . . firing bridges, blasting rail lines, cutting off lines of retreat. It gave me a great respect for explosives, and a lot of knowledge. When the war ended I decided to put the knowledge to use. My father was living with the Pawnee by then; he was a self-sufficient man and didn't want me hanging around. I'd heard of the work being done in Sweden by a chemist named Nobel. He was trying to mix nitroglycerin with something to make it more stable. As a liquid it's damn tricky stuff. You know, it's illegal, now, to move it by rail. If I want to use it, I have to mix it on the site.

"Anyway, after the war I hopped a boat and went to Stockholm. It wasn't hard to get a job at Nobel's factory. I lied about my age, and he'd lost so many men, including his own brother, that he was in need of experienced people. They put me to work testing various mixtures. The following year Nobel came up with dynamite . . . really just nitroglycerin mixed with kieselguhr, a kind of earth. Still dangerous stuff, but not unpredictable like nitro."

"Is that when you came back to the United States?"

"I stayed in Europe a few more months, learning what I could about engineering and chemistry. Nobel was a first-rate chemist; he studied in the States. I came back, eventually, to see my father. He'd always been strong as an ox, a mountain of a man, but I had this notion things weren't quite as they should be. I found him dead, an accident while trapping. I stayed and lived with the Pawnee for several months."

Daniel spent a silent moment remembering a part of his life that he would not tell Cat: the young Pawnee girl who had been his squaw, and to whom he had been faithful during her life. She had died, she and the child she had been bearing in her womb. She had been fifteen, the only other virgin he had ever taken; he had been twenty.

"After that I returned to my first love . . . explosives. I went to work for the Union Pacific. And that's all there is to tell."

"It's such a dangerous life."

"But the only one for me. You can see why I don't like emotional ties; they always end in disaster. Look, see that Steller's jay? Making off with the leftovers from our lunch. Damned impertinence."

He stood up and stretched in his long limber way, then stooped down and scooped up a small bunch of lavender mountain daisies.

"For you, for listening," he said, presenting them to Cat.

She refused to reach for them, and at last he dropped them into her lap.

"How much longer, Cathryn?" he asked gravely.

"I don't know." She bent her head to hide a sudden sting behind her eyes. But she had not cried for nearly a year, not even at her grandfather's funeral, and she did not cry now. "Maybe never," she said in a low voice.

And why should she have thought she wanted to cry? A woman with a frozen heart and a frigid body had no right to be in love with any man.

"Why didn't you just stay at the other camp?"

The young fierce voice was a woman's. She was standing in the entranceway of a tent, holding the flapped door open, staring without appreciation at a night sky as close and clear as only a mountain sky can be. Her straw-colored hair was looped into a coil at the back of her neck, but long wisps escaped, framing her Nordic cheekbones. She still wore the clothes she had worn all day, a rough practical gown suited to the rigors of the advance camp where she had been living for these past months. A heavy shawl had been added for the chill night air.

"Inge—" In the shadowed tent lit by a single lantern,

Daniel came up behind the girl and dropped his head into the hollows of her throat. His palms moved soothingly and seductively over her shoulders and her breasts and her hips, with the absolute self-assurance of a man taking a woman he knows is willing.

"No more talk," he murmured huskily. "Come to bed."

"Is that all you keep me here for?"

"I've never pretended. You know I want no ties."

"Damn you for a bastard!" But she allowed him to pull her back into the tent, and moments later she was undressing Daniel with an impatience that equaled his. She was moist and ready, and he mounted her at once.

"There, sweetheart," he muttered into her ear, "you see? You wanted it, too. Oh, God, how I want you. I've been thinking all day about this."

"Have you?" she hissed, at once angry again, and beginning to squirm beneath the hard body that penetrated hers. "How nice that you've been thinking about making love to me! But why do you—"

Suddenly, breath-stoppingly, her angry lips were bruised apart. Daniel ignored her raking fingernails. His mouth possessed her punishingly, and so did he, driving in with a passion that resembled rage. Her own response turned her wild and weak with wanting, and gradually, as her hips arched higher, her fingernails forgot their task.

Only later, when Daniel at last rolled away, and Inge saw the vivid weals she had raked into his muscled shoulders, did she remember the question that she had been about to ask.

"Why do you always want me on days like this, Daniel? After you've seen *her?*"

13

The next day, Wednesday, Daniel traveled light, taking only a rifle, a knife, a thin bedroll, a coil of stout rope, some dry biscuits, and a couple of small traplines. He also took a full bottle of whiskey, and a water flask.

The trails were roundabout and strewn with fallen rock. He was unalarmed by the small clues—the bent grasses, the broken twigs—that told him someone had recently traversed the territory. There were Indians and trappers in the Sierras, and prospectors, too, at times. He reached the top of the mountain that was his goal in late afternoon.

"Damn fool thing to go alone," Yancy had grumbled.

"Stop being an old woman, Yancy," Daniel had said. "There are times a man needs to be alone. To think."

He had started into the whiskey an hour before the sun set over the cathedral spires of the Sierras. A long time later he was still drinking, his mood as black as the night that engulfed him. He felt none of the biting chill in the air. Before the moon rose the bottle was half empty; its level continued to drop.

At length, thoroughly inebriated, he lurched to his feet. For a time he swayed on the naked moonlit crest of the summit, and then for long moments, like a mighty bull moose bugling in pain, he roared his wordless rage to the mountain-tops.

"I wonder what's happened to Jake," Cat said to Laura Brody with a worried frown. It was Thursday morning, and they were standing with Laura's eight-year-old daughter, Charity, watching the train unload. "He should have been back yesterday."

Laura Brody was some fifteen years older than Cat. She was a handsome woman, one quarter Cree, gentle and reserved in manner, and devoted to her husband and four young children. No particular camaraderie had developed between Laura and Cat. There was the age difference, for one thing, and Laura, large again with child, was far too busy with her young brood to indulge in easy friendships. But a respectful liking had developed, and the two often chatted at times like this.

"Perhaps his father's taken ill again," Laura suggested, concerned but reassuring. "He's sickly at the best of times. Don't worry; Jake's probably stayed in the valley to help him."

Cat decided then and there that she would ask Daniel's permission to go into the valley tomorrow, should Jake fail to appear. Daniel's initial injunction to stay on the site had been relaxed somewhat, but he had extracted from her a promise that she would not go on the train without his knowledge.

"Good heavens," Laura said, "look at those Chinamen."

Cat turned and saw a circle of Orientals seated on a shelf of rock. One of their number, who had just come back on the morning train, was walking slowly from one man to the next. He was a small wiry man, pig-tailed, pockmarked, older than the other men. He appeared to be blowing some kind of powder from the palm of his hand into the nostrils of his compatriots. The recipients, each in turn, were inhaling deeply.

"I wonder what they're doing," Cat said. "I hope it's not something like opium."

"I wouldn't think so. More likely it's medicine of some kind. Sam Yee is usually in charge of administering such things. He told Yancy once that he knows of two thousand different drugs, everything from ginseng to powdered pearls to snow-toad jelly. He even gave Yancy something for wind in the bone and, would you believe, it worked?"

"Wind in the bone?"

"Rheumatism," laughed Laura, and then turned her attention to a two-year-old who had stumbled and burst into screams of angry pain. "There, there," she soothed, swooping low to gather the child to her shoulder.

"Did you hear that odd noise last night?" Cat asked, when the child's tears had at last been comforted away.

"Who could sleep through that? It must have been a wounded animal; they can sound almost human at times. Miles away, I imagine, but sounds do travel in the mountains."

124

"I hope the poor thing is out of its misery by now," Cat observed abstractedly. The haunting howling had disturbed her, and although she had been sleeping more soundly since coming to the Sierras, she had not done so last night, for the noise had lingered in her mind long after a cathedral hush had been restored. But at the moment, she was far more worried about Jake.

Daniel groaned himself awake. His tongue had turned to sourdough on the rise; his head felt like the aftermath of one of his own explosions. A blinding pain seized his eyeballs from behind, and a pair of brands seared them from in front.

He rolled over onto his stomach so that the morning sun could no longer penetrate his lids. The movement turned the rock to a roller coaster. "Water," he moaned.

And at last, as he rummaged for his water flask, awareness and remembrance began to crawl over his flesh like a thousand clammy lizards. Had he really drunk himself into such a state over a woman?

He spent the next half hour nursing his hangover. His stomach recoiled at the thought of food, but he drained the water flask. And at last, because he knew men would come looking for him if he did not return to camp by nightfall, he set about the task he should have finished yesterday. A surveying team would come later; his main concern at the moment was the composition of the rock and a general overview of the tunneling problems that might be encountered.

He walked to the cliff edge, hunkered down on his heels, and studied the mountain face. Starting some fifty feet below the top, a long fissure ran down the surface, and because this natural fault might affect the blasting, he decided to have a closer look, despite the raw state of his nerves.

There were no good anchors near the precipice. He secured his rope to a large boulder at some distance, tied the other end around his waist, and lowered himself gingerly over the edge.

He had descended a slow twenty feet, every bone complaining, when he heard the small noise above his head, and looked skyward.

"Well, well, Savage," said the face leering over the edge, "nice of you to leave your rifle up here."

In Daniel's pain-beleaguered brain, one tiny core turned clear and calm, like the eye of a tornado. He wetted his lips, took a firmer grip on the rope, and braced himself against the smooth wall of rock.

"Target practice, Mosley?" he said thickly.

Mosley laughed, his teeth white against the stubbled chin. "Guns aren't my style, Savage. I'm an explosives man, and a helluva good one, too, and I won't stand for any man branding me a public coward. I figured you'd be over this way sooner or later. Very thoughtful of you to come alone. Saves me the trouble of blowing up a whole mess o' men."

Daniel's legs clenched the rope tightly. His right hand edged warily toward his knife sheath, under pretext of steadying his body against the rock. "What do you intend to do, Mosley? Drop a little firecracker or two?"

"Hell, no. Something much better. There's a little stick o' dynamite attached to your rope, over by the boulder, and the fuse is already lit. How long will it take you to shinny back up, Savage? Twenty seconds? I'll give you ten . . . maybe less." He glanced over his shoulder toward the boulder which would protect him from the small explosion, then turned back. "Now *there's* a short fuse for you! And I'll be here, watching you try to make it back u—"

The knife caught him in the throat, and for one astonished millisecond before blood spurted, Mosley's face registered incredulity but no pain. His voice was a croak. "You bas—"

But the word was never finished; Mosley was already dead. His head slumped and blood began to pour freely, staining the rock face.

There was no time to go up; so Daniel went down. The long slide took seconds only. He had just reached the narrow fissure, and jammed his body sideways into the fault, when the small charge of dynamite detonated.

When the echo of the explosion had died down, Daniel tested the rope above him. It had gone slack. Ruefully, with hands stinging from rope burns, he pulled it over the edge. It snaked down and swung limply in the air—about a hundred feet of rope in all, and attached to nothing but himself.

In early afternoon Cat strolled to the site of bridge construction, a note for Daniel in her hand. In it she requested permission to go down to the valley tomorrow. There was a workman approaching the top of the rope ladder leading down into the gorge, and Cat addressed him. "Have you seen Mr. Savage about?"

"No, miss," he said, pausing.

"I wonder if someone might be going across to the other camp?" she asked hopefully.

"Coupla hours," he grinned, "everyone an' his uncle will. Look!"

Cat did. A team of men were still hoisting a huge timber into place on the bridge, but it was clear to see there had been great progress made in the last few days.

"By tomorrow we'll be back to layin' ties, an' soon on to the other side. Hear tell the tunnel's about to break through, too," the man noted pleasantly, and returned to his assigned task, pulling up the rope ladder which would no longer be needed in this location.

By the end of the working day the last of the timbers were spiked into place. "Who was that jest crossed over?" asked Yancy, as he surfaced back onto the bridge via another rope ladder from which he had just conducted a last swaying inspection of his handiwork.

"The young 'un, Miss Kinross," a spiker informed him.

"Shee-it," said Yancy as the swirl of brown skirt, now no more than a speck, vanished over the mountain trail that led to the site of the forward camp. Well, hell—if she was asking for Daniel, someone would tell her he was off camping. "Jest hope it ain't Inge," he muttered to himself.

Cat did not ask for Daniel; she asked for Daniel's tent. There were some curious stares from the men who had just broken off tunneling operations for the day, many of whom did not know her by sight.

"Sure like to git me a piece o' that," observed the man who had just given her directions. "She the new gal at Liza's?"

"Naw, she's the young 'un the boss is lookin' after. Keep yer hands off . . . eyes, too! Boss put the word out hisself, near four months ago, when he brought 'er into camp, before you was on this job. She ain't to be tetched."

"Can't stop a man from lookin'," came the complaint.

"Think so? Boss tore a strip off one fella who jest looked sideways with his tongue hangin' out."

"Sweet on the gal, is he?"

"Naw, more like he's her pa. No hanky-panky there! Boss ain't in need. He gits his, reg'lar, with Inge."

"Lucky sonuvabitch," griped his companion. "Wisht I was

in his shoes." He watched, enviously, until Cathryn Kinross had vanished along the trail that led to the tent camp.

"Is Mr. . . . . oh, I'm sorry. I must have the wrong tent," Cat said to the top of a bent-over flaxen head.

The woman at the tent entrance was seated in the late sunlight, on a low stool simply fashioned of a sawed-off section of Sequoia log, washing her face in a pan of water set at her feet. She was clad only in chemise and petticoats; her possessions were strewn over the earth. Through the open flap of the tent, Cat could see her gown casually thrown over a large low iron-framed cot.

At Cat's words, the woman looked up. Droplets of water gleamed on the sun-bronzed high cheekbones, competing with the light freckles summer had sprinkled across a shapely nose. Cat recognized her at once.

"You're . . . Ingrid, isn't it?" she said with a slight frown. By now, Cat knew all the inmates of the bordello by sight, and many by name. There was a considerable turnover of girls; many could not stomach the life. She had assumed this one had returned to more civilized circumstances long ago. But perhaps she had set up her own headquarters here in the forward camp?

"Inge," came the corrected name, with a decided lack of warmth.

"I thought you must have gone back to town."

"As you see, I didn't. I'm living here now."

"I must have mixed up my directions. Can you please tell me which is Mr. Savage's tent?"

There was a moment of uncomfortable silence as Inge appraised Cat. Then she began to dry her face; the towel muffled her words. "You won't find him at his tent."

"Would he be at the tunneling site?"

"You won't find him there either. He's not around."

Cat felt her hackles rise in response to the animosity she sensed in the other girl. Now there was a sharp edge to her voice. "Nevertheless, I'll take my chances, and if I can't find him I'll leave a note. If you would just be good enough to direct me to his tent."

Slowly, the towel came down, revealing an expression of open hostility. Inge compressed her lips for a moment; fought a short struggle with herself; and lost.

"You're there," she said, a measure of satisfaction creeping into her voice.

Cat felt as if a blow had just been delivered to her midsection. Unable to find words, she started to turn away.

"Don't go yet," Inge said quickly. Having lost the battle with her conscience, she now wanted a different kind of victory. "Now that you're here, you might as well leave that note. I'll see that Daniel gets it, as soon as he returns."

Cat came to a halt, her spine rigid. "Perhaps I'll see him before you do," she said. "If he's not here and he's not at the tunnel, he must be over with Yancy. I probably missed him in passing."

"No, Daniel's not with Yancy. He camped out last night. He went to have a look at the next tunnel site. Didn't he tell you?"

"No."

"If your message is so important, you'd better leave it with me. This is the one place he's sure to come as soon as he returns."

After a slight pause, Cat turned back, shoulders squared, face devoid of reaction. "When do you expect him back?"

Inge's expression pretended no warmth. "Tonight by bedtime, I'm sure. After all, it's his first night away since I became his woman." Then, with eyes intent on Cat, she added slowly: "I *am* his woman. You do understand that a man like Daniel needs a woman."

"So he's told me, more than once," Cat said as coolly as possible, "although he didn't mention he already had one."

Hatred grew like a snake inside Inge. Cold, horrid little baggage! Butter wouldn't melt in her mouth! And this was the woman Daniel thought about while he made love to *her!*

"Oh, doesn't he talk about me?" Inge said, lifting her brows. "Well, I suppose a man like Daniel wouldn't do that. He'd hardly talk to *you* about the things he does with *me*, would he now? He's not the type to brag about his sexual prowess. But," she lied, "he does talk to me about *you*."

"Oh, really?" Cat managed to look disinterested. "I should have thought, from what you said, that you and Daniel don't have time to talk. Now if you'll excuse me . . ."

"We do talk . . . after," Inge interrupted, realizing Cat would not give her the satisfaction of asking questions. She knew, also, that whatever she said next must be close to the truth; this Kinross girl was apparently not a fool. Inge knew little about Cat, but with the intuition of a woman in love, she could make her guesses.

"Daniel told me he wanted you for his woman, but you weren't . . . willing. Why aren't you willing, Miss Kinross? Why don't you want him to touch you?"

Cat could not believe she had heard her ears properly. Would Daniel really talk about such intimate matters with another woman? Would he discuss her reluctance so freely?

"For a man like Daniel women have only one use, the use he puts me to. Oh, I know my place, and it's in bed! Your unavailability is just a challenge to him, that's why he wants you. At the moment you're a distraction to him, and a dangerous one at that. Men in Daniel's occupation can't afford dangerous distractions."

Then, sensing that she had pricked some part of Cat's cool surface, she added with a smile: "Let him take you to bed, Miss Kinross. I won't even be jealous, for I know that once he's had you, he'll come back to me. Warmth and passion and no demands, no commitments, that's what Daniel needs in a woman, and it's what I give him. God knows, if there's one thing he doesn't need, it's a woman like you! Make up your mind, Miss Kinross. Get into bed with him, or leave camp! Either way he'll forget you soon enough. As it is he forgets you anyway . . . when he's with me."

Cat turned and walked away, praying she would not stumble on the stones she could not see in her path.

Going up was out of the question; going down was the only way. And he would have to save the rope for as long as possible—certainly until he found some safe place to anchor it in. Daniel had had some small experience in mountaineering, and he had read a good deal on the subject: Whymper had conquered the Matterhorn back about the time Daniel had been in Stockholm.

He coiled the rope over his shoulder, and worked his way down to a somewhat more hospitable niche. He peered down, examining as best he could the sheer drop and the way the cracks ran over its face. The fault in which he was now lodged continued for about ninety feet. At the top, this chimney in the rock was wide and shallow. A man must inch his way down, braced into place by the sideways pressure of knees and spine and arms and feet. The technique was called "jamming," and Daniel had used a mild version of it on easier climbs.

Braced in this inhospitable place, he spent some time

examining the contents of his pockets, and the various effects he carried upon his person.

One knife sheath. No knife. It was a loss he did not regret.

One water flask, empty. It only served to remind him of his raging thirst. He dropped it, and counted the seconds until it landed; then spent a few moments of mental arithmetic with Newton's laws. About seven hundred feet straight down to the jagged rocks below.

A stray railroad spike he usually kept in his pocket. He sometimes used it as a marker, for scratching rocks.

Some wooden matches.

Other than that, nothing useful. He grimaced when he saw the spool of thread Cat had given him the day before yesterday; he'd forgotten to pass it on to Williams. Willing away the thunder in his head and the lightning in his stomach, he began to descend.

Free climbing down the crack system was slow, difficult work; once or twice, his knees began to shimmy violently with the effort of maintaining pressure against the sides of the chimney, and only the strength of his arms and the sheer gut will to live kept him suspended in the fissure.

When the crack narrowed and deepened, his technique changed somewhat. Now, he moved by jamming his hands and feet into the crevice, a method scarcely less dangerous, and one that afforded little relief to his pained muscles. It also offered the new torture of scraping his knuckles raw. By mid-afternoon he had covered eighty feet; lost too many needed body fluids in sweat both hot and cold; and the river in the rock was about to give out.

He started to climb sideways. It was the only irregular surface he could see, and he managed to cover it slowly by using what fingerholds and toeholds he could find. On one particularly difficult traverse he used some of his rope—burning off an appropriate length and tying it to a jagged outcropping of rock. That piece of rope had to be left behind.

He had spotted a shadow on the rock face, to the right and about a hundred feet down. It could be a ledge, and, if so, he might be able to reach it before nightfall. By the time the sun threatened to sink, he had worked himself to a precarious point above the shadow. The ledge, if there was a ledge, was now about eighty feet directly below him, he judged. From here down, the cliff face appeared sheer and smooth.

It was time to use the rope—what remained of it. He took

his single railway spike and jammed it sideways into a small rock-cleft, like the rung of a ladder. The first crack did not hold; he tried a second and a third before finding a suitable anchor. He tested it as well as he could while clinging to the toeholds on the mountainside. He gave it his full weight. It ground down into place, and held. Then, with infinite caution, he began to lower himself.

Soon he could see the ledge clearly, a dozen feet below where he was suspended. It was about two feet wide, not generous, but adequate to harbor a man until rescue came.

If rescue came.

And if a man could reach the ledge.

The sun was about to sink; there was not a fingerhold or a toehold in sight; Daniel's arms and legs were cold and numb; his hands scraped raw; his mouth bone dry and his head like a blast furnace.

He had twelve feet to go to his goal, and the rope had just run out.

14

Before nine o'clock in the morning, Cat was at the unloading area, watching anxiously as the smoke feathered up the loops of the rising track. She was wrapped in a shawl; today the uncertain sun was doing little to add to the warmth of the air.

It was not only the cold that had turned her features pinched and drawn. It had been another sleepless night, a night of self-recrimination and remorse; and added to that she was worried about Jake. She felt in need of Jake; he was the only real friend she had made during her sojourn in the mountains, the only person to whom she had confided the reason she had sought refuge in the Sierra Nevada. Jake knew about Julian Gow, or he knew part of the story. Whether she would speak to him about Daniel and Inge she did not yet know, but she did know she could speak to no one else.

And so she stood by the track, watching, and determined to leave for town when the train departed, if Jake did not materialize. But seconds later she sighted him, leaning out from the observation platform. When the train stopped he swung off at once. Cat's relief was swiftly followed by alarm: Jake's eyes were haggard, his shoulders defeated. At the signs of suffering in her friend's face, Cat pushed her own troubles temporarily aside.

"What's the matter, Jake?" she asked quietly, taking his arm.

"Let's get away from here," he said in a choked voice, and it was only when they reached the privacy of Cat's cabin that he told more.

"It's my father . . . he's dead." Jake dropped onto the edge of the bed and buried his golden head in his hands. There was agony in every line of his youthful frame. "Smallpox. He'd been sick for a whole week, since about the time I was there last. . . . Oh, God, if I'd known."

Cat's arms went around Jake's shoulders, offering what little comfort they could. "You couldn't have done anything, Jake."

"I don't know that, do I? There was no one looking after him when I arrived. He was delirious . . . fevered. He died Wednesday night. I buried him yesterday."

"Oh, Jake." And because there was little more to say, Cat spent some minutes cradling him in her arms, much as a mother might cradle a child.

"There's more to it than that, Cat," Jake choked out when his wrenching sobs had come to a halt. "The things he said before he died. . . . Oh, God, I need to tell somebody, and there's nobody I can tell."

"You can tell me," Cat comforted.

"No, I can't even tell you . . . it's too hard . . . oh, Cat, I want to die, too. I want to kill myself."

Cat insisted that Jake stay in her cabin for the day. She went in search of Yancy to inform him that Jake would not be working; she was told that Yancy had left camp at first light this morning, with a party of men. She was not told where they had gone, or why; and so she remained unaware of the fact that Daniel Savage had not returned to camp yesterday, as expected.

The balance of the day was spent watching over Jake. He wept until he exhausted his weeping, and then he slept; he woke again not long before dusk.

Cat had prepared a light supper for him, knowing he would not want to eat with the track gang tonight. Jake sat up on the bed for the meal, and Cat perched herself beside him. He swallowed no more than a mouthful of food, although he took some liquids. He looked dreadful, his face flushed and his eyes somehow sunken and swollen at the same time.

"I should go," he said, struggling to his feet as Cat lit lamps against the encroaching gloom.

"No, stay for a while," she told him, gentling him back onto the bed. "It's not as though it's hard to find your way back to your own tent from here. What are friends for if you can't share troubles?"

"I can't share mine. My father . . . the things he said . . ."

"He was delirious, Jake." Cat sat down on the edge of the bed, and touched his hand comfortingly. "If he said something to upset you or hurt you, I'm sure he didn't mean it."

"It's not that," he choked out. "It's what somebody said to him, about me. About the kind of person I am. And it's not true, not really true, at least I don't think it's true. But I couldn't tell him that, he was too far gone."

"Tell me, Jake. Talk about it."

"I can't. You'd be horrified."

"There's nothing you could say that would shock me," Cat said ruefully, and her mind made an unwilling detour into the life she had led with Julian Gow. "There are some things that can't be helped, Jake. Maybe your father knew that. Maybe he understood more than you think. And anyway, if what that person said wasn't true . . ."

"But in one way, it was." In Jake's tortured face there was an agony more real than any tears. And at last, as gloom deepened beyond the cabin windows, he began to talk.

About noon, some time after Jake had succumbed to sleep in Cat's cabin, one of Yancy's rescue crew shinnied down a long knotted rope suspended from the rocky shelf where they had found Mosley's body, head dangling over the edge and knife still embedded in the throat, a gory testament to part of what had happened.

"Ohmigod," he whispered, and then shouted up to the concerned faces that peered down over the edge: "About thirty feet to the right, on a ledge."

"Dead or alive?" Yancy bellowed. To all the shouts of the rescuers, there had been no answering call from Daniel.

"Don't know," yelled the first man. "Can't see no more'n an arm dangling out, but he must be damn near naked. Climbed the last few feet on his own clothes, from the look of it. Lower a rope ladder!"

It was a needless injunction, for the men above him were already working with feverish haste to anchor the rescue apparatus into place.

Yancy himself went down on the rope ladder. With heartfelt gratitude, he breathed a single word, and then shouted it to the mountaintops.

"Alive!"

Daniel's inert body came up in a sling fifteen minutes later; but another half hour passed before the chafing of limbs and bundling in blankets and rubbing of whiskey on his lips restored consciousness.

"Water," he tried to say, and the word would not pass his cracked lips. Yancy was pillowing his head and offering a flask. With difficulty, Daniel swallowed a few drops, and grimaced to find it was whiskey.

Yancy seemed to understand, and a water bottle followed.

"Helluva stunt," Yancy said after another few minutes, when some kind of groggy reason had been restored to Daniel. "What the Christ happened? Or can you tell me yet?"

"Later," slurred Daniel, and went to sleep.

The men strapped him onto a makeshift stretcher, well bundled against shock, and started the long trek back to camp. It would be slow going with this new burden, but they should make it by sundown. Daniel woke occasionally and called for water, and by late in the day he had recovered strength enough to take food. Yancy trudged beside him, and gradually the story came out.

"Sonuvabitch yellowbelly! Reckon he was skeered to face you right out, even though you was drunker'n a skunk. And you . . . Christ! Not a piton to your name! An' lyin' on that ledge, naked as the day you was born!"

"No rope."

"So we figgered," said Yancy. "Musta been some trick, doin' a striptease in the air."

"Tied m'self," explained Daniel.

It had not been easy work to climb back up the rope in a state of near-shock and with every limb shaking, but Daniel had done it. He had secured himself by the waist while the shirt and trousers had come off, and these, tied to the end of the rope, had given him just enough length to reach the ledge. The last light of dusk had warned him he had no time to waste, and so he had used the whole cloth, without tearing and braiding as he might otherwise have done.

"Good thing you got long sleeves," Yancy observed morosely, "or you'da never made it."

Daniel managed a wry laugh. "Legs, too."

"Can't figger one thing, though. When we found you, yer hand was clenched into a fist, tighter'n a man in rigor mortis. Had to pry the dang fingers open. Figgered there was somethin' inside. But there was nuthin'. At least, nuthin' you coulda used on the climb, even if you was twice as crazy as you are. Yet, sweet Jesus, you hung on like it was a lifeline brought you all the way down."

As they started up the slopes that led to the forward camp, with the sun sinking fast in the west, Yancy squinted his puzzlement at his friend's bruised and bloodied face.

136

"What the *hell*," he asked, "were you doin' with a god-damn spool o' thread?"

"My father was one of those rough and ready men," Jake told Cat. "Scornful of me because I was puny, a weakling. He'd earned his living hauling cartage at the age of thirteen, and he thought I should be able to do that too. I wasn't strong enough. He made my life miserable . . . called me a sissy. I ran away from home when I was fifteen."

Jake's voice was low, barely audible at times, but Cat knew him well enough to follow the indistinct narrative.

"A lot of men were starting to hop the freights then. It was back in '73, at the start of the depression. I took to the rails too, riding the tops of baggage cars, hiding in boxcars, hanging on to the brake rods. Oh, it was dangerous, but I thought if I could live the rough life, the life the hoboes led, I could become a man . . . prove myself to my father. How I wanted to prove myself! For the first few months it was all right. I was hungry, but it was all right."

Cat waited in silence, knowing Jake would go on with no urging now. Her hand clasped his, offering silent encouragement.

"I didn't know about hoboes then. They're not quite like the other men who ride the freights nowadays . . . the migrant workers, the men who are desperate because they can't find work anywhere. Hoboes are different. They ride the rails all the time, live in shack camps near the freight yards . . . they call them jungles. And like jungles they have their own law. The hoboes are tough and rough and, and . . . oh, God, I can't tell it. . . ."

"Try," Cat said quietly.

"There are no women hoboes," Jake said in a low tortured voice. "They learn to . . . to get along without. I didn't think about that when a gang of them, big tough men, invited me to join their campfire for some mulligan stew. I was flattered, thought I was being accepted at last. I thought I was becoming the man my father wanted me to be."

After a silence that lasted too long, Cat said gently: "Is it so hard to tell, Jake? I know what you're going to say."

"They held me facedown and . . . oh, God, I wanted to die."

"Jake, you were raped. You couldn't help that."

"You don't understand. No one can understand."

137

Cat pulled his head against her breast, and everything inside her ached in silent empathy.

"It hurt so much," Jake sobbed.

Cat stroked the gold head, and felt his tears dampen the fabric of her dress. "I know," she whispered.

"One of the men kept me after that. He was my jocker, I was his road kid. He taught me to panhandle, and scrounge for food, and steal chickens, and . . . mostly he was good to me. I grew to love him, and I felt real bad when he fell one day when we were trucking . . . hanging on to the metal between the wheels, on a car's underside. He was mangled to death. It was horrible. I went back home then, and found my mother dead. She had died the year before, and I hadn't known it. My father was living alone. He was a sick man by that time, unable to work."

Again Jake was silent for a time, and he was calmer now. When he spoke again, his voice was level. "I thought if I took this job on the track gang I might find out about myself. I didn't know if I was a man, or if I even wanted to be a man. But I wanted to try. I went to the bordello once, and . . . and I made a fool of myself. Even though Inge was young and fresh and not like the others, those women with faces like nails, she, well . . . I didn't have any feeling for her. I was scared, too, for I'd never been alone with a woman, and I was afraid to tell her that."

"Does it matter so much?" asked Cat.

"Yes."

"And is that what someone told your father?"

"No . . ." Jake lowered his head, ashamed to recount the rest of his story. "There was a man named Mosley. He's gone now, he was fired. But for a short while, he was in charge up at the forward camp, before you came here. I'd see him when I ran errands up that way. And then one day he forced me to go with him, to do things. . . . Oh, how I hated him. The first time he did it with a knife held to my throat, and after that he, he . . . threatened to tell my father, so I kept doing as he asked."

"But he told your father anyway."

"Yes, because I wouldn't go with him when he was fired. He went down in the valley and he said things, dreadful things. My father kept them to himself all this time but he was . . . Well, I couldn't understand why he was so cold, so nasty to me. Now I know. And by then I had begun to think

138

those things weren't true. I didn't think I was like Mosley, I didn't want to be like Mosley."

"Jake . . . whatever you are, you're not like that."

"I wanted more than anything to prove myself. And my father died, thinking . . ."

"Jake, your father was wrong to care so much."

"But he did care, don't you see. Oh, Cat . . . I've spent so many years not knowing about myself, not understanding. I can't bear it anymore. Help me, Cat, help me."

They clung together like orphans seeking comfort in a night storm. "You don't know what it's like not to know about yourself," agonized Jake. "Oh, Cat, I need so much to know for sure, and I don't know anyone to help me but you."

Cat's heart bled, as much for herself as for him. "How can I help you, Jake, when I don't even understand about myself? Sometimes I think I love . . . someone, yet I can't bear for him to touch me."

"Daniel," guessed Jake bitterly. "How can you feel that way about Daniel? He has his own woman. Everyone in the camp knows it but you! I've thought of telling you a thousand times. It's Inge right now, and before that it was someone else, and after that it will be another woman. No wonder you don't want him to touch you! Touching a woman means nothing to him, *nothing* . . . not like it means to me. You don't know how much it means to me, how much it would mean, now, tonight. . . ."

"Jake, I can't."

"Would it be so hard? You spent months with Gow. You must have allowed *him.*"

"I don't want to, Jake."

"Please, Cat, please," he whispered. His voice was muffled against her breast, and already his hand fumbled at her petticoats as he pulled her to a prone position on the small cot. "No other woman can help me, and if I don't find out, now, tonight, I'll never have courage to try again."

And I'll never be a whole woman again unless I find some courage, too. And I want to be a whole woman for Daniel. And I can't bear for Daniel to touch me. But Jake's touch is soft and slow, and I'm not afraid of him. Is it so terrible to do as he asks? And might it make me a whole woman again?

"Please, Cat, help me. Help me."

It was a cry from a purgatory no less desperate than her own, and when Jake began to fumble with the fastenings of

139

his clothes, Cat did nothing to stop him. Neither undressed more than was necessary; and what followed had more to do with comfort than with love. Watching her own actions from a detached and distant promontory, Cat felt no warmth, no cold, no panic, no repugnance. She felt only compassion.

And after it was done, there was only a vague feeling of relief. With no more words they lay for a time, cradling each other on the cot, sad and spent, clothing still awry. Cat's back was to the door. The sound across the room was quiet, and because it took her a moment to remember that she had not slipped the bolt—she had, after all, not expected the night's events—she did not look around at once. But Jake's widening eyes and the ominous silence warned her.

She turned, and saw the tall apparition that was Daniel. Daniel, looking like death.

"Get out, Jake," he said at last, his voice gray and flat as if with some emotion too terrible to voice, "get out before I kill you."

15

At Yancy's insistence and to Daniel's impatience, the first hour back in camp had been spent in his tent. He had been given a hot meal, and then Yancy and Inge, ignoring the stream of imprecations he flung at them, had spent some time examining the bruises and contusions, and applying alcohol to the worst of the damage.

"Christ. You make it hard for a man to feed himself," complained Daniel in disgust, surveying the new white gauze beneath which his fingers and palms had nearly disappeared.

"I'll feed you, then," soothed Inge, secretly pleased at the prospect of Daniel's coming dependence. "And dress you too, if needs be. Now lie still, and I'll shave you."

"The hell you will!" snorted Daniel, swiftly rolling his naked length out from the bed where it had been blanketed during this past hour. His resilient body, rested during the return trip, was now capable of functioning; the throbbing in his swollen hands was painful, but bearable since dressings had been applied. He pushed aside Yancy's attempts to restrain him.

"Ain't no reason to git dressed now," Yancy frowned, as Daniel started to rummage through an iron-bound chest for shirt and trousers to replace those lost on the mountain.

"I'm going across to the other camp," Daniel had said, and nothing—not Inge's pleas nor Yancy's deep disapproval—had swayed him. Obdurate, and with no one's help, he had dressed himself, finding his fingers capable of some movement despite their bindings.

He was hardly aware of the fact that Yancy accompanied him across the bridge with a lantern. He was hardly aware of the murmured congratulations and condolences of the men they passed in the night: The story had traveled around camp like wildfire. He was hardly aware of the moment when Yancy passed the lantern to him and parted company, at the door of the Brody's mobile home.

He was aware only of the light that still burned behind the

141

fresh new curtains, in the cabin that was his goal. He needed to see Cat; God, how he needed to see Cat. . . .

And then, he opened the door, and saw.

"Daniel," she whispered, her eyes huge.

"Get out, Jake," he said again, swaying in the doorway with some of the same sensations he had felt on the mountainside. His mouth was tight and sick with the effort of self-control, the clefts in his cheeks drawn into deep implacable lines. A jagged cut across one cheekbone and the two-day growth on his jaw added to the ghoulishness of his appearance.

"Jake's done nothing wrong," Cat said, finding some dignity as she pushed her skirts back into order, and struggled to a sitting position. "Daniel, you don't understand. It's not—"

"Get out." The voice was cold and quiet and lethal as a stiletto, and the words were flung not at Cat but at Jake.

Jake at last recovered enough to fumble his clothes back to decency. His face was pale, with a fevered flush high on his cheekbones. He said nothing as he scrambled off the bed.

"Get out of this cabin and get out of this camp," Daniel said as Jake went to the door. "Go on tomorrow's train. If I ever see you again I won't answer for my actions."

"Daniel, you can't be so harsh!" Cat flew across the cabin and seized Daniel's arm, an action which made her dimly aware of the bandages that wrapped his hands. "Jake's not at fault. If you'd only listen, I'll explain—"

"OUT!"

Daniel bolted the door behind Jake's retreating form, and leaned against it. His eyes swept Cat with a heat and a hatred so intense that she backed away across the room. She had said she would explain, but what was there to explain? Daniel's eyes had not lied. And to tell Daniel of Jake's self-doubts seemed a sordid thing to do. How could she tell him that she had allowed Jake's caresses because of the experiences they had shared? Because of the bond of common suffering? Because of the woman she had seen in Daniel's tent? Because of her own consuming need to become whole again?

Her face composed itself, and her chin tilted into the lines of pride that had become second nature during the months with Julian Gow. Her eyes that had been huge and sooty with alarm grew calm, a gray emotionless glass.

"Jake's done no more than you yourself wanted to do. You can't fire him for that."

Daniel did not bother to answer. He started to advance slowly toward her, unbuttoning his shirt as he came, his eyes darkened with some emotion so stark and primitive it chilled her to the bone.

"How can you condemn Jake, or me? I know about Inge, Daniel."

A bandaged hand slashed her down onto the bed, and Cat gasped with the force of the blow. She stared at him in shocked disbelief. His face was a cruel mask. This was a Daniel she did not recognize, a remorseless stranger with a visage terrible to see, doom-dark as an angel of destruction.

Without another word he removed his clothes, his eyes not leaving her for an instant. She saw the bandaged hands clearly now, and other scrapes where alcohol had been applied, but these things seemed unimportant in the light of what was happening. She tried to twist off the bed, only to find herself thrust savagely back against the covers. She gasped again with pain and shock.

"Stop, Daniel, you don't know what you're doing. Stop! You—"

He crushed down on top of her, driving the breath from her lungs, and pinioning her into place. Like Jake, he did not try to remove her clothes. He thrust her skirts roughly to her waist, and crudely yanked her legs apart. His knees intruded in the space between; his bandaged hands immobilized her arms against the pillow, in readiness for his assault upon her flesh. There was no need to wait for arousal. The blood already pounded in his veins and crazed his brain and swelled his manhood and turned his body to a weapon of vengeance for the terrible thing she had done.

"Daniel, don't . . . You're hurting me, *hurting*. . . . Don't do this. . . . I'll hate you forever. . . ."

Her plea held a desperation that reached him in some way. The red haze of rage still blinded his eyes; the hatred and the pain and the awful drive to punish still pulsed in his sex. But on the threshold he halted, torn by the horrible conflicts of his own particular hell.

Cat did not try to fight him. Rigid, paralyzed beneath the press of that vengeful, virile body that was poised for rape, she stared in horror at the agonized face so few inches from her own. Daniel had closed his eyes. His lips were drawn back tightly to bare the vicious, shuddering clench of his teeth. His face was gray, his nostrils white with the flare of effort. A cold sweat had broken out on his shoulders and on his brow; droplets of perspiration slid unchecked into the sandpaper texture of his jaw. It was as if a titanic tug-of-war was being waged for possession of his heart and body and mind and soul. Cat turned her eyes away, unable to bear the naked tortures written on that face.

"Do it if you must," she whispered as he started to draw away. "I won't stop you."

The harsh explosion of his breath broke against her cheek. He did not release her pinioned wrists. His lips sought hers and seized them, forcing her face to turn once more to his. His mouth parted her unresisting lips, claiming them with a vehemence and thoroughness that turned Cat's blood to ice.

And as the hard length of him at last drove home, that part of her that had long since learned to turn cold and fastidious at any assault upon herself became separate, apart, inviolate, despite the violation that Daniel was perpetrating on her flesh.

He came into her with a force and a ferocity that made the ordeal on the mountain pale into insignificance in his mind. Damn her, damn Jake, damn himself for caring . . . oh, *God*. Why did he still want to hurt her, to destroy her for what she had done to him? Why did he feel no relief?

But Cat, feeling his seed pour into her, did feel relief—a detached relief, a thankfulness that it had been swiftly over. She longed for him to withdraw, ached for him to withdraw.

But he did not. He lay sprawled over her, pinning her to the bed, throbbing and diminishing within her. His stubbled face rasped against her throat, and his bandaged hands still shackled her wrists against the pillow.

"Please leave," Cat said frigidly after several minutes had passed, her voice echoing the cold distaste she felt at the stickiness between her thighs. For answer his grip on her wrists only tightened; the head buried in her throat did not even stir. With a sense of growing uneasiness, Cat realized that he was asleep, that the tightening of his hands had been involuntary. His weight was heavy on her frame. Several times she tried to ease herself out from under, but even the slightest movement brought a further steeling of the shackles on her wrists, and the shifting of her hips did not dislodge his sex. Even in sleep, he would not let her go.

Her throat stung with bitterness as she contemplated what had happened between them. Rape? No, it could not be called that; not with consent. And yet it had been a violation all the same. Cat knew she had told Daniel to proceed, and yet, she found it hard to forgive him for doing so. She had survived rape in the past, and although she could not remember it in full, she knew it had been far worse than anything she had been subjected to this day. But she had thought she cared for Daniel; and in that lay the real horror of tonight.

Why had she thought she loved him? Why had she not realized he was capable of such brutality? Why, why, why? But at last exhaustion overcame the hatreds and the hurts, and despite her discomfort beneath the heavy burden of his naked weight, she slept, still clothed.

She woke to the feel of him swelling, filling her deeply once again. The light that still burned and the suddenness of awakening put panic in her eyes; they opened to find his face hovering above hers, his eyes topaz chips that smoldered with dark destructive passions. Her gaze fled. The panic caused her to struggle briefly as she had not struggled last night, and he jerked both her hands above her head, pinning them together beneath one bandaged palm. He used his freed hand to bracket her jaw, dragging her eyes back to his.

"Don't fight me," he said thickly. "For the love of heaven, don't fight me now. Don't make me stop."

She moaned. "I won't fight you. I'll let you, Daniel, but—"

He freed her wrists and sank his white-swathed fingers into her hair. "Then kiss me," he commanded, his voice a rough rasp, his grooved cheeks deeply slashed with the pain of his inner damnation. "Be willing with me, as you were with Jake."

"No, Daniel, please—" Cat shuddered and tried to shrink away. The ice that had so often protected her was elusive now. Unwanted sensations began to course through her thighs, a partner to the panic she seemed unable for the moment to control. "Take me if you must, but don't ask me to . . . respond."

"Make love to me," he gritted through his teeth. "Put your arms around me and kiss me of your own accord. Now!"

And when she did not at once obey, he groaned from the depths of his soul in purgatory. "You made love to Gow," he grated into the edge of her lips. "You made love to Jake. Now make love to me!"

"Just take me, Daniel," she begged. "Take me and be done."

"Pretend, damn you!" Cat felt herself riven by a penetration that brought a pained gasp to her lips.

"I can't," she started to say, but his mouth clamped down over the words. His angry tongue filled her, gagged her, trying to extract by force the response she was unable to give. His hands bruised down to her hips, thrusting aside the petticoats that still confined her. He clasped her hips roughly in his bandaged palms, and crushed them to his own.

And at last, as he drove toward his unshared climax, she retreated gratefully into the frozen empty wastes of emotion from which she had wanted, so recently, to escape.

It was dawn before he rolled away, freeing her imprisoned body. He came to his feet and stood naked beside the bed, looking down at her, hating her, hating the way she turned him inside out, hating the fact that his possession of her had been no possession at all, hating the silvery impenetrable eyes.

"From now on," he said slowly, "you're my woman. You'll lie with me when I choose."

"And what about Inge?" Cat asked icily, rearranging her skirts. The inelegant thrusting of petticoats to her waist had been demeaning, a part of the indignity against which her entire being still revolted. There had been no love in Daniel's kisses, no tenderness in his hurtful hands. The possession had been brutal and animalistic—as though he were driven by devils instead of human desires.

"She served her purpose," Daniel replied with a cruelty that was deliberate. Why should he explain now that Inge had been no more than a precaution, an insurance that he would not impose his needs on Cat?

"I won't take Inge's place. If you make me do that, I'll hate you, Daniel."

"Hate me all to hell, you're still my woman." Daniel retrieved his trousers now, and stepped into them, at last covering the hard flanks and removing from Cat's view the disturbing presence of his masculinity. He pushed his feet into the soft moccasins he had chosen to wear last night in order to avoid the complications of laces.

"What happened to your hands?" she asked coldly, as if she did not care.

He stopped midway through putting on his shirt, and looked at her for a few smoky moments, his eyes hooded and enigmatic. At last he frowned downward, buttoning his shirt as best he could to cover the rough tangle of his chest. "I held onto something when I should have let go," he said tonelessly.

"Explosives?"

He paused and looked at her again, face deliberately voided of expression. "Do you really give a damn?"

"No."

"I didn't think so," he said, and slammed out the door.

16

This morning Yancy's men were back to laying track. Despite the chill, sweat glistened on men's foreheads and darkened their shirts as they seized the weighty sections of rail that had been brought to the bridge by horsecar. Working in teams, they trotted forward at a run, and at a shout of command, the heavy burden clanged into place over the previously laid ties. The bolters followed close behind, and the spikers—men with the shoulder meat to drive the great metal spikes into place with three mighty blows of a sledgehammer. Ten spikes to a rail, four hundred rails to a mile, a hundred miles still to go.

"Can you please tell Mr. Brody I need to speak to him?" Cat had to call loudly to be heard over the metallic din, and the resonant shouts that echoed through the mountains. "It's very important. I must see him at once."

Five minutes passed before Yancy appeared, called back from a short distance away, where he had been supervising the gauging of the track.

"Sumpin' the matter?" he asked, peering at Cat's pale face. "Look like you seen a ghost."

"It's Jake," Cat said at once. "I thought you should know. I went to his tent this morning, and found him ill and fevered. There's no rash, yet, but . . . I think there may be smallpox in the camp."

"Sonuvabitch," said Yancy, his normally lugubrious face fretting with a frown deeper than usual. "You sure he ain't jest pinin' over his pa? Heared about that this mornin'."

"Reasonably sure. Jake would have been exposed some days ago, when he saw his father on the regular weekly trip. Yesterday I thought he was just upset, but today . . . Well, I think it's just a matter of time until the rash appears. I thought you should know at once."

"Sonuvabitch," Yancy repeated.

"I'll look after him," Cat offered. "He can be isolated in his own tent. He hasn't seen anyone much but me since he got back, and I've been vaccinated."

"You know what to do?" frowned Yancy, trying to remember which of his own children had received the cowpox vaccine.

"No, but I'll find out. On the way here I spoke to one of the Chinamen, the one with the badly pitted face."

"Sam Yee," Yancy reminded her.

"Yes. He's had smallpox, and he'll help me. He tells me the Chinese knew there was smallpox in the valley, and used their own method of protection the other day."

Yancy's pouched eyes asked the question, and Cat told him about the sight she and Laura had witnessed. "Yee ground up the crust of some dried blisters from a mild case," she explained. "Evidently it's an old method, but he says it works. They'll all have smallpox soon, but not the dangerous kind. He says they won't be very sick, and most of them won't even miss a day's work."

"Crazy sonuvabitch Chinks," Yancy said, but there was some admiration in his voice.

"There's one other thing." Cat's face was set. "Can you please tell Daniel I'm moving into Jake's tent to look after him? Daniel fired him yesterday, but, of course, he can't leave now."

"Don't say!" A real surprise widened Yancy's eyes. "Now why'd he do a thing like that? Mountain musta addled his wits. Reckon he told you about that last night?"

Before Cat returned to Jake's tent, Yancy gave her a brief account of the ordeal on the mountain. It explained some of Daniel's behavior, but not all; she had not heard about the spool of thread.

But if she could not yet forgive she could in part understand, and when Daniel appeared at the entrance to Jake's tent late that afternoon, she tried to temper her judgment of him with a remembrance of the things Yancy had told her.

"Jake can't leave now, Daniel," she said quietly, looking up from the bedside where she had been applying cooling cloths to lower the fever. Jake was sleeping restlessly, tossing and moaning, his eyes sunken and his face flushed.

"So I see." There was a grim white line about Daniel's mouth; he moved no farther into the tent.

"Yancy told me what happened to you, Daniel," Cat said after a short uncomfortable silence haunted with the ghosts of what had passed between them. "I'm sorry I didn't know about it last night."

"It's unimportant." His voice was flat, colorless. "It had nothing to do with my behavior. Under the circumstances I'd have . . . behaved just as badly, any other time."

She lowered her eyes, and went back to sponging Jake. "Is that intended as an apology?"

"Of sorts."

"Then I'll apologize, too," she said in a low voice, still avoiding his eyes. "Jake and I . . . there's nothing there, Daniel. It didn't mean anything, and it had never happened before. I had reasons for allowing it last night, reasons that seemed right at the time."

"I don't want to hear the reasons." The black hatreds in Daniel's heart turned his voice to gall. He controlled himself with difficulty. "Now come back to where you belong. Back to the cabin."

Cat looked up then, her face pale but determined. "No," she said.

"Sam Yee can look after Jake," he told her tersely.

"I'm staying here. I've borrowed a bedroll, and I'm moving in until Jake's better."

"There won't be a repeat of last night."

"Don't you understand, Daniel? Jake needs me."

"I need you, too."

"Do you?" Her eyes searched for the truth of what he said. His hands were out of view, braced on the outer canvas of the tent; only the tall powerful frame and the strong planes of his tanned face were visible from here. The fresh jagged scar on his cheekbone seemed not a sign of weakness, but of endurance. Fresh in her mind was the story of the mountain. What she remembered was the resourcefulness and self-sufficiency; what she saw was the virile length and strength and the face of a man who needed nothing she could give.

"Do you?" she repeated more bitterly. "I don't think so, Daniel. All you want from me is what you took last night, and that's a need I'm not prepared to fill, a need I'm incapable of filling. If you need a woman, go to Inge."

"I take it you choose to stay with Jake," he stated flatly.

"Yes."

Without another word he dropped the tent flap and left, and that was the last she saw of him for two weeks.

They were long, difficult weeks. The rail-laying did not move on, as planned; too many of the track gang were invalided. Smallpox swept the camp. Unlike city folk, many of the men had not been vaccinated, and Jake had not been the only person to suffer exposure. Within twenty-four hours a half dozen others were prostrated with the high temperatures and bodily aches and pains that presaged the appearance of a rash on wrists and face; others soon succumbed.

Jake's skin erupted on the fourth day, and the raised red spots soon turned to pustules. His temperature rose dangerously, and scratching became a problem. Cat tied his hands to prevent it, and bathed the blisters with unguents provided by the Chinese man of medicine. By the twelfth day, when crusts had started to form, he seemed for a time to be taking a turn for the better.

"Cat," Jake murmured, coming awake. He tried to move his hand that was pinned to the blanket, and Cat covered it with her own.

"It's starting to go, Jake," she told him reassuringly. "You shouldn't have too many pockmarks."

"No?" His eyes closed tiredly, as if he did not care. Cat thought he had dozed again, but when she started to withdraw her hand a few minutes later, he said faintly, without opening his eyes: "I . . . never said . . . thank you."

"Oh, Jake, it's not necessary. Sam Yee has done as much to help you as I have."

"No, I mean, for . . . before."

"You don't have to thank me for that," she said, with a twist of pain for the remembered brutalities of two weeks ago.

"It . . . wasn't any . . . good. Not . . . for you. Not . . . for me."

"Oh, Jake. It doesn't matter."

"It wasn't . . . good, but . . . I love you, Cat."

"I love you, too, Jake," she said truthfully. It was platonic, the love she felt for Jake; she believed herself to be capable of no other kind.

Jake opened his eyes and smiled weakly. "Why did you . . . let me?"

"Because—" It took Cat a moment to formulate her answer. She felt the need to be honest with Jake, as she could never be with Daniel. "It was because of what happened to you when you were fifteen. Something like that once happened to me. Oh, not exactly the same, but . . . There were guards that held me down and . . . I don't remember much of what was done that first time, but I know some things happened, because they happened again. I understood how it could warp a person's insides."

The pain, the humiliation, the wanting to die. The sickness inside because she had not had the courage to kill herself. And all the months of trying to find dignity in spite of the indignities that were being committed on her flesh.

"I've never been the same person since," she said. "I think I needed your help as much as you needed mine."

"Truth . . ." Jake's eyes flagged wearily, and something that could have been a smile ghosted across his lips. "I . . . liked it."

He lay for a time with his eyes closed, and then opened them again to find Cat's face. "Still . . . love me?" he said, with a worrisome little rattle to his voice.

"Yes, I do," she said with no hesitation, touching a fingertip to his lids. "Now close your eyes, Jake, and rest."

He slept after that. He was not rational again; pneumonia set in as a complication. Two days later, with a full heart but no tears, Cat closed his eyes for the last time.

"I did love you, Jake," she whispered.

The body was removed by mid-afternoon; Daniel arrived at dusk. He stood as he had stood once before, tall and unsmiling in the tent entrance, regarding Cat with unreadable eyes. Although he did not speak, she knew what he wanted. Her cloak was already donned, not for the chilled air, but because she had known he would come. She picked up her small bundle of possessions, gathered together some hours before, and followed him without a word.

In the cabin Daniel took Cat's cloak and lit lanterns and pulled curtains and bolted the door. He spent more silent moments stoking the fire which he must have laid before coming to Jake's tent; the cabin was already warm.

He turned to face her at last. He was standing, and she was standing. A half dozen feet and a great gulf lay between them, a gulf that might never be bridged.

"Undress," he told her. There was no softness in Daniel's eyes, nor in the deep clefts that bracketed his mouth. "Take off your clothes and let down your hair. I want no barriers this time."

But there were barriers, perhaps more than Daniel knew. Would she, could she do as he asked? Oddly, what had happened two weeks before made it easier tonight. She knew now it was possible to submit to his touch without succumbing to remembrance of all the things she did not want to remember. Yet, it was not easy to bare herself to Daniel's view.

Slowly, she unpinned her hair. The fringe over her brow was long and straight, the rest fell in a dark cloud to her waist. Slowly she loosed the fastenings of her gown, and allowed it to fall in a crumpled heap at her feet.

And slowly, with a sense of detachment learned long ago because of the low-cut gowns she had once been forced to wear, she lowered the straps of her chemise. With the same sense of detachment, she watched the changing expressions of Daniel's face, undressing no more because she was sure now it would not be necessary.

"Oh, God," he breathed at last, his eyes mesmerized by the sight of her breast. Her right breast.

"It happened the first night," she said in a voice so remote she might have been talking about events in the life of a stranger. "I don't recall how it happened. I suppose Julian had the guards do it. He called them into the compartment . . . several of them. There were half a dozen on the train, some in his own car, some in the next car forward. I don't remember them arriving. I only became conscious of them later, and of this."

Daniel's voice was thick, sick. "Did he brand you anywhere else?"

"No," she answered with perfect self-possession. "Shall I dress now? You can't want to see any more."

"No, I—" His eyes, tortured, rose to meet hers. "I won't make you undress. But how can I know you're telling the truth?"

"There are no more marks."

"All these months, and—" Daniel spoke with effort, as if in pain. "Why didn't you tell me?"

"I didn't think you'd want to know," Cat said coolly. How easy it was, tonight, to remain apart. Already she had donned her armor of ice. Now, she could not be touched, not even by the look in Daniel's eyes—disbelief and pity and all the things she had seen too many times, in too many eyes. The ornate W that marked the upper curve of her right breast was placed so as to be visible above a low-cut gown, and Julian had taken a perverse pleasure in forcing her to display it.

"Cathryn! Don't you think I *care?*"

"I suppose you do care." She sounded as if she herself did not. "It's not pretty."

Ye've a bad failing, Miss Cat, and that's vanity. How many lifetimes ago had Hannah said that? How many lifetimes since Cat had laughed and laved the water over her breasts and accepted the flawless flesh as her due? She had retched the first time she had seen her breast. It had been fresh then, angry, ugly; and there had been pain, searing pain, pain that drove daggers into her flesh. That much she had not forgotten. It had been all over by then. Julian had been standing over her, his mouth cruel and sensual, his eyes like dry ice. Several guards flanked him. "Whore! Now do you admit you came to me unclean?" Retching, she had been too sick to answer.

The mark had healed since then; now it evoked curiosity rather than horror from those who saw it. But to Cat, because the scar reached into her very soul, the breast was not pretty.

"Do you think I give a good goddamn whether it's *pretty?*" Daniel came across the space between them in two strides. His hands came up as if to seize her shoulders, but with some terrible effort of will the fingers tightened only over empty air, and fell to his sides again.

"Why did he do it, Cat? Why?"

"Can't you guess? W for whore, Daniel. Julian wanted me for himself alone, just as you do. He was willing to share me no more than you are. He wanted a virgin, and I had been with a man. With you."

Daniel's hands balled into fists, betraying some of the particular brand of hell he was suffering at this moment. Remorse and rage and nausea washed through his body and his brain.

"Now do you understand why I don't enjoy lying with a man? Julian destroyed a part of me that night."

"Oh, God," Daniel said in a curdled voice. And had he destroyed the rest? Remembrance of his own violence lay like acid in his entrails. Was he any better than Gow? He had wanted to kill her that night, to destroy her. If he had had a brand in his possession he might have used it.

"Forgive me, Cat," he said thickly. "I didn't know. The things that happened between us . . . I didn't want them to happen that way. I don't care if you lay with Jake."

"Don't you?" she said indifferently. She stooped to the

floor, recovered her fallen dress, and turned her back while she restored herself to decency. When she had done so, she turned to face him again, her neck proud.

"I felt no more with Jake than I've felt for many months. I felt nothing. Nothing! I'm not a whole woman anymore, Daniel. I lay with Jake because I had reason to think he might be able to help me. But now . . . ."

The shadow of Julian fleeted through her eyes, and in that moment some part of her forgave some part of what had transpired between herself and Daniel. It had not been so very hard after all, and he had been patient for many months, and perhaps he had suffered some of the same emotions she had felt upon finding a woman at his tent. That was a necessity she had understood; even so, it had been difficult to accept. And although she could not explain it to Daniel now, it was part of why she had allowed Jake's caresses.

"Now," she said slowly, "I don't think anyone can help me. I'll never be whole again."

In the days that followed there was no time to grieve for Jake, or for the little death she had died that night, when Daniel had turned and walked out of the cabin, sick-faced but without another word. How was it possible to have one's heart frozen in ice, but to feel with it all the same?

But hearts had to be forgotten when there were bodies to be cared for. By now, many dozens of men were ill, and the Chinese who had been doing most of the nursing were in need of help. There were feverish foreheads to be sponged, hands to be restrained, bedpans to be administered, soiled bed linens to be changed. One of the men's dormitories had been turned into an infirmary, and the triple tiers of bunks were filled with the groans and the rantings of men half mad with the torments of the flesh. Hell-on-Wheels. Now, the name seemed a fitting one indeed.

For a month Cat spent much of her time at the infirmary, not leaving until exhaustion claimed her long past dusk. She took her meals, now, with the track gang; cooking for herself was a luxury she could no longer afford.

There was smallpox at the forward camp, too; Yancy told her that.

"And Daniel?" Cat asked. "Is he all right?"

"Right as rain," Yancy said glumly, because it was not really true. Daniel was protected by vaccination, sure

155

enough, but there was something in his friend's manner recently that gave Yancy cause for concern.

"He hasn't been around for a long time," Cat observed, with a dull ache that told her she had now forgiven him entirely. But she had not seen him since the night of Jake's death, and so she had been unable to tell him so.

"Playin' nurse, same's you," said Yancy, without adding that Daniel's absence was caused largely by Inge's illness.

The epidemic ran its course; time did, too. Too many men, and a few women from the bordello, were maimed by the ugly facial disfigurations that time could never erase.

And there were too many deaths. Other markers joined Jake's grave in the nearby mountain meadow where there was earth enough to bury men—the same mountain meadow that already held too many bittersweet memories for Cat. And it was here that Daniel found her one afternoon in early November, when the epidemic was nearly at an end. With the smallpox diminishing in virulence, the campsite was at last about to move elsewhere.

"Hello, Cathryn."

She turned at the sound of his voice, and saw him standing a short distance away, tall and somber and somehow older now. He looked as if he too had suffered during these past weeks.

"Still grieving for Jake?"

"I suppose I am. I miss him. He was a good friend."

"Friend?" The word was faintly sardonic, and Daniel apologized at once. "I'm sorry I said that."

"It's true, he was more than a friend." I loved him, but not in the way you mean." She turned away and spent a final moment laying late-blooming flowers on Jake's grave. Then she turned her eyes from Jake's rough marker to others, and finally to the silent spires that steepled against a sky heavy with snow. "So many men, so young some of them. And the markers so insignificant next to the mountains and the sky."

Daniel remained silent. The Sierra Nevada was not the only range to be dotted with the graves of the men who had built the railroads. Men conquered mountains, and the mountains conquered men.

"Will the train ever stop here?" Cat asked.

"No," he said quietly, "not once we move on."

"That's sad."

"Not sad. Necessary. What's done is done and has to be

put behind. It can't be changed. Nothing can be changed. Life goes on."

They started to walk toward the trail, slowly, each conscious of the other and of the things that had held them apart, that still held them apart.

"The forward camp is moving to a new location," Daniel told her as they went. "I came to tell you I won't be around anymore."

"We'll be moving, too."

"Yes, but not as far or as fast. Yancy has another difficult bridge to build, and I'll be tunneling in easier rock. Soon I'll be twenty miles ahead. I came to say good-bye."

"Daniel—"

Cat came to a halt at the edge of the meadow, and put her hand on his sleeve in a tentative gesture—the first physical approach she had made in all these months.

"Daniel, if you still want me for your woman . . . well, I'm willing to try. I'll come with you to the forward camp. I can forgive and forget if you can too."

He was silent for a little too long. "It's too late, Cat. What's done is done, and can't be changed. It wouldn't be right for you, or for me."

She searched his face, knowing he spoke the truth yet not willing to admit it. "So much has happened in these past weeks. So many deaths, so much suffering. Can't we put a part of the suffering behind us?" She paused, then went on. "I know now why you behaved as you did that night. Laura Brody told me about the spool of thread. She didn't understand, but I did."

He turned away, shoulders tensed and spine rigid. "Then you misunderstood," he said bleakly. "I was half delirious by then. I suppose I thought the spool might serve some purpose. Hanging onto it was reflex, pure reflex."

"I don't believe that's true," Cat said slowly.

"Dammit, of course it's true," he snapped, suddenly angry. "Emotional involvements are a weakness I can't afford, I've told you that before. I can't deny I wanted to take you to bed, quite badly, for a time. I had memories of a very passionate young girl, and I wanted a repeat performance. I've lost interest now. Why else do you think I've been staying away from this camp?"

Cat was taken aback by his vehemence. "I didn't know, I—"

157

"Well, now you do know!" he said savagely, and without waiting to see if she followed he took several long strides up the rocky trail. He slowed moments later and waited for her to catch up, but he did not speak again until they had reached the main camp.

"Perhaps I was too frank," he said in the moments before he veered off for the bridge. His expression was controlled now, remote. "I apologize for that. And for everything."

"There's no need to apologize for telling the truth, or for anything else."

"Yancy's agreed to look out for you. He has money for you . . . your money, so don't be shy about using it. I'll replenish the supply once in a while."

Cat nodded her acquiescence.

"You can always send a message if anything important comes up. There'll be men and mules running a supply line to the forward camp, at least until the snow sets in. I'll be back this way once in a while, if I can make it. It might not be until spring."

"Spring . . . oh. Then there's nothing to do but say good-bye, is there?"

"No." He stood there for another moment. In his face there was an expression Cat could not read, a strength and silence and something else, something akin to the mountains, a quality that for the moment eluded definition. "Good-bye," he said, and swiveled on his heel.

Spring. Cat walked slowly to the cabin, unthinkingly resting one hand on the flat of her stomach, below her breast. What was the thing she had seen in Daniel's face? Surely not loneliness. She had asked Yancy, yesterday, if Inge was still at the forward camp. Yancy had been markedly evasive at first, and Cat had decided directness was called for.

"Yancy, tell me the truth. Yes or no! Is Inge still living in Daniel's tent?"

Yancy had screwed up his face into doleful lines, torn between loyalty to his friend and an innate honesty that prevented him from lying. As Daniel's friend, he sensed many things he had never been told.

"Is the answer yes or no?" Cat had persisted.

"It ain't no," Yancy had confessed reluctantly.

No, not loneliness. Endurance, perhaps? A certain grimness? These were the things she had seen in the face of the mountain.

Before entering the cabin, she turned to the sound of the train whistle. She could not see it from here, but she could imagine the smoke billowing to the sky; the great rods starting to churn, slowly, slowly, then more rapidly and rhythmically as the locomotive backed out and vanished down the slope. Within a few days she would be on it. San Francisco seemed a likely goal. If she needed help, she could always try to find Deirdre. San Francisco . . .

Perhaps it was for the best. A man who wanted no emotional ties would certainly not want the kind of emotional tie she had been suggesting. A half a woman, and a whole child that might not even be his own. It was a poor bargain, and one that she should not have offered.

And in spring . . . Where would she be by then? She, and the life that grew inside her womb?

BOOK II

The Will

17

In the fifty-second year of his life, having learned by devious extraordinary means to control the once-compelling fires of his loins, Julian Gow concluded he had no more to fear from his vision.

"Who are you?" he asked of the shadowy woman whose face he had never seen.

"I am Revenge," she whispered.

"Foolish woman! Do you think to kill me by my own seed? By my own blood?"

"I am Revenge," she moaned, and then again: "I am Revenge."

"I sow no more seed," he answered, with echoes of triumph. "You cannot destroy me now."

"I have the weapon," came the soft inexorable answer.

His pillow began to dampen with sweat. His eyes flickered compulsively. He looked more closely at his vision, and trembled to see that the seed in her was not the seed of his loins, but the seed of his destruction.

"I have the will," she whispered.

In a trance, without volition, he began to peel the glove away from his right hand.

"I have the way. . . ."

In the morning, Julian Gow had his bloodied right hand fitted for a new glove. It was well padded, and made of the toughest leather. It was not unlike the gauntlet worn by a trainer of peregrine falcons, except that a small padlock at the wrist locked the glove into place.

During the daytime, in order that he might wash his hands when he chose—a thing he had taken to doing with great frequency—Julian Gow kept the key to the padlock on a gold chain, in his watch pocket. At night the key remained in the care of his most trusted bodyguard.

The vision that caused this extraordinary measure took place in April of 1883, twenty-five years to the day after its first manifestation. In the same month Julian Gow set out in earnest to determine the whereabouts of a number of women who had cause to hate him, including the wives and daughters and mothers of many men he had ruined over the years.

On the list was Cathryn Kinross, then twenty-five years of age.

18

"En voiture, messieurs! En voiture, s'il vous plaît!"

At the cry of the stationmaster, several tardy passengers hastened their good-byes, and turned to board the train pulled alongside the platform. Beneath the recently installed electric lights in the station, the teak sides of the polished coaches gleamed, and so did the raised bronze lettering above the windows: *Compagnie Internationale des Wagons-Lits et des Grands Express Européens*.

On the platform the usual complement of people milled—ladies in bustles and hats that grew more astonishing by the year; gentlemen whose fashions had not changed so very much in a decade, although the straw boater and the Norfolk suit had joined the silk topper and the frock coat; conductors frowning at turnip watches; porters attending to bulge-topped trunks and the various paraphernalia of travel. The acrid smell of train was in the air.

Tonight, the Gare de Strasbourg—later to become the Gare de l'Est—attracted no unusual crowd, as it had on one memorable night the previous October. Then, speechmaking and champagne and top hats had been the order of the day, and it had seemed that all of Paris, all but the lovers whispering in the shadows of the Pont Neuf and the Pont des Arts, had bent its footsteps to the Right Bank to witness the departure of what had become, even before its inaugural voyage, the most famous luxury train in the world.

"Trois minutes à six, messieurs! Trois minutes!" At the cry, a tall man with tawny eyes and grooved cheeks murmured a farewell to his pretty companion, planted one last effective kiss on a pair of very receptive lips, and stooped to pick up a well-traveled portmanteau. He strode toward the train, pausing only to flick a coin toward a news vendor. The date on the newspaper showed a midsummer's day in 1884; it was more than a year since Julian Gow had taken to wearing his extraordinary gauntlet.

The tall man glanced quickly at the headlines before

folding *Le Figaro* under his arm. Only more bad news from the Sudan, with Gordon still hemmed in at Khartoum—or to be more exact, no news at all: The Mahdi's fanatical followers had cut telegraph lines between Cairo and Khartoum some months before.

But at least the headlines did not talk of soup lines and starvation and business failures; these were prosperous years.

"En voiture, monsieur! Dépêchez-vous, s'il vous plaît!" And then, as the stationmaster recognized him: "Ah, Monsieur Savage! Quel plaisir de vous revoir!"

"Bon soir, Monsieur Gris. Il fait chaud ce soir, n'est-ce pas?" Daniel also exchanged a brief word of greeting with the uniformed conductor who stood smartly at the door of his sleeping car, and swung onto the train just as the whistle sounded. Moments later he was following the conductor along the carpeted corridor. He considered asking the name of his compartment mate, and then thought better of it. Unless a person traveled in tandem on the Orient Express, he took what the fates dealt out.

The conductor came to a halt at a door, just as the train trembled into life. "Numéro sept! La bonne chance, n'est-ce pas? Ah, l'amour—"

And before Daniel had time to reflect on that odd observation, the door into the luxuriously appointed compartment swung open, and he saw the woman's silhouette against the window. Daniel's eyes widened. Black silk, a slender waist, a great swoop of outrageously feathered hat—and a lot of self-possession, since she had not turned at his arrival.

With a haste that could only be called conspiratorial, the conductor backed away to retire. "Monsieur, madame, on dine à huit heures. Et maintenant . . ."

"An unexpected pleasure," Daniel said dryly in French, when the door had at last closed them in together. He spoke with a fluency honed by some years of living on the continent. Without taking his eyes off the woman's shapely back, he busied himself in depositing his portmanteau and his newspaper in the gilt rack provided for the purpose.

"It's a rare thing to find a woman traveling alone in Europe, and I confess it's a pleasant surprise. Perhaps introductions are in order, and as Georges did not stay long enough to perform the task, let me—"

"Hello, Daniel," said a cool voice, in English.

Daniel turned totally still at the sound of the woman's

166

voice. His face tightened perceptibly. She turned, slowly, smiled, and threw her large muff onto the Spanish leather seat that would later be transformed into a lower berth. Then, unhurriedly, she unpinned her hat and tossed it beside the muff. Her dark hair was exquisitely coiffed. Maturity had ripened her breasts and added elegant little hollows beneath the high cheekbones. She should have been lovelier than ever, but for some reason she was not. There was an emptiness in the gray eyes—a flatness that robbed them of appeal.

Daniel recovered swiftly from the moment of deep shock. He watched in silence, not yet trusting himself to speak. A wary stillness concealed the still-raw jangle of his nerves. She began to peel off the mauve kid gloves that matched the elaborate ostrich plumes in her hat, and that were the one remaining touch of color in her outfit. It was as if she had consciously waited to perform the act until she knew that his eyes were upon her. Her movements were slow, sinuous, seductive.

"Aren't you glad to see me, Daniel?" A tip of tongue appeared and bedewed the ripe curve of her lips, leaving them moist and provocative. The second glove began to come off, as cunningly as the first. "Oh, darling, if you knew how I've ached to see you all these years. It's been so—"

"Cut the act, Cathryn," he broke in with a brutal directness that was as deliberate as the artful stripping off of gloves she had just undertaken—a gesture that seemed to Daniel oddly cold and contrived. Some part of him recoiled at that gesture; he wanted to punish her for it. Perhaps it was a legacy of the half-forgotten tortures she had once put him through.

"Act? Daniel, darling, after all these years how can you—"

"It won't wash, Cathryn," he clipped in brutally. "I remember the past too well. You were never very glad to see me then."

"Perhaps not, but . . . Oh, Daniel, how can you be so cold, so callous?" She moved across the compartment, and placed her hands over his lapels. "Yes, perhaps I should have tried to find you long ago, when I first heard that Inge had died."

Daniel's eyes were unfriendly, conceding nothing. "Then you did know I married Inge," he said.

"Yes, I heard." She smiled upward, but even the brief batting of lashes touched none of the nothingness in her eyes.

"Trapped, despite yourself, Daniel? How sweet of you to give Inge some happiness in the last months of her life. I take it you knew you'd be a widower soon."

Daniel knew a moment of cold rage. It was true enough that he had married Inge out of pity, not out of love. But that the smallpox had aggravated a blood condition was something neither he nor Inge had known; her death had been unexpected. All things considered, it had not been a joyless marriage. Another emotional tie ending in disaster? True—but this time there had been rewards, and a lesson to be learned. With him or without him, Inge would have died; and she had been touchingly content for a time.

But he had no intentions of discussing his brief marriage with Cat. "Inge died nearly seven years ago, Cat," he snapped. "If you were so anxious to get in touch with me, you could have done so long ago. My whereabouts have never been any particular secret . . . as yours have. Yancy could have given you my address at any time."

"Yancy! He's becoming quite the railroad magnate, isn't he? That little line covers half of California now. You must be sorry you sold out." Her parted lips trembled expectantly; an expensive perfume hovered in the air. "I didn't need Yancy to tell me you were living in Europe, Daniel. I read that long ago, in a little railroad journal, and that's where I read you were a widower, too. I wanted to see you then, but it's taken me all this time to work up the courage. If you knew how I've dreamed of you, dreamed of you in my arms . . ."

Daniel unlaced the fingers that had crept around his neck, and returned them forcibly to her sides. "That won't wash either," he said cuttingly. "If there's one thing you never lacked, Cathryn Kinross, it's courage. Now can we talk like adults? What the hell are you doing on this train? In this particular compartment? I don't believe in coincidences."

She pretended to pout, and fluttered her lashes again, although she made no further attempt to embrace him. "I'll admit it's no coincidence. But it's true I wanted to see you, Daniel, to hold you. . . ."

He sighed, with deep aggravation. "Didn't I tell you, Cat, I don't believe that? You're desirable, charming, maddeningly beautiful . . . and you might fool some other man. But not me."

She looked affronted; her chin tilted haughtily. "I don't know what you're talking about," she said coldly.

"At least that's an honest voice," he noted with acrid sarcasm. "Now stop pretending you're here because of my irresistible attractions. There isn't a sexually fulfilled bone in that icy body of yours. Arch, artful, enticing . . . There are many words for that little game you just played, but honest isn't one of them."

Her lids languished briefly; he could almost see the thoughts clicking through her head. Seconds later a small brittle laugh escaped her lips, and as her eyes came up her smile became bright, artificial. Her eyes remained untouched.

"You've seen through me, Daniel. All the same, that's a very cool greeting for an old friend."

"There's water under the bridge. Eight years is a long time."

She shifted her muff to one side and dropped gracefully to the seat beside it, then studied him with a small watchful smile. There was a coldness in her movements now, a total lack of seductiveness. "Not quite eight," she corrected him, "since that day you said good-bye. You must have been planning to marry Inge even then. Were you afraid to tell me, Daniel? I would have congratulated you! I heard two or three days later, and by then you'd already left for the East. You were very close-mouthed about that, too! But Laura Brody guessed it was a honeymoon trip."

It had been far more than a honeymoon trip; but he had no intentions of discussing that with Cat either.

"Laura Brody had no right to make guesses," he said brusquely, "Is that why you ran away?"

"Absolutely not. I had already packed when I heard that piece of news. I was growing very bored with the rail-laying camp."

He remained standing, his long legs adjusting easily to the rhythms of the train, his eyes hooded. "You've changed," he observed. She *had* changed. Hardened. That she had paid some kind of price for the intervening years showed in a thousand small ways—the little intransigence about the lines of her beautiful mouth, a touch of rigidity in the prideful posture, a certain brittleness of expression. And those dead eyes. Was this the same Cathryn who had once made her girlish advances in a perfumed September night? Then, she had been child and woman all at once, shy and bold and vulnerable and in the end—during one last wordless, urgent coupling—memorable enough to twist herself into his heart for several years thereafter. But time had given him some immunity, after all.

"Changed? Perhaps. But you haven't. I saw her kissing you good-bye on the platform. Another blonde, Daniel?" Cat's voice was artificial; the arch of her brows maddening. She smiled too sweetly. "Why isn't she on this trip with you?"

"Change of plans," he said. His nerves grated at that terrible fakery in her voice. Did she not have one shred of real emotion left? "There was some mix-up in the tickets. At the last minute I couldn't get accommodation for her."

Cat's lashes drooped briefly, spiking against her cheeks. "Now you know why," she said, satisfied.

Daniel's anger surfaced, putting blazing pinpoints in his eyes. "How the hell did you arrange that?"

"My grandfather's name still means something in railroad circles."

"Add to that that in France a little bribery goes a long way," he flared.

She did not deny it. "My contact told me you'd be on this run, and that you'd reserved for two people. I didn't know who your companion would be, but I did guess that she might be . . . dispensable. It was simple enough to arrange to take her place."

He glared at her, hostility unconcealed. "Didn't it occur to you that I might be angry? That *she* might be upset?"

"Of course it occurred to me. I decided to risk your anger. And about *her?* Well, frankly, I'm sure there are more where she came from. Is she good in bed, Daniel?"

"You bitch," he grated, his knuckles whitening and his voice shaking with outrage. "She's a hell of a lot better than you."

Cat's smile faded, and her face became cold and closed. "You can go back to her, Daniel, as soon as I'm through with you. If you cared for her so much, why didn't you miss this train, and go on a later one?"

"Because this is a business trip," he snapped. "I've been hired by the Ottoman Sultan to consult on a railroad job. She was only accompanying me as far as Vienna. Now please explain why you've decided to turn my life topsy-turvy after all these years. Frankly, I find it unamusing."

"I have a perfectly good reason, Daniel, but I'll come to that. First let me tell you I *don't* intend to turn your life topsy-turvy. Why, I've hardly thought of you for years. But then, several weeks ago something happened to catch my eye. A little story in the newspaper. It reminded me of your existence. And that's when I decided to come to you for help."

"Help—" A sudden wave of concern washed through him, surprising him with its intensity. His eyes probed her, but with less animosity now. "Are you in trouble of some kind? Financial trouble? I used to worry about that. . . ."

She raised her brows, and cocked her head, and regarded him coolly. "Did I say I was in trouble? I assure you I'm not. I'm a wealthy woman now, Daniel. I've done very well for myself."

But all the old concerns had come tumbling back, along with a deep curiosity to know what she had been doing all these years. "Where did you go when you left the Sierras? And where have you been living since?"

"I don't think you need to know that."

His eyes traveled to the slender hands that remained elegantly motionless in her lap. They were ringless, but a slight change of skin color and the indentation created by many years told him that a ring had recently been removed.

"Divorced," she said without a flicker of hesitation. "Yes, Daniel, a divorced woman. A very wicked thing."

"Then you're Cathryn Kinross again?"

"Legally, yes, but I still use my married name. I was married for many years; it seems easier."

"What name?"

"I don't think you need to know that either."

Daniel swooped down and claimed the muff that lay beside her on the seat. "I see you have no intention of satisfying my curiosity, so I'll have to do it for myself." He opened the muff and peered inside; the initials CK were embroidered in the lining.

"You won't find my married name on anything in there," she told him, and remained unperturbed when Daniel began to pull out the contents one by one. She had expected such a move, and had removed a number of personal items, leaving only those that could be explained in some easy manner.

First a little chain-link snap purse; his eyes widened at the amount of money it contained. Her passport: nothing there. Various other papers that also gave her name as Cathryn Kinross. A locket: he snapped it open, but the likeness had been removed. Some perfume in an expensive cloisonné

171

flacon. And finally, a carefully folded newspaper page that had begun to fray at the creases.

Daniel replaced the other items, handed the muff silently back to Cat, and unfolded the news sheet. "New York," he muttered, "so that's where you've been living."

She did not correct his mistake. It was on a last thought that she had left the newspaper amongst her possessions, thinking to deceive him. "That's the story about you," she said.

"This paper's over a year old," he said, noting the date: May 25, 1883. "And you only saw it several weeks ago?"

"I had used it to line a drawer," she returned smoothly, for she had expected such an observation.

Daniel's eyes coursed over the sheet. It was a front page graced with a drawing of the Brooklyn Bridge, which had opened the previous day. It was a great accomplishment marred by many tragedies. In the building, the bridge had killed twenty men, including its designer, John Augustus Roebling; it had also crippled his son, the man who had brought the project to completion. The younger Roebling, part blind and half paralyzed with caisson disease caused by work in underwater cages deep below the East River, had witnessed the ill-fated opening from his house on Columbia Heights.

"Not that story," Cat said levelly, as if she knew which item had caught his eye. "It's the little story at the bottom of the page, the one about this train."

Daniel's eye slid down and found the article, and after a moment he smiled sardonically. "'Rumor has it,'" he read out loud, "'that only one American citizen is to be included in the glittering list of prestigious personages joining the inaugural run of what will undoubtedly soon become the most famous train in the world. If truth be known, it is a list which along with other distinguished guests will include this humble correspondent. . . .' Stuffy old windbag!"

Daniel crumpled the newspaper and threw it back into Cat's lap. She opened her mouth angrily, some emotion for the first time touching her eyes; then controlled herself and began to straighten the paper.

"Prestigious personage hell! Very evidently, I wasn't on the inaugural run of the Orient Express."

"But the article did remind me you were still around." Cat refolded the paper along well-worn lines, but this time in such a way that the little article remained face-out. She herself began to read. "'It is rumored that Mr. Savage, a noted explosives expert, is to be included because of his work on the St. Gotthard Tunnel, first great railway tunnel through the Alps, an accomplishment which helped make possible the present route. . . . ' Oh, it goes on a bit about that, and about your other work. It mentions too that you were in the Hardanger Mountains working on the Oslo-Bergen line. That's how I managed to track you down. It wasn't so very hard. So you see why I saved this paper." She began to smooth it with her fingertips, and kept it in her lap, not returning it to the muff.

"New York," Daniel said thoughtfully. "Then I take it you're not in hiding from Julian Gow anymore."

He watched her closely for any sign of the shadow that would once have passed through her eyes at mention of Gow's name. There was none—but then, Cat had always been good at hiding her emotions, and she had had many years to practice the art.

"No, I'm not," she said with perfect self-control. "Julian has known where I am for more than a year."

"And he hasn't troubled you?"

"No, not really. Oh, he keeps sending messages through his lawyers . . . some piece of paper he wants me to sign . . . but he can't really hurt me now." She simulated a laugh. "I don't worry about Julian anymore. So you see, Daniel, that's not why I've come to you for help. And it's not money. I have everything a woman would want."

"Including a child," said Daniel flatly.

Her face froze; she had not expected this.

"Oh, come now, Cat. You were married a long time, you said. Is it such an unlikely conclusion? And that locket. It doesn't have a portrait in it, but it does have a lock of hair. It's not dark enough to be your own, and it's soft and downy . . . baby hair. And the locket's relatively new."

Swiftly, her gaze fell to those slender naked fingers, so pale against the black silk stuff of her dress. "There was a child," she said in a low emotionless voice. "She died."

Daniel felt a strong pang of regret for the unfriendly attitude he had adopted since Cat's materialization. "I'm sorry, Cathryn," he said quietly. That explained the black, then. Or did it? Despite the high collar, the gown did not

173

appear to be a mourning outfit, and certainly the ostrich plumes and mauve gloves were not. Nor did the little striptease she had done earlier fit in with the image of the grieving mother. Had the death of the child contributed to her marriage break-up? Manlike, wanting to avoid a topic that left him feeling vaguely uncomfortable, he changed the subject.

"Tell me what kind of help you want," he directed, gruffness concealing a certain uneasiness. "If I can give it, I will . . . for old time's sake."

Cat's eyes came up again, void of emotion, barren as desert sands. "You're still angry that I tricked you into this," she stated.

"I don't deny it," he admitted, but his tones were not as testy as before. "You say you knew my whereabouts. So why all the duplicity? I wouldn't have been angry if you'd approached me in any other way."

She hesitated only briefly, and then picked her way through the careful words. "I didn't want you to refuse. It would have been too easy for you to refuse if I'd come to you in the Hardanger Mountains, or elsewhere."

"Hell, Cathryn, I'm not heartless. I'd have listened. You didn't need to go to such extraordinary lengths."

"Yes, I did." Her fingers tightened fleetingly on the clipping, as though if were a lifeline. "You see, Daniel, it may take three days for you to give me the help I need, and . . . I think you're the only man who can give me that help. You're the only man that ever succeeded in giving me that kind of help before."

Good lord. Daniel stared at her disbelievingly, wondering if she could possibly mean what he thought she meant. Wondered, too, if he even wanted to help: to renew those deep, driving, soul-tormenting frustrations he had once felt because of his own terrible and towering need for the flesh of a woman who was not only frigid, but acutely afraid of his touch. He knew she was right: If she had come to him in Norway, or anywhere else, his answer would have been no. Very definitely, no.

"You can't possibly have misunderstood me. You were quite right, Daniel, when you said there's not a sexually fulfilled bone in my body. I'm still cold."

"And you don't want to be cold anymore," he stated flatly. Now, at last, he sank into his own place on the Spanish leather seat, and ran his fingers wearily around the back of his neck.

Something in his manner told Cat she could count on his help. She looked down, ostensibly to restore the clipping to its silken niche. Behind the dark veil of lashes, satisfaction gleamed. "I don't want to be cold anymore," she agreed.

It was not true; but Daniel did not need to know that.

19

"So much for gas light on trains," remarked a corpulent and prosperous Englishman, peering around the dimly lit salon-wagon restaurant. On the Orient Express, gas light had at last made its debut as the form of illumination on trains; but because the gas mantel had not yet been invented, the naked flames of the elaborate cut-glass chandeliers had to be turned very low, as a precaution against fire.

"Ah-là-là!" proclaimed the French table-mate, fingering one of his several Baccarat crystal wineglasses. "But if there were more women on the train, like she of the dark hair, then the little light would be so romantic, n'est-ce pas?"

Indeed it was romantic. Every detail was loving and lavish: the wall panels painted by artists such as Delacroix, the spotless napery, the heavy gleaming silver. Even the waiters balancing laden trays wore velvet breeches and silk stockings and buckled shoes; and had a long-forgotten passenger not once complained about powder in the soup, they would have been wearing powdered periwigs, too.

The train was traveling smoothly, and on schedule, through a moonless night. By morning, musical place names like Châlons-sur-Marne and Igney-Avricourt would have given way to names with a harsher ring: Strasbourg and Baden-Baden and Stuttgart. The potpourri of passengers was cosmopolitan indeed: Germans, Finns, Italians, Greeks, a Transylvanian duke, several urbane Turks homeward bound. There was even a dark-eyed turbaned Indian *raj* and his retinue, for whom the beleaguered chef de cuisine had somehow produced a mountain of specially concocted curries and sweets. And this—miracle of miracles!—despite the ten courses, each worthy of Escoffier, that had also been produced in a tiny kitchen where every curve of the track could, and often did, send the contents of some scalding copper pot flying over a luckless sous-chef. On the Orient Express, scalds were a badge of honor.

At the moment, the occupational hazards of the kitchen

staff were the last thing on Cat's mind, or Daniel's. Both toyed with their food and with their own thoughts, too conscious of what lay ahead to do justice to the chef's superhuman efforts. Long before the three-hour meal was over, they left their table, and wended their way back along the plush corridors that led to their own compartment.

"I see the scene is set," Daniel murmured with a glance at the eiderdown-filled comforter and the pure silk sheets that were one more luxury on this most luxurious of trains. Soft gas light glowed on rosewood inlays and carved cornices. At the window, the novel spring-loaded blinds had been lowered, and the damask draperies released from their gold-tasseled sashes.

In their absence, the embossed leather seats had been converted for the night. On Daniel's instructions, only the lower berth had been prepared. This was wider and more comfortable than its counterpart on a Pullman car, and because the upper remained nested behind its marquetry disguise, offered considerably more headroom.

He came up behind Cat, and his knuckles trailed a slow sensuous path down the length of her spine. His mouth moved into her hair; his hands slid around to rest lightly at her hips, soothing them for some slow moments before he adventured further. And even then, it was only his thumbs that gentled the very verges of her breasts.

"Slender as a young girl," he muttered into her hair, "except in the right places."

Cat did not shrink away as she would once have done, but she remained stiff until the moment when one strong hand moved back to stroke the nape of her neck. She knew instinctively that Daniel's next move would take him to the fastenings of her dress.

"No, Daniel." Spine rigid, she moved steps away from him. Swiftly, almost too swiftly, she began to disrobe. "It's time you undressed, too."

"Why not?" With a shrug and a brief lifting of brows, Daniel obeyed. His garments were less complicated than hers; by the time she had undressed to her corsets and begun to unpin her elaborate coiffure, he was naked. She turned away from him. Was it the freeing of his erection, Daniel wondered with some amusement, or was it a sudden access of modesty for her own state of undress?

And then in a few swift movements she was naked: black

hair streaming down the silken back, the curves of her soft, womanly, well-formed. She pulled her hair over one shoulder and turned to face him at once. With a sudden shock of remembrance and some surprise at how much a man could forget over the years, Daniel realized why she had turned her back. The long fall of hair now almost concealed one breast.

She folded back the comforter and slid quickly between the silken sheets. She lay with eyes closed, sheet pulled high over her breasts, not troubling to conceal the tension in her limbs. Daniel would expect this; he had been told there were glaciers to melt. "You can extinguish the lights now," she suggested.

"Why would I do that?" He came down on the bed beside her—his frame too long, too warm, too threatening. A part of Cat receded; she began to watch the scene from a distance. He smoothed her hair over the pillow, away from her shoulder, and kissed her collarbone without pushing the sheet from her breast.

"I'd prefer the light off," she said.

"And I wouldn't. Don't you remember one of the first lessons I ever taught you? A man likes to look at what he's making love to."

And so, Cat steeled herself, using lessons learned long ago, and some learned since. It was only a game, after all. . . .

Daniel withdrew his mouth from her throat. Very slowly and expertly, with his head propped on one hand so that he could see, he put his other hand to work. Still, he did not push the sheet away. His featherlight touch smoothed and soothed its way over the fabric, slowly exploring the curves beneath—lingering nowhere, sparing nothing, deliberately molding the silk to her contours as he traveled. His eyes lingered where his fingers did not, praising the flesh revealed yet not revealed. As he touched each part, he talked. His voice was low, slow, intimate.

"How beautiful you are. Those breasts, so full . . . the little peaks of them . . . the way your waist flares into the bones of your hip. The way that ridge of bone flows down. No, it's not bone, it's ivory. Ivory and satin. And the way your body dips again, here . . . and rises here . . ." He touched lightly where a little crispness of hair rounded the sheet, and then, deftly, with one finger, drew a line that settled the silk between her tensed legs. "And here . . . and *here* . . ."

"Can't we dispense with this part? It would be faster if you'd just get under the sheet."

"I'd rather dispense with the sheet first." But he did not do so; the sheet remained in place. But now, his head made a move, and his tongue touched briefly where a rise of nipple lay in outline. Then his slow fingers began to stroke where moisture gave the supple fabric some transparency, and a darkness of flesh gleamed through. She remained unaroused.

"Let yourself float, sweetheart. There's no need to do a thing. We don't have to make love if you don't feel like it . . . not tonight. I can enjoy doing this, just this. . . ."

His teeth caught the nipple gently and fleetingly; and then, leaving that nipple, he turned his attention to the other. Cat spent a moment glaring at the bronze-streaked hair bent so closely to her breast, but then she resigned herself. She closed her eyes and willed for it to happen. . . .

Her low moan was Daniel's first signal that any changes were taking place. Then, as if of their own accord, her fingers laced themselves into the vital texture of his hair. She began to writhe beneath the moist trespass of his mouth, slowly at first, then with a fervor that increased in tempo as he folded the sheet back and stroked the bared softness of her thighs. She gasped and trembled beneath his hand.

"Daniel, don't keep me waiting . . . not now . . . oh, my darling, it's been so long. . . . I want to feel you inside, you you you. . . ." Urgent now, her pliant fingers traveled to his sex. He levered himself between her legs. As he plunged, a sob of relief and satisfaction broke from her lips. "Yes, oh, yes. Oh, my darling . . . so deep, so wonderful, so *right* . . ."

A tigress in her reawakening, she moaned and groaned and sobbed, and twisted her head from side to side, and clutched his spine and wrapped her legs around his muscular flanks; and at the ending, as her hips strained convulsively upward, she cried: "Now, Daniel, *now* . . ."

"Quite a renaissance," Daniel remarked, rolling away and coming to a sitting position on the edge of the bed. She, too, pulled upward and propped herself against the pillows, all modesty flown to the winds. Her mouth was dewy-soft and grateful.

"Oh, Daniel," she breathed. But then she saw the enigmatic eyes contemplating her thoughtfully, and her lashes fell.

"That was very well done, Cathryn. You must be very pleased with yourself."

She stiffened instantly at the sarcasm in his voice. "Of course I'm pleased. I didn't think it would be so—"

"You little bitch," he broke in, in the most callous of voices. "You didn't feel a damn thing."

Her slender hand cracked across his face with the suddenness of a striking cobra, and with every ounce of strength in her body.

And his hand, with equal swiftness and even greater force, struck back.

For an instant shock streaked her eyes with silver. Anger followed swiftly, as her fingers rose to the face where his fingermarks were already rising red.

"How dare you!" Every part of her quivered with venom—her voice, her body, her breasts.

At least this emotion was true, Daniel thought grimly, unlike her earlier fakery. It was that that had angered him, that pretense, not her lack of response. Why in hell would she inveigle him into this situation, and then *pretend* to be aroused? The inevitable conclusion of the lovemaking had left him with a bad taste, and a curious sense of unfulfillment gnawing at his vitals—as though the plateau just reached had been a prelude to passion, and not the climax of it. His man's pride demanded that she give some response, especially as he had tried to exercise a patience he would have used on no other woman. But she had given nothing, nothing, nothing—nothing but a cheap simulation of desire.

"How dare *you?*" he retorted rudely. "That performance might have come right from a brothel."

Conscious of the way his eyes drooped insultingly to the letter emblazoned on her breast, Cat stiffened. Rage ripped through her. The years had fortified her defenses in many ways, for she had had to claw for survival in a sometimes cruel world; and the defenses were not entirely to do with sex. The mask she wore was nowadays seldom cracked, except in the teeth of a temper, something else the years had sharpened, too. She glared at him, hating him at this moment with every fiber of her being—hating him for the present and for the past, and for decisions the anguish of which he could never know.

"Perhaps it did come from a brothel," she blazed.

His smile was sour. "Not you, Cathryn Kinross . . . never

you. You have too much distaste for human contact. Brothels aren't your style."

"That shows how little you know about me, Daniel Savage. I'd be a whore, if I had to. I'd do anything, if I *had* to!"

He laughed, not pleasantly. "You could have been a whore, but I don't believe for a minute that you were. Good God, no wonder your marriage failed! The miracle is that your husband stayed around long enough to produce a child!"

Her eyes fell swiftly, and something in her seemed to sag, as if the anger had evaporated. She spoke without raising her eyes to his. "How did you know I was pretending, Daniel? I thought I did a good job."

"Oh, yes, you did a good job . . . too good, considering that your artful little body didn't come up with a single one of the right signals. Hell, you wouldn't even keep your mouth still long enough to be kissed. A man can read a woman's body like an open book, if he takes the time to do so, and if he cares."

"I suppose I should be flattered that you care," she said stiffly. "Or do you care?"

He was a time answering; perhaps he was wondering himself. "I care whether you feel. If this were a chance encounter I'd put the whole thing from my mind . . . take my pleasure and run. But you asked for my help; you told me you wanted to feel, and . . . dammit, Cat, there's some pride involved! A man doesn't like to be duped, and he doesn't like to think he leaves a woman cold."

"Your pride needn't suffer." She gave a small and totally brittle laugh. "I'm no worse off than I was before we made love."

"Why *did* you pretend? If you really wanted to feel you'd have waited, perhaps tried too hard or not tried at all, or . . . good God, Cat, why *did* you embroil me in this charade? I don't think you want to feel at all."

She had been expecting this conclusion for some moments; and behind her shuttered lids possible answers had been clicking through her mind. It had been wrong, she recognized now, to think that Daniel could be easily deceived: He was far too experienced. She had taken the wrong tack, and too soon. Nor could she fob him off now with some easy lie. No: The truth, or part of the truth, was better, and it would serve just as well.

She met his penetrating gaze, and smiled faintly, sadly.

"You've reached some of the wrong conclusions, Daniel, but you're quite right about one thing. I hated every minute of what we just did. But I do want to be whole; I wasn't lying about that." She paused, poised in a delicate balance between truth and fiction. "At least I *did* want to be whole . . . but then, after it started, I wanted it to be over with as quickly as possible." She allowed herself a small sigh. "By the time I realized how distasteful it was, I owed it to you not to call a halt. I had disarranged all your plans, after all, and I hate that coy kind of woman who leads a man on, and then tells him to stop."

Daniel remained silent. He hated that type of woman, too, but he also hated pretense.

Faced by his uncompromising expression, her head dangled; her long hair streamed over her breasts. Her hand began to pluck uncertainly at the edges of the sheet, and then, in a small and inspired gesture, she seized it and once more draped it over her breasts, not looking upward to see if he was watching. "I'm sorry I asked for your help. I only wanted to put an end to my . . . emptiness. But it's hopeless, quite hopeless."

Daniel's eyes had softened; her air of defeat had touched him as nothing else had done. "If at first you don't succeed . . ."

"I'm not sure I want to try again," she answered with seeming despair. "And you can't possibly want to help me now."

A strong tanned hand joined hers at the edge of the sheet. Gently he released the silk from her nerveless fingers, and let it fall. His knuckles brushed back and forth against a nipple. Beyond a faint cringing of the flesh, the action triggered no response in her body. But then, Daniel had expected none. The only thing that surprised him was the immediate resurgence of his own sexual drive.

"It's not only fair to you," she whispered, noticing this and exulting, for reasons that had nothing to do with any need for her body to be freed from its long sleep. And yet, she had not lied to Daniel. She did indeed want to be whole again, but over the years her definition of wholeness had changed. Frigidity suited her very well. What she wanted from Daniel was not a thaw, but a child.

A child that would be Daniel's child, and, therefore, a brother or sister to the little girl who had died, for Jenny, with her amber eyes and her streaky brown hair, could only have been Daniel's child. A child who would not be a replacement —there could be no replacement for Jenny—but a new joy and a new purpose and a new fullness and . . . yes, at times, a struggle and a heartache and a headache, too. Cat had not lied about wanting to feel, but it was her heart she wanted to feel with, not her body. She wanted to feel; she wanted to fill the void in her life; she wanted a child to blot out the terrible memory of the way Jenny had died.

Daniel eased her back against the sheet, and lowered his newly aroused body beside her. He started to stroke her hair, gently. "I'll help you, Cat . . . if I can. But this time you must promise not to pretend. Just lie back, relax, let the motion of the train take you. Look at the ceiling; think of other things. . . ."

20

Think of other things. Cat lay on the bed, forcedly limp beneath Daniel's hands, doing just that. Her mind was totally detached from what was happening to her body. The steady rhythm of the train affected her, physically, far more than the erotic patterns Daniel's lips were laying on her ears and on her throat.

He touched her in no real way, and it was easy enough to submit to his caresses, knowing that sooner or later—sooner, she hoped—Daniel would be forced to give in to his own physical arousal which, like his patience, appeared to be mighty. It was the right time of month to conceive, and Daniel the right father; but she could not count on a single encounter to do the trick. Some innate fastidiousness prevented her from wanting a child fathered by a man for whom she had never had any feeling. And all these years had produced no man for whom she did have feeling—except Ryan. And that was a different kind of feeling: a father feeling.

Of course Daniel would not be pleased to think he was serving only as a stud: But then he would never know. Just as he would never know the truth about Jenny.

Would things have been different if she had told him she was pregnant, that day so long ago? Perhaps. But then, she had not known that Jenny was Daniel's child; and by the time she knew for certain, she also knew that Daniel was married.

She had found that out the day she put the Sierra Nevada behind. It had come from an unwitting Laura Brody, who, not being privy to Daniel's innermost feelings, or Cat's, had revealed something Yancy had been loathe to tell.

"The money Daniel left for you? Wait a minute, it's locked in the safe. Thank goodness Yancy trusts me with the combination! Are you sure you need *all* of it? There's quite a lot, enough for several months. Daniel did say to give you whatever you asked for, but . . ."

184

"I have no winter clothes at all," Cat improvised. "I need so many things, and . . . and I want some new furniture for the cabin, too. I'll bring back what I don't use. Daniel won't mind. He said to send a message to the forward camp if more money was needed."

"As long as it's not needed for the next few weeks," Laura informed her, leaning her head into the heavy metal safe where Yancy kept the cash for payrolls. "But of course, if you run short before Daniel gets back from his trip, Yancy will lend you some."

"His trip?"

"Yes, he's gone east. He left yesterday. Didn't he tell you?" Laura located the envelope containing Cat's funds, clicked the safe closed, and rose from her crouched position. She handed the envelope to Cat. "He said he had something he wanted to do—something very important, and it might take him quite a time. He was very close-mouthed about it, but I *know* it wasn't railroad business. Why he was so secretive I can't imagine, for everyone's bound to find out sooner or later."

"Oh?"

"Yes . . ." Laura Brody looked uncertainly at Cat, and evidently decided that this particular secret could be shared. Laura's little glimmer of triumph was human; it was fun to impart gossip. She lowered her voice. "He took a lady friend with him. And . . . imagine this! . . . They're going to be married, as soon as they reach a preacher. I wouldn't doubt the knot's already tied! Personally, I think the trip's a honeymoon. Fancy that, Daniel married! Daniel of all people!"

Daniel married. But why? He wanted no responsibilities, no commitments; he had said so a thousand times. Cat hid the coldness that clutched her stomach, and murmured an appropriate question.

"You wouldn't know the woman," Laura said. "She's been living at the other camp for some time. Before that she was . . . well, it does seem odd that Daniel would marry someone that half the men in camp have . . ."

Laura bit her lip; she was telling too much. "What I mean is, she's nice enough, but it seems odd he would marry the woman when half the camp knows he's been living with her for months, without benefit of clergy. Although I suppose it's not so very odd, considering."

"Considering," Cat repeated faintly, resisting an urge to put a hand to her stomach. "Is she expecting his child?"

"I doubt it very much; Inge would know how to prevent that. And besides, she's been far too sick. Smallpox. Why, she very nearly died, and now, I suppose Daniel feels an obligation. Her face is very badly pocked, and with that kind of thing she can't very well—" Again Laura changed course slightly: "She can't very well, er, support herself. And no doubt Daniel feels he can't throw her out the door. Well, his devil-may-care days are over now, although I never thought I'd see it. Responsibilities do have a way of creeping up on a man, even when he doesn't want them!"

Yes, responsibility had a way of creeping up on a man. It was sad, and human, and ironic, that the woman who had awakened such chivalry in Daniel should have been of a profession that allowed most men to forget the vows of marriage—for a time, at least. Poor Daniel.

How terrible to shackle a man with responsibilities he did not want! Not even for the sake of a child would Cat have wanted an unwilling husband. Poor pock-scarred Inge . . .

How lucky that she had not told Daniel about the pregnancy! It was not until Jenny was a year old that Cat discovered the sequel to the story, when she saw a tiny item in a railroad periodical, announcing that Daniel's share in the California line had been sold out to Yancy Brody. The story also made mention of the fact that Mr. Savage, a recent widower, was now residing in Europe.

Jenny had been born toward the end of May, in San Francisco. She had always been on the frail side, and the doctor Cat had consulted several months after Jenny's birth had been blunt about the reason.

"Malnutrition," he said, looking angry and harassed. Work in the free clinic gave him little reason for joy. "Malnutrition plain and simple. Not hers . . . *yours*. You're not eating the right things, and add to that you're overtired. What the deuce do you expect? You carried her in your body, didn't you? You're nursing her, aren't you? If you go without she goes without. It's as simple as that. Rest! Let the housework go!"

"It's not housework. I have a job." There was not even a house at the time; only a dingy rented room, and a landlady to whom she owed a considerable amount of money.

"Quit the job. It must cost half your wages to get the child cared for while you work."

"I can't quit," Cat said, "or we wouldn't eat at all."

"Look, Mrs.—"

"Miss," she reminded him stubbornly. Officialdom demanded the truth; the truth was on the form the doctor held in his hand. Despite what she had told Daniel, there had been no husband—not then, not later.

"There are agencies here in San Francisco that can help in cases like yours," the doctor said gruffly. "But I suppose you know that. Charitable institutions. Homes. Give the child up!"

Cat had been told the same thing too many times; her eyes turned defiant.

"One of those stubborn types," muttered the doctor beneath his breath, writing out some instructions he knew would never be followed. He handed the paper to Cat, and looked her straight in the eye. "You're not helping your baby, you're depriving her. An unwed mother can't bring up a child. What do you expect from me, miracles? Next!"

That had been the nadir, a black hour of despair and self-recrimination. But Cat had come too far to give Jenny up now. The next day she resigned from the position she had considered herself so lucky to get, so soon after Jenny's birth, over many other applicants. And jobs were scarce back then: '76 had been one of the worst of the depression years, with soup kitchens and tens of thousands near starvation. The salary was low, but no lower than other women earned; the ten-hour day was standard. And the job was in a large office close enough to the rooming house to permit a quick trip home during the half-hour lunch in order to feed Jenny, who remained too tiny and too sickly to start on solid foods.

"We'll raise your salary," she was told, "if we decide to get one of those new contraptions, the, er, typewriting machines. Mr. Jones saw one at the Philadelphia Exposition, and he's looking into it now. Quite an invention! Quite an investment! I don't believe there's another such machine in San Francisco. Well, now, Mrs. Kirk, isn't that worth waiting for? It would be quite an honor for you to be allowed—"

"How much more?" she interrupted, her jaw set.

"Fifty cents a week." A bland smile greeted her. "If we decide to buy one. And if you can teach yourself to operate it. You'll have to do that on your own time, of course, after hours. We couldn't—"

Too little, and too late. Without another word Cat stood up

and walked out. She already knew her next goal: She had been there once before, shortly after arrival in San Francisco. There had been a sign beside the door then: GIRLS WANTED TO SERVE DRINKS. The sign had been fly-specked, as though it was always there.

Last time, with money in her purse, she had gone by hansom cab, and the driver had demanded double fare for braving the outskirts of the Barbary Coast, where even the police ventured only in well-armed pairs. On that occasion Cat had suspected the driver of traveling a roundabout way in order to further increase his fare. The maps showed a much less circuitous route, and today, as she must travel on foot, Cat took it. Too late she realized her mistake.

"Hey, you! Wanna job, sweetie?"

"Ain't she the snooty one! C'mere, darlin'—"

"Ah, forget her, sailor. She ain't got tits. Now lookit *these!* Look, but don't touch; six bits to shag. . . ."

Cat hurried along, ignoring the crude suggestions and hiding her revulsion at what she saw. Fortunately, as it was mid-morning, most of the leering tars she passed by were too glutted with last night's pleasures to present a serious obsta-cle. Occasionally a rough pair of hands tried to pull her into a doorway, but most of the doorways were already occupied with sleepy and scantily clad prostitutes crying out their wares. She kept her eyes lowered, partly to avoid stumbling over drunks or stepping in mudholes or slipping in the vomit that spattered the streets; partly also, to avoid direct views of the uncurtained windows where sex acts of various sorts were taking place in full view, crude advertisements for the dubious entertainments to be had within.

And then, as she drew closer to the House of the One-Eyed Irishman, the neighborhood began to improve dramatically. The cribs and cow-yards with names like Nymphia and Ye Olde Whore Shoppe vanished; so did the signs advertising circuses and various strange diversions; so did the creep-joints and dives with names like Hell's Kitchen and Bucket of Blood. It was with relief that Cat finally reached her goal, and asked for Deirdre's uncle. Ryan was in his office: The House of the One-Eyed Irishman did not open until later in the day.

"Aren't you the one came months ago, looking for that poor dear niece of mine?" Ryan squinted at Cat thoughtfully. He was a big, tough, handsome, likable man in his mid-forties, with no Irish accent and both eyes intact. The eye-patch was worn only when Ryan was at the gaming tables; Cat later learned that it had little pinholes Ryan could look through. Ryan's tables were thoroughly dishonest, and this was only one of a number of devices designed to put men off their guard.

"Didn't I tell you before it's not safe to come here, my pretty miss? What was your name?"

"Cathryn Kirk."

"Well, you've wasted your time, Miss Katie, and a cabfare, too. Can't tell you where she is. Probably still off in South America with that sweet-talking son of a Drumm Street pimp that fed her his pack of lies. By heaven! I'll have his neck. Seducing a sweet, pure, innocent girl like—"

"I'm not looking for Deirdre. I'm looking for a job."

Ryan stared at her in open-mouthed amazement. A widower and the father of two pale, proper daughters who were now full grown, he made very clear distinctions between a slut and a lady. His own womenfolk were ladies, and so were the friends of his womenfolk.

"Not in my place," he objected. "Not *here*. I wouldn't have a friend of my nice little niece working *here*."

"I need a job."

"Then go get a decent one! This is no place for a lady. Why, I'd never let my daughters on the premises. Look what happened to Deirdre. Walked in here just once, next thing you know she's been picked up by a . . ." Ryan paused, then said brusquely: "Nice girl like you wouldn't want to work in a crummy dive like this."

"You have girls working here," Cat persisted. "Your sign says you need girls to serve drinks."

"Sure, I always need girls. But serving drinks is just the start. A decent girl like you wouldn't know what else they do."

"Of course I know what they do. I could do it, too. And night work would suit me very well."

Ryan looked shocked, and then shook his head firmly. "No. You're a friend of Deirdre's, and you're not the type. You haven't seen my girls. A dirty bunch of raggle-taggle rowdies, ugly as sin most of 'em."

"If they're so bad, your customers might be glad of a change."

Ryan backtracked swiftly. "Oh, you'll find none better along the street, if truth be told. Mine have their teeth, and I

189

won't hire 'em under sixteen, and the girls are *clean*, if you know what I mean. But they're out there slinging drinks without their, er, unmentionables, and any man wants to look, he lifts a skirt, and looks. And if he wants to buy, he buys."

"How much does the job pay?" Cat asked patiently.

"Half what a girl earns, and she keeps her own tips. But you're not hired!"

"That will be quite satisfactory."

"You're not hired!"

"I'll start tonight."

"Not a chance!" roared Ryan, turning purple. "On the ravaged honor of my dear wronged niece, I swear I'll never allow such a thing!"

"Are you afraid I can't do it? I'll prove to you I can. Tonight I'll work for nothing."

"No! How could I live with my conscience—"

"For a week, then. But in that case I'll keep all the tips."

"No!"

"What time shall I report for work?"

Ryan just glared at her ragefully, making sputtering sounds in his throat.

"Would eight o'clock be soon enough? I'm busy at supper time."

"Be busy until hell freezes over! You're not working here!"

"I'll turn up tonight, Mr. O'Brien, and if you don't let me stay I'll simply walk to the place next door. They'll hire me. And if your girls are as bad as you say, why, perhaps some of your customers will start walking next door, too." She stood up to go, and smiled ingenuously. "Eight o'clock, then?"

"Don't come!" he shouted as the door clicked closed behind her.

But he gave in, glumly, when Cat reported for work that night. "Not as one of the girls, though," he told her morosely, pushing off the eyepatch as he ushered her into the little back office. In the seedy smoky gaming house, action continued at half a dozen small tables manned by dealers other than Ryan. "How could I explain to my sweet sainted niece if I turned her friend into a whore? The poor girl would have a fit of the vapors. No, I'm going to teach you something else, Miss Katie. Ever dealt cards?"

"I used to play poker with my grandfather. Not really

poker, for there were only two of us, but I do know some of the rudiments."

Ryan looked gloomy. "A babe in the woods, then. But you'll learn. You'll learn!"

And she had learned; she had an aptitude for cards. Within a month Ryan had declared her ready for a tryout at a table of her own—not poker or dice but vingt-et-un, easier for a beginner.

"A low-cut gown," he decreed. "That'll be your distraction . . . your eyepatch, so to speak."

"I'd prefer not," Cat said, and with some initial hesitancy explained the reason for her reluctance, describing it as a birthmark. But Ryan's eyes had only lit up.

"Some eyepatch! By God, that'll be a distraction! And you'll be showing no more, in fact, a great deal less than you'd have shown if I'd sent you packing next door. Let 'em ogle and wonder, and while they wonder and ogle, we'll win! All the ladies wear low-cut gowns, even in high society. Fact is, the higher the society, the lower the gown! Even my own niece goes a shade low now and then, and she's pure as the driven snow . . . or she was, until that offspring of a Sutter Street whore whisked her off to Valparaiso with his two-tongued promises. And her too innocent to see through his lies! No, this time, my little Katie, you're not winning the fight. Low-cut gown it is. Twist me around your little finger you do, but not this time. Not this time!"

And because Ryan had been good to her, and because the work was easy and paid well, and because the hours suited her very nicely with Jenny sleeping through the night, and because she was grateful that she was not working next door, Cat relented.

"On one condition. If I'm to wear a low-cut gown, I need more money." Cat was determined to acquire a proper nursemaid for Jenny, and a decent place to live, a place with light and air and parks nearby.

"I'm not paying you another cent!" Ryan's ready temper rose. "I don't want you here as it is, and you haven't even dealt a card yet!"

"But I'm good. I'm going to be good, and you know it. I have the hands for it, and I practice all the time at home. If you won't give me more money, I'll—"

"Then go next door!" thundered Ryan, who had heard such threats before.

"—I'll take less," she finished calmly, while Ryan's jaw dropped with amazement. "Cut my salary, and cut me in on the profits."

"Like hell!"

"I won't cost you much. I want none of your usual profits, not a cent of them." She smiled innocently, and cocked her head. "Just half of the extra profits that come in from now on. I think I'm going to be a draw, Ryan."

"Half of nothing, you mean," snorted Ryan, but with a financial gleam in his eyes. He knew a bargain when he saw one. "It's a deal, then. But don't come sniveling to me when you change your mind."

Cat had never looked back; nor had Ryan. She chose to dress in black; the air of cool mystery suited her style. The Widow, as she swiftly became known because of the mysterious mark on her breast, had drawn customers like flies to honey. Her unavailability was a challenge on a street where virtually every woman could be had for a price.

She had conceded the battle of the necklines to Ryan, but she had not conceded the next battle. It took place about a year later, shortly after Deirdre returned from South America, tearfully repentant—in Ryan's hearing at least—but considerably richer. Cat had long since admitted to Ryan that she did not know Deirdre very well; that Deirdre would probably not even remember her name.

"Oh, what that shameless snake did to the poor heartbroken girl. Sweet thing doesn't understand what happened, even yet. My own brother's orphan! Why, he'd turn in his grave! A sweet, innocent colleen! A virgin!"

"Not anymore," smiled Cat.

"No thanks to that Bull Run Alley blackguard!"

"It occurs to me," mused Cat with an apparent change of thought that was less of a non sequitur than Ryan could have guessed, "it occurs to me that there's something drastically wrong with this place."

"Wrong! The busiest gaming house on the Barbary Coast? Why, they're lined up to get in here now!"

"It's time we made some changes," Cat said. The "we" had become habit; by now, the extra profits far outstripped the usual ones. Cat's share had become very large indeed, enough to pay for a respectable house with a large bright nursery for her daughter.

"Changes?" Ryan groaned. "You've talked me into all the

changes we can afford. Better-looking girls . . . that doesn't come cheap, you know. And buying the house next door so we can expand next year. Hiring some fancy decorator. Could buy half of Telegraph Hill for his fancy price."

"That's when we should make the *real* change, when we expand," Cat said thoughtfully. "This part of the Barbary Coast isn't at all bad, Ryan, not like some of the streets. Why, it almost borders on respectability, but not too much respectability. This could be quite a place. It could have class."

Ryan glared. "It's classy enough for me," he said.

Cat chose to ignore the warning signals that told her Ryan was growing annoyed. "The trouble with this place is that the tables are dishonest, and the girls aren't. They're far too honest. They show everything at the flip of a petticoat. It should be the other way around. Girls that practice more deceit, and tables that practice less. Let the girls keep some mystery and dignity! That's the only way we'll get a better clientele . . . men who are willing to spend really big money. Think about it, Ryan. We'll make a fortune. Dishonest girls, and honest tables."

"Sweet mother of God. Well, it had to happen. Success has stolen Katie's wits away. Honest tables! I won't listen to another word."

"You'd better listen, or—"

"You can't threaten to go next door now! There is no next door!"

"—or I'll start my own business, in competition. You know that empty lot across the street? I bought it. I know my way about now, and I could get backers. Are you listening?"

Ryan opened his mouth, snapped it closed, and nodded his head furiously, glaring all the while. Assured of his attention, Cat resumed her suggestions.

"Your girls could pretend different things. There are Virgin's Rooms everywhere around, yet I'll wager there's not a virgin on the whole of the Barbary Coast." By now, Cat knew the trick was done nightly with blood pellets—often three times nightly, by the same girl.

"If a clever girl can pretend she's a virgin," smiled Cat, thinking of Deirdre, "she can pretend other things, too. Can't you see it, Ryan? The Nun's Room. The French Room. The Room of the Seven Veils . . . that would be Salome, dancing."

"More likely someone called Gertrude," Ryan scoffed.

193

"Gertrude by day, Salome by night. Does it matter? The illusion, that's the thing. Men like a little mystery in a woman. Think how they wonder about me!"

"Maybe there's something to it at that," Ryan conceded, grudgingly, after a full hour of argument on the subject. "But honest tables! . . . I might as well scrap my eyepatch!"

"What a good idea," Cat said firmly. "We need a new name anyway. Something more dignified . . . something to appeal to judges, politicians, important men. House of Mystery, House of Illusion . . . no, House of Games. That's it: Ryan's House of Games. Games downstairs, and games upstairs. Very expensive games. The girls will need a lot of instruction, but believe me, Ryan, if they're properly coached, the men will play . . . and pay."

"And who, milady Katie, is going to coach those Devil's Acre doxies? Not you! Your table is the busiest in the house."

"No, not me," Cat said with an upward twist of the lips that told she knew certain secrets. "But I think I know just the person. . . ."

At first Ryan had ranted and raved; but that was when Deirdre was brought into the business. Ryan's House of Games, refurbished and renamed, had been a great and instant success. Ryan in charge of the poker tables and the various dice games; Cat in charge of the vingt-et-un and the roulette; Deirdre in charge of the girls.

But Ryan had kept the eyepatch, and because it was always good to let a man think he had won, Cat conceded that point, and even presented him with a new velvet patch. And, she had to admit, the patch did look very distinguished with his new evening clothes.

Yes, Cat had done very well for herself, and for Ryan, and for Jenny. Home soon became a big gingerbread mansion near Nob Hill, where the neighbors knew nothing of the respectable Mrs. Kirk's nightly occupation. There were carriages and cooks and nursemaids and clothes, and during the day there was always time for Jenny. There was the joy of seeing Jenny thrive with good food and fresh air, although she remained extra susceptible to the ills of childhood. But in the final analysis, the money had not helped. . . .

Cat shifted restlessly in the bed; why didn't Daniel get on with it? These past ten minutes, with his mouth and his hands caressing her breast as if he had all the time in the world, had seemed an age.

"This is very boring, Daniel. Can't we call a halt soon?"

"I'll stop anytime you say," he murmured against her flesh.

"I didn't mean *stop*. Just do it. Make love to me, and get it over with."

"I'll stop when you say, but I won't make love to you until you're ready. And you're not ready."

"I won't be ready tonight. But you've earned your reward, so . . ."

"Shall I stop? Yes or no?"

A deep sigh; sooner or later Daniel would have to give in to his man's body, and allow himself the natural conclusion.

"No, don't stop. But don't curb your own impulses, either. You must be very frustrated, and quite fed up with trying."

He laughed, softly. "I haven't even started trying," he said.

Jenny had just turned four when tragedy first struck. "Infantile paralysis, Mrs. Kirk," the doctor had said gravely, settling his stethoscope into its case, after listening to Jenny's labored breathing. It had been no free clinic this time, but the best medical practitioner money could buy.

"Poliomyelitis is the medical term. It's always bad at this time of year; I've seen several cases in the past week, and the summer's barely started. I'll call in a colleague for consultation, of course, a specialist. But I think he'll say the same thing."

The specialist did say the same thing. And then, the high temperatures, the ineffectual medicines, the long nights—Ryan's was forgotten for the time being—the watching, the waiting, the praying. Most of all the praying. And then the relief, the unspeakable relief.

"God willing, your daughter will live." The fever had broken; the worst was over. "She's a fighter like you, Mrs. Kirk. There's little danger of respiratory failure now . . . that's always the worry. You mustn't expect too much. But I reassure you, Mrs. Kirk—"

"I don't want reassurances, I want the truth."

"In these cases one can never . . ."

"The truth!"

The truth had been ugly; Jenny's motor nerves had been

195

seriously afflicted. "Your daughter will be a cripple, Mrs. Kirk. She'll need a wheelchair. She won't be able to use her legs; they'll be paralyzed, and far too deformed."

"If she can't move them, I'll move them for her!"

"There'll be no miracles, Mrs. Kirk. We don't usually manipulate the legs; we usually try to keep them as immobile as possible. But I suppose you can try."

Try. Jenny could not move her painfully twisted little legs, but Cat could—and did. Hour after hour; day after day; month after month. Up, bend, straighten, down, up, bend, straighten, down, and Jenny at first crying with pain of it all. There were no miracles, but at least the little muscles did not atrophy altogether; even the doctor was surprised.

And there were good times, too, and rewards. With her daughter Cat shared a kind of closeness she had felt for no other human being in her life. Then, as the pain diminished, Jenny could be distracted. Cat made a game of the endless passive exercises, and there were word games, too, and that brought other rewards, as the light and laughter returned to the gold-touched eyes that were so like Daniel's.

Games all day, and games all night. Evenings were once again spent at Ryan's. Business paid the bills, and could not be ignored forever. There was no time for fatigue; life was far too full.

"Please, Daniel, this has been going on for nearly an hour now. It must be close to midnight, and I'm *very* tired."

"Calling a halt?"

"No . . . wait! Don't roll away. Make love to me, but do it quickly. I don't mind, really."

"What? And admit failure? You don't know what a challenge you've handed me, Cathryn Kinross."

"You can help me tomorrow. Perhaps I'll be ready tomorrow. But *you're* ready now."

"I'm quite prepared to wait. And hell, a little willpower is good for the soul. Don't think about what I'm doing. Think about the motion of the train; some people say it's a wonderful aphrodisiac. The train, that's the thing. . . ."

She had rented a private car for that train trip a year ago May, so that the exercises could be continued en route. The train had taken the whole entourage to New York in comfort —Cat, and Jenny, and a nurse, and three bodyguards provided by Ryan, big, tough Barbary Coast bouncers all of them. In the new life she had built for herself, Cat seldom thought about Julian Gow, but on that trip discretion seemed the better part of valor.

The reason for such extraordinary precaution was very simple. The wealthy Mrs. Kirk was going east for one purpose only: To prove that Cathryn Kinross was not dead.

It was seven years since Cat had escaped Julian Gow's dubious protection; there was a move afoot to declare her deceased. A San Francisco lawyer had made discreet enquiries on Cat's behalf, and discovered that a distant cousin was claiming the Kinross estate—what estate there was; Kirklands had long since been sold to pay debts.

But the Peekskill and Tarrytown shares still remained. The move to declare Cat dead was being spearheaded by Gow's lawyers—not, Cat gathered, because of any desire to acquire the shares, but because of the long-empty seat on The Trunk's board of directors, a seat guaranteed to Jared Kinross's heirs. Loyalty to her grandfather dictated that the shares should not be lost. And so, as she wished to protect her San Francisco identity, she decided the only recourse was to claim her shares in person, in New York; and because the round trip would take three weeks or more, she decided to take Jenny with her.

On her first day in New York she paid a surprise visit, unaccompanied, to the lawyer who had handled her grandfather's affairs. To this startled man she issued instructions for the handling of the shares. The income was to be shared by Angus McBride and his daughter. The seat on The Trunk board was to be kept, for although Cat had no intentions of filling it, neither did she have intentions of signing a release for Julian Gow to use the directorship in any other way.

She also wrote a short will to provide for her daughter, something she had never done before under her real name. Ryan was named guardian. In the case of the railroad shares, which would only be a burden to Jenny, her beneficiary was to be the United States of America, a move calculated to put a government appointee on The Trunk's board in the event of her death. It was a small piece of revenge but a well-considered one, for it ensured her own safety. The very last thing Julian would want was a government watchdog on his board of directors!

A copy of the will, duly notarized, was also prepared, and

mailed to the Attorney General, a man Cat knew to be inimical to Julian Gow. She made sure the lawyer understood her intent, for she suspected it would be only a matter of time before Julian was apprised of her actions—as, indeed, he was, and with more dramatic results than Cathyrn Kinross, even in her most vengeful daydreams, could have foreseen. Will! The very word was to trigger in Gow a reaction out of all proportion to reason.

But at the moment, Cat did not know that. She left the lawyer's office breathing more easily, although caution dictated that care be exercised for the remainder of the New York visit, in case it took time for the news to filter through to Julian. A number of swift surprise visits to former acquaintances followed, in order that there be a number of people who could testify to her reappearance. Hannah she did not visit; she had decided to leave that emotion-charged reunion until the homeward trip.

The next few days were devoted to Jenny. New York was a changed city, and in showing it to her daughter Cat discovered for herself a place that was far removed from the hushed opulence of Fifth Avenue.

Change! It was the very life's blood of New York. In seven years the pulse of the city had quickened; New York had grown northward and skyward. On Wall Street, six-story buildings were being leveled to make way for structures ten and even eleven stories high. Electric lights were strung along some streets, and although San Francisco had electricity, too, Brush arc lamps, the lights in New York were different—Mr. Edison's invention—and they cast an eerie fairyland glow over the jostling crowds and prancing horses along Broadway and the Bowery. And there were other things strung along the streets. In places telephone wires nearly obscured the sky, yet seven years ago the telephone had not even been heard of. Never mind that the streets were still muddy and the pavements pitted; never mind that ownerless pigs rooted in some of the alleys; never mind that the "els"—there were several elevated steam railroads now—racketed around corners, showering sparks and causing horses to bolt. There were people chattering in a dozen languages, and the Fulton Fish Market, and windows in stores like Macy's, and any excuse for a parade. . . .

Jenny was enthralled. And when she grew uncomfortable in the wheelchair, there was always a pair of strong arms to carry her for a time. One of the bodyguards, big and rough-mannered though he was, had grown very fond of the little girl.

They were to leave New York immediately after Jenny's birthday. And for that, because a sixth birthday was a very special thing, and because three bodyguards should be more than enough to protect a small girl in a wheelchair, and because Jenny had been entranced by glimpses of the swooping steel cables magically spanning the East River, Cat had planned a very special treat.

The Brooklyn Bridge was to open on that day, almost as if the whole great wonderful structure had been planned as a very special birthday surprise for a small shiny-eyed six-year-old. There were to be streamers and flags and fireworks and a regimental band, and gun salutes, and all the men-of-war of the North Atlantic squadron anchored in the river, and President Arthur himself in attendance.

The birthday outing, so successful at first, had swiftly become a nightmare. First they had been jostled by a group of men—longshoremen, they looked to be—as big and rough as Ryan's bouncers. They had been somehow swept into the thick of a crowd they had tried to avoid. Above all other cries in that crush of humanity, Cat had heard her own child's suffocating screams, and although she had been no more than a few feet away she had been powerless to help. If even the big Barbary Coast bouncers had not been able to withstand that human tide, how must it have been for Jenny, frail six-year-old Jenny, whose bones would have broken so easily?

At the opening of the Brooklyn Bridge, twelve people had been trampled to death, and one of them had been little Jenny Kirk.

21

It was as well the train was traveling at full speed. The short rageful shriek that pierced the night did not penetrate beyond the tightly closed doors of Compartment 7; only Daniel Savage heard it.

"Stop that, Daniel, at once! I won't be kissed in that way!"

Cat jerked her body to a sitting position, freeing her thighs and for the first time trembling all over, but with outrage, not with desire. Her wandering consciousness had at last become aware of where Daniel's slow downward trail had led him, and the improper ministrations of his mouth seemed an affront to her innermost privacy. She had been subjected to many things in her life, but never this. Some women might like it, but she was damned if she'd put up with the indignity; it offended her sense of fastidiousness. And it had nothing—absolutely nothing—to do with conception.

She scrambled to her feet over the side of the bed, sacrificing some more of her dignity, and kicking Daniel's shoulder in the process.

"I've had enough now," she said tautly. "We'll stop for tonight."

"Oh, no you don't." Daniel's hands shackled her waist at once, twisting her back against his naked body. "That's the only twinge of feeling you've displayed in the last hour. You can't give up at the first sign of success."

"Yes, I can. I've had enough."

"Well, dammit, I'm not giving up . . . not now." His own long-bottled sexual needs only firmed Daniel's resolve; his grip tightened. "You can't have this all your own way. I was just beginning to enjoy myself, really enjoy myself."

"Enjoy yourself in the usual way, then!"

"This is usual enough for me." There was laughter in his eyes, and a mockery in his mouth that only annoyed Cat further.

"I won't let you do it, Daniel. It's vulgar."

"Get down on that bed," he ordered, pushing her. "Maybe vulgar is what you need."

His persistence and his use of superior physical strength infuriated her. She began to struggle, not in panic but out of stubbornness. With no further ado, Daniel thrust her down bodily on the rumpled silken sheets, and pinned her into place.

"You said you'd stop if I gave the word," she hissed. The short earlier scream had escaped her lips only because her undignified position had impinged so suddenly on her drifting consciousness; it was a mistake she would not repeat. But she had no intention of submitting so easily to a caress she considered humiliating.

"Then you should have given the word earlier. I'm not normally such a patient man, Cathryn Kinross, and there's a limit to my— Ouch! Damn you, you little hellion!"

And with that, he dragged her legs apart by brute force and hoisted them over his shoulders, ignoring the way she stiffened with outrage. With the palms of his hands he raised her buttocks upward. He lowered his head; his lips touched. Furious that he should so ignore her wishes, she squirmed and swore and tore at his hair, wrenching his head forcibly away from her thighs.

"It takes two to play this game, Daniel Savage! I *won't* cooperate!"

"By God, if you think you're going to stop me now! . . ."

And with that, his hands were no longer occupied in raising her hips to his lips. They shot upward, beneath the bend of her knees, and manacled her wrists. He squeezed until her fingers released their grip on his scalp; then he dragged her hands to her sides and pinned them there. Her heels drummed against his well-muscled back, but he did not free his hold. He watched with narrowed eyes until her ineffectual pounding came to a halt.

He laughed softly, triumphantly, his eyes alight with little golden fires. "Are you sure it takes two to play this game? I can do it perfectly well without your cooperation, even if it means tying you to the bed. And as for kicking, my back can stand a lot of punishment."

She lay panting, knowing he had won. It was best to accede. What Daniel wanted to do was an indignity, but she had submitted to other and worse indignities in her life. And

201

perhaps, when he realized the futility of his efforts, he would take her in the way she wanted—the only way she wanted.

"Give in, my sweet, and I'll free your wrists. I could proceed without your help, but I'd prefer not to cover your pretty body with bruises. Besides, I can think of better uses for my hands. Surrender?"

"Surrender," she sighed, and let her body, and her mind, go limp. He released her forearms at once, planted his hands on her breasts, and watched for a moment to make sure she continued to acquiesce.

"That's better," he murmured, at last lowering his mouth so that the words could be felt stirring the soft dark patch of her thighs. "That's all the cooperation I need. You don't have to do a thing but look at the ceiling. Or even better, watch. . . ."

Even before his mouth had returned to its task, her mind had receded. She watched with a curious detachment that left room for no emotion but one of faint distaste, wondering abstractedly how long it would take Daniel to realize that her surrender was no surrender at all. Nothing stirred her—not the hands that stroked her breasts and toyed with her nipples; not the expert lips, not the invading tongue.

The humiliation went on for a time; Daniel did not give up easily.

At long last, he raised his head and eased himself away from her thighs. For the past few minutes he had sensed no stirrings in her, not even the restless shifting of legs on his shoulders. By now, his own frustrations had become acute and painful; the throbbing in his groin unbearable. Cathryn Kinross's needs could obviously wait until tomorrow, but his could not.

"My turn now, sweetheart. I enjoyed every minute, but . . ."

Daniel's words trailed to a halt. Cathryn Kinross had gone to sleep.

He quelled the first instincts of annoyance, and the impulse to proceed. To awaken her now in order to slake his own desires was more of a concession of defeat than pride would allow. So, grimacing, he pulled a counterpane over her naked form, sat down beside her, and waited for the fires licking at his loins to die down—a painful process, but a necessary one.

And when his body was at last quiescent, he did not succumb at once to sleep. He sat on the side of the bed, comtemplating the slumbering woman. She looked younger, more defenseless now. Sleep softened and slackened the jaw, and the dark sweep of lashes shuttered those once-beautiful eyes that life seemed to have emptied of warmth and humanity. With the womanly ripeness of her breasts and the terrible secret they displayed hidden beneath the counterpane, she might have been seventeen again. Seventeen, a soft, clinging, passionate seventeen, and trembling in his arms . . .

Certainly, and to his own sure knowledge, nature had intended this to be a passionate woman. Yet she had been frigid for—how long? Probably since her first encounter with Gow. The reason for her frigidity was buried somewhere in that period of her life: undoubtedly in the night Gow had had her branded. It was a night she claimed, truthfully he believed, not to remember. Yet the memory must lie locked deep within her, and with it the passion that had bloomed so briefly, so long ago.

She had come to him for help, and he intended to help her, whether she really wanted help or not. Call it male pride, call it stubbornness, call it remembrance of things past—but for reasons buried deep in his own subconscious, he intended to rid her of her frigidity; he would blast her out of it if necessary.

And so, as the train sped through the night-shrouded vineyards of France toward the borders of Germany, he sat naked on the edge of the bed and studied Cathyrn Kinross in sleep. His expression was thoughtful, much as if he had been considering what manner and potency of explosive to use on a particularly difficult rock face.

22

"Tell me about what happened that night, Cat."

"Last night? I do apologize, Daniel. That was very rude of me. But surely now you realize *that* way won't work."

"No, not last night," Daniel said genially. They were seated in the privacy of the compartment, recovering from a breakfast almost as munificent as their dinner of last night had been meager. Daniel had drawn a cheroot from his pocket; it remained unlit. He was toying with a sulphur match, studying it.

"Then I can't think what night you mean," said Cat.

"The night Gow took you. You told me once you'd forgotten most of it."

Her little smile remained perfectly in place. "If I've forgotten, how do you expect me to describe it?"

"Just describe the parts you do remember," he persisted. "You don't have to talk about the more unpleasant aspects."

Her manner grew a shade cooler. "I couldn't even if I wanted to. Those parts are a total blank. But I don't want to talk about any of it."

"Have you ever enjoyed lovemaking since that night?"

"No."

"Then surely you must see it's important. If you remember, it may help. Describe the setting. You must recollect that much."

"I prefer not to."

"I hear Gow's private car is very opulent."

"I didn't say it was on a train."

"Yes, you did, Cathryn, years ago. I've forgotten none of what you told me. Guards on the next car forward, you said. That doesn't sound like Fifth Avenue."

"Nasty memories aren't very conducive to lovemaking! If you want to help me, you'll leave them alone."

"Soft lights and soft words don't work so very well either. His compartment or yours? Or did you share one?"

She shifted on the seat, and stared out the window at the ordered fields of Germany whizzing by. "Does it matter? It happened, that's all."

"Did you have your own compartment?" Daniel persisted.

"Yes. No. Yes and no. There was a wall that slid back. At first, I was alone."

"I take it the partition slid back, and he came through. What time of night did Gow come to you?"

"I don't remember."

"You must have some idea."

"No, I don't. I was sound asleep. He just . . . arrived."

Daniel considered that for a moment, rolling the match thoughtfully between his thumb and forefinger, and remembering the night he himself had appeared by Cat's bedside. Then, her panic had been very real. "That must have frightened you out of your wits. To have a man suddenly appear by your side, in the dark."

She remained silent, hostile, not correcting his error.

"You never did sleep well in those days. I imagine it must have been very late at night, perhaps in the early hours of the morning. On the first night you would have been lying awake, waiting for him. Did Gow always appear like that, like an apparition out of nowhere?"

"Are you determined to make me remember everything?"

"Was he naked?"

A fleeting vision of Julian returned, clogging her throat briefly. She didn't answer.

"Naked, then," concluded Daniel.

"No, he wasn't," she denied tightly. "So much for your guesses! I remember that much very clearly. I opened my eyes and he was standing there, wearing a silken robe. None of these memories are going to help me, so please—"

"Standing there," Daniel reflected, "and you saw him clearly. So the lights hadn't been extinguished. Perhaps he'd been watching you for a time. Were *you* naked?"

"I really can't remember," she said with an airiness that led Daniel to conclude she had been.

"Was Gow already aroused?"

"No!"

"But your fear aroused him at once," Daniel guessed. Gow enjoyed fear in his business rivals; why not in a woman? "Did you try to hide your fear?"

"Why do you have to know?" she cried. "It's not important now."

"That night is the key, Cathryn. If you could remember, it might help you."

"In that case I don't want to helped!"

"Then you've put me to a lot of trouble for nothing, haven't you? We can quit this experiment right now. Making love to a block of ice is not my idea of a grand experience."

Slowly Cat's hostility subsided, and she made a brief effort to cooperate. "I couldn't entirely hide my fear that first night. Later, I managed. So you see, you're wrong. Fear isn't the only thing Julian is interested in."

But other things might accomplish the same purpose, Daniel mused to himself. That was Gow's way in the business world: Rivals who could not be intimidated would be subjected to public humiliation. There had been fear that first night; had there been humiliation, too?

"When did you first become conscious of the guards?"

"I don't remember."

"Liar. You told me you didn't remember their arrival, that you only saw them afterward, when you were recovering. That means you and Gow were alone, at least until you blacked out. Do you remember him taking you?"

"No," she said, frosty once more.

"What was the last thing you remember?"

"Really, I—"

"Tell me," he ordered.

"Julian was angry."

"Then he got far enough to discover you weren't a virgin."

"I told you that long ago."

"So you did. Did you struggle that first time?"

"I don't remember."

"You told me once you never struggled."

"Then I suppose I didn't!" But in this she lied; she had struggled that first night. "Really, Daniel, it's a long long time ago, and very distasteful to think about. I'm totally blank on the subject."

"Not totally blank," he said agreeably, "just evasive. I'm going to ask some blunt questions and I want some blunt answers. You say Gow discovered you weren't a virgin; you say you didn't struggle. So there must be at least one moment you remember . . . the moment of penetration."

206

"I remember no such thing," she replied tautly.

"Then he didn't penetrate?"

"I don't remember! Now leave the subject alone, Daniel. This isn't helping, it's harming. If you really wanted to help you'd never mention that night again."

"Perhaps he found out with his hand," Daniel continued with a clinical detachment, as if he had not heard her. He studied the end of his unlit sulphur match as if it fascinated him. The unsmoked cheroot had long since been tucked back in his waistcoat pocket.

"His hand," he repeated thoughtfully. "It's a well-known fact that Gow wears a leather gauntlet on his hand. Yes, that would be very hurtful and humiliating."

"Keep your guesses to yourself, Daniel Savage," she said with a tight-lipped warning in her face. "He didn't wear a gauntlet in those days."

"Then he used his bare hand?"

"No, he—" Cat bit her lip; she had not planned to admit so much.

Daniel smiled grimly; he had tricked her into revealing one small detail. "So he was wearing the kid glove. I believe it was a kid glove in those days. Did you ever see him without the glove?"

Cat's eyes turned to the train window. She felt drained by Daniel's persistence, but at least now that he had left the topic of that terrible night, she felt she could answer with some equanimity. "No," she said in a low level voice. "He never removed the glove in front of anyone, although he changed it several times a day, in privacy. He never wore the same glove twice. He had gloves made by the hundred, just for his right hand. He had a thing about cleanliness."

"Was he that fastidious about everything?"

"Nearly everything."

"I can see," Daniel remarked conversationally, "that a man like that would prefer virgins. I suppose he considered you soiled goods. You told me once he didn't like to share."

Cat stared out the window without answering. Oh, God, did Daniel have to remember everything she had ever said?

"Did he strike you, Cat? Hurt you in any way when he

207

discovered the truth? Something must have turned your mind to a blank. Violence seems likely."

She closed her eyes, willing Daniel to stop. But perhaps he would not, without some small sop to his curiosity. "Yes, Julian struck me."

"Hard?"

"Yes, hard. He called me a whore and a slut. And that's all I can remember, all, all, all. . . ."

It was all she was going to tell, but it might be enough. There were some things he did not need to ask: The brand mark spoke for itself. With an expression that might have been satisfaction had it not been so grim, Daniel struck the match and watched it burn, paying close attention to the flame and the glowing tip it left behind.

Only at the last minute, as the flame licked at his very flesh, did he blow it out. Cat opened her eyes in time to see the final gesture.

"You almost went too far," she said, staring.

"Just practicing," smiled Daniel.

He made love to her in the early afternoon, lowering the blind to shut out prying eyes in the passing station house at Munich. Today, thank goodness, Daniel paid more attention to his own pleasures than to hers. To Cat's immense relief he did not importune her to repeat last night's unfortunate experiment. The lovemaking was swift and efficient: Last night had been an immense strain on Daniel's self-control.

Afterward, he would not let her rest for the afternoon, as she wished to do. He had made special arrangements for the chef de train, a picturesque man with gold-encrusted uniform and a white Van Dyke beard, to take them on an exhaustive and personally conducted tour of the train; and because Daniel had gone to considerable trouble to make the arrangement, Cat allowed herself to be coerced.

Dinner was an intimate meal brought to them at an early hour, in their own compartment, again by special arrangement. Daniel plied her with wine.

"A great ice-breaker," he noted with a small smile playing in the grooves of his face.

"Wine doesn't lower my defenses. It only makes me sleepy."

208

"Then you mustn't drink too much," Daniel agreed affably. But he picked up the bottle of Chablis and refilled her glass.

Brandy followed the early meal, and even before she undressed for the night, Cat had to hide a yawn or two. She was immensely relieved when Daniel extinguished the Pintsch gas lamps before he climbed in beside her. Perhaps, tonight, he would not notice if she dozed.

23

"Cathryn," said a low voice out of nowhere.

She woke immediately but without opening her eyes; the old habit had never died. Light shone through her lids. She knew at once where she was: There were the smells and sounds and the rhythmic creaking of the train to remind her. She knew where she was, but she knew something was different; every vibrating instinct told her so. There was a changed atmosphere in the compartment. The very air was charged with it.

She had gone to sleep naked in the dark beneath Daniel's hands, yet the light was on and Daniel no longer lay beside her. She opened her eyes slowly, not moving her head, refusing to give in to intuition.

"Daniel?" There was no answer. "Daniel?"

Perhaps he had left the compartment? He was not within view. She turned her head slowly, and realized with a small jolt that he was standing in silence close against the door. She could not see his face, only the tall outline, but she knew it was him. She recognized his dressing robe. And then, she heard the door click closed.

She quelled a fleeting sense of unease, and turned her head away from the shadowed figure. He must have just entered. He had only been down the corridor to the washrooms, after all. How silly she had been to think otherwise! And that first whispering of her own name must have been imagination.

"Daniel, really, you gave me such a start. Why didn't you answer? And why so many lights just to—"

And then the second jolt, a bigger one. He advanced into view, still silent. The gas light threw long shadows on the opposite wall. His face was cold and cruel, the face of a stranger. She stared for a moment, then forced a light laugh, and maneuvered herself into a sitting position on the edge of the bed.

"Daniel, this is ludicrous. Wearing a glove in the middle of the night! I can see exactly what you're trying to do, and you can't trick me into remem— Damn you, stop that!"

The gloved hand shoved her roughly back into a prone position on the bed, and she sprang back up immediately. She was not afraid now, she was angry. Reflexively her hands searched for a sheet to cover her nakedness; there was none.

Damn Daniel! How far did he intend to go with this cruel game? Well, she understood games, too, perhaps better than he did!

"It won't work, Daniel," she choked out in her rage. "I know now why you asked me all those questions. I know precisely what your moves will be. Well, this is one charade I won't play out. If you keep it up I'll scream. I'll—oh—"

She had not expected him to move so suddenly, so swiftly. He caught her by surprise, muffling the scream with his ungloved hand before she could voice it. He ignored the raking fingernails and the flailing legs, and forced her down on the bed, his long limbs pinning her into submission while he extracted a silken scarf from the pocket of his robe.

Cat knew he intended to gag her, and she was damned if she wanted to be gagged. She bit. And when that didn't stop him, she bit more deeply.

Daniel's curse and the swift sucking-in of his breath gave her only a moment's satisfaction. The bitter taste of blood was still on her tongue when he drove a handkerchief deep into her mouth, forcing the cries back in her throat. Then the silken scarf over that, biting into the edges of her mouth. He flung her on her stomach and kneeled on her spine while he tied it into place, ignoring her wild struggles.

But this isn't the way it happened, she wanted to scream ragefully, this isn't the way! Curse Daniel for his wretched plan! There had been no gag that time. There had been screams, screams, too many screams. . . .

But how could she tell him that, with the silk cutting into her mouth? And now he was tying her hands, too, lashing them together behind her back, so she could not fight him. The cord sliced into her wrists. Then the legs—those more loosely, around the ankle, to prevent kicking.

She struggled as much as she was capable of struggling, but his hands were too strong and his intent only too clear. Ungently, he rolled her trussed body over once more, and she tried to tell him with anger-sparkled eyes: *It didn't happen this way; it didn't!*

But Daniel was not, for the moment, looking at her. He was examining the deep teeth-marks that had broken the flesh on his hand. Hell, he thought; why hadn't he driven the gag into place while she still slept? He had considered doing so. He did not need Cat to tell him that his first moves were at fault. But tonight, a gag was a necessity. He was under no misapprehension as to Cat's vocal powers, or her ability to resist.

He had planned the whole evening quite thoroughly, starting with the lovemaking episode earlier in the day— that, to ensure that he would not become seriously aroused tonight, a thing that tended to interfere with judgment. And now, *this;* and the wound would have to be attended to. Human bites were like rat's bites: damn dangerous. He frowned fleetingly at Cat's bound and naked form, and decided she would have to wait. Who knows, the wait might increase her apprehension. At the moment she didn't look frightened at all, just furious. And if the situation had not been so fraught with perils—for himself as well as for her—he might have allowed himself a smile at the angry color flaming in her cheeks, and the silver daggers dancing in her eyes.

He procured the brandy bottle he and Cat had broken open after the evening meal; it was still more than half full. There was a porcelain bowl hidden in a concealed cupboard, for night emergencies, and this, too, he found. These, and matches, he placed on the middle of the floor, far from anything that could catch fire. And because even the smallest accident could turn a wooden-sided railway coach into a traveling inferno, he removed his robe, and the kid glove, too. He came down on his heels, naked, beside the brandy bottle, and set to work.

He gritted his teeth as the stinging liquid splashed over his bloodied hand. Holding the match to his own flesh took an even greater degree of willpower. But pain was preferable to blood poisoning, and he managed to repeat the feat three times. Cat remained, for the moment, ignored.

At last he pushed aside the brandy bottle, wrapped his hand in an improvised bandage, and rose to open a window, intending to air away the sickening smell of scorched flesh. He spared a glance at the trussed figure on the bed—and froze in his tracks.

Cat was not watching him, as he had expected. She was lying rigidly on her back, staring at the ceiling. Her eyes were

212

fixed and very wide open. He walked closer, and leaned over the bed. She seemed not to see him. In her wide gray eyes was terror, true terror.

And suddenly Daniel knew he had stumbled on a part of the truth. *Gow had had her branded first;* the rest had followed. The smell of burning flesh must have triggered her memory. He watched her for some moments, certain that she was now reliving that night, and the look on his face firmed to one of grim resolve. He stooped down to the floor, retrieved the recently discarded glove, and donned it.

The glove crawled over her breasts, her hips, her thighs. She was too terrified to move. She wanted not to see the ceiling but it was there, telling her what was demanded of her this night, what was expected of her in all the nights to come.

A hand separated her ankles that had been clamped together. Inexorably the hand drew her legs apart, spreading her in readiness, widening the space between her rigid limbs. The fingers too cold to be human flesh slid toward her thighs. They reached their goal, and probed.

The hand was snatched away at once. It yanked her to a sitting position, and she saw his expression, inhuman in its vengefulness.

"Whore! Slut!"

She tried to scream as the hand slashed across her face, her throat, her breasts, the stinging force of it connecting again and again, driving her back against the pillow. . . .

Daniel stood still and tall beside the bed, his mouth taut and his eyes compassionate as he watched Cat's wild flinching and writhing. Certainly, it was clear that she had fought Gow every inch of the way. It had not been necessary to strike her to bring back her tortured recollections of the towering rage to which she had once been subjected. Two simple words had done the trick—words which Cat herself had suggested this morning. Would he be able to bring back all of her forgotten past by using the power of suggestion? To do so would mean more guesswork as to the probable happenings of that hellish night. When had the guards arrived? Now?

She rolled away, insane with the need to escape, and fell on the floor. Unvoiced screams tore at her throat. Why could she not scream? Why could she not fight? She had screamed then, she had fought then, she had clawed then like a cornered wild creature. And that had brought the guards. . . .

They did not return her to the bed. She tried to struggle up, fighting, fighting, fighting, gasping and crying, but she was too well pinioned to the floor. The lights were bright, the scene too horrible for description. The tall figure loomed above her like an angel of vengeance.

"You've been with a man. Whore! Slut! You come to me unclean! I'll teach you to wear the mark of another man! *Brand her!*"

No, she tried to scream as she saw the white-hot brand descending. *No!* Her body cringed, and then arched violently upward as the pain, the terrible terrible pain, seared through her breast and scorched through her body and her brain. And the smell, that sickly unforgettable smell . . .

She fainted.

Daniel stood grimly watching the naked figure on the floor—the shrinking, the arching, and then the sudden stillness. She had not really fainted, but he could imagine that she was reenacting such a thing. He could only guess what had happened after the branding, and to recreate that scene entailed more risks than tracing a mark on her breast with his fingertip. How submissive would she be after reliving the shock of that dreadful experience? How submissive had she been that night?

It had to be chanced; the gag would have to be removed. But he must try to ensure her silence in any way he could.

"Scream again and feel my wrath on the other breast! Silence, you strumpet! *Silence!*"

The guards dragged her to her knees. She could breathe again, but she dared not scream. Her head hung low over her breast. Half-blinded with sweat and with the hair that streamed into her eyes, she could see only the ankles of the man, the strong legs planted apart.

"If I can't use you one way I'll use you another! Serve me like the whore you are!"

She had seen the ceiling and knew what was wanted. Nausea and pain wrenched through her limbs. She was too weak to fight anymore, even to save what remained of herself. She was in deep shock, icy-cold despite the drenching of sweat that trickled between her breasts. There was nothing now but pain and fear. Fear and pain. Pain and fear. Ever and ever amen.

"Raise your head! Obey!"

She was too weak not to obey, too sick and too weak to obey. And then, a hurtful hand twisted into her scalp, seizing a hank of hair and dragging her head upward.

And as she had done once before, she bit.

Coming down on his haunches beside her, Daniel grimaced at the heel of his hand that Cat had just assaulted for the second time with her teeth. Thank God for the bandage that had protected it this time! He had guessed earlier, from the suddenness and ferocity with which she had used those sharp little weapons, that she must have used them that night, too—and how.

He gathered Cat's limp naked form into his arms. She flinched from his touch as though he had administered blows, not embraces; from the shuddering of her body beneath his hands Daniel was sure the blows had been real enough on that nightmare night so long ago. She continued to whimper despite the soft, soothing murmurs with which he tried to comfort her.

"No," she sobbed, "no . . . no . . . no . . ."

And what had happened next? Gow demanded submission and subservience, and she had not given it. Gow was aroused and wrathful. Would he have repeated that particular experiment? How *could* he have repeated it, after an encounter with Cat's teeth?

Yet the rape must have proceeded; Gow never conceded defeat. How would a man so fastidious have taken Cat? A man who would not even wear the same glove twice? Yet he *must* have taken her; he had kept her as his mistress for seven months. But how? How? *How?*

Daniel could make only one guess; and that guess soured his mouth and seared every sick cell of his imagination. It was time to stop playing this morbid game.

The hands that laid her on the bed were gentler than she remembered. There was no struggle, no strength, no will left in her now. Her eyes were closed, the lids flagging with fatigue and despair. Her body was a vessel in which only pain remained. She let the hands do as they wished.

"I *know* what must have happened, Cathryn," choked out

215

a man's low voice. Incongruously, it vibrated with some deep, wrenching emotion that echoed a part of the agony in her own soul. "It's over now. It won't happen again."

"No . . . no . . . not again. . . ." Her words were scarcely audible, and interspersed with other sounds, little animal sounds uttered deep in her throat. She could feel the prickling and the heat of the man's chest upon her breasts. A muscled arm encircled her, holding her closely, the grip soft even in its strength. Was this gentleness only another kind of torture, testing the mind the better to destroy it?

"Sweetheart, it's over," he murmured urgently, his warm breath stirring against her mouth. Why was he stroking her hair so tenderly? She tried to turn her face, to stifle her anguish into the pillow. But his insistent fingers followed, twisting into her tangled mane, allowing no escape—forcing her face to remain turned so that her pain and her abject terror and her humiliation could be seen. Julian wanted to witness that; he always wanted to witness that.

"Don't you understand, darling? This time it's happening only in your mind." The voice seemed very far away—low, urgent, oddly fierce and tender all at once. An arm tightened briefly, achingly, around her waist. "It's all done with now. Those things that happened, they won't happen again."

Why did he torture her so with his insidious lies? "Ohgod-ohgodohgodohgod," she whimpered. "Let me . . . die . . . I want to . . . die. . . ."

"Come back, Cathryn, *come back*. It's me, darling . . . Daniel. *Daniel.*" Gently he cradled her shivering and unre-sisting form, and cupped her fevered face, and bathed her closed eyelids in tiny, soft, imperative kisses, as if each one of them might cleanse away the horror that was in her soul, and the sickness that was in his. "I won't let him hurt you any-more. He'll never hurt you again. Come back, sweetheart, it's all over. This is Daniel, and I love you. I love you. *I love you.*"

In the dark tunnel of her mind it was a tiny light, too far to reach. She moaned her weakness, her inability to reach that light.

"Daniel . . ." She crawled toward the light; she almost reached it; she failed.

"Daniel. Daniel. Not Julian. *I'm not Julian.*"

"Not Julian . . ."

Suddenly on his lips he tasted the salt of tears. He held her

216

close, willing her back from the purgatory she had been reliving in her mind. "Cat, Cat, I won't let him touch you. Julian will never touch you again."

"Not . . . Julian . . ."

"It never was Julian, darling. Not tonight."

"Never . . . was . . . Julian . . ." She shuddered convulsively. Sobs made a staccato of her anguished words, and tears began to flow in earnest. "Never . . . was . . . Julian . . . he used to . . . watch . . . he liked . . . to watch . . . but . . ."

Daniel's heart turned to a cold clutching fist. "Watch," he repeated numbly, seizing her jaw so she could not turn her tear-streaked face away.

"It was . . . the guards . . . Julian . . . gave me . . . to . . . to the guards."

The damburst had come; Cat's secret was out.

24

She cried for hours in the circle of Daniel's arms. There were tears for the twisted time with Gow, and tears for those unshed on her grandfather's grave, and tears for Jenny, and tears for the wasteland of her life. There were tears of grief and tears of relief and tears for the things that had been. And there were some tears, too, for the things that would never be.

She cried until there were no more tears. And because they were the tears of the years, the tears unwept for a decade, it was nearly dawn before she slept, exhausted, in Daniel's close and undemanding embrace.

Only when he had assured himself she could not be readily awakened did he ease himself away from her clinging arms. Exhaustion stamped his face; his eyes were haggard and haunted. He had no conviction that he had been right in invoking Cat's remembrance of things past. *Someday you'll go too far,* she had warned yesterday morning, and perhaps her words had been prophetic. She had cried all night, and none of his murmured endearments had seemed to comfort her at all.

Daniel raised the blind a few inches. During the night Austria had been put behind them. Although Hungary was a part of the same empire, there was a different feeling about the countryside, a faintly Oriental flavor in the way the dawn streaked the sky.

With a frown he lowered the blind again, and dressed quickly. The gas lights were still burning, as they had been all night. He spent some brief moments with a pencil and paper before extinguishing the lights; then he slipped soundlessly into the corridor.

The conductor was dozing, fully uniformed, in his small room at the end of the sleeping car. He was awake and alert on the instant at Daniel's arrival: The Compagnie Internationale des Wagons-Lits et des Grands Express Européens demanded a high degree of competence in its employees. The conductor snapped to attention as he answered Daniel's question.

"Budapest?" He consulted his watch. It was accurate to the minute, but still set to Paris time, as were all watches on the Orient Express. The route traversed too many countries, and to follow their haphazard time zones—often different from one city to the next—would have created unspeakable confusion.

"Budapest in forty minutes, monsieur. You were afraid that I would have failed to wake you? But I would not have forgotten. An employee of the Compagnie never forgets. Perhaps you wish some coffee? A croissant, before you leave the train?"

"No, Georges, that won't be necessary."

Daniel had never planned to go to Constantinople; Cat had only assumed it. He had indeed been hired in the service of the Ottoman Sultan, and had even been given the honorary rank of *bey* in order to expedite his work. But his goal was not, and never had been, the Bosporus.

In 1884, for all its vaunted luxuries, the Orient Express still subjected its passengers to some discomforts, and not least of these was the final fifteen hours of the trip, which was not by train at all. It was a voyage by ship, over an often-stormy Black Sea, between the Bulgarian port of Varna and the promised goal of Constantinople. Only one thing prevented a more direct overland route via the network of European railroads further to the south, and that was a gap in connections. From Nish in Yugoslavia to the Turkish railhead at Tatar Pazardzhik, through a stretch of wild, mountainous, bandit-infested country, no railroad had yet been built.

The Turkish-ruled Balkans were Daniel's goal, and to reach them, via Nish, meant changing trains in Budapest.

"It's all right, Georges, I've decided not to get off at Budapest after all." In his hand Daniel held the letter he had written this morning, and peeping out from beneath the letter was a franc note of very large denomination. He spoke in rapid-fire French, but it was the franc note that carried his message. "You can arrange to extend my ticket as far as Varna, can't you, Georges?"

Georges, discreet as only a Frenchman and an employee of the famous Compagnie could be, did not let his eyes stray to the half-concealed note. What this traveler asked would be difficult, very difficult indeed. For the money, he would not consider doing it. But this man had connections. He was a frequent traveler on the line, and it was said he had even been invited on the inaugural run, although he had declined the honor.

"It will be hard; the train is fully booked. But for you, Monsieur Savage, I will try. As as you are acquainted with the chef de train, perhaps . . ."

"It's very important, Georges. The course of love is not always smooth. You're a man of the world, Georges, you must understand." Daniel paused delicately, knowing Georges was bound to see Cat's tear-swollen face sometime today. "The lady needs some . . . consoling."

"It will be arranged," Georges said more positively. He was a romantic at heart.

"We wish all meals to be brought to the compartment, all day. Other than that, no interruptions."

"I understand, monsieur."

"Splendid, Georges. I knew I could count on you. And one more thing—" Daniel shifted the things in his hand perceptibly, but not blatantly, to show that the first franc note concealed another, equally large. "There'll be a man waiting for me in the station at Pest: a Turk. Undoubtedly he'll be in fez and official dress, and accompanied by several underlings. He's an emissary of the Ottoman Sultan. Zoltan Pasha is the name."

"And you wish me to deliver to him the note? It shall be done."

"I wish you to convince him that I'm not on this train at all," Daniel said dryly. "Zoltan Pasha speaks several languages; you won't have trouble communicating. Tell him I gave you the letter back in Paris, that there was a mix-up in reservations."

That much was partly true, Daniel reflected wryly. Zoltan Pasha would froth at the mouth, but he could wait. He would have to wait.

"Perhaps this . . . Zoltan Pasha . . . will wonder that you have not telegraphed," Georges pointed out, with indisputable logic.

"Let him wonder. I'll make some excuse when I finally connect with him. Tell him I'll be in touch as soon as I make alternative travel arrangements, which may take a day or two yet. Didn't you say, Georges, that the Orient Express is fully booked?"

220

"Toujours," said Georges, his face still straight but more conspiratorial now. He loved intrigue, and the Orient Express seldom failed to provide it. "Seldom, on any run, an empty place! A man might wait for weeks!"

"Then even better, tell him I'm traveling an alternate route; that I may come some roundabout way. Be convincing, Georges, I don't want him trying to reach me on this train."

"Have no fear, monsieur," assured Georges, accepting the letter and surreptitiously shifting the franc notes so that they could not be seen at all. With total delicacy and with the very pads of his fingertips, he determined that there were not only two of the notes, but three, possibly four. For the first time he smiled, a discreet smile befitting an employee of the Compagnie. "Have no fear at all! Zoltan Pasha will be convinced."

A short time later the train sliced slowly between the twin hills of Buda, and the atmosphere of the Orient grew very strong. The legacy of Tatar, Mongol, and Turk invader lay over the town in the fortress that dominated one hill, and in the neobaroque palace that crowned the other. Bridge timbers groaned as the train crossed the Danube, putting Buda behind and entering the more modern town of Pest.

The train stopped at Pest for only eight minutes, but it was more than sufficient for Georges to accomplish his mission. Zoltan Pasha was not hard to locate. Although the small group of aides were all in civilian dress, a concession to their presence in a foreign country, Zoltan Pasha himself wore fez and military decorations. On the nearly empty platform, his uniform and his authoritative bulk could not be missed.

Georges must have been convincing, for after the delivery of the note and a short conversation, Zoltan Pasha and his party turned to leave the station house at once.

All the same, Daniel reflected as he resettled the window blind in his compartment to shut out the tiny crack of light, it might take some doing, a few days from now, to cool Turkish tempers. Zoltan Pasha had looked convinced; but he had also looked very, very angry.

When Cat awoke it was mid-afternoon, and Daniel was perched on a low stool at the bedside.

"How are you feeling?"

"Fine." She sat up in bed, not troubling to cover herself with the sheet, or tidy her straggling hair. She smiled. Almost at once tears sprang to her eyes—slow tears now, but they slid down cheeks still puffy from last night's weeping. She tried to stem them, unsuccessfully, wiping away one only to find it replaced by another. "I must look a fright."

"You've never looked more beautiful," Daniel said gravely, and for him it was true.

"I don't know what's the matter with me. I don't usually do this. Oh—" She pressed fingertips to her eyelids, staunching the flow. "I can't seem to stop."

"Let it go, Cat. You've got some catching up to do. How many years since you've cried?"

"I don't know." She dashed away another tear, and with female unpredictability laughed through it. "I've always hated weak weepy f-females, and now I'm one of them."

"Perhaps it's time. Nature demands it now and then. And it's not a sign of weakness. Even strong men weep sometimes, or they should. You've kept too much locked inside, and for too long."

There was a moment of silence during which Cat looked away, and a brief anguish crossed her face. The tears stopped at once.

"I won't let you lock it in again, Cathryn," Daniel said quietly. "I know everything now. I know you were never Gow's mistress, and it takes very little imagination to realize what those seven months must have been like." He paused, and when she did not answer, he persisted: "You do remember last night, don't you?"

Her eyes still evaded his. "Yes, I remember," she said in a low voice. "It seemed very real. I should be aching in every limb, but I'm not, so I suppose most of it was in my imagination."

"Most of it," Daniel agreed, "but not everything." He held up his bandaged hand and laughed ruefully, with a lightness he did not feel. "This triggered it. From there I made guesses, all the wrong guesses as it turned out, but they accomplished the right purpose."

"I'm sorry I bit you. I—"

"I'm not," Daniel said fervently, with a remembered gratitude for the warning it had given him. Better a hand than what one of the guards had suffered.

The tumbling-out of Cat's secret had solved so many inexplicable mysteries.

It explained why the multiple rape had been able to continue, despite Cat's teeth.

It explained why Gow, a man obsessed with virginity, a man fastidious to the point of sickness, a man who conceded nothing and forgave nothing, had taken a woman who was no virgin at all—and kept her for seven full months. Daniel had guessed yesterday that such a man would not settle for used goods; that he must have had his pleasure of Cat in some abnormal way. That line of reasoning had been right to a point, but even in his wildest imaginings he had not guessed how perverted Gow's pleasures—the pleasures of a voyeur and a jaded man—had been.

And above all, the revelations of last night detailed with appalling clarity the reasons for Cat's frigidity, the depth and the height and the formidableness of it. She was not a whole woman; how could she be? The miracle was that she had survived with any part of her mind intact at all.

Cat dressed. She was controlled now, no longer on the verge of tears. Meals were brought. Daniel learned more, gradually, as the miles and the hours sped by. They talked; they sat in silence at times watching the scenery; they talked again, sometimes of other things but occasionally of her life with Gow. Guardedly at first, then more easily as relief loosened her tongue, she began to reveal other details that fleshed out the nightmare skeleton in Daniel's mind.

"After the first night he had the guards place a chair for him, beside my bed. One of the guards would shake me by the shoulder, and he'd be there, watching, a little smile on his lips as he told them exactly what to do. . . . He made them turn my face so he could see. That's what he wanted to see . . . my face."

Fear, thought Daniel. Gow had wanted to see her fear and her pain.

"I thought if I could learn to show none of the emotions Julian wanted to see, he would tire of watching. But he didn't, at least not for several months. It was something new for him, and for some perverted reason I think he liked it better than . . . than what he had done with his other mistresses."

"Then he hadn't done that sort of thing before. The watching."

"No. I know that, because of things I overheard. But he did

223

like to humiliate his other mistresses, in other ways. I think he really hated women; it was as if he always had to prove that he was better in some way. Oh, I suppose it sounds silly, but I always had the feeling that once he had been very afraid of some woman. And that's why he liked women to show fear."

"And when you learned not to show it? Did he still want to watch your face?" And when she was silent for a short time, Daniel added quietly: "Tell me everything, Cathryn. It's better. Then you can start putting it all behind you."

Cat's eyes remained trained on a distant vista beyond the moving window. "Yes, he still wanted to see my face, my expression," she replied levelly, betraying emotion only in the tight clasp of her laced fingers. "Even though I tried to show nothing, I think he enjoyed my humiliation."

Perhaps yesterday's guesses had not been so very wrong after all. A bitter bile rose in Daniel's throat. "And how did Gow plan to ensure your silence, when he was through with you?"

"I don't know. I used to wonder about that. An accident, perhaps? Possibly he knew I could never testify in court to what had happened. To have to describe those things in public . . .' She shuddered, visibly. "I'd never have had the courage to do it. Do you understand now why I was afraid Julian would look for me, so long ago? Why I'm afraid to face him, even now?"

"Yet you said you weren't afraid of him anymore. That he's known your whereabouts for over a year."

Cat explained, briefly, the measure she had taken to ensure her own safety. "Ever since, he's been sending messages through his lawyers; he wants me to rewrite that will. But what can he do? I've simply ignored the messages. In fact, I told the lawyers I'd deed my grandfather's railroad to the government outright, if Julian didn't stop bothering me. No, Julian can't do anything to hurt me now . . . but I still wouldn't have the courage to face him in person. I'm not like you, Daniel. I'm a coward."

"A *coward*—" There was an uneven timbre to Daniel's voice. What kind of courage must it have taken for a woman—no, a young girl not yet twenty—to hold her head high through those terrible months with Gow?

They were in Rumania now; Hungary was only a memory. Budapest had long since given way to Temesvar, Temesvar to Orsova, Orsova to Turnu-Severin. From the foothills of the

Transylvanian Alps they sliced toward the Carpathians and the Miroch range of the Balkans that loomed ahead. By nightfall the train was testing the shaky trestles along the narrow defiles of the Iron Gates, for such was the name of the pass that breeched these mountains. And now, the Danube was sighted once more, at a spectacular plunge beneath the precarious tracks.

When Cat retired along the corridor to wash for the night, Daniel ordered that both berths be prepared, a directive that caused Georges, romantic that he was, to conclude that the lovers' quarrel had not yet been resolved.

On the contrary, several things had been resolved, in Daniel's mind at least. He had made grim resolutions today, but thawing a frigid woman was not one of them. That the breakthrough had helped Cat in some important way he did by now sense; but at the same time he was sickened by his own success. Male pride had been replaced by shame for the whole male sex; by compassion; and by a great humility that forbade any further effort.

He had rid Cathryn Kinross of some of her defenses; let her keep the rest.

Had Daniel been given to interpreting the symbols of nature, and had he been paying more attention to the train's breeching of the Iron Gates at sunset, he might have taken heart. For here, as it had not been at Budapest, the Danube was wild, torrential, tempestuous, magnificent—perhaps a presage of things to come.

25

When Daniel returned to the compartment, Cat had already retired into a berth—the upper. She had not pulled the curtains, and he could see she had donned a nightgown, a plain white lawn garment of no particularly erotic design.

"I intended to sleep up there, Cathryn. That's a man's place."

"I prefer it this way. Do you mind?"

So: She too had given up. Not very surprising, after all. He treated the matter lightly, not wishing to discuss her change of heart. "Usurping male prerogatives again, Cat? Shall I extinguish the lights?"

"Yes, please."

He did so before slipping out of his clothes, and sliding into the berth below.

"Daniel?" came her voice in the dark, a few moments later.

"Yes?"

"I want to thank you for some things . . . things you did years ago."

"You don't need to thank me for anything."

"Yes, I do." Perhaps, for more than he would ever know, but how could she thank him now, for giving her Jenny? "That money you provided back then, for one thing. It didn't come from my grandfather. I found that out last year, when I saw grandpapa's lawyer. Grandpapa could have given you nothing. He left almost nothing but debts."

"Oh, hell, forget it. It wasn't much."

"It was enough. It supported me until I was able to get a job."

There was a short span of silence during which Daniel felt relieved that she did not offer to repay the sum.

"And I want to thank you for the past few days," she went on.

"That doesn't need mentioning, either."

"Yes, it does." Time lapsed: enough time that Daniel had believed Cat to be asleep when her low voice sounded again.

"I've given up on the thing that brought me here, Daniel. I realize now it was wrong of me, and not at all necessary. I can live a full life without it. You've given me that much, Daniel, and I ask you to remember it, because I don't want you to feel you've failed me in any way. No matter what."

"Do you want to talk some more? I could light the lamps."

"No. No, I don't want to talk." A small sigh sounded in the darkness, competing with the steady creak and groan of the train. "Good night, Daniel."

He lay awake for a time, staring into the black space above him, and thinking not of Cat, but of Julian Gow. Of how he would kill Julian Gow. Of the degree of slowness and cruelty he would use. Of how he would watch Gow's face as Gow had once watched Cathryn's.

The exercise took an hour, and exorcized none of the hatreds that lay like a tapeworm feeding in his gut. But the previous night had been sleepless, and so in time he and his hatreds coiled together in the dark, and dreamed.

If Daniel was certain in his resolutions, Cat was uncertain in hers. She, too, lay awake. Tonight, for the first time in years, she felt unsure of her own needs and wants, and yet, paradoxically, she felt oddly at peace with the world.

What she had said to Daniel was true: She had given up all thoughts of the thing that had brought her here. A child no longer seemed a goal in itself. That was vicarious living, and the long night's reckoning just past had forced her to recognize that it was her own life she wanted to live, not someone else's. She had existed for and through her daughter for years, and she regretted no part of it; but it was a sad commentary on herself that Jenny's death had left such emptiness behind —not a person at all, but a shell of a person. Was there anything left inside that shell?

It would be farfetched to say that sexual drives kept Cat awake. Such drives had been too long repressed to surface easily. But tonight there was a very real need to reach out and touch some warm and feeling person, to find out if she was more than a shell. Daniel. She needed Daniel.

It was an asexual craving, a need for closeness and for the bodily contact from which she had recoiled for so many years.

She did not wish him to make love to her: That would be begging for failure. Nor did she believe that Daniel would be keen to repeat his experiments. Undoubtedly he felt compassion, but compassion and passion were poor bedmates. And what man would desire a woman who had been handled in such ways?

She waited until the even cadence of his breathing told her he was well and truly asleep, and then she lowered herself quietly from the upper berth, and slid in beside him.

He muttered and stirred, and threw one muscular arm across her body. The arm tightened involuntarily around her waist, but he did not wake. Contented, Cat curled her spine into the curve of his body, and started to drift, drift, drift, feeling warm and safe in a way she had not felt since childhood.

It stole into her subconscious when she was in the never-never land between waking and dreaming. There was a warmth in Daniel's loins, a stirring and growing, very gradual at first. He moved in no other way, and neither did she. At first she thought he was still asleep—that this, too, was involuntary, as the arm had been.

But when the length of him burgeoned into full hardness, and surged against her with unmistakable suddenness, she knew he was not asleep.

"I'm awake, Daniel," she whispered, wanting to satisfy that need in him, not for her own fulfillment but out of a sudden gratitude that made her heart feel as if it had swollen to bursting point.

His answer came, but not in words. Briefly, his arm re-staked its claim to her waist until she nestled even closer into the spoon of his body. Satisfied that she would remain, he freed her waist and used his hand to smooth her hair against the pillow. The gesture was not erotic, and soon his hand grew still.

No part of him touched her breasts or her thighs or her ears or her throat; those sensitive areas of the body were left to make discoveries for themselves.

It was a very long time before his lips, closed and dry and demanding nothing, touched the shoulder of her nightgown. It was the lightest of contacts, not even a kiss. "Go to sleep, sweetheart," he murmured, evidently determined to put his arousal to no use. But by then, every expectant nerve ending in her body forbade sleep.

The heat had begun in her thighs—slow, stealing, taking her by surprise. By now her breasts tingled with aliveness, the nipples of them erect and trembling, waiting for the touch that never came, except in her imagination. The nape of her neck prickled where his warm breath had stirred her hair, but where his lips had not. Through the lawn nightgown her skin felt sensitized in every inch that lay pressed against the flesh and blood of him. And every one of those crisp chest hairs had ignited its own small fire along her spine.

The suspense and the sexual excitement had become unbearable, and it took only Daniel's murmured words to bring the culmination. With a sob she turned and clung, seeking his mouth with a wildness and a desperation that took Daniel totally by surprise.

Even before he had time to deepen his kiss or free her from the nightgown, she was shuddering and arching and crying out. The climax was sudden, shattering, violent—all the more surprising because he had done nothing to encourage it; and all the more explosive because it had been so long contained.

The ice had not been cracked, it had not been melted—it had been blasted out of existence.

"Oh, Daniel, Daniel, Daniel—" And at once she was clinging and floating and flying and laughing and crying, and the tears were those of pure release and joy.

He rained little kisses on her lids and on her hair, and gloried in the arms wound around his neck, and in the yielding silk of her, and in her joy, and in her laughter and in her tears, and in the release of her body from its long winter.

"You should have told me you wanted to make love, sweetheart. Were you trying to put my willpower to the test? Good God, my readiness must have been obvious enough for this past half hour. Why didn't you ask?"

"I thought you mightn't want to now, not really. That is—"

His throat, and his embrace, constricted fiercely. And because her meaning was so very clear to him, and because he could express himself in no better way at this moment, he kissed her again. The kiss was hard at first but it grew soft, and without ending it, Daniel stripped her gently of her nightdress, and began to worship her flesh with his hands. He had not thought to prepare her body for his entry, but no urging was needed now. Eager to rediscover what had bloomed so briefly and been lost so young, she trembled with readiness. Her legs sprang apart to receive him almost before his fingers found the secret touchstone of her womanhood.

"Oh, Daniel, I didn't know, I'd forgotten. That feels so wonderful . . . like velvet when you move inside me. I think I want you inside me always."

"I want it too, love," he murmured into the ear where his tongue had been toying for his own pleasure, as much as for hers. "But it can't be arranged. I can't hold back much longer."

"You don't have to hold back at all," she exulted with a surge of wild excitement to know that he, like she, had been trying to prolong the joining, and the journey to forgetfulness.

He drove in swiftly and surely, pacing his own moment of release to the exquisite shiverings that told him she had reached the pinnacle of hers.

They slept after that, locked in each other's arms, only to wake before dawn and make love again. Cat had a good deal of catching up to do. She reveled in the way Daniel kissed her breasts and stroked her thighs and fine-tuned her flesh like an instrument, drawing from her time and again the chords of response that had been too long unheard.

Daniel himself had no such needs, but perhaps that was best. His lack of haste gave him great patience and stamina. And if he could not fully share every moment of quivering awareness, he enjoyed the exercising of his new and seemingly extraordinary powers over the reawakened woman in his arms.

At last, as a new day gathered its forces beyond the window blind, he dampened a cloth and set himself to sponging her body.

"Why are we stopping?" she murmured contentedly, lassitude at last stealing through her limbs.

"You may not have to stop, but I do." He bent over to plant a light kiss in the wake of the dampened cloth. "There are limits to a man's endurance, my lovely wild-woman. I couldn't possibly make love to you again."

"*Never* again?" she teased, lacing her fingers around his neck.

"Not until—" But Daniel stopped. There would be no tonight; Varna would be reached before nightfall. By now the Turks had very likely learned that he had boarded in Paris, and there were reckonings to face. The cloth hovered, not completing its task.

Cat appeared not to notice Daniel's sudden thoughtfulness. She stretched lazily, with a sensual awareness of self that was a new and joyous discovery all its own. "I couldn't do another thing, even if you could. I'm worn out. Isn't it wonderful! No, I meant why is the *train* stopping."

"Bucharest. You can sleep for a hour now, but no more. We have to change trains at Giurgiu." Ahead lay another inconvenience in the route of the Orient Express. The train was about to confront the winding, wandering Danube once again; and this time, the river presented an obstacle that could not be overcome without a change of train. Between the border towns of Giurgiu in Rumania and Ruschuk in Bulgaria, there was no bridge, only a ferry boat.

"What a nuisance!" declared Cat. "But after that, I plan to rest all day. One more night, Daniel! I'm not going to let you sleep a wink between Varna and Constantinople."

Daniel frowned, knowing there was no easy way to break the news. "I'll have to leave you at Varna, Cathryn. My ticket only goes that far, and frankly I'm supposed to be somewhere else. I should have left the train twenty-four hours ago, at Budapest. I'll have to turn around and go right back."

Cat's face fell, but only briefly. "I'll go back with you," she said decisively, sitting up. "I didn't want to go to Constantinople anyway. Twenty-four *hours*, Daniel."

"It can't be done, Cat," he said firmly. "I managed to get return space on this train, but only for one, and I pulled every possible string to get that. There's no other way, except wretched local trains, and that can take days. Hours of waiting at every border, and likely no sleeping car at all. And there is some urgency involved. No doubt there'll be a stream of politely furious messages waiting for me at Varna. You see, Cat, I was supposed to meet someone in Budapest."

A woman, of course, thought Cat. All defenses slid back into order easily; the habits of years had not been shed in a night. "Well, then, I concede." She smiled brightly. "One can't argue with train schedules and such! Anyway, I doubt I could move a single muscle for days. Good heavens, I'm hungry as a horse! Do you think Georges would—"

"Cathryn," he interrupted fiercely. "Stop it. I know you too well. The only thing waiting for me in Budapest is a bunch

of restless Turkish soldiers who want to get on with plans for a tricky mountain railway. If I'd followed instructions, I'd be in the Balkans right now, and for all of the next month. And there'd be no woman with me."

All at once she was clinging to him, defenses and pride put aside. "Then let me come with you, Daniel. Please. I'll be no trouble. I'll make no demands."

"It's no place for a woman, love." He kissed her nose gently, lightly, not encouraging her impetuosity. "It's rough country, bandit country. That's why the military escort. Oh, I'll be safe enough, but—"

"If it's safe for you, then it's safe for me." She drew back from him; this needed thinking. Was Daniel exercising caution lest she become an unwanted burden in his life? Had she thrown herself at him too eagerly? Did he think her demands unreasonable?

"And after the Balkans I have another little job to do." *A very big job to do.* "It's a job I must do by myself; I can't have a woman along. So you see, Cat, it's impossible. I have commitments, and I can't burden myself with any woman."

"A month," she said carefully, "one month, Daniel. I can't spare more time myself. I've built another life, and I want to go back to that life."

"Back to what life?" His eyes narrowed, probing her guarded expression. "You said you were divorced."

There was a brief skipping of beat as she considered her answer. "That's true, Daniel, but perhaps I can save my marriage even yet. You can imagine why it failed, and now that things have changed, my husband may be willing to take me back."

Daniel's mouth tightened. But with Gow to be dealt with, how could he ask her to share his future? "Do you love him?"

"Yes, I do. He's very—"

"What's his name?"

"Ryan." The answer came in an eyeblink; it was the first name that occurred to her. "He's been very patient, considering everything. And I do love him; it was for Ryan's sake that I wanted to put an end to my . . . problem. I came to you in desperation, when everything else had failed."

Daniel brooded for a moment, and then stood up and started to pull on his clothes. His back was turned for a time, and Cat watched him, feeling a tightness in her throat that

232

told her she wanted to cry again. How easy it had been to fall in love with Daniel this time. How easy, and how wonderful, and how terrible.

At last he turned to face her again, his expression totally enigmatic. "I think it's time you told me the whole story of these past years . . . *Mrs. Ryan.*"

Cat's smile was bland and unrevealing; her mask was well in place. "Ryan's his Christian name. And I'm telling you no more." She propped her elbows on bent knees and studied Daniel, wondering what could be read in the expressionlessness of his face.

"If you loved him so very much you wouldn't be thinking about a month with me."

This was a trickier observation to handle; Cat studied her toes for a moment before coping with it. "It's a different kind of loving, but that doesn't mean it's any less real. My marriage was never successful physically. Perhaps it never will be. There have been so many tries, so many failures, so much futility. After last night I feel confident with you. But with Ryan? I don't know. I can't bear to fail again, at least not yet. Not yet . . ."

She looked up, her eyes calm. "One month, Daniel. One month to make up for those failures, those frozen years. One month of feeling and healing and . . . Is it too much to ask?"

He thought about the past and about the present, and most of all he thought about the future, and the day of reckoning with Gow. "No," he said slowly, "it's not too much to ask."

"Oh, Daniel!" She left the bed and threw her arms around his neck on the instant. "I promise you won't regret it!"

He detached her fingers and kissed them thoroughly, one by one. "But not in the Balkans; I won't take you there. I'm taking a month off, and to hell with the Turks. I'll send them a telegram telling them they have to wait. We're getting off the Orient Express altogether."

She laughed happily, delighted at his impulsiveness. "Permanently?"

"Permanently for a month." He smiled down at her, his eyes warm. "Why should I go on to Varna only to find a lot of angry messages, and perhaps an importunate Turk or two? No, my love, I'm going to sweep you off this train, and we're going to vanish into nowhere. Now get dressed."

Cat practically danced across the compartment to her own

233

clothes, shedding years with every singing step. "One month!" she lilted. "One whole month, and the rest of the world can wait!"

"Indeed they can," agreed Daniel. But behind her back, his eyes glinted dangerously. He was not thinking of the Turks; he was thinking of Julian Gow.

26

A necklace of memories, strung on a string of beautiful days, wonderful days, falling-in-love days. Had any woman ever fallen in love so deeply, or been loved so well? It was an arrogance to believe it, but in the fine flush of love and discovery she believed it all the same—deliriously, exquisitely, arrogantly.

Did it matter that Daniel did not include her in his future? He told her he loved her, and that was all that mattered for now.

For a whole month Cathryn Kinross fell in love. They left the train in Giurgiu, and crossed the Danube into the wild lands of the Bulgar. She fell in love on the little ferry boat crossing the Danube. She fell in love in the public diligence that transported them toward the River Yantra; and when one of the leather underslingings that supported the body of the carriage broke, and for lack of a bed they had to sit up all night in a town with the odd name of Dve-Mogili, she did not even care, for she fell in love in Dve-Mogili.

She fell in love along the River Yantra; and on a well-remembered night in Veliko Turnovo and another in Adrianople and three or four memorable nights between; and on a sun-baked street in an unremembered town in Thrace; and in Svilengrad; and in a big featherbed in the tiny Turkish village of Cherkes Keui, where Daniel described a trail of fiery kisses to her navel.

"Don't stop there," she murmured to his invading head, closing her eyes at the premonitions of ecstasy that were already shuddering down to her thighs.

"I wasn't planning to," Daniel informed her with as much of his mouth as he could spare.. "This is just a way station. A very pretty little way station, and it's worth a short stop. . . ."

This time, when he worked his way down to his destination, there was no holding back. She arched and gasped at that shock-wave moment when she felt his lips descend.

And with his fingers encroaching at her nipples, he taught her very thoroughly what he had not been able to teach her once before. She grew wild and wanton beneath the inroads of his tongue; she twisted her fingers in his hair to shackle him far too well to her thighs. And at the ending, when it was very very right, she cried out wildly and . . .

Or was that in Sarköy, where the same thing happened all over again, and the innkeeper's wife arrived in a black shroud of a veil to see if anything was wrong?

They had gone to Sarköy impetuously, to catch a steamer to somewhere. In Sarköy they argued about whether to go to Corinth or Crete or Athens, and then caught the very next steamer that came through the Sea of Marmara, which was on its way to Nice. Why not? They had time for a few days in France.

Before they embarked for Nice, proof arrived that Cat's indiscretions had so far resulted in no pregnancy; she realized on reflection that she must have miscalculated. And so for the several days of sea voyage through the Aegean and the Ionian and the Mediterranean, they slept like spoons in a cramped stateroom with a grimy porthole, and did not make love at all.

She fell in love in Nice. And she fell out of love, temporarily and tempestuously, on the one night they spent in rival Monte-Carlo. Although there were finishing touches still to come, the new casino was already very grand with its wedding-cake exterior and its palms and its marble foyer and its bird-cage elevator. The salons and gaming rooms had been in operation for some years, and their stunning Belle Epoque decor had begun to draw a glittering crowd of Russian nobility and impressively titled English peers.

Daniel was holding the counters, and after Cat lost too much at roulette—there had been a run on the red—he would not give her more.

"It's not a gift, it's a loan!" She looked daggers at him, and cursed herself, too, that she had been too easily persuaded to put her own money into safekeeping, back at the hotel. "I told you, I'll pay you back later!"

"Not a chance. You've played enough."

"Damn you!" she blazed, when the argument had been going on for too long. "Damn you all to hell!"

Daniel only looked amused, despite the shocked glances from bystanders. "I'll win for both of us, love," he said mildly. "Just watch."

"No, just *you* watch!" And she turned to outrageous flirting, until a total stranger placed a counter for her, on the black. She won, and kept winning, first at roulette, then at chemin de fer, in the Salon Privé. Daniel lost.

"Quite the cardsharp," he said afterward, narrowing his eyes at the winnings she had thrown triumphantly on the hotel bed. The stakes in the Salon Privé had been high.

"I always win," she gloated.

"Then you should stop playing." He came up behind her, and started to loosen the pinnings of her coiffure. "You know what they say. Lucky in cards!"

She slapped his fingers away, vigorously. How dare he be so arrogant as to think he could touch her tonight! "I don't give a damn whether I'm lucky in love or not! After refusing to stake me, you can just . . . just go to *hell!*"

"Tsk, tsk. Very loose language for a lady. Do you know what a sensation you created tonight?"

"Bastard!"

"Unoriginal, too."

"Son of a Bull Run Alley whore!"

All at once, Daniel caught her by the waist and flung her on top of the bed, scattering the evening's ill-gotten gains. He pushed one shoulder of her dress down far enough to expose the nipple of her unmarked breast. "For a female," he said, hovering above her bared flesh, "you have a shocking vocabulary. And to think I've been avoiding bad language because I thought you were a lady."

"I am!"

"Not! Very definitely not! Now take back what you said about my lineage." He bent and seized the nipple, and spoke through the edges of his teeth. "Take it back now!"

"I will not! Ouch!" Her knee aimed for his groin; he scissored away in time.

"Put me out of commission, will you?" His teeth tightened.

"Ouch! I'll never give in! Bastard! Born in a Clay Street stewpot! Ouch! Your father was an Iodoform Alley pimp! Ouch! Your grandfather was—"

He at once released her nipple, and rolled away from the bed.

"Ha! I won again," she smirked.

"The hell you did." Slowly, and with an exasperated expression, he removed his formal evening clothes, and hung them over a chair. Then he came down on the bed beside her, and seized her shoulders in a grip of steel. "We've hardly started the battle yet."

"Using a man's weapons!" she cried angrily, for she thought he intended to force her into the lovemaking she did not want.

"No! Using yours. I'll teach you who's master of this game, my foul-mouthed bitch. Now just lie there and listen. I'm going to pay you back in kind, Miss Cathryn Kinross, and my gutter language is more complete than yours—"

And so began the Battle of the Words. When it was over, because she had surrendered somewhere along the way, he said admiringly: "You may not be a lady, but you're a woman, all woman! That was very exciting . . . you flinging the words right back in my face. Why did you concede?"

"Because I wanted you to win." She basked in the warmth of his gaze, and melted inside. "Oh, Daniel, I *am* lucky in love. So very lucky . . ."

With more than a week to spare they found berth on a small Italian steamer heading back toward the Bosporus. Daniel had secured reservations to Budapest on a new run of the Orient Express, this time via Constantinople. In a second telegram to his Turkish employers, he confirmed the date of his proposed arrival.

She fell in love on that last night in France, and told him so by twisting down suddenly in bed, and taking him in a way that Daniel would never have asked of her, knowing of her warped life with Gow. Afterward, he pulled her upward in the bed and held her fiercely close. For a time he could not trust himself to speak.

"This is where you belong, Cathryn," he said at last in a choked unnatural voice. "Here in my arms. You didn't have to do that."

"I didn't have to, I wanted to," she said in a breathless flush of love for his consideration. "I had to know if it made a difference."

Again a poignant pause, during which he bathed her eyelids in tender explosive kisses. "And did it?"

"Yes," she said simply, "because . . . because it's a part of *you*. I love you, Daniel, every part of you . . . the taste of you and the touch of you and the texture of you, and most of all I love you you you. . . ."

And then, the next morning, when they woke early in their hotel room: "A little longer, Daniel. A few more days. Send

238

the Turks another message, tell them you'll be another week."

"No, love, I can't. And it's not just the Turks, it's the thing I have to do afterward."

"What thing?" she insisted for the hundredth time. "You've been so mysterious about it. Is that job dangerous, too?"

He tried to distract her. "No more mysterious than that other life *you* plan to go back to. Why won't you tell me about that?"

But Cat would not be sidetracked. "If it's not dangerous, why won't you let me go with you, then? You asked me once to be your woman, Daniel, your mistress."

"I wouldn't ask it now."

"You know I don't care what people think."

"No, no, no, sweetheart." Gently but firmly he dislodged her fingers; and there was a return of the brooding expression that always came over his face when she mentioned such things. "I told you, I can't take a woman along on that job. It's simply not allowed."

"Then after that job's over," she suggested, putting pride aside and fighting for the man she loved, with the desperation of a woman with only a few more days of happiness left.

"You know I won't plan that far into the future," Daniel said curtly, wondering how brutal he would have to be. How could he ask Cat to wait for him—to marry him? There were too many risks in killing Gow. How could he involve Cat in an uncertain future that might mean death—or even worse, incarceration? Time enough to think of the future when he knew what that future held.

"I'll go when you tire of me. I won't ask more."

"Dammit, no! You know I want no commitments in my life." He sounded vicious now, and his lips were drawn back in something like a snarl. "I'm damned if I'll let myself be saddled with responsibilities of any kind."

"I didn't ask you to be responsible for me! You took on responsibility for one woman, and I know you don't want to do it again. Do you think I'm angling for marriage? Well, I'm not. If I wanted marriage I'd go back to Ryan and try to make that work. Ryan would make a second attempt, I know it! And he's the kind of man a woman wants for a *husband!*"

"Then perhaps that's what you'd better do," Daniel said in a peremptory voice.

She sat up and dropped her feet over the edge of the bed, reaching for her wrapper. When she turned back to face him, decently covered now, her face was totally calm in a way that made Daniel's heart contract.

"It would have been kinder if you'd just admitted the truth. If you're tired of me now, I don't see any particular point in going on with this charade. I told you I'd go quietly, and I will. I see no point in going to Constantinople; I may as well head directly for Calais, by train."

"Cat!" He scrambled over the side of the bed, and seized her shoulders. "We still have a week."

She made no effort to shake him away, but she remained apart—untouchable. "I don't think I can stand another week of being told how much you love me," she said.

"Cat, I *do*, I love you to distraction . . . oh, Christ. Things may work out better than I expect, and if they do I'll come looking for you. Just let me know where to find you."

"I'll think about it," she said coldly.

"And if your marriage hasn't jelled by then . . . well, perhaps someday we can talk about the future."

"I don't care about the future! I care about now. And I won't stay where I'm not wanted. Not for one—"

He stopped her mouth with a kiss whose ferocity expressed some of his feelings. At last he drew his lips away. "Can't you tell that I want you? Come to the Balkans with me, darling. It'll be a rough life but it won't really be dangerous, not with a military escort. If you can put up with that kind of hand-to-mouth existence . . ."

"Yes, oh yes!" she cried happily, soaring with joy, and throwing herself against him. "I promise you won't regret it!"

"I already do," he muttered against her mouth, and then put her aside in order to get dressed.

"I won't let you out of it now. I won't be a bit of trouble. You'll see!"

"Yes, you'll be trouble, The soldiers will be sick with envy, for one thing. Besides, bustles and horses don't mix."

"Then I'll buy some boys' clothes in Constantinople. We have almost two days there, don't we? I hate bustles anyway. And if necessary, I'll cut my hair so the soldiers think I'm a boy."

"The hell you will!"

"Are you afraid they'll think you're in love with a boy?" she teased, singing inside.

"You'd never pass for one, even if you bound your breasts. And I wouldn't let you do that either. Do you know how to ride?"

"I'll learn," she said determinedly. "In one day, if I have to."

"And I do believe you would! But for the first week you'll be so damn sore you'll hardly be able to sit down, let alone do anything else with that prettily turned bottom of yours. Most nights I'll be too damn tired to do anything anyway. The trip will hardly be worth your while. *Now* will you change your mind?"

"No, I won't. I don't care if we don't make love all month! Those nights we do nothing . . . I enjoy them too, just curling in your arms. You're right, that's where I belong. Oh, Daniel. I love you so. . . ."

And because the springtime of her life was spent, and because the autumn bore no thinking about, this summer blooming was all the more intense. She loved with the kinds of loving that for most women would be spread over many seasons. She loved with the tumbling, trembling ardor of her arrested adolescence; she loved with the tumultuous passion of a woman for the only man who has ever awakened her; she loved with the indiscretion of a mistress and the abandon of a whore; she loved with the mature unswerving love of a woman for the man whose child she has borne. She loved him poignantly for the past and selfishly for the present and desperately for the future.

Another month of falling in love? It was all she asked.

27

"Oh, Daniel, isn't it beautiful?"

The exotic spires and fantastic rooftops of Constantinople gleamed before them in the sun as the steamship threaded its slow way through the fishing boats and ferries anchored in the narrows of the Golden Horn. Here, where the Bosporus created a narrow dividing line between Europe and Asia, silhouettes strange to the eye pierced the cloudless sky—the cupola and the clustered shapes of the Basilica of St. Sophia, the huge dome and the six slender minarets of the Blue Mosque.

"What's that?" Cat asked, pointing to a vista of domed roofs closer to the quayside where they were about to dock.

"The Kapali Carsi," Daniel noted absentmindedly. "The covered bazaar. It's a whole city of shops, thousands of merchants all together. You can buy anything there."

"That's where I'll buy my boys' clothes, then."

"No, you won't," objected Daniel. "I'll do the shopping. Westerners aren't always welcome here, and unveiled women can't move freely in public, except in the Pera . . . the quarter set aside for foreigners. It might be different if we were official guests of the Sultan, but we're not. Not unless I let them know I'm here."

"I won't closet myself in a French hotel, in a Turkish city," declared Cat, and made up her mind to do exactly as she pleased. "Other tourists are coming here all the time now. It can't be so very dangerous."

"Ah, but they go on organized tours. You can do that too. There's lots to see: the Roman hippodrome, the Topkapi . . ."

His voice trailed off as his attention was suddenly riveted by something on the quayside.

"What is it?" asked Cat, noting the direction of his gaze.

"Zoltan Pasha," muttered Daniel, frowning. The face last sighted in the station at Pest was this time wreathed in polite smiles, but the Turkish general was recognizable enough, with his military bearing and his glittering of gold braid. This time, the attendant soldiers also wore uniform. "Damn. I wonder how he knew to expect us in Constantinople."

"It wouldn't be so hard. You did send a telegram from Nice, informing them when you'd be arriving in Budapest," Cat reminded him. "No doubt they checked into reservations between those points. I imagine they've been anxious ever since you failed to turn up before. Perhaps they thought you would let them down again."

"I suppose that's it." Daniel brooded. "Well, there's no help for it now. There goes our last few days of privacy."

"Don't be such a pessimist, darling! And don't look so angry! *Now* we'll be official guests of the Sultan. With a military escort I imagine we can go anywhere we please. Oh, Daniel, it's going to be a *wonderful* two days!"

Daniel pushed aside twinges of unease. He smiled down at her, drinking in the sight of her as if to fix it forever in his mind.

These past weeks had changed Cathryn Kinross, and in no subtle way. The pride was still there in the graceful tilt of throat, in the confident carriage. But now, her body was vibrant with promise fulfilled. She wore the self-awareness of her own sensuality like a badge. It was there in the assured swing of her limbs, in the curve of her lips, in the suppleness of spine, in the shine of eyes. Luminous with happiness, she had at last become what nature had intended her to be—a truly beautiful woman.

And because he knew he had put that radiance in her face, Daniel's throat tightened. "I suppose you're right," he said. "But I'd rather have had you to myself."

The Sultan Abdu-l-Hamid, Emperor of Powerful Emperors, Sole Arbiter of the World's Destiny, Refuge of Sovereigns, Distributor of Crowns to the Kings of the World, and Shadow of Allah upon the Earth, was a sickly and frightened man. Everything was a plot: the shadows gliding behind fretwork screens; the hush of the noiseless Oriental carpets; the sumptuous untouched meals that might have known a poisoner's hand.

It was as well that his great palace of Yildiz Kiosk had many scores of bedrooms; he seldom dared to use the same one twice.

For what dire fates might not lurk when a man has deposed

243

his own brother? When he has ordered the murders of his grand vizier, his ministers, his generals, his officials, his courtiers, and even some of his own family? When he has massacred Armenians, and plans to massacre more? When the menacing Russian bear, despite its victory in the Russo-Turkish War, still snaps at the territories of the tottering Osmanli empire? When Walachia and Moldavia have been lost, and Serbia and Montenegro, and Bosnia and Herce-govina too? When the Bulgars are eyeing Eastern Rumelia? When there are brigands in Thrace and bandits in the Balkans, and a great restlessness in the vassal state of Egypt? When even the Mahdi, rising like a sandstorm in the faraway deserts of the Sudan, shouts a battle-cry not against Egypt, but against the Turk?

Abdu-l-Hamid, known to the world as Abdul the Damned, ruler of the vast and foundering Ottoman Empire, lived in constant terror of his life. And so did those around him.

It was for this reason that the smiles on Zoltan Pasha's face, as he watched the docking of the steamship in the Golden Horn, were not at all feigned. True, he had been angry once; but in a month his orders concerning this American infidel had changed. If the Savage Bey had not turned up today, as spies had promised . . . why, a man's life could be forfeited for less.

"Savage Bey?" Zoltan Pasha straightened his broad chest to full military dignity as his soldiers presented arms. He ignored the woman for the moment, although there were definite orders concerning her, too. But a woman should know her place, and this one evidently did not. Her recent carryings-on, as reported by the spies, shocked Zoltan Pasha to his proper Muslim core.

"Allah be with you, Savage Bey, and with your issue! Greetings in the name of the Emperor of Powerful Emperors, Sole Arbiter of the World's Destiny, the Shadow of Allah upon the Earth . . ."

"Oily? Really, Daniel. Personally I thought Zoltan Pasha was very attentive, and very polite. He didn't seem at all angry about your failure to turn up before."

"Mmm," said Daniel.

"You couldn't have asked for a friendlier welcome." Cat did a small pirouette, her long skirts brushing against a priceless Bokhara. "And such a splendid suite! Why, I heard someone say it had been decorated for the Sultan himself."

After a brief tour of Constantinople by calèche, the Turkish escort had brought them to the palatial new Grand Hotel of Pera. At a word from Zoltan Pasha, the simple rooms reserved in advance had been changed to a luxurious royal suite, and the French management had sent gifts of fruit and flowers.

"It may have been done to Abdul Hamid's taste, but he'd never use it. He's terrified to leave his palace. Fact is, he's afraid of his own shadow."

"He can't be that terrified or he wouldn't have asked to see you tomorrow. An audience with the Sultan! I wish I could come along too."

"A woman? Not a chance. Besides, if you were with me, you wouldn't get your other wish . . . a trip to the covered market. So you see it's worked out very well. You'll be safe with Zoltan Pasha and his soldiers." Daniel advanced toward her, eyes gleaming wickedly, and a mock menace in his steady pace. He forced Cat to back up toward the piles of silken cushions in one corner of the room. "And that's where I want you . . . safe. I wouldn't dream of letting Abdul Hamid clap eyes upon you, in case he took a notion to sample Western wares."

"Are you so sure I'll be safe with Zoltan Pasha?" she teased. "He might want a new decoration for his harem. I could see him undressing me with his eyes, and he's very impressive, with all that gold braid. Quite handsome, too."

Daniel gave her a light shove, and Cat pretended to lose balance. She landed in down-soft mounds of cushion, laughing happily as he fell over her body and pretended to growl tigerishly at her throat. She started to undress him at once.

"Zoltan Pasha," she murmured, pushing aside Daniel's shirt and starting to work at the fastenings of his trousers, "has four wives and twenty-two concubines. He seemed very surprised when I asked if they were satisfied with their lot. Very satisfied indeed, he said! I wonder what kind of *lot* he meant."

"You she-devil." Daniel faked a savage bite on her chin. "You're trying to make me jealous . . . and I am. I'm insane with jealousy."

"And for very good reason." She stroked him with her

pliant fingers, then clasped and began the slow movements that she knew would drive him to a frenzy. "I like it when you're jealous; it seems to produce the right effect. Twenty-six women! I wonder if Zoltan Pasha could handle twenty-seven."

"Not if one of them was you." Daniel started to work impatiently at the fastenings of her dress.

"I think I'd look well in a harem. Henna on my hands, and those wonderful loose trousers, all floaty and transparent."

"Buy some tomorrow at the market, " Daniel ordered. "Blast this western garb! Female fastenings and whalebone stays!" Losing patience, he flung her skirts upward and loosened the undergarments from her limbs.

"So impetuous today? Jealousy *does* have the right effect."

"It's the thought of you dressed as you should be . . . in damn near nothing." With his fingers he probed deeply, sending a soaring ecstasy through her thighs. He nuzzled his mouth into her throat. "If I had you in a harem I'd rip the clothes from your limbs."

"I'm sure Zoltan Pasha wouldn't let a few fastenings stop him," came the breathless reply.

"What do you want me to do, tear them from your limbs?"

"I thought you'd never ask," she murmured, closing her eyes and arching against his hand.

And to the sounds of rending hooks and eyes, the Western dress came off. For a time no more was heard but the soft sounds of love, and the whisper of cushioned silk.

"Make sure it's very transparent," Daniel muttered the next morning, for Cat's ears alone. Zoltan Pasha and his contingent had appeared at the door of the suite bright and early for the promised expedition; they stood nearby now, waiting while good-byes were said. Despite last night's playful words Daniel had no fears for Cat's safety. Despot though he was, Abdul Hamid was already under considerable international pressure because of his failure to send a Turkish army to the Sudan, still a nominal part of the Ottoman empire. To arouse questions about the safety of visitors to Constantinople would only bring more criticism from the Western powers. As the official representative of the Turkish government, Zoltan Pasha would take good care of his charge.

"I can hardly wait until tonight," Cat whispered to Daniel,

and stood on tiptoe for one last fleeting kiss—an indecently public gesture that offended Zoltan Pasha's sense of propriety in no small degree, although the disapproval was well masked by his stoical expression.

"And buy some kohl for your eyes," Daniel added sotto voce, before he relinquished Cat into the care of the Turkish soldiers.

He himself would have preferred to join the shopping expedition, too; but he was to be picked up at the hotel little more than half an hour from now, and taken by guard of honor to the palace. Damn Abdul Hamid and that blasted audience! What interest could the Sultan possibly have in a foreign employee, and in a small railroad to be built in some farflung province of his crumbling empire? But in the Ottoman Empire one did not disregard the imperial wishes, and so half an hour later Daniel was waiting, as ordered, outside the front door of the hotel.

"Effendi?"

Daniel turned to the voice, only to see that this was certainly no envoy of the Sultan. The man was not in uniform. He wore the habiliments of a street beggar: the once-white shirt tattered and baggy, the whiskers untidy, the feet bare, the loose folds of his trousers not concealing the bow of his legs.

Thinking the man wanted a handout, Daniel shook his head firmly, and indicated that he did not speak Turkish.

"Effendi, you come," said the beggar urgently, in passable English. He started to pluck at Daniel's sleeve. "Come at once."

"I think you must have the wrong man," Daniel said. He was not too surprised that the man spoke some English. This past year, since the inauguration of the Orient Express, had brought many wealthy Europeans to Constantinople.

"I come for you, Savage Effendi," came the urgent reply. The man darted a frightened and furtive glance along the street, in the direction that Cat and Zoltan Pasha had taken half an hour before. "Come! The lady cries for you to help."

Daniel was instantly on the alert, every warning bell jangling. "The lady? Why?" He seized the man roughly by the shoulders. "What's happened? Isn't she at the bazaar?"

"No, effendi." The man cringed beneath the fingers digging deeply into his flesh. "Be merciful, effendi! I come to help! To tell you the things I have heard!"

"Then tell me, dammit!"

"A poor man like myself might starve, if he is not shaken to death! To think I came so far to help, and at such great risk to myself! With no reward but the hands of an infidel to shake the wits from my head! Now I have forgotten. For the love of Allah, effendi—"

With a curse Daniel released the man, and drew some coins from his pocket. "Now, for God's sake, talk."

"Allah be praised that he should bring my memory back!" The beggar grinned a broken-toothed smile. "It was the woman. I heard her cry your name, as they dragged her through the portals."

"What portals? *Where?*"

"Into the courtyards of an important man."

"What man?"

"How can a poor beggar like me remember all? My wits are still in flight from the violence of your hands."

Some more silver appeared magically from Daniel's pocket. "Whose house? *Where is she?*"

"I could find the place, Savage effendi, but of the name of the man I am not sure. Perhaps, if Allah smiles upon me once more, I could take you to the very spot."

"Then take me—" Daniel halted suddenly. Amongst all the danger signals sounding in his brain, there was one that told him this might be a trap of some kind. But why? He had no enemies in Constantinople. "How did you know where to find me?" he asked suddenly.

"The lady screamed your name. She spoke the tongue of an infidel. The infidels of other lands always stay at this hotel. The man in the door of the hotel pointed at you, when I spoke your name."

Once again, Daniel seized the man by the scruff of the neck. "You're lying. She had an escort of soldiers; no one would have dared attack her."

"But, effendi, it was the soldiers who seized her!" The mendicant's teeth chattered at Daniel's renewed violence. "Be m-merciful, effendi, do not destroy a poor man who only thought to make the price of a night's lodging from what he had overheard!"

Daniel's brain raced. If the man told the truth, there'd be

no help from the authorities, not even from the Sultan's guard. To become involved with Turkish officialdom at all might only delay getting help to Cat, wherever she might be.

And if the beggar lied, then it must be a trap. A ruse to draw him into a dark alley and rob him, perhaps?

"Take me to where she is, and you can have all my money." Daniel spilled a variety of copper and silver coins from his pocket, and thrust them into the beggar's outstretched hands. The man's liquid Turkish eyes rounded at the sight of so much manna from heaven. "Allah is merciful!" he cried. "The day brings many riches!"

Daniel pulled the linings of his pockets right out, so that the man could see no more remained inside. He breathed a silent prayer of thanks that his passport and other papers of importance had been left, yesterday, at the hotel desk.

"Now you've got everything, every damn piastre. You can keep it, all of it, if you tell me what really happened. The truth and the whole truth! *Is the lady in danger or not?*"

Joyfully, the beggar thrust the cache of money into his shirt, where it joined the sum that had been given to him a short time ago by another man. "But I have told the truth, effendi, as Allah is my witness. The woman is in trouble. Come, Savage Bey, and I take you to her. Hurry!"

And so, with one grim glance at the small procession of Cherkees cavalry and Imperial Guards that was even now rounding a distant corner along the sun-baked street, Daniel took off after the beckoning beggar. In the conflicting tattoo of danger warnings, it did not occur to him to question that the man should have addressed him as Savage Bey. It was a title indicated in no way by the Western clothes he wore—and certainly one that Cathryn Kinross would never have thought to use.

At a jog, he followed the beggar's fleet and naked feet along the broad sun-dazzled avenue, dodging Europeans as well as Turks, Kurds, Celts, and Greeks. Then, as the quarter of the foreigners was put behind, the streets became more Byzantine. Ruins of ancient moated and turreted walls were passed, and now only Turkish and Arabic were heard. In the doorways of primitive whitewashed inns, old men sat gossiping and sucking at waterpipes. Peasant women wearing pantaloons clutched their veils and their water jugs more closely, and backed into shadows as Daniel loped by.

And then, as the beggar turned into a narrow crooked alley where houses hunched together in dismal poverty, a new alarm sounded. No rich man's house lay in this dirty lane. . . .

He turned, but it was too late; a blinding pain exploded in his neck.

28

The trip to the covered bazaar had been a picturesque confusion of sights and sounds and colors and smells. How delightful it had been! Artisans beating brass and forging fine ornaments; mounds of shimmering silks; rows and rows of little shops where a person might haggle, over tea, about the price of a carpet or a piece of pottery decorated in Kufic characters, a pair of curly-toed slippers or a sugary confection of hazelnut and honey.

But with Zoltan Pasha at her side there had been no haggling at all. A curt nod from the Turkish general seemed to determine the price, as merchants cowed either by his rank or by the attendant soldiers seemed to halve their demands.

Cat's shopping trip had been a wonderful success, untouched by any incident of the type described to Daniel. For her, the first twinges of alarm did not begin until a small party of grave-faced officials met the returning expedition in the lobby of the Grand Hotel of Pera. Zoltan Pasha listened while explanations proceeded in Turkish, and when he turned to Cat his face was stern.

"What foolishness! Your American friend was seen following a beggar along the street this morning, shortly before the escort arrived to take him to the palace. The Sultan Abdul Hamid will be most displeased. There must be apologies when Savage Bey returns."

"Apologies!" Alarm was followed swiftly by anger, and at this moment all Cat's emotions showed on her face. "Don't you see it must have been a trap? Daniel wouldn't vanish like that! Send your soldiers looking!"

"All day men have searched, for it is no light thing to disobey a Sultan's bidding. The Emperor of Powerful Emperors will be most—"

"*Damn* the emperor of powerful emperors!" cried Cat, growing desperate. "Can't he even keep the streets of his own city safe? *Do* something!"

Zoltan Pasha stiffened. Tongue of a mother-in-law! Had

251

the woman no discretion? If she continued to speak in that way, and if it came to Abdul Hamid's royal attention, the order to see to this woman's safe departure from the country would most certainly be rescinded.

He fixed a placatory smile on his lips—things had, after all, gone very well today. "No doubt Savage Bey will return before the sun has set . . . if Allah so wills."

But Allah did not so will. A week later Daniel had not been found. The reservations on the Orient Express went wasting. Cat tried everything: desperate pleas to the consuls of half a dozen countries, to the hotel management, to all the local officials who would listen and some who would not. She even requested an audience with the Sultan himself, and when it was refused she hired a carriage to take her to the gates of the palace of Yildiz Kiosk, and it was there that Zoltan Pasha found her, in late afternoon. For once he looked unnerved, whether from the long hunt for Cat, or from the proximity of the palace.

"I'll come with you now," Cat told him stubbornly, "but I intend to stand here every day until the Sultan sees me. *He* might be able to do something, if he's as all-powerful as you say. I can't understand why everyone's trying to discourage the search, even *you*. Oh—"

Tears of sheer frustration stung behind her eyelids, but she fought them back as Zoltan Pasha saw her to the calèche. Beyond the shadow of the palace, he grew more expansive and self-assured again. "You must give up and return to your own land," he told her, stroking his strong jaw as the calèche clopped its way southward past sleepy villas, toward the quarter of the Pera. "I have used my influence to procure a new reservation for you, on the Orient Express. The steamer leaves for Varna tonight. There is nothing you can do for your friend. Nothing! The beggar has been found, and questioned. . . ."

"Found? Where? When?" Cat clutched at Zoltan Pasha's arm, in an attitude of supplication.

"He was found a week ago."

"Why didn't you *tell* me? Oh, and I thought you weren't even trying—"

Zoltan Pasha shifted in his seat to free himself from the importunate hand. Although he had been ordered to have this conversation with this woman now, it was best not to be too friendly with her—there were soldiers accompanying the

252

calèche on horseback, and they could see. "You were not told, because at first our efforts to pry the man's tongue loose met with little success. Although, when the kirbaç . . . the lash . . . was applied to the soles of his feet, he did confess that he had been paid to lure Savage Bey away from the district of the foreigners."

"I've always known *that!* Is there no more to be found out from this man? You must take me to him. I'll offer a reward, anything—"

"It is useless, mademoiselle. The man is dead. He died on the rack."

Cat stared, horrified, rage ripping through her breast. "How could you *kill* him! The only person who could have helped!"

"If we had known by whose orders he acted, we might not have done such a thing. If it is true, what our spies now begin to suspect, then the man was only loyal in all things, a faithful servant of Muhammad, may Allah's peace and blessing be upon him. But of course we will never know."

"What on earth are you trying to imply?" Anger and frustration put an hysterical edge on her voice. *Loyal?* To whom? Was Zoltan Pasha suggesting that the beggar had been acting on orders of someone important?

"I imply nothing, for I know nothing. But it seems the dirty beggar was seen conversing one time in a dark corner, with a man who had been known to speak with other men who are . . . or might be . . . agents of one so powerful that I dare not whisper his name. Oh, it is a rumor only, and very roundabout, and those whose names are mentioned have vanished too. It is difficult for me to say, for even though I am loyal to the Sole Arbiter of the World's Destiny, I am not told all secrets that lie within the palace walls. So you see, mademoiselle, it is best if you leave this country. There is nothing you can do . . . if there is even a whisper of truth to these things."

"Are you implicating the *Sultan?*"

Zoltan Pasha looked shocked. "Of course not! You imagine things, mademoiselle! But if it should transpire, as spies also report, that this man Savage was plotting to overthrow the Shadow of Allah upon the Earth . . ."

"Plotting! You're mad!"

"The throne has many enemies." Zoltan Pasha's lids turned heavy. "May Allah protect the Refuge of Sovereigns

253

from the dogs who snarl around his feet! Whether your friend was plotting or not is unimportant. It is necessary only that such a thing be hinted, and a man might vanish forever into some dim dungeon, hidden from the eyes of all. I, even I, have no access to such information. To seek for news of a political prisoner is to drop a coin in a deep well indeed! A man might be torn limb from limb before the splash sounded . . . or even worse!"

Cat stared at him in total horror. Daniel seized on the orders of the Sultan himself? Zoltan Pasha could be implying nothing else, despite his evasiveness. "Even worse?" she repeated in a choked voice.

"I could not describe such a thing to a woman," he hedged, although he had been ordered to do exactly that. "Not even to my own wives would I disclose that such barbaric practices exist."

"I'm not one of your overprotected wives, Zoltan Pasha. I must know everything . . . now! Tell me what fate is planned for Daniel."

"Did I say I knew what fate was planned? I do not even know if the man still lives! If I ask more questions my own life may be in jeopardy! But I have heard of the cruel practices of a certain jailer, a man of Arab extraction . . . oh, such things are not meant for gentle ears."

"Tell me!"

"Perhaps Allah in his goodness will protect Savage Bey from such a fate. Perhaps he was seized by foreign powers? By thieves and cutpurses? By wretched Armenians or filthy Bulgars, who would be merciful enough to slit a captive's throat? It is best that you do not know, especially as it is very unlikely that Savage Bey is in a Turkish dungeon at all—"

"Damn your two-edged Turkish tongue! Tell me!"

Zoltan Pasha's sorrowful sigh hid his deep satisfaction. The woman deserved some punishment for her unseemly and unsubmissive behavior, and for the trouble she had put him to. She had been a thorn in his flesh for this past week, and the camping out at palace gates had been the very final straw.

"May Allah forgive me that I utter such things to a woman. There are certain parts of a man's body, the parts without which he is no man at all."

"No," Cat whispered, feeling a wave of nausea flow from her stomach to her throat.

"Ah, if it were only that. To leave a man a eunuch would be

merciful in the eyes of the prophet, for a man who is a slave and a eunuch can lead a useful life. But there are those, the filthy Arab jailer for one, who take such parts and put them in an unseemly place, and then sew a man's lips together so he cannot spit them out. But perhaps there is some mercy to the torture after all, for with his mouth sewn together, a man will not live long."

"Are you telling me Daniel's dead?" asked Cat whitely, as the calèche drew up at the hotel steps. "And that he died in that way?"

"I tell you no such thing, for I know nothing of his fate, and never will. In this city one must train one's eyes to see only what is safe to see. Now will you not take my advice and return to your own land? Rest assured there is nothing more you can do for your friend . . . unless you are acquainted with men of power in your own country, men who might make representations to the Ruler of Europe, Africa, and Asia, the Shadow of Allah upon the Earth . . . who, although he knows nothing of this matter, might be prevailed upon to save a prisoner from torture. . . ."

Too sickened to speak more, Cat somehow stumbled her way to the hotel suite, hardly listening when Zoltan Pasha assured her he would return some hours later, after the hour of prayer, to escort her to the Austrian steamer for the overnight trip to Varna. "I took the liberty of telling the hotel management you will no longer need the suite, and also of passing along to the grand vizier your personal thanks for the hospitality of the throne. A maid will arrive soon to help you pack. As for Savage Bey's effects, if you wish to leave them I will personally arrange for their disposal. I assure you, mademoiselle, this is best. If there is any help to be gained for your friend, it must be gained in your own country. To stay here now is to stay at your own risk. The Sultan himself has expressed a wish that you depart."

Cat just stared at him. Leave now, when no one seemed to care about Daniel's fate? And if she could not help him here, she could certainly not help him by returning to the United States!

Zoltan Pasha started to leave with his guardsmen, then turned back at the last moment. A smile touched his lips, but his eyes were cold. "Ah, by the way. I nearly forgot." He pulled a piece of yellow paper from the breast pocket of his uniform, and unfolded it. It was inscribed with a short handwritten message. "This morning, when I came to find you at the hotel, the manager gave me a message for you. It arrived, he said, by transatlantic cable. I confess I read it, for I thought it might contain some clue in the distressing mystery of Savage Bey's disappearance. But there is nothing in it, nothing! And the stupid French pig who took the message even put the words in wrong order. *Will reconsider* . . . I believe that makes more sense."

A message? No one on the other side of the Atlantic knew she was in Constantinople. Every intuitive bone in her body vibrated with the instant knowledge that Zoltan Pasha was lying again: that this message did have something to do with Daniel's fate.

She accepted the piece of paper from Zoltan Pasha's hands, but pride told her not to read it until the door had closed between them, shutting out his oily watchful smile.

The message was not signed, and for a fleeting moment she thought Zoltan Pasha had been right—that the first two words had been transposed. But then she knew.

RECONSIDER WILL, it read. WHAT CAN HAPPEN TO TWELVE CAN HAPPEN TO ONE.

Twelve? The number had a significance for Cathryn Kinross that it would have had for no other person. There had been twelve people killed at the opening of the Brooklyn Bridge.

And in that moment she knew, with a blinding certainty and a horror that passed all utterance, exactly who was responsible—not only for Daniel's fate, but for Jenny's.

BOOK III

The Way

29

Suddenly, a shaft of morning sun fell like a sword along the length of the polished boardroom table. Julian Gow stared at it, transfixed. But he blinked away the fleeting presage; it had only been caused by the opening of the great double doors at the far end of the darkly paneled boardroom. This was not the vision. His bodyguards stood beside him, phlegmatic and reassuringly bulky, and the chairs along the sides of the table were filled with the members of The Trunk's board of directors, their faces all turned to see what might have caused this untoward interruption.

Gow rose in his chair, cold with fury, as one of his lesser lawyers entered. "What is the meaning of this? No one comes in this room during our meetings! You have my orders!"

And then, the silhouette of the woman came into view, backlit in the doorway. She wore a mantle, but it did not fully conceal the fact that she was heavily pregnant. Gow's face turned ashen.

"I couldn't very well keep her out, Mr. Gow," said the lawyer.

"I won't have a women in this room. And above all that woman! Take her out!"

One of the guards moved to execute his master's orders, and Cat said in a low fierce voice: "Don't touch me, Olin. I have a legal right to be here!"

"It's true." The lawyer intervened, hurriedly before the guard could make contact. His Adam's apple bobbed with nervousness; his eyes skated toward Gow. "Miss Kinross *does* have a seat on the board."

Eyebrows all along the table flew skyward. So this was Miss Kinross! They had all heard of her, of course; most had known her grandfather. They knew the long-empty seat on the board was rightfully hers. They knew that she had brought court action against The Trunk, some months before, in an attempt to break the lease by which Gow held control of her grandfather's railway, her grounds that Gow himself had been breaking the lease for many years. They knew that the case had been heard the previous week and that the action had failed, a foregone conclusion to those who understood Gow's methods in the courts.

But *Miss* Kinross? They had not known she was pregnant. Why did she still use her maiden name, with not even a pretense that she was married? And did she not know enough to stay away from Wall Street, this enclave of men and power? Did she not know to stay away from *Gow,* who grew apoplectic at mere mention of her name?

"Mr. Gow, need I remind you that since Miss Kinross returned to New York she has been most, er, recalcitrant. I thought perhaps as you had won the court case recently, she might be coming here to accede to your wishes. . . ."

But the lawyer's words trailed away as he became aware that the feared Trunk president was not listening to him at all. As if in a trance, Gow had sunk back into his chair at the head of the imposing table. He sat there now, stiffly, with his hands on the table—the left hand naked, the right hand locked in its leather gauntlet. He stared wordlessly as Cathryn Kinross advanced to the far end of the table. She did not make any move to take the empty seat so long unused.

"You've been asking me to change my will, Julian," she said in a bleak voice. "And now that you've won the court case, I've come to tell you that I've done it."

Gow made visible and shuddering efforts to shake away the terrible sense of fatality that had seized him. It mattered not that his body had grown ice-cold, that his brow was trickling sweat; Cathryn Kinross had come to surrender.

"Your lawyers promised you would intercede with the Sultan if I do as you wish. They said you had influence and armaments dealings with the Ottoman empire. Is it true, Julian? Can you save Daniel?"

"I can if it pleases me." Gow's voice had an odd timbre; his left hand had started to stroke the gauntlet that encased the right. "I have the power."

"I don't believe that, Julian." Her voice had turned suddenly hard and scornful; her eyes glittered.

Gow took control of himself, and the right fist crashed down on the table, causing a small collective jump, and drawing all eyes. "Abdul Hamid will do as I say!" he thundered.

"The Sick Man of Europe and the Sick Man of America?

Between the two of you, Julian, I don't believe Daniel is alive at all. And if he is only one thing has kept him that way . . . my refusal to do as you wish. Yes, I lost the court case, but I still refuse to give in. I *have* changed my will, Julian, but in no way that you'll like. I don't need to tell you what it says; you'll find out soon enough. Pray that my child is born alive! Pray there's no cholera, no scarlet fever, no tripping over stones! I may not be strong enough to fight you and win, but others are. And if anything happens to me or mine, my weapon goes into their hands."

Fear prickled at the necks of men along the table, not because of anything Cathryn Kinross had said, but because of Gow. The word weapon had been a trigger. He now sat like a man hypnotized, his colorless eyes wide and fixed in their sockets. The beads of perspiration that had collected on his brow began to slide unchecked into the edges of his cruelly chiseled mouth. Others in the room, trying to make themselves small in their chairs, received the distinct impression that The Trunk's president believed himself alone with the woman.

"Yes, I lost the court case. How many judges did you bribe? But I'm not through with fighting you yet, Julian. I have another way."

"Way," whispered Gow, in a toneless ghost of an echo. He had begun to blink very rapidly. As if obeying some deep inner command, his left hand traveled to the watch pocket of his waistcoat. The fob he drew out, without looking at it, was attached not to a watch but to a golden key. His left hand holding the key traveled unerringly to the lock, and still his eyes did not leave Cathryn Kinross. He inserted the key at the wrist of the gauntlet, and turned it. The lock came free.

And then, slowly, still in a trance, he peeled the gauntlet from the right hand men had never seen.

"Oh, my God," whispered one director, sucking in his breath; and all along the table men's eyes were riveted by the sight.

Julian Gow's right hand was covered with deep, crescent-shaped scars; scarcely an inch of unmarked skin remained. Only one thing could have caused those scars. Even as men watched in fascinated horror the right hand began to travel to the mouth.

Suddenly the mangled fist smashed down on the table; men jumped. "Get her out of here!" Gow screamed to his guards.

"Get her out! I won't be ruined by a woman! I never want to see her again!"

This time several guards hastened to do Gow's bidding, swiftly striding the length of the table and seizing Cat by the arms.

"Gently!" cautioned the lawyer with some urgency, seeing the rough way they bundled her toward the door. "Careful! Mr. Gow's orders are that she is not to be hurt!" His eyes darted nervously to Gow, seeking direction. Could it be true that this woman had some power over the man all Wall Street held in awe?

But Gow's attention had left the scuffle at the other end of the room. He was staring at his scarred hand, as if he could not credit that he had uncovered it in public.

The hand was never seen again. On the afternoon of that same day, it was fitted for a very special kind of glove. This glove was made of chain mail, in the manner of medieval armor. It had no key. It was fastened to a band of steel forged around Gow's wrist, so that the glove could never be removed, not even for the washing of hands, a ritual which now occupied much of his time.

262

30

"What were ye thinking of, Miss Cat, to beard the lion in his own den? Now ye'll have the full power of Gow's wrath brought down upon ye, for certain!"

"Hannah, I've told you a thousand times," Cat answered tiredly, "fear is the only real power Julian holds over men. The only way to break that power is to show others they don't have to fear him. If I'm not afraid, why should they be?"

While Hannah examined the bruises on her arms, Cat's heavily pregnant body was lowered into a chair in the neat parlor of the small New York home she had rented some months before. It was a far cry from Fifth Avenue: It had an outdoor privy, for one thing, as many Manhattan homes still did, and electricity had not yet come to this street. But if the home was not exactly elegant, it was clean and comfortable enough, and since Hannah had come to help her, there was no need for other servants.

Were it not for the coming battle with Gow, Cat could have afforded a great deal more. Her half share in Ryan's gaming house still produced a very generous income. But recently, the money had gone to pay a huge battery of high-priced lawyers, many of them seconded from their duties with important men.

Yes, Cat had allies, and for months all her energies had gone into recruiting them. First of the allies was Hannah herself, and it was Hannah—the first person Cat had gone to see after returning to America—who had unwittingly suggested the weapon to be used against Gow. Hannah had still been living at Angus McBride's country home then, but the brood of stepbrothers and stepsisters had grown; for the first time in years, Hannah had the freedom to choose a life of her own.

Cat had poured out the full story, holding back almost nothing of what had happened in the intervening years. There had been no thought, even then, of giving in to Julian's demands; Gow had overplayed his hand.

Hannah had wept and railed, and called the curses of the earth and the skies and the seven seas upon Gow's head. "Och, Miss Cat, to think what ye've suffered! I'll na' condemn ye for the life ye've led. And I'll na' condemn the child ye carry. Puir fatherless bairn!"

"Will you come with me?" Cat asked simply. "I'll need you, Hannah. My baby will need you."

Hannah's spinster soul had long since tired of minding other people's children, but that was forgotten now.

"I told ye once I'd come if ye were in hell," she grieved. "Aye, and it's there ye were, wi' the devil himself. Mister Jared must turn in his grave a thousand times each day. He'll na' rest in eternity until that wicked man is paid for his sins. Aye, sins against you, and sins against others!"

At last Hannah, seeing the pale determination in Cat's face, had controlled her own tears. And in time, she had spelled out to Cat what some of those other sins were.

"During the depression it was, back in '77, the year old Commodore Vanderbilt died. No doubt ye read of troubles on the rails. First Mr. Gow cut wages: firemen, engineers, brakemen, switchmen, gandy dancers, ticket sellers, porters earning scarce enough to keep body and soul together, conductors with small bairns to feed. Thousands upon thousands of men, though The Trunk dividends had na' suffered one whit! And when that made trouble, he called in the militia, and others . . . big strong men with sticks. Aye, there were riots, and men with skulls bashed in! There's one ye'll remember, an engineer who worked for Mr. Jared. You call him to mind, a Mr. Flood."

"Uncle Ernie," said Cat woodenly, feeling a wave of nausea that was not due to her pregnancy.

"Aye, that one. A nice, kind man, and a fine engineer."

"He was killed?"

"Nay, but he's no more driving engines. He's a fireman now, with another line, for he's half-blind from the beating they gave him, though there's none would dare testify to that, at the time. An accident in coupling cars, they said! And how could that be, when Mr. Flood was no brakeman? And when there were brand-new automatic couplers on the cars? A hundred 'coupling' accidents they had that week! Men with arms crushed, or legs, or faces! And when the week was over, Mr. Gow fired every last man that ever worked for Mr. Jared."

"But he couldn't do that," protested Cat. "It was in the lease. Their jobs were promised."

Hannah, grieving for the past, began to rock back and forth. "Troublemakers, Mr. Gow said. It was na' true; many had made no trouble at all. But Mr. Jared's men were na' afeared to lose their jobs, as others were. So Mr. Gow made an example of them. And who was to say him nay? By then he'd already broken the terms of the lease a thousand times in other ways, and na' been stopped."

"What ways?"

"There's been no Peekskill and Tarrytown train since your grandfather passed along. The little local runs . . . Mr. Gow stopped them, every one, the day Mr. Jared died. There's naught to be seen now but Trunk colors, maroon and black. And if he could break the lease in one way, why na' another? Aye, Mr. Gow's promises are thinner than the paper they're penned upon."

The conversation had started a train of thought. The next day Cat acquired a copy of the lease. She spent the better part of a week closeted with it, until every term was engraved on her memory; and after that she acquired a copy of the original charter issued by the State of New York to her grandfather's little railway. That too she studied. What would her grandfather have done? What would *Daniel* have done? Gradually a plan formulated in her mind, and soon thereafter she filed an action to break the lease with The Trunk. She did not expect success: Julian had too many judges in his pocket.

Once the action had been started, Cat had taken a trip to the West Coast, to see Ryan. There was no attempt at secrecy. Julian, she knew, would be kept informed of her whereabouts, but what could he do? It was clear he did not want her dead. She told Ryan less than she had told Hannah, but it was enough.

"I'll come east," Ryan shouted, slamming a great tight fist on his desk. "By God, I'll tear the be-jesus bast—er, pardon, I'll tear him apart with my bare hands."

"No, Ryan, someone has to run the gaming house, and run it well. I'll be needing income. That's how you can help . . . by doing without me here. In fact, it's better if Julian believes I've sold out altogether. Can we arrange to make it look like that?"

Ryan had offered to send a number of Barbary Coast

toughs, paid for out of his own pocket, to protect Cat's person.

"It won't be necessary. If Julian wanted me dead I'd be dead already. No, he wants me alive, Ryan, at least until I've changed my will."

"Then, by Jesus, don't change it!"

"But I must sooner or later, to provide for the child I'm expecting. Besides, I've thought of a better beneficiary for my grandfather's railway. A consortium of railway men, Julian's rivals, all of them. If anything happens to me, or to my child, or to anyone I care about, and that includes you, the railroad will automatically go to them. If I can't break that lease they will! They'd like nothing better than to see The Trunk without access to New York. And tomorrow I'm off to see the first of those men: Yancy Brody."

Yancy was by now an important man in West Coast railroading, but access to him was easy: He had not turned into a desk executive. He had been blind with rage at what Cat had told him, especially as some of it confirmed old suspicions. It was then, during that visit with Yancy, that Cat learned for the first time why Daniel had left the United States, and why he had sold his half share in the California railroad.

"Sure he married Inge. But that goin' east, that was no honeymoon. Figger Dan'l musta had a score or two to settle with Gow even back then, for that's what he set out to do, though he never let on a word of why to me, or to any other soul. Jest set out to git Gow, real quiet . . . and git him he nearly did. Stalked the sonuvabitch until he got through the bodyguard. It was in the big train shed at Forty-second Street, platforms all crowded with folks catchin' trains. Took a coupla smart swings, Dan'l did, connectin' with Gow's private parts, I hear. An' then, the guards moved in. Dang near beat Dan'l to a pulp! An' they'da finished him off fer sure, but fer the people gawkin' about."

"Oh, Yancy," said Cat, grieving that Daniel should have suffered so for her sake. "I wish I'd known."

"A week later," Yancy went on, "out goes a warrant fer Dan'l's arrest. Attempted murder, they said. Claimed he had a gun. Gun, hell, it was the guards had guns!"

"There must have been witnesses!"

"Sure there were witnesses. All with their eyeballs in their pants pockets, time Gow was through with 'em. Though I

266

figger Gow musta known it was chancy to come to court, fer there was no real manhunt put on, an' the thing was hushed up some. Gow's lawyers tole Dan'l to git outta the country. An' he had Inge to think about by then, so he did. An' then, when the trouble started on the line, sold out his share to me."

"Trouble on the line? Oh, Yancy."

"Gow-type trouble. Leastways, it seemed mighty like it. Runaway train in the mountains? Now that don't seem likely, what with airbrakes nowadays. Yet we had two runaways in two weeks. The engine, an' then the helper engine. Two! An' then, we bought a third, an' that dang near went, too! Freight mostly, but some crew was killed. An' other things. Bolts loose on the tracks. Snowshed timbers sawed near through, bridge timbers, too. Couldn't prove a thing, but accidents? Hell! They stopped when Dan'l sold out. So you see, I got a few scores to settle m'self. Need help against Gow? You got it!"

"It won't save Daniel," Cat pointed out. "I imagine he's dead."

Yancy agreed. "An' if he is alive an' kickin', givin' in to Gow ain't no insurance to do anything but put him six feet under. Sonuvabitch snake in the grass . . . murderin' so's you can't prove a thing in the courts."

"Don't come east until I'm ready to fight him," Cat warned. "Julian will know I've come to see you, and I don't want him taking any more reprisals against your railway. Let him think I've met with no success. Early April, that's when the court action comes up, and it's after that I'll need you. By then my grandfather will have been dead nine years."

"Sure you'll be on yer feet?" asked Yancy dourly, with an experienced glance at Cat's thickening waistline.

"Certainly," she said calmly. "I'll still have six weeks to go. There'll be plenty of time, Yancy."

After Yancy there had been others to see, some of them important men she had met during her stay on Fifth Avenue so long ago, others who had made more recent marks in the worlds of high finance and railroading. Access to men with names like Drexel and Morgan and Loeb and Hill and Harriman and Vanderbilt was not easy, and it had taken great persistence. Of the era's great East Coast railroad barons, she avoided only Jay Gould, whom she personally disliked and mistrusted.

To reach these men she used Yancy's name, and in some cases her grandfather's name, and in some cases even Julia's name; and each successful interview made the next a little easier to arrange. Once past the fierce denizens who guarded the outer gates she found there were many who were only too willing to pounce upon the carcass of The Trunk, should it become a carcass. Most expressed doubt; some laughed openly at the thought that a woman should be so presumptuous as to fight the power of The Trunk.

"Julian Gow doesn't own the whole Trunk, he only controls it," she said time and again. "I intend to bring The Trunk to a standstill, and when I do, the price of Trunk stock is bound to be driven down. You'll be able to buy it for a song."

"Bring The Trunk to a standstill!" Sometimes the answer came in a guffaw, sometimes in a polite but disbelieving smile. "And how do you plan to do that? Surely not with that laughable little lawsuit?"

"You don't need to know my plan; just rest assured it will work. I ask only that you remember how Cornelius Vanderbilt acquired control of the New York Central, twenty years ago. When I have done all I can, then it will be time for you to step in . . . you, and the State of New York."

As the men she approached were not asked to provide money for the battle about to be joined, or take part in any overt way, what was to be lost? A few had suggested top-flight legal help, and as Cat was well aware that Julian Gow would know of her various visits, she had hired the lawyers forthwith. The upcoming court case was a very good cover for seeking the legal advice she so badly needed.

Yes, the battle was about to be joined. Her grandfather had given her the weapon. Julian by his actions over the years had given her the will. And Daniel, Daniel who had never backed away from any man, perhaps he had given her something, too. . . .

"And were ye na' afeared, Miss Cat, to face those big rough men again, and that . . . that *satan* wi' the evil sickness in his soul? Ye're a fool if ye were na' afeared!"

"Yes, Hannah, I was afraid. But Daniel always met a challenge straight on. He had a special kind of strength for facing fear. And I don't want my child, *his* child, to be born in the shadow of fear. Oh, Lord in heaven—"

Cat had not lost her ability to cry; a tear or two splashed down on Hannah's freckled and comforting hands.

Hannah ached inside. To her, Cathryn Kinross was the firstborn she had never had. "There now, Miss Cat," she soothed, "it's no shame if ye have na' the courage for what ye plan to do tomorrow. There's many a man would let the devil lie well enough alone. If Mr. Gow did na' harm ye today, he'll na' harm ye ever . . . nay, nor your bairn. Forget your plan!"

"Oh, Hannah, I can't. I must do what I have to do, for I never want to be afraid again . . . for my own sake, for my child's sake, for Daniel's sake. But I'm such a coward. I'm afraid, so very afraid. . . ."

31

In nine years Fifth Avenue had changed. St. Patrick's Cathedral had long since been completed; wall-to-wall Vanderbilts had built mansions rivaling Julian Gow's own; the rich and the superrich now papered the once-countrified blocks bordering Central Park.

Inside Gow's marble-pillared mansion there had been some changes, too. The household staff had been doubled so that each dust-mote might receive instant attention. A new sculpture gallery filled one vaulted space. Electricity had arrived. A fencing room and a fencing master had been added. A world-renowned Dutch artist had been employed to repaint a certain ceiling; and when his work was judged too tame, a world-renowned French artist was called in to repaint it all over again.

In the study that housed the sword collection, there had been additions, too, and one was not a sword at all. It was that miracle of miracles, the telephone; it sat like a strange black spider on one side of Gow's enormous desk.

To the sword collection had been added a sabre that had once belonged to the Emperor Napoleon; a rare crusader's sword of the twelfth century; a ruby-encrusted scimitar that was the gift of Sultan Abdul Hamid himself. Excalibur remained, but now it was bedded not in a block of stone, but in a larger-than-life statue of a naked woman, kneeling with bowed head in an attitude of submission.

"Who do I pay to run my legal affairs: lawyers, or fools?" Gow glared at his chief legal adviser—not the man who had been present in the boardroom yesterday, but an apple-cheeked man with pince-nez and an air of Victorian respectability. The lawyer's name was Phair, and despite his appearance he was a clever, subtle, and unscrupulous sharpster who was well accustomed to walking tightropes with Gow. He was also one of the very few men whom Gow would see alone, with no bodyguards present. Phair knew enough to wait, not answering while Gow vented steam.

"You claimed you could coerce her into signing a new will once the court action was through. And what does she sign? A threat! And now, you have the audacity to tell me she still wants to break the lease!"

The lawyer examined his well-buffed fingernails. "Normally, Mr. Gow, a small matter like this would not be brought to your attention. But some special circumstances have arisen. It seems that Miss Kinross is distraught by her failure with due process of law. Brain fever, perhaps? She still insists that you honor the terms of the lease. Five hundred dollars compensation to each man you fired, she suggests. She further suggests that you could make up the deficit in local runs in one year, by ensuring that all trains using the track into New York bear Peekskill and Tarrytown colors. Telegrams were received at our main terminals this morning, outlining her demands and her intentions."

"I hire a hundred lawyers!" Gow stood up and paced the room, halting in front of Excalibur and glaring at the statue balefully. "Can't you deal with one weakling of a woman?"

Phair polished his pince-nez and restored them calmly to his nose. "Not this time, Mr. Gow," he said carefully, "as you yourself gave the order that she is not be bodily abus—er, bodily threatened. She's barring the track out of New York, and she can't be moved. Since the telegrams advised us of her intention, your regular Trunk runs have been backed up all day."

"What?" Gow slammed his mailed fist on the hilt of Excalibur as if to drive it farther into its female scabbard. Fury stained his eyes almost to pink. "Then have her lifted off! Bodily! At once!"

"It will be difficult, Mr. Gow. She's in a locomotive."

A vein stood out in Gow's forehead, turning blue. "Then order the men running the train to move along!"

"But, Mr. Gow," said Phair with a deprecating expression, *"she's* running the train."

The Trunk engineer who had been given the order to shunt Cat Kinross to a siding drove a powerful brute of a freight engine, a consolidation 2-8-0 that far outweighed the small locomotive that had been provided by Yancy for Cat's use. The engineer braked to a crawl as he approached the bend in track where she was parked. He had been directed to do this carefully, and he would; his own sympathies lay with the woman. And he had heard that the man acting as fireman for Cathryn Kinross was a respected compatriot of his—Ernie Flood.

Cat had chosen a place where, due to the configuration of the hills, the roadbed was too narrow to allow for the laying of double track without further blasting. Normally this created no problem; stretches of single line track were common, and scheduling allowed northbound and southbound trains alike to share the line.

It had been easy enough, with Yancy's cooperation, to bring a locomotive onto Trunk line. All railroad owners extended courtesy privileges to other railroad owners running private trains. Permission had been an automatic thing, handled by employees at a low level, without reference to their higher-ups.

The engineer kept his hand steady on the throttle, easing the huge freight locomotive into the bend. At five miles an hour, the locomotive shuddered with leashed power at every thrust of the enormous rods.

In his slow progress the engineer noted that a number of locals had gathered to watch from a nearby hill, at a safe distance. Two small tents had also been pitched, giving the scene a faintly festive air. He also noted the lanky, grizzle-haired man who dropped to the ground from the parked train, and loped along the track to meet him at a lazy pace.

"Wouldn't do that if I was you," said Yancy, swinging up to join the engineer in the cab of the 2-8-0. "See that ole wooden boxcar behind the tender? She's loaded. Fact is, whole dang train's loaded—with explosives."

"What?" The screech of great wheels sounded as the attacking train ground to a noisy halt, twenty yards from its goal. A hiss of steam escaped, and the engineer gaped at Yancy.

"Set to go off like a firecracker," confirmed Yancy with a mournful face. "Dynamite, an' blasting caps, an' fuses all over. Phial of nitro, too. Jolt that stuff, you got yerself a helluva big bang."

"Je-sus," said the engineer.

"Mighty determined lady. Sweet-talked me into riggin' the whole thing," claimed Yancy, who had called Williams in to do the job. "Says she ain't gittin' off the track fer nuthin'. Fact is, she's wired in, too . . . attached to some mighty tricky

272

fuses. An' she's all set to camp there. Got a bedroll in that engine cab, an' little lace curtains. Jest like home."

"Je-*sus*," said the engineer, popeyed.

"Might as well turn tail," suggested Yancy. "She ain't movin' till The Trunk shells out hard cash to her grand-daddy's trainmen that Gow fired. An' till The Trunk rollin' stock is painted blue an' gold, every dang car. All set to have her baby in that engine cab, if needs be."

"*Je*-sus," said the engineer, mopping his brow with a kerchief. "A baby."

Without cracking a smile, Yancy directed a knowing wink at the engineer. "Noo York papers sure would like to hear about this, I reckon. Man could git hisself a passel o' publicity, gittin' dang near blown to kingdom come, like you jest did. An' if you ain't willin' to spill yer beans, I'd be right grateful fer a hitch back to town. Though I'd rather stay with the little lady."

"Je-sus-Christ-a-mighty," said the engineer, and his face grew into a slow grin as he contemplated the prospect of imparting this news to the brotherhood of railwaymen, haters of Gow one and all. "Reckon the lady needs you here, mister. Je-ho-sephat, what a story!"

Yancy dropped back down to the ground, and the engineer made to move the giant locomotive into reverse. He issued an order to his fireman, who had been listening agape, and then leaned out and called to Yancy: "Remember me to Ernie Flood, will you? And wish the old bugger luck!"

Within two days the nearby hill had taken on some of the aspects of a fairground. In the fine spring weather, the sun shone on a half-dozen tents, some gaudily striped, that had been added to those previously pitched. The crowd had swelled to several hundred, and the enterprising local farmer who owned the hill had taken to hawking hot meat pies. Reporters were out in force. Photographers wandered around with big black box cameras which, due to the recent invention of roll film, had been somewhat simplified since the day Cathryn Kinross had boarded Gow's special train, a decade before.

A week later Ryan, too, appeared on the scene, despite Cat's injunction to stay away. Hannah relayed to him the message that Cat preferred not to publicize her San Francisco life. "Then I'll stay away from the train," he agreed. "But I'm sticking it out. Came east as as soon as I heard she'd lost the court case. Hell, if a man can't—"

"I'll thank ye to mind your language in front of a lady," Hannah said tartly, thus beginning a little battle-within-a-battle that raged for the duration of Cat's extraordinary sit-in.

"Whoo-ee!" grinned a reporter from a very large New York newspaper, who had just come from talking to the pregnant woman ensconsed in the locomotive cab. "Says she used to be Gow's mistress, too. Told me to ask *him* for the details about that."

"Making a spectacle of herself," someone sniffed. "Breaking the law."

"But she got no justice in the courts," argued another. "And Mr. Gow . . . well, he's been breaking the lease for nine years, and that's law, too. And it's not just herself she's fighting for; it's those fired men, too, and the ones Gow's ruffians beat up back in the depression. What was it you called him in yesterday's newspaper?"

"The Man in the Iron Fist," answered the reporter, who was an admirer of Dumas. "Seemed to fit."

"Big railway running roughshod over a whole lot of little people. What's this country coming to?"

"But a woman should know her place," grumbled another. "Unmarried, and in a . . . a family way. She should be hiding in shame."

"That's half the story right there," said the reporter cheerfully, licking his pencil and poising it over paper. "Anyway, times are changing. An illegitimate child didn't stop President Cleveland from getting in last year, did it?"

"Ma, ma, where's your pa," someone chortled delightedly, bringing back one of last year's Republican chants, and then himself giving the Democratic answer: "Gone to the White House, ha, ha, ha! Well, personally I'm all for the little lady. If the courts can't protect a person's rights, there's something wrong with the courts. I say to hell with The Trunk! I hope she gets her way!"

"So do I," said the reporter fervently, and started to scribble.

By the end of another week Cat Kinross's allies included not only the press, but half the country, too. That she was young and beautiful added to the spice. Souvenir photographs snapped a safe distance from the locomotive cab were hawked on the hill, and in the streets of New York; and the stiff little sepia cards found a ready market amongst those anxious to see if she matched the glowing descriptions in the press, and the highly imaginative drawings in the *Daily Graphic*.

True, many were shocked by her unmaidenly behavior, but as time wore on even many of those began to feel a sneaking admiration for the young woman who had almost unaided taken on the power of The Trunk. Reporters avid for fresh angles interviewed everyone, including Cat's half-blind fireman Ernie Flood. Gradually stories old and new came out: stories of competitors Gow had crushed; stories of wage-cutting during the depression; stories of strike-breaking; stories, some sad, about the men who had been fired; stories of Gow's shady armaments dealings during the Civil War, and now with unpopular foreign powers; investigations into the shocking conditions on immigrant trains. There were even stories that hinted in veiled ways at certain goings-on in Gow's Fifth Avenue mansion, and in his summer home at Newport. Debaucheries, perhaps? Lecheries that even the muck-raking Newport scandal sheet had not detected?

A picture began to emerge in the public's eye, and it was not a pretty picture.

"The public be damned!" roared Gow, echoing the much-reported sentiments of one of his most famous rivals. His mailed hand brushed aside the sheaf of unfavorable press reports, and seized on the reports of lost revenues Phair had just brought to his study. "Damn public opinion! I care about *these*. Freight contracts canceled! Passengers using other lines! I won't have it! Approach Vanderbilt and see if the New York Central will carry our traffic until that woman gives in. As she will! As she must! Pay what Vanderbilt asks. Pay anything!"

Phair leaned forward in his chair. His expression was guarded, but less obsequious than two weeks ago. "Vanderbilt's railroad is already carrying your traffic," he said with meticulous enunciation. "And very happy with the state of affairs, too. They've put on extra runs to handle freight and passengers out of New York. And it's rumored that with Trunk stock down on Wall Street, one of the biggest buyers is Mr. William Vanderbilt himself."

"Fool!" shrieked Gow. "Don't you see he's trying to take control?"

"So are half a dozen others," said Phair phlegmatically. "It's even rumored there have been some clandestine approaches to your board of directors, to see how they intend to vote their stock at the next annual meeting. Public sentiment is with the woman, Mr. Gow, despite the fact that she's breaking the law."

Gow's metal-clad fingers began to drum on the desk. "Has the warrant been issued for her arrest?" he snapped.

"Why, yes, Mr. Gow. But the law can't act until she moves the locomotive, and detaches herself from the explosives."

Gow looked as though he would choke. "Then send a locomotive north again, and this time shunt her from the track! I don't care if she explodes!"

"It's too late for that, Mr. Gow," said the lawyer, emboldened to see that Gow had begun to blink rapidly. "The whole country is watching now. People are placing bets on the sex of the child. The *New York World* has started a pool on the exact moment of birth. The *Sun* is doing an exposé on the judge who handled the recent court case against The Trunk . . . oh, no proof of bribery yet, but innuendo, Mr. Gow, innuendo! Mrs. Curtis herself has come from the new *Ladies' Journal,* and wants to run a naming contest, if she can get Miss Kinross to agree. Miss Kinross is receiving messages of support from all over the world. Nothing official of course, but some of them well known. Lillie Langtry—"

"A courtesan! A person of scandalous reputation! A *woman!*"

"—Mark Twain, Joseph Pulitzer—"

"I've heard enough!" Beads of perspiration stood out on Gow's brow; his left hand began to pluck at the metal sheathing on the right. "Do what must be done! *Get rid of her!*"

"That's not possible now, Mr. Gow," said Phair with a very real deliberation to his words. "Miss Kinross has won."

For the next few moments Phair watched with dispassionate eyes while Gow disintegrated visibly. He had witnessed several episodes like this over the course of the past two weeks, with Gow lapsing into a nearly catatonic state. Phair was at this moment judging the state of Gow's readiness, and also—with another part of his mind—considering how to vote his own sizable block of Trunk stock.

"I prepared some papers for you to sign, Mr. Gow," he said at last, when he judged the time was right. He drew two documents from his briefcase. As chief legal adviser not only to The Trunk but to Gow himself, Phair was privy to all his employer's shady dealings. "First a message to the Ottoman Sultan. Last week I took the liberty of trying to determine whether the man Daniel Savage is still alive in some Turkish prison. Personally I doubt such a thing; Abdul Hamid is ruthless with suspected conspirators. To date there has been no reply. This second message, therefore, is more strongly worded. It spells out your firm intention of canceling the next arms shipment to Turkey unless the man Savage is produced alive. It is possible, of course, that his condition will negate any advantage to be gained; however—"

Seeing that Gow had now subsided into an unblinking and totally trancelike state, the lawyer discreetly pushed one of the papers across the desk. He placed a quill pen in Gow's mailed fist, nudged the fingers, and watched while the signature jerked onto paper almost of its own accord.

"And this"— Phair's eyes glittered briefly as he produced a second document —"this is an order to do with routine Trunk matters. Sign here, Mr. Gow."

Gow obeyed reflexively, his eyes fixed not on the paper, but on some nonexistent point in space.

Moments later Phair left the study, and only when he was past Julian Gow's guards and out in the Fifth Avenue sunlight did he breathe with total ease. Thank God the deliberate prodding of Gow had produced the desired result! Gow might be enraged later, but that didn't matter; Phair intended never to see him again.

And thank God Gow had signed the second order! That had been the important one; the first had been merely to test Gow's reactions, for he would never have signed it under normal circumstances. The second order—that was the thing. It confirmed a directive issued in a secret meeting of The Trunk's board of directors, a meeting at which Gow had not been present. Not that it mattered in any material sense, except as a legality. The compensation had already been paid; the repainting of The Trunk rolling stock had begun this morning.

In acres and acres of switching yards and sheds and roundhouses, the work went on at a feverish rate. Trunk maintenance crews who had never wielded a paintbrush were called off other jobs and ordered to do so now; and because they had been following the front pages with secret delight, they set to work with a will. Scores of signpainters and signpainters' assistants began to apply the hasty gold lettering almost before the powder blue was dry. The power of The Trunk could work wonders, and a job that should have taken months was done in only two weeks.

There was no need for Cat and Yancy and Ernie Flood and Hannah and Ryan and others to wonder about what was going on. The press had reported on everything, and with the greatest of glee.

"By the sweet Virgin, here she comes," reported Yancy, squinting at the streamer of smoke tailing slowly toward them. They had all been warned of the locomotive's approach; they knew it bore Peekskill and Tarrytown colors. Yancy leaped up beside the fireman, who had already joined Cat in the cramped locomotive cab where she had lived and eaten and slept for a full month now. Ernie Flood had started to shovel coal some time ago; the steam was already up.

At first sight of the approaching train a great cheer rose from the hillside, where more than five thousand had gathered to witness the surrender of The Trunk. Cat hardly heard it. For once, she was not thinking of Gow, or of Daniel, or of the crowds, or of the death with which she had lived so intimately for these past weeks. She was watching the slow approach of the train, a blue streamer unfurling against the bright soft green of spring, its plume proud in a nearly cloudless sky. Tears stood in her eyes.

"That's my railway," she whispered, with her hand placed below her breast, on the mound of her stomach. "Your great-grandpapa gave it to me. My railway! And someday it will be yours!"

"Steam's up!" cried Yancy exultantly. "Fer Chrissakes, git goin'!"

And with a grin remolding the normally lugubrious lines of his face, he seized a double handful of lace curtain.

"Let 'er rip!" he shouted, and to the wild cheers of the crowd, and the tumbling of lace curtains, the locomotive began to grind slowly backward.

32

"And the woman?" Gow asked frostily into the telephone. He was in a foul rage. He hated the telephone for one thing; it was impossible to see a man grovel on the telephone. And he intended to make Phair grovel before the conversation was through. The man would be fired, of course, in time: Gow already relished the prospect of Phair coming crawling back to Fifth Avenue, begging for his high-priced job.

But for the moment, Phair was needed to answer questions, and follow through on various directives Gow had issued.

"Did the law apprehend the woman?" Gow repeated in a steely voice, further angered by Phair's long pause.

"The warrant for her arrest was executed," Phair returned with a coolness of manner he would not have used some weeks before. "The law was waiting at the next siding. As soon as the explosives were detached, she was taken into custody."

Phair did not bother to add that Cathryn Kinross had been taken directly to hospital, where she was under nominal custody only, while a nation eager for news awaited the imminent birth. Already, the press and the public were crying out for the dropping of charges—or at the very least, a fine and a suspended sentence.

"You've handled this very badly, Phair. Now at least see to it that she comes up before one of my own judges," snapped Gow, making a mental note to ascertain personally that the man on the bench would be one of those in his pay.

"Certainly, Mr. Gow," came Phair's answer, with a promptitude verging on impudence.

"Call a meeting of the board of directors for tomorrow. Nine sharp! Vanderbilt will suffer for accepting my freight on his lines! Rates, secret rebates, everything . . . I want all the information in my hands for that meeting."

"Ah! A rate war," came the answer, a little more sardonic

than Gow cared to hear. The chain-mail glove began to drum ominously on the speaker half of the telephone, clattering against black metal.

"I'll hold you personally responsible, Phair, if we don't get every contract back within the month," Gow snarled. "I want every Trunk car working at full capacity."

"Every Peekskill and Tarrytown car," corrected the lawyer with an odd sound in his throat that might have been insolence, although it could have been merely the static on the receiver in Gow's left hand.

"I gave orders those cars were to be repainted, beginning the instant the woman was removed from the track! The work should have been started yesterday."

"Ah, Mr. Gow," returned Phair as if butter would not melt in his mouth, "that's not possible. When the order was given the maintenance workers went on strike."

"Break it!"

"The press is watching, Mr. Gow. The world is watching. A public subscription is even being taken up so the men won't suffer financially. Moreover, the men could not do the work even if they wished. That shipment of maroon paint that was ordered last week . . . well, there was a switching accident in the yards; the whole train was derailed and turned on its side. Paint all over the tracks; men are still trying to clean up the mess. Very odd; it was a top crew on the job. More supplies have been ordered, but there seems to be some problem at the paint factory, too—"

"Enough!" shrieked Gow. "I want all Trunk trains back in service by tomorrow, no matter what color they're wearing!"

"That will be difficult, Mr. Gow. Very difficult." This time the insolence in Phair's voice could not be misinterpreted. "The Trunk will be unable to complete any of its New York runs for some time to come."

Gow's lips thinned; his voice shook with uncontained fury. "That's an impertinence! With the track cleared and the woman in custody, I won't hear of any more delays. See to it!"

"This time it's not the woman, Mr. Gow," came the smooth-as-oil reply. "This time the State of New York is your adversary, and there are powerful men behind the move. You are aware, Mr. Gow, of the little legal twist that allowed Commodore Vanderbilt to gain control of the New York

Central, twenty years ago? The Central was an upstate system then; it terminated at Albany. Its passengers used to reach New York by transferring to the New York and Hudson River Railroad, which Cornelius Vanderbilt owned. Now, in the original charter of Vanderbilt's line there was a small clause . . ."

It was a story well known to the moguls of Wall Street, and Gow did not need to listen to know what disaster had befallen him now. Gradually, as Phair droned on, a glazed look came into those pale eyes; he blinked several times. He felt chilled to the bone. Sweat broke out on his brow.

". . . the clause permitted operation east of the Hudson River only; it specifically forbade crossing of the river itself. For years the clause had been ignored. Then one day Cornelius Vanderbilt pointed to that clause, and refused to take his trains across the river to meet the New York Central. In effect, this cut off the Central's access to New York. . . ."

Gow started to tremble violently. The shutter-speed of his eyes increased dramatically. Without volition, and with agonizing slowness, his unsheathed left hand transported the receiver back toward its nest. Phair's words seemed to come from a great distance now.

"The details here are not an exact duplication, but the principle involved is the same, and the Peekskill and Tarrytown charter is on the law books of New York State, just as it was in the other case. As long as your trains bear Peekskill and Tarrytown colors they are forbidden by law to cross the Hudson River. Need I tell you what this means? Back then, Vanderbilt used that little clause to bring the Central's traffic to a virtual standstill. Stock prices tumbled; Vanderbilt gained control. And have no doubt about it, there's a little of the old Commodore in young William, too! Of course, there's no proof that there's a Vanderbilt behind this, Mr. Gow. It might be any of half a dozen men. Or perhaps a consortium. In any case, considering the present circumstances, it will be hard to change the law without a lot of lobbying and bri—"

The receiver clicked home at last. Gow's staring eyes were fixed on just one thing now. Across the room, beyond the desk, only the jeweled hilt of Excalibur projected from the belly of the naked marble woman, but what Gow saw was the whole sword, the shining sword, the sword he had so often seen in his mind's eye.

With his stare never leaving the sword or the statue of the woman, his left hand began to claw at the chain-mail glove that encased his right.

A short time later, Cat Kinross gave birth in a hushed hospital room, bringing to an end the terrible pains that had pierced her belly for too long. She had gone into labor nearly thirty hours before, shortly after Yancy's explosives man, Williams, had detached her cautiously from her death-trap.

"'Tis the strain has brought it on early," Hannah clucked worriedly when Cat was safely in the hospital await-ing delivery. To have a baby in hospital was still an unusual thing, but in this case various officials had insisted that Miss Kinross's condition be supervised. Hannah had been allowed into the dim room to help through the period of waiting.

"Not early, Hannah." Cat had managed a shaky laugh, between pains. "I lied to you by a week or two."

Hannah raised her eyes to heaven. "Och, Miss Cat, ye're a sinner born, and I'll trust ye never again!" And then she rolled up her sleeves, and tore up a piece of her own clean petticoats for Cat to bite down upon.

Despite the prominent doctor attending the birth, it fell to Hannah to impart the news to Cat, who had been groggy in the final stages.

"A fine boy, Miss Cat, and I would na' be surprised if he tipped the scales at nine pounds or so! No wonder ye were so long in labor! They'll be washing him now, and soon . . ."

"He looks like his father," murmured Cat when the newborn had been nestled into her arms. Two tears slid slowly as far as her lashes, and trembled there without falling. Happiness and sadness. Must every wonderful accomplish-ment be paid for in pain?

"Will ye be calling him Daniel, then?" asked Hannah, and then informed Cat that a small crowd of reporters waited with bated breath to hear the news.

"No," Cat said with a twist of the heart. "I couldn't bear to do that. I don't want Daniel's name brought into this at all."

"What will ye call him, then?"

"Can't you guess, Hannah?" Memories welled back, and the two waiting tears slid down Cat's cheeks, but they were followed by no more. She smiled through vision that still swam a little. "Jared. Jared Kinross. Oh, I think grandpapa would be very, very proud!"

In a certain sumptuous foyer on Fifth Avenue, there were no smiles. The French master chef of Julian Gow's household was conferring, or to be more exact, arguing, with Gow's senior bodyguard.

"You know Mr. Gow's standing orders," said the rock-hard man with impassive eyes and cruel mouth. His name was Olin, and he alone of all the guards had been with Gow nine years before, during Cat Kinross's sojourn on Fifth Avenue. "No interruptions. Mr. Gow's orders."

"Vous êtes un sot!" The chef threw up his hands. He was losing temper; the argument had been going on intermittently for more than an hour now. "Monsieur Gow has the order that is standing about mealtimes, too! He would think nothing of doing that!"—he snapped his fingers—"to all of us, if the pheasant is not quite perfect. Fou! Imbécile! You have the head of a donkey! Did you ever know Monsieur Gow to be late for a meal? To go so long without the washing of hands? The butler tells you! The majordomo tells you! Now I, Armand, tell you!"

"My standing orders are—"

"Merde! You are a man of small brain and smaller imagination! What if he is not well?"

"He was well two hours ago," Olin said stoically. "I saw him myself."

"Then as you are the last to see him, perhaps you have yourself to blame! Perhaps he has had an attack of the heart, non? Perhaps he has suffered the stroke, non? Perhaps he has broken the neck, non? And perhaps he will fire you for not rushing to him the doctor, non?"

And at last, reluctantly, Olin allowed himself to be persuaded. The two men approached the door of Gow's study, flanked by two guards as motionless as potted palms. A discreet knock aroused no answer; nor did a louder rap. The chef Armand darted an aggrieved I-told-you-so look at Olin, and opened the door.

"Mon Dieu," he whispered, blanching and backing away.

Olin walked through and studied the scarlet-soaked scene with emotionless professional eyes, taking care not to tread on the fine Turkish carpet where Gow's life's blood must have spurted away in seconds. He motioned to one of his underlings. "Fetch a coroner," he directed, "and don't touch anything."

And although Olin was indeed a man of little imagination, he was already wondering how he would explain away the fact that he had been the last person to see Gow alive, a circumstance to which there were several witnesses.

For who would believe that Gow had killed himself, and with one hand, when the sword Excalibur could barely be raised with two? Yet there lay the evidence. The sword was near Gow's left hand, lying where it had been released in death.

And on the rug, some distance from the drained body, was another hand—this one severed at the wrist, and still clad in its chain-mail glove.

33

"Liberté Éclairant le Monde. It means Liberty lighting the world," remarked the exceptionally pretty female passenger leaning on the rail of the steamship as it entered New York harbor. On Bedloe's Island, teams of men like small black ants were swarming over scaffoldings, working to raise a gigantic statue atop a huge granite-faced pedestal. The copper sheeting, not yet greened by age, gleamed in the sun. Soon, the famous statue would rise higher than the tallest building in Manhattan.

"Even though she's a gift," the woman went on gaily, "Congress wouldn't pay for that base. Personally I believe it's because Liberty isn't a man. But Mr. Pulitzer's paper raised the money. And you, sir, are you in favor of putting a woman on a pedestal?"

The woman trained a devastatingly flirtatious smile on the fellow American beside her. How distinguished he looked in his Inverness cape, with that gauntness around his cheekbones, and that slight limp that added to his air of mystery. He had been the subject of not a little speculation on this transatlantic trip, and the general consensus was that he must have been serving abroad, perhaps as a soldier of fortune. Wounded, too, and convalescent for some time. His face had been white as a sheet three weeks ago, before sun and sea air had bronzed it back to vitality. Perhaps he had been with Gordon at Khartoum? Taken prisoner? With Gordon and the Mahdi now dead, it was said that a few men had been released.

"A gift?" asked the man, ignoring her leading question.

"From the French. My goodness gracious, sir, where have you *been?* Now don't tell me; I'll guess. In the Sudan?"

But the tall man was abstracted; he appeared not to hear. Then it was true, thought the pretty woman; she'd heard that this man had no time for any of the women aboard. Vanity had prevented her from making the attempt to intrigue him earlier on the voyage; vanity had driven her to see if she could

285

succeed at the last minute where others had failed. And vanity now caused her to decide that despite the man's virile appearance, he must be one of *those*.

But Daniel Savage did have his mind on a woman—the one woman who had been on his mind through the nine months in a vermin-infested Turkish prison, and then during his long fevered stay in a Turkish hospital that was hardly better.

He had been half-dead when they moved him to the hospital. His back had been raw with beatings, and infected, too. His ribs had been skeletal. His left leg had been freshly broken by a brutish jailer, so that for two days he had not been able to reach the slop buckets, or scramble for a place at the trough that was filled with food for the prisoners once a day, the only sign in that sunless place that another mark could be scratched on the dank stone wall. When carried from the prison, he had been far too ill for the Turkish authorities to send home; and so he had spent many months mending since the day the lawyer Phair had forwarded the formal request for release.

Although Daniel did not know it or appreciate it, the only thing that had kept him alive at all was Julian Gow's technique of overkill. Gow's messages to the Ottoman court had impressed too well on Abdul the Damned that Gow wanted Daniel Savage dead. Abdul the Damned trusted no man alive; why should he trust a man from a distant and infidel country? And so, Daniel Savage had lived—but barely.

During the stay in the Turkish hospital no communication with the outside world had been allowed, perhaps because the Turkish authorities had preferred not to put the handiwork of their dungeons on display. But the American embassy had been informed that Daniel was alive; and when he was finally escorted to the quayside to catch the steamer to Varna, a long letter from Yancy had been placed in his hands. He had read it as the Bosporus receded in the distance, and he had read it a thousand times since.

He knew now that Gow had been responsible for his incarceration. He knew that Gow was dead, murdered by one of his own bodyguards, who had been convicted despite protestations of innocence. He knew that the battle for The Trunk was still raging on Wall Street. He knew that old charges against himself had been reinvestigated and dropped, as witnesses no longer cowed by Gow revised their stories. He knew what Cathryn Kinross had done. He knew she had borne his son.

And he knew that shortly after the birth of the boy Jared, upon payment of a fine in lieu of sentence, she had vanished completely—and that, despite a good deal of trying, Yancy had been unable to find her since.

Yancy Brody's string-bean height stood out amongst the crowd of greeters awaiting the docking of the liner. The reunion was at first wordless, and charged with emotion. The pretty woman who witnessed the way the two tall men clasped decided then and there, much to the satisfaction of her vanity, that her surmise must have been correct.

"Tried everything," Yancy told Daniel some time later, after they had reached a hotel. "Shee-it. Lawyers, investigators, you name it. Nuthin'. Noospapers tried hard to find her, too . . . nuthin'. Even old Angus McBride that worked fer her grandpa, he ain't got a clue."

"And Hannah McBride?" asked Daniel. "If anyone knows, it would be Hannah."

"She ain't Hannah McBride now," divulged Yancy. The previous year he had become reasonably well acquainted with the homely flame-haired spinster who used to bring meals to the train for himself and Ernie Flood and Cat Kinross. "Up an' married some Irish fella she met, whilst campin' on the hill. She's Mrs. O'Brien now. Mighty surprised when I learned that, fer they was like cat an' dog, or so I heared tell. Never met the gent but once, fer I slept on the train, back in the baggage car with Ernie Flood. Allus figgered Gow might take a notion to throw in a firecracker. An', sonuvabitch, I think he would've, if he could've. But by then, too many folks was keepin' their eyes glued."

"Have you been in touch with Hannah?" Daniel reiterated patiently.

"Sure. Her pa gave me the address. She's livin' on the West Coast now. Paid a call near three months ago, in San Francisco. Witch-tongued woman! Expectin' too, an' big as a house, though she's pushin' forty now. She gave me my walkin' papers. Tole me Miss Cat's been through quite enough. Says you ain't got marriage on yer mind, an' she ain't contributin' to Miss Cat's life o' sin, especially as you ain't got sense to stop fatherin' brats out o' wedlock. Two's enough, she says."

Daniel stiffened, instantly alert. *"Two?"*

287

Yancy shot him a peculiar look. "Didn't you know? Took me back some, too, when she said that. But I figgered you'da bin told."

"I knew there was a child that died," Daniel said thoughtfully, subsiding.

There was little more to be found out from Yancy, beyond a long recapitulation of all the events of the year before. And later that night, when Daniel lay tossing fitfully in bed, his fist balled over his brow with the effort of concentration, he examined all the clues he possessed to Cat's whereabouts.

A husband called Ryan. Ryan what? Or *had* there been a husband? Out of wedlock. Life of sin. Hannah's chance phrases suggested that Cat had never been married at all.

The first child dead. A girl? Yes, a girl—Cat had definitely told him that much. He remembered now that he had avoided questions, and cursed himself for it.

What last name was she using? Certainly not Kinross. Something that started with the same initial, possibly—the initials in the muff suggested that much. What name? Usually people picked something that had meaning for them.

What city was she living in? New York? Not if she wanted to avoid recognition. Yet she had been living in New York before . . . *or had she?* He recalled now that he himself had made the assumption, because of the newspaper in her muff. The newspaper: That was another odd thing. Why would a rich woman use newspaper to line a drawer, when there were perfumed papers and oilcloths available?

Had she returned to the life she had been leading before the European trip? It seemed likely; she had been very close-mouthed about those years. According to Yancy, nothing of that life had been breathed, not even at the height of the publicity surrounding the battle with Gow.

She was not just hiding from the press, she was hiding from him, and he thought he knew why. Damn that Kinross pride! It would be the very devil now to convince her that he was not motivated by a sense of obligation.

Hannah knew the truth, and by God he'd wring it from Hannah if he had to. But perhaps there was something else, some clue Cat had unwittingly revealed during that memorable month in Europe. . . .

In Ryan's glittering House of Games, the woman once known as the Widow was no longer seen at the tables. It was a necessary precaution; too many wealthy Easterners now patronized these halls. There had been sketches in West Coast newspapers, too, and although these had been highly romanticized, there was always the chance of recognition.

Cat was adamant about protecting her anonymity, and Ryan was content to let her become a silent partner. Deirdre was decoration enough for the house, and the reputation for running honest tables ensured a steady flow of moneyed clients. Nowadays some even brought their bejeweled wives, for the rooms upstairs remained discreet—available only to certain select customers who could afford to pay the price.

Cat came to Ryan's only once a week now. On these occasions, she hurried up the great broad staircase heavily cloaked, to meet Ryan in his office. There were accounts to be gone over, suggestions to be made for various innovations —customers always wanted to be titillated with some slight change of scene—and in these matters, Ryan still tended to defer to Cat. But now, he had a new adviser to contend with: Hannah wanted him to abandon the upstairs operations altogether.

Hannah and Ryan married! Cat had been told of their plans right after Jared's birth, while she was still in the hospital. She had laughed out loud when she heard the news, thus offending Hannah mightily.

"And what's sae funny, pray tell? Though I'm plain as a picket fence and past the age of marrying, there's a feeling or two in this flat chest! Aye . . . laugh all ye want, my pretty one, but for all your looks and all your lovers, how many men have walked ye to the altar? Oft bedded, never wedded!"

"Oh, Hannah, you misunderstand." Cat wiped away a tear of laughter. "I've always thought the male population didn't know a good thing when they saw it! But you and Ryan have been like chalk and cheese. You've been scrapping since the first day you met!"

"Aye, well, down in that big black engine ye didn't know everything," snorted Hannah, who—perhaps because she herself had been living close to death, carrying meals to the train—had put some of her straight-laced ways behind her during the sojourn on the hill. It had come about one night after a particularly wild argument with Ryan. But those memories were too close and too personal and too thrilling to be shared, even with Miss Cat, and Hannah hugged them to her bony breast.

"So you called a truce to the fighting," Cat remarked delightedly.

"Truce? Never! The man has bad gambling ways and a wicked temper, and he's black Irish to boot. And though he's manly enough, I'd na' have agreed, but that I have a mind to become a wedded woman before ye do. So *that* for all your fine looks, Cathryn Kinross! *Miss* Cathryn Kinross!"

And Hannah was a mother now, of two months' standing. The date of her little girl's birth had caused Cat to do some private counting on fingers, although this time she kept her smiles to herself. All the same, it was nice to know there had been some happiness up on that hill.

And her own child . . . Jared was ten months old, a fine strong boy who showed every sign of developing his father's long athletic limbs. He had a resistance to childhood disease that Jenny had never had, and Cat gave thanks every day for the strength of his sturdy, straight little legs.

And Daniel was alive. . . .

Cat knew that now; the news had come through Hannah, after Yancy's unfruitful visit some months before.

"I sent Mr. Brody packing, for I did na' know how ye felt, Miss Cat. Och, I know how ye feel about the *man*. But it's a mistress he wants, not a wife, for ye told me so yourself."

Cat was still in a swirl of delirium and speculation from the news. Daniel alive! Alive! *Alive!* She longed to see him. But did she want him offering marriage out of some sense of duty, as he very likely would? He had done so once before, to another woman. And he could not fail to learn of Jared's existence—through Yancy, or through a thousand stories in old newspaper files. This time there would be no question of paternity; Daniel would know very well whose child she had borne.

"You did the right thing, Hannah. If Yancy Brody comes to see you again . . . or if Daniel comes . . . stick to your story. Or better still, say I've gone back to my first husband."

"First husband?"

"Oh, I told Daniel some such tale. Just say things worked out between us; he'll understand. Tell him we've gone to live in Europe. Or South America. Or anywhere . . .'

Yes, it had been a very difficult choice, and there were many nights when she lay heartsick in her lonely bed, regretting it. But this was not one of them. This was the night she went to Ryan's and counted the week's take, and discussed the various problems of administration.

Cat hurried up the broad red-carpeted sweep of stair, eyes turned downward and hood pulled close about her face. At the gaming tables spread below, a large crowd of fashionably dressed people milled. Ryan had objected to the idea of making evening dress *de rigueur,* but that change, like others, had turned out very well. Everyone wanted to be seen at Ryan's now, and everyone included some very important somebodies. The buzz of their voices mingled with the cries of the croupiers and the click of balls in the spinning roulette wheels, drowning all other sounds. Thus it was that she did not hear the footsteps behind her, taking the stairs two at a time in order to catch up.

As she reached the head of the stairs where a great circular balcony overlooked the gaming tables, fingers shot out from behind and curled around her wrist, causing her to gasp with surprise. She whirled around, and the insistent fingers kept their hold.

"Daniel," she whispered, her eyes huge.

"I could almost believe you're not glad to see me," he smiled.

"Not glad! Oh—" Joy and relief and love and a whole tangle of emotions welled inside her, and some of these spilled into her expression. Her eyes clung to him shamelessly, and had it not been for the crowds below and the several watching attendants on the balcony, she would have been clinging, too.

"You made yourself very difficult to find," he said. "Surely, after all that's happened, you weren't hiding from *me?*"

Small nagging cautions returned—not too insistent yet, but they were there. "How did you . . . ? Did Hannah—"

"No, not Hannah." Daniel's smile feathered his eyes and grooved his cheeks into well-remembered and well-loved lines. There was a new scar on his temple, white against the recent tan. She bled a little to see that mark, and the slight limp as he drew her away from the staircase.

"Isn't there someplace private we can talk?"

Cat's eyes darted around the dozen doors that opened onto the broad balcony. Occasionally one of the rooms was not in use for one reason or another, and the placement of potted plants gave the clue. One room was empty. But to take

Daniel into a whore's bedchamber seemed a very obvious thing to do; pride forbade it. "There's Ryan's office," she suggested. "He's in there now, but I don't suppose he'd mind if we—"

"I don't want to meet the man," Daniel interrupted brusquely. "It's you I've come to see, not your husband. I take it he *is* your husband again."

Cat opened her mouth to correct the misapprehension, and immediately changed her mind. Why not? *Why not?* There was no need for Ryan and Daniel to meet. And at least Daniel could not believe she had marriage on her mind. Somehow, that made the use of the bedchamber more acceptable.

"Come along then," she said, still guarded in public, and allowing herself only a fingertip touch on his sleeve. She turned her footsteps toward the unused room, stopping along the way to give one of the attendants a message to relay to Ryan.

As the door closed them in together, Daniel's eyes swept the space, taking in the virginal bedhangings, the little-girl look of the room, the bearskin rug at the hearth where a friendly fire chuckled. He clicked home the lock on the door.

Cat shrugged off her cloak and threw it on a chair, not trusting herself to speak, not daring to look directly at Daniel now lest he see too much of her soul. She felt very young and unsure of herself, just as she had so long ago, on that first night at Kirklands. To hide the sensation and the tears of happiness that glittered on her lashes, she turned to the fire, and started warming her hands.

Daniel's emotions too ran deep, deeper than words could express. But he had decided he must not try to tell Cat of those emotions, not yet. And so he came up slowly behind her, and slowly placed his hands on her shoulders, and slowly turned her to face him.

"Oh, Daniel," she spilled out tremblingly, with no thought now of pride or of hiding the shimmer of her eyes as they searched his face. "When I thought you were dead I wanted to die, too."

"Cathryn," he murmured huskily, and brought both his hands up to caress her collarbone, the touch an anguish to his fingertips. "You *might* have died, with the thing you did. And if you had—" His words choked to a halt; he had not meant to say so much.

And now her hands rediscovered the contours of his face—the bones too prominent now, the hollows too deep. "Dying seemed a very little thing," she whispered, "when I thought what they might be doing to you. Oh, darling—"

"Hush," he muttered, forgetting for the time the course of action he had intended to follow. "The words can wait." And then he began in earnest the lovemaking he had intended to leave until later. He pulled her close and sealed her mouth with aching kisses, winding his fingers in her hair, and telling her with his hands the true things he could not yet say with his lips.

And then the nakedness, his and hers; and the soft soft bed; and the singing and the soaring of the flesh. And for a time the words did wait, as the sweet savage language of love was spoken with urgent mouths and urgent hands and limbs grown wild together.

"So many scars," she whispered in the poignant after-sweetness of release. She stroked his spine, tracing the marks and sorrowing for every one, telling her love with fingertips grown infinitely gentle. "They must have beaten you terribly. Oh, Daniel, when I heard you were alive, I . . . I can't tell you how I felt."

He rolled away, at last withdrawing. With a firm hand under her chin he turned her face to his. For a short time he allowed himself to bask in the warmth of those eyes where love spilled luminously out, for the moment quite unmasked. But he understood Cat well enough to know that the unguarded moment would not last.

"Won't your husband mind that you're entertaining another gentleman in here?" he asked finally, breaking the spell.

Cat tensed almost imperceptibly, and took her time with the answer. "Ryan's a very understanding man," she said. During the moment's pause pride had reasserted itself, along with the remembrance that she wanted to make no demands. She began to detach herself, slowly but surely, from Daniel's embrace. "I believe Ryan is even grateful to you, Daniel, for what you did for me . . . just as I am."

He permitted her chin to leave his fingers. "How about my son? Does your husband accept that small condition too?"

"Oh, yes." Cat's answer came a little too quickly; deliberately she slowed herself down. She bestowed a calm smile on Daniel, who now lay with his head propped on one hand, regarding her enigmatically. "I imagined you would have heard about Jared. I assure you, Daniel, your son is very well taken care of. Ryan adores Jared as if he were his own, and Jared adores Ryan. I'd prefer you didn't—"

"Don't worry," Daniel said coolly, "I won't disturb the status quo."

"I could arrange for you to see him someday, from a distance. I take him to the park nearly every morning."

"As long as he's taken care of," Daniel shrugged unconcernedly, "I think it's better if I don't see him at all."

Cat fought away a swift stab of anger. How dare he be so unfeeling? "How did you find me?" she asked, with some measure of coldness in her voice.

Daniel's eyes turned mildly mocking. "I have a very strong memory of a certain time you lost your temper," he reminded her. "Your defenses are very good most of the time, but when you lose your temper all hell breaks loose. Clay Street, Iodoform Alley, Pacific Street, and a few other places, too. Hell, it didn't take much imagination to realize those were actual street names, and that you hadn't pulled them out of a hat. And they didn't come from a nice sedate small town either. So I found me a street map of San Francisco . . . and, frankly, I wasn't too surprised when all those names turned up on the Barbary Coast."

She stared at him, and turned a little cold inside. "And you went through all those streets looking for me?"

"Some," he lied. "I take it Ryan removed you from all that. That wasn't very nice company you were keeping, sweetheart. You should be ashamed of yourself. Couldn't you have supported yourself in some more seemly manner after leaving the Sierras?"

She turned her eyes swiftly to the ceiling, facing him no longer. Gall and wormwood rose in her throat as she fought a brief desire to scratch his eyes out. How dare he deign to pass judgment on her!

"As you say," she said at last, decidedly chilly, "I've muddied my skirts a little on the way up. I'd do it again if I had to. Now you know why Ryan doesn't question whom I choose to entertain."

Beyond her vision, Daniel smiled grimly to see that his needling was bearing fruit. "I also remembered that you played a mean game of chemin de fer. One might almost say a professional game. So I made enquiries along those lines, too."

"And that's how you heard about Ryan's."

"That's right," he agreed imperturbably, and with total truth. That was exactly how he had found Cat. Despite what he had implied, he had spent no time at all searching in the more wretched districts. Men got rich on Pacific Street, but women did not. "Naturally, when I asked for you downstairs no one admitted to knowing you, although someone remembered a woman of your description from two years ago. If I'd realized Ryan was so understanding . . . I'd have approached him directly. But . . ."

"Instead you decided to watch for me," Cat concluded without warmth. "I'm surprised you were permitted to come upstairs."

"Ah, but I paid heavily for the privilege. There was a very pretty hostess downstairs. She offered to come up with me herself."

"Deirdre," frowned Cat, not entirely liking that small piece of news. "You should be flattered. Deirdre dispenses favors only when she chooses."

"Jealous, love?" With the palm of his hand Daniel began to soothe her waist suggestively. He marveled that two pregnancies had left her so smooth, so supple, but he kept those thoughts to himself. Instead he murmured the words he knew would hurt: "You needn't be jealous. I was going to suggest we might arrange to do this every Saturday night. It's worth the price of admission."

She stiffened, more markedly this time. "You couldn't keep coming here. But I could meet you once in a while, somewhere else. A hotel, maybe."

"I thought you said Ryan didn't mind a little adultery on the side. But hell, yes, a hotel would suit me better too. We could make a standing arrangement. I could come down from Sacramento once a week."

"Sacramento?"

"That's where I'll be living. I've bought back in to Yancy's railroad, and that's where it's headquartered now. I have a mind to settle down. I've had enough danger to last me for a lifetime."

"I see," said Cat thoughtfully. Sacramento? It was a thriving rail center, becoming a little too industrial perhaps, but there were some beautiful residential districts. And there were excellent rail connections with San Francisco; it would be easy enough to keep an eye on her investment in Ryan's. She knew a moment of quick regret, and put it firmly aside. One night a week? It was better than forcing a man into a marriage he did not want. And evidently, as Daniel cared so little to see his son, his attitude to long-term responsibilities had not changed so very much.

"That's where I've spent most of the past few months," he said with studied casualness. "I've been scouting for a place to buy. I have my eye on a nice estate, just out of town."

"You've been in Sacramento? But I thought you'd been here, looking for—" She bit her lip, and refused to go on.

Casually, Daniel began stroking his fingers back and forth against a nipple. "I've been in San Francisco just for the past few days," he said lazily.

"Oh?" She shifted in the bed, half-turning to make her breast unavailable. "Exactly when did you return from Europe?"

"About three months ago . . . a few days after Yancy approached Hannah. Well, hell, Cat, it was clear you weren't anxious to take up where we left off."

"I see," came the distinctly frosty reply. She rolled farther, presenting her naked spine to him.

"Getting a little chilly in here." To punctuate his sardonic remark, he gave her an easy pat on the buttock, yawned audibly, and left the bed altogether. She could hear him padding barefoot across the room; could hear the movement of the fire screen; could hear the sounds of the coal scuttle being raided, and the fire being poked back to life. His callous contempt for her sensibilities fueled other fires too, and they had built to a fine flame before he returned to bed.

"Very fancy room," he remarked. "Why all the white?"

She could feel the mattress once more crushing beneath his weight, and shifted a little farther to the other side of the bed.

"It's part of the illusion," she said succinctly, pulling a sheet over her nakedness. "This is called the Virgin's Room."

"Couldn't Ryan find a virgin to put in it tonight?"

"No," she replied frostily, not bothering to add that the current virgin had been absent for two weeks, nursing a three-year-old through the mumps.

"Why so angry?" Daniel came close against her and began

to nuzzle the nape of her neck. "And I thought we were just on the threshold of a wonderful new relationship."

"I'm not angry," she declared.

"No? Well, that's a relief. I wouldn't want a silly misunderstanding to interfere with what promises to be some very exciting adultery. I've never met another woman, darling, who makes love quite as well as you."

"How very charming. I'm flattered. I suppose that's why you finally came looking for me?"

"I don't deny it," he agreed equably, refusing to rise to the tartness in her tone.

"Are there no women in Sacramento, then?"

He hesitated deliberately. "Ah . . ."

"Good heavens, Daniel. Surely you don't think I'll mind? I'm not a child."

"Well, then, I may as well admit it. It's Charity."

Cat's reclining body grew very still—like a coiled spring, thought Daniel with some amusement. But her voice came back, totally casual now: "Charity? Not Charity Brody! Why, she can't be—"

"She's eighteen now," said Daniel. "Marrying age."

A false little laugh came from the face he could not see. "Oh, Daniel! You can't be serious! She's twenty years younger than you."

"I told you I had a mind to settle down," he murmured agreeably, pecking a line of kisses along her shoulder, and letting his hand slide over her hip, under the sheet, to tangle in damp curls. He tugged, gently.

"And I suppose now that you've decided to settle down, you want a nice little virgin. I take it she is a virgin, or you wouldn't be here in San Francisco, working out your frustrations on me."

"Ah, Cat," he said soothingly, "don't think of it that way. Even if I were already married to Charity I'd have come to find you sooner or later, and suggested some sort of arrangement. I can't expect a decently brought-up girl like Charity to make love as inventively as you."

She scrambled out of bed, sheets flying, hair flying, caution flying, too. "You'll marry her but you won't marry me!" she screamed like a harridan. "The mother of your child! Wouldn't you consider me?"

She yanked open the drawer of the bedside table, grabbed

297

a handful of its contents of scented sachets and flung them in Daniel's face. He ducked the perfumed hailstorm that rained against him.

"Take that . . . and that . . . and that! And take a hundred virgins for all I care! But never let me see you again!"

She fled across the room and started flinging things around in a furious search for her clothes. Daniel came up on one elbow and watched her, amused.

"Come back to bed, you stubborn bitch," he said in a lazily affectionate voice, "and we'll start talking business. To begin with, I accept."

"I wouldn't talk to you if you were the last man on earth!" Tears of frustration and humiliation stung at her eyes and began to stream down her face, unchecked. She stamped a bare foot. "Oh d-damn! Where are my clothes!"

"I burned them." Daniel's mouth twitched; his tawny eyes crinkled. "And mine, too, so you couldn't decide to flee out of here in a pair of trousers. Dammit, Cat, will you calm down long enough to listen? I accept your proposal of marriage."

"You . . . *what?*" She froze.

"I heard you perfectly clearly. You asked if I wouldn't consider marrying you. Well, yes, I damn well would. Fact is, I've been considering nothing else for a helluva long time. The only question in my mind was how to get you to propose."

"You—" She sputtered; she looked stunned. "You bastard," she choked out.

"Ah, Cat. You silly proud stubborn woman. If I'd asked you, you would have refused. Don't you see I had to trick you? The only time your defenses crumble is when you're really angry. Now come back to bed. Charity means about as much to me as Ryan means to you. Less in fact, for I haven't seen her since she was eight years old."

She remained standing stock-still, dumbfounded, naked, and unconscious of her nakedness. And so Daniel began some of his explanations: the return to New York only two weeks before; the searching of old newspaper files; the locating of Ryan that had been accomplished without difficulty yesterday; the talk with Ryan himself.

"And with the last name of O'Brien? I knew at once he was Hannah's husband, for he'd certainly never been yours

. . . *Mrs. Kirk*. Yes, I know what name you've been using! I found that out in New York too, by reading up on the Brooklyn Bridge disaster. Jenny Kirk, celebrating her sixth birthday . . . mathematics has always been one of my strong points, love. When I asked Ryan yesterday, he confirmed my guess. About that, and about a lot of other things, too."

"How . . . did you . . . know," whispered Cat, who had gradually make her way back to bed, looking thoroughly defeated.

"You would have never used that paper to line a drawer. You, a rich woman? Besides, I could see it clearly in my mind's eye, yellowed in small squares that had been turned to the air." Daniel pulled her down beside him, crushing dried lavender and old rose petals in the process. "Oh, sweetheart, I relived every moment of that trip a thousand times over in my imagination. It was the only thing that saved my sanity in Turkey. Now tell me about my daughter."

And she did, without tears, and without telling him that Gow had been responsible for Jenny's death. The hatreds of those lost years had to be put behind, and neither cared to mention Gow now. Daniel cradled her in his arms, not interrupting the memories.

"I know it's hard to believe, Daniel, but Jenny was a happy child, somewhere deep inside. And that's what I try to remember."

"I saw Jared yesterday," he said suddenly. "Both of you . . . in the park. It was all I could do to keep from approaching you then. But I knew I mustn't, or you'd have said no."

"Oh, Daniel." She turned her face into his shoulder, filled with a wonderment of love beyond the telling. "You don't have to marry me, you know. I'm willing to be your mistress."

"Now don't try and take back your offer, for I won't let you." His mouth parted over hers, sealing the pact with the gentlest of kisses, as if to dispel forever the hatreds and the hurts and the heartaches of the past.

Cat sighed contentedly, and wrapped her arms about his neck. "Are you sure you wouldn't rather have a nice little virgin?"

"Not a hundred virgins, when I can have a woman like you." On her breast, he traced an outline with his finger.

"That's for Woman, sweetheart, and that's what you are . . . all Woman. Oh, Cathryn, I love you so much, so very very much. . . ."

And as the ghosts of long dead petals crushed beneath their twining limbs, he took her once again, renewing with his body the brand he had long since placed on her heart.